DR. BRINKLEY'S TOWER

Also by Robert Hough

The Final Confession of Mabel Stark
The Stowaway
The Culprits

DR. BRINKLEY'S TOWER

ROBERT HOUGH

First published in Canada in 2012 by House of Anansi Press, Inc.

For information about permission to reproduce
selections from this book, write to:
Steerforth Press L.L.C., 45 Lyme Road, Suite 208,
Hanover, New Hampshire 03755

Cataloging-in-Publication Data is available from the Library of Congress

ISBN 978-1-58642-203-5

This novel is a work of fiction. Names, characters, places, and incidents are either
the products of the author's imagination or are used fictitiously. Any resemblance to
actual persons, living or dead, events, or locales is entirely coincidental.

First U.S. Edition

1 3 5 7 9 10 8 6 4 2

As always, to Suzie, Sally and Ella

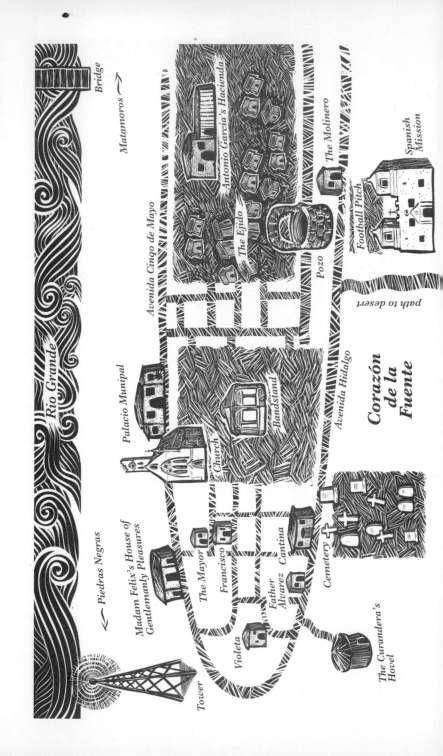

{UNO}

{1}

FRANCISCO RAMIREZ STOOD FRETTING BEFORE AN antique full-length mirror framed in strips of shellacked mesquite. It was a fine piece of craftsmanship, hand-built and intricate with detail; if you looked closely, you could see deer heads carved into the frame, each one gazing bemusedly in a different direction. The mirror, one of the family's few notable possessions, had come to the Ramirez clan almost a century ago, when Francisco's great-great-great-grandfather presented it to his reddening fourteen-year-old bride on their wedding night. *Mi querida*, he'd reportedly told her, *you are growing lovelier each and every day. Now you can watch it happen as well.*

It was now 1931, the long, bloody years of the revolution still a fresh wound. The mirror, meanwhile, had been put to daily use by five generations of the family. While it had generally been well cared for, the passage of time had nevertheless taken a toll. There was a spidery hairline crack near the bottom, the result of its having been dropped during one of its many relocations, and the surface was beginning to undulate slightly, not unlike the Coahuilan desert itself. The glass had also started to acquire a dull copper patina, such that it now cast reflections of a slightly seaweed hue. As a result, more than one Ramirez had looked at his or her reflection and erroneously concluded that the carne seca served at dinner had somehow been tainted.

The mirror's real dissolution had occurred during the revolution, when government soldiers were continually requisitioning goods for the war effort, only to spend the proceeds in houses of ill repute. In an attempt to save the mirror, Francisco's father had placed it in an old municipal grain hopper, where it was hidden beneath a mound of wheat that had been deliberately left to ferment, thus repelling tax collectors with its ammonia reek. When the family finally retrieved their cherished artifact, the wood had permanently absorbed the aroma. No amount of scrubbing, they soon discovered, could stop it from emitting the sour, vinegary odour of a gringo scouring product.

Given these shortcomings, the mirror had been relegated to the bedroom used by Francisco, who was now assessing himself in the turbulent, hypercritical way of all adolescents. It was mid-afternoon, and the thin chambray curtains over his bedroom window, drawn to keep out the brutalizing heat, glowed orange.

The problem, as he saw it, was his nose. Three years ago, in a game played on the municipal pitch out by the old Spanish mission, Francisco had inadvertently used it to stop a drive by a muchacho known for the lethality of his right foot. While doubled over in a pained, breathless silence, Francisco had grabbed the appendage, which now extended laterally from his face, and instinctively pushed it back into place. The other players looked on, amazed that he was still on his feet.

The accident had rendered the bridge of his nose some- what lumpy in appearance, not unlike the backbone of a spiny armadillo. It was the mildest of disfigurements, and one that had not bothered him in the ensuing years. (In fact, if you asked the majority of the town's young women, they would tell you that the accident had only added to Francisco's rug- ged appeal.) In recent months, however, the equanimity with which he regarded his appearance had vanished, along with his ability to concentrate, sleep soundly, or generate anything resembling an appetite.

Ay, he thought to himself. *You need the help of an expert.*

He took a deep breath, crossed the room, and left the dank, crumbling row house in which he lived with his father, his grandmother, and his two young brothers. Walking with his head down, a means of avoiding the many pits and chasms in the street, he moved along Avenida Hidalgo, which formed the southern border of his native town, Corazón de la Fuente. He then bisected the town's arid main plaza, causing several neighbouring busybodies to wonder where Francisco Ramirez might be heading. Upon reaching the east side of the plaza, just beyond the town's pitiful church, he entered a narrow side street that led to Corazón's second, smaller plaza. Little more than a mounding of dry, sun-baked earth, it was surrounded by a traffic circle that serviced a trio of similarly dry and sun-baked laneways.

Facing this plazita was the home and business of an eighty-eight-year-old Casanova named Roberto Pántelas. For decades he had made his living by grinding corn, wheat, and coffee beans, and for this reason was referred to by most as the molinero. Yet he was best-known for his understanding of the fairer sex, having bedded somewhere between seven and eight thousand specimens during his long, virile life. Francisco found him sitting on a low wooden bench. Feeling the cool thrown by Francisco's shadow, the molinero lifted his craggy, age-weathered face.

— Francisco Ramirez, he croaked. — My young compadre. You startled me.

— Hola, Señor Pántelas.

— Please, sit down. Keep an old man company.

Francisco lowered himself, a comfortable silence settling between the two. Finally, Francisco felt compelled to speak.

— Señor . . . I was wondering if you might help me.

The molinero slowly looked in the teenager's direction.

— Help you? How?

— Could you tell me . . . How do I . . . win the affection of a young woman? A young woman who is showing no signs of interest?

The old man thought for a moment. — By any chance, are we talking about the lovely and serious-minded Violeta Cruz?

Francisco nodded, for some reason feeling foolish. In a town with only eight hundred or so residents, all it had taken was a few indiscreet glances, along with an ill-timed blush or two at the mention of her name, and the understanding that Francisco Ramirez was yet another young man who had fallen for Violeta Cruz now followed him wherever he went.

— Sí, he answered dejectedly.

The molinero chuckled warmly. — Nothing like setting your sights high. She'll be a tough nut to crack, that one. Of course, if my old eyes are still working as they should, it'll be worth the effort.

Francisco couldn't help himself. He grinned and nodded.

The molinero pondered, his milky eyes gazing into the middle distance, his spotted hands quivering in his lap. His breath slowed so considerably that Francisco feared the old man had chosen that moment to enjoy one of his several daily siestas. Yet just as Francisco was about to touch the molinero on the shoulder, he turned slightly and began to speak.

— Why not invite her to tomorrow's festivities?

— I was thinking of that. You think she might accept?

The molinero shrugged his shoulders and grinned. — Ay, Francisco, she's a woman. How would I know? They're as unpredictable as desert fire. If they weren't, they wouldn't be worth the bother.

Francisco chuckled, thanked the old man, and prepared to take his leave. Just as he was rising to his feet, the molinero spoke up.

— There is one other thing you could try.

— And what is that?

— A little prayer wouldn't hurt.

{2}

THAT NIGHT, A BAND OF DRY HEAT, ORIGINATING somewhere in the saguaro fields of central Arizona, settled like a tarp over Corazón de la Fuente. During the hour or two before dawn, the town's pink and blue adobe houses began to warm up prematurely, causing many of the residents to rise early. Francisco awoke in darkness and lay motionless in the thick, gloomy air. He finally rose and splashed water on his puffy face. He then swept the stoop, started a low fire with dried huizache branches, and treated the family pig to a slop of fruit peel and millet. Shortly afterwards the sun rose, blazing. By nine in the morning the local crows had all taken refuge in nests made of pirated string, the desert vultures had stopped looking for carcasses, and even the crickets, normally lovers of incinerating heat, had become too listless to convincingly rub their hind legs together. This pitched the town into a dense, ominous silence. Everything stilled, and waves of heat rose from the dusty, pitted laneways. The breeze vanished as though it had never existed, causing the palo verde trees lining the central plaza to cease rustling and turn quiet.

Francisco spent that morning at home, attempting to move as little as possible. After a lunch of chicken soup and tortilla, he turned in for a siesta, only to find that his heart would not permit the arrival of sleep. He lay looking up at the ceiling, spotting shapes in the swirls of lime wash, listening to his little brothers snore like hamsters in the bed next to his. Gradually he surrendered to the lightest form of sleep, whereby the mind, although still conscious, creates the most addled of thoughts.

Around five o'clock that afternoon, a light breeze arose and downgraded the day's intolerable heat to one that was merely sweltering. Though movement was now possible, it was accompanied by a sprouting of moisture on the brow, beneath the arms, and in the hollows behind the knees. Francisco dressed, washed his face with basin water, and combed his hair. He then nodded a goodbye to his father, kissed the portrait of his mother adorning the sill of the living room window, and stepped into the dusty street.

He paused and watched the village slowly come to life. If he wasn't mistaken, there was a cautious expectation in the air, a simmering anticipation that had not been felt for years. Whereas Saturday-night fiestas had once been part of the municipal routine, one had not been enjoyed since the outbreak of fighting, a date so long ago that many of Corazón's children had no idea that such a tradition existed. Yet tonight, thanks to the efforts of twin brothers named Luis and Alfonso Reyes, the town would gather on the most festive night of the week, the men dressed in clean white shirts, the women in ruffled, clinging dresses. Already families were making their way towards the centre of the village, clouds of hot white dust rising into the air as they walked.

Yet there was another, more germane reason why those walking towards the plaza exhibited a certain spryness in their step. About six months earlier, a wealthy American business-person had contacted both the town's mayor and, apparently, the governor of the state of Coahuila. The gringo's name was Dr. John Romulus Brinkley, and he was planning to start his own radio station just over the border, in the town of Del Rio, Texas. To achieve his broadcasting aims he intended to build an immense radio tower in a field just outside Corazón de la Fuente, so that the strength of his signal would not be compromised by what he felt were limiting, small-minded American broadcast regulations. (Here is where the information strayed into the territory of rumour, rumour so juicy and salacious that the old women of the town couldn't repeat it without girlishly tittering: it seemed that Dr. Brinkley had grown rich performing some sort of operation that treated the most humiliating problem a red-blooded Mexican hombre could experience.)

Francisco walked west along Avenida Hidalgo until he reached a small street running northward. Midway along this block was the tiny two-room house occupied by Violeta Cruz and her widowed mother, Malfil. Like every home in Corazón, it was not in good repair. Chunks of adobe were falling from the facade and ceramic tiles were missing in the roof, such that when it rained, the floor had to be decorated with buckets and large basins. Adjacent to the house was a tiny dead-end street called the Callejón de Perros, so named because the town's stray dogs all gathered there after a long day of rooting through garbage and spreading canine-borne infections. Ordinarily they slept so tightly clumped that, in the dark, the laneway looked as though it were surfaced with a lumpy burlap matting. On this afternoon, however, the alley was empty, the dogs already at the central plaza, awaiting the scraps and litter that the crowd would surely leave behind.

He knocked.

Violeta answered. — Francisco, she said. — What brings you here?

— Violeta . . . I was just heading to the plaza, and I was wondering if you'd come with me.

As Francisco awaited an answer, his world gained a hallucinatory glimmer, with small movements magnifying in scope, intensity, and colour: Violeta sweeping a lock of jet-black hair off her face, Violeta taking a portion of ruby lip between her white teeth, Violeta turning to see if her mother was watching. Time slowed, and the air around him grew thin.

— Ay, Francisco. It's just that . . .

— That's all right, he interrupted. — I understand.

She peered at him for a moment or two. — No, she finally said. — I mean that I just have to get my shawl.

Ten minutes later, Francisco and Violeta entered the central plaza, the site of so many roving gun battles during the throes of the revolution. Many of the houses ringing the plaza were still marred by bullet holes, and the remaining trees in the square all had a grey, denuded quality, their trunks perforated with shrapnel. The town hall, which occupied an entire block along the north of the plaza, was still aerated by the cannon fire directed towards it during a battle between government forces and a splinter group composed of Villistas, anarchists, and American-born mercenaries. But the worst off was the town's church, lovingly erected by the Spanish in the mid-1600s. During that same skirmish, a grenade had landed in an open window of the spire, causing the tall conical structure to fall away from the rest of the building and land in ruined, tamale-sized fragments. The spire had not yet been rebuilt, the townsfolk reasoning that at any moment the lingering embers of the revolution could reignite and their beloved town church might yet again become a magnet for lobbed explosives. Of course, this reluctance was compounded by another, withering fact: nobody had any money for bricks.

As Francisco and Violeta neared the bandstand in the centre of the plaza, they saw that someone had wrapped scissored paper around the four wrought-iron columns that marked the corners of the elevated stage. In this way the stand was transformed into an ersatz wrestling ring, the laboriously produced papel picado taking the place of ropes.

Already spectators were beginning to seat themselves according to their status in the town. Occupying the black wrought-iron benches nearest the bandstand were the town's most important persons, a roster that included the mayor, the village priest, the town's wealthiest man, and, it goes without saying, the owner of the local cantina. On the next row of decorative benches sat the town madam and her working girls, a privilege honouring their status as the town's most significant businesspersons. While every member of Madam's infamous stable was named Maria, each had a different surname, selected by Madam Félix herself. These included Maria del Sol, Maria de las Rosas, Maria de los Flores, Maria de los Sueños, Maria de la Mañana, Maria del Mampo (who happened to be a transvestite from the state of Oaxaca), Maria de las Montañas (a name earned because she was blonde and angelic, as though descended from the most altitudinous tips of the Sierra Madres), and last but not least, Maria de la Noche (who, due to the suggestiveness of her name and the sinful burst of her hips, was a favourite amongst Madam's gringo clients).

Behind them were the town's rank and file: women, mostly, their men lost to armies raised by both the rebel Pancho Villa and the dictator Porfirio Díaz. Though many of them were still young, the collective impression they gave was one of age; mourning had caused their shoulders to hunch, the corners of their mouths to point downwards, and their once olive skin to turn ashen. Their sadness was so ample, in fact, that it was not adequately contained by their individual selves but seemed to emanate from their bodies like the glow of a kerosene flame, infecting the tenor of the entire town. Seated with them, however, were the promises of the future: sons and daughters who had been too young to fight and who, unlike many of the adults, possessed all their limbs and the whole of their sanity. These included Francisco and Violeta, who were moving towards a pair of unoccupied seats.

The last row contained the town's impoverished, most of whom lived in a collectivized settlement called an ejido in the east end of the town; squat and dark-skinned, they were mostly of Indian descent, with wrinkles so deeply etched into their faces they looked like devices intended to collect rainwater. Finally, at the very back of the gathering, standing on an overturned crate, was a wrinkled gnome of a woman whom the fine people of Corazón de la Fuente referred to as either Señora Azula or, more commonly, and with a slight derision in their voices, the curandera. While she was generally feared — there were those who believed she had mated with the devil, producing a demon child who had gone on to become one of Villa's most psychopathic lieutenants — she nonetheless played a key role in Corazón's antiquated and otherwise non-existent medical system. Those suffering from maladies not associated with embarrassment — colds, stomach disorders, broken limbs, vaporous infections — donned their Sunday best and crossed the border into Texas, where they consulted one of the doctors in the town of Del Rio. Those suffering, however, from venereal disease, unwanted pregnancy, emotional illness, alcohol addiction, or any brand of genital sore would, under cloak of darkness, sneak to the cottage of the curandera, who kept hours befitting an owl. Distrustful of money, she accepted chickens, bolts of cloth, and root vegetables in return for a consultation.

The show began with a musical presentation: a group of local students who called themselves Los Inconsolables del Norte. Armed with accordion, trumpet, snare drum, and armadillo-shell guitars, the students lurched through renditions of "Mi Capitano," "Mi Estrellita," and, in a nod to Madam's assembled employees, the popular bolero "Mi Hermosa Maria." And while the music wasn't enjoyable per se — it was vastly atonal, with an articulation not unlike the grunting of an estrous sow — the audience nonetheless hummed along, overjoyed that the town's youth had somehow generated the lightness of soul necessary to make music.

When the students finished, everyone applauded with a vigour as genuine as it was polite.

It was now time for an address from the mayor, a weary veteran named Miguel Orozco. Burdened with an ill-functioning left foot, he clambered awkwardly onto the stage, trying his hardest not to tear any of the papery ropes. Applause rose when he succeeded, yet another sign that a small degree of hopefulness had infected the town.

— Señores and señoras, he began in a tremulous voice. — I would like to welcome you all to the very first lucha libre in the history of Corazón de la Fuente. Though I have never attended such an event, I am assured that it is a most enjoyable spectacle, and I think that the Reyes brothers deserve our gratitude for providing such an unexpected diversion.

There was polite clapping, followed by a pause in which the mayor's face turned serious.

— As you all know, these past years have not been easy ones, or prosperous ones, or happy ones, for the people of México. Many of us lost loved ones during the revolution, and all of us have suffered from great upheaval. And yet . . . it is my belief that those days are over, and that prosperity and happiness are poised to return to our humble village.

Though he didn't have to, he gestured towards a large field beyond Madam Félix's House of Gentlemanly Pleasures. With any luck it would soon be visited by gringos wearing hard hats and steel-toed boots.

— It is my humble opinion that sunny days are coming to both our town and the grand state of Coahuila, and it is also my belief that this optimism is symbolized today by the wonderful efforts of Luis and Alfonso Reyes, who

spent an exceedingly hot morning constructing this beauti-
ful ring and who organized this wonderful concert by Los
Inconsolables del Norte. And so, it is with this in mind that
I ask you all to give an enthusiastic Corazón welcome to . . .
Los Hermanos Reyes!

The mayor gestured towards the opened doors of the
town hall, where the Reyes brothers appeared in the arch-
way, hands on their waists and chests thrust forward, wearing nothing but cowboy boots and wrestling trunks. Alfonso
wore a white mask, Luis the black mask of a villain. As the
brothers strutted through the plaza towards the ring, Luis was
already calling to members of the audience, accusing them of
being idiots and pendejos and stupid, bug-eating campesinos.
The onlookers cheered and whistled, as was demanded of an
aroused lucha audience.

The brothers climbed into the ring and went to their corners. While waiting for the bell, Alfonso kneeled and prayed
to Jesús, the Lord above, the Holy Spirit, and, last but not
least, his mother, who at that moment was looking on from
the plaza while nervously chewing a lock of dark hair. Luis,
meanwhile, stomped his boots and jeered his opponent by
calling him señorita and asking if he'd enjoyed his fiesta de
quinceañera. This last remark inspired laughter within the
audience; even Violeta chortled, causing Francisco to wonder
whether she might be enjoying herself in his presence.

There was a lull. The audience quieted. Consuela Reyes,
standing immediately outside the ring, struck the back of a
cast-iron pan with a large metal spoon that she ordinarily used
to lift cricket fritters out of simmering oil. The hefty sixteen-
year-olds circled one another, legs bent and arms at the ready.

Alfonso feinted, Luis jabbed, and they returned to their slow, predatory rotating. Suddenly there came a muffled, high-pitched battle cry. Luis charged, his arms windmilling. When he collided with his brother in the centre of the bandstand, those seated closest to the ring heard Alfonso say — Lift me in the air, Luis, just like we practised.

Luis paused as though thinking hard, a moment that caused all the Marias to titter behind their fans. He then bent at the knees and, employing the strength for which the Reyes brothers were known, lifted his brother into the air. For a moment he held him aloft, like a Mayan priest displaying the entrails of a ram, before throwing Alfonso to the floor of the stage. Alfonso landed properly, right on the flesh of his shoulder, and then rolled away while moaning theatrically. As his brother lay writhing, Luis paraded the ring, gesturing malevolently at the crowd. By this time some of the younger audience members, who had seen lucha bouts in the nearby city of Piedras Negras, began yelling, *Kill him, kill him!*

Luis stopped and cupped his hand over his ear, as though struggling to hear. His supporters switched their cheer and began yelling, *The guillotine! Give him the guillotine!*

Luis paused, let out a war cry so visceral that many of the Marias shrank into their seats, and charged his still moaning brother. When he was a metre away, he leapt skyward and then dropped, his rotund backside leading the way, the back of his fleshy left leg appearing to strike his brother across the face. Alfonso rolled away, feigning injury by groaning and holding his nose. Luis leapt to his feet and circled the bandstand, ranting against his detractors and inciting his supporters. Above the din, he heard, *the propeller, hombre!*

Luis again cupped his ear to the audience.

The propeller! shrieked the adolescents in the crowd. *Give him the propeller!*

Despite the presence of his mask, the whole town could see that Luis was grinning. He circled the ring a few more times, stomping his boots for effect, before approaching his downed brother. Luis bent, grabbed Alfonso's feet, and hooked them under his armpits. He then gripped his brother's knees and began to turn. One second later, Alfonso was airborne and spinning, his masked head whirling though space, his arms tight to his stomach so as not to disrupt the aerodynamics of the move. Yet as Luis accelerated the spin, their mother, who understood that her sons suffered from both an excess of might and a deficiency of common sense, began to wave her arms in the air and yell — No, no, Luis, put him down. Luis, por favor, put him down!

It was too late. In the muggy heat of the evening, Alfonso's legs had grown slippery with perspiration. Luis's grip loosened and Alfonso came free, at which point he soared through the air like a bag of flung sorghum. The crowd silenced as he arced, face towards the twilit sky, over the confines of the ring. His flight ended in the lap of Los Inconsolables' accordion player. A thunderous minor-key squelch, not unlike the screech of a ram being neutered, echoed off the walls of the village, drifted over the surrounding plains, and was heard by a tribe of Kickapoo Indians who were out hunting that evening for desert voles.

The second noise to ricochet through the streets was the clang of a dropped pan. Consuela Reyes ran to her son. The accordion player, having been protected by his now battered instrument, merely looked as though the wind had been knocked out of him. Alfonso Reyes, however, was lying on his back, completely still save for a quiver in the fingertips of his left hand. Luis came running, crashing through the paper ropes he had laboriously erected that morning, and stood fearfully behind his mother.

Consuela gingerly peeled off her injured son's mask. Alfonso looked pale and disoriented.

— Mijo, she said gently. — You can hear me?

— *Errrrrrrrr* was the reply.

— Do you know your name?

Alfonso mumbled and seemed to fully come awake.

— My back hurts.

— Can you move everything?

— Sí, he sighed, and to illustrate he rocked his feet from side to side.

Consuela Reyes glanced up just long enough that the townsfolk of Corazón de la Fuente could see that her eyes were glassy, her lips trembling, and her face, once so youthful and pretty, was now marred by lines and red blemishes. They each took a step forward to offer assistance, for each and every one of them saw in Consuela what they saw in themselves: the way in which accumulated sorrow can be caused by years of strained coping.

And then, slowly, as though hefted by an unseen crane, Alfonso Reyes rose shakily to his size-twelve feet, one arm draped around his beleaguered mother, the other around the humped shoulders of his relieved brother. The people of Corazón raised their hands into the dwindling light and emitted a hearty *Qué bueno!* Most then stopped to slap the Reyes brothers on the back and congratulate them on an evening of high-calibre lucha. This in turn caused the brothers to smile, and to promise that they would be back the following Saturday with a new display of wrestling prowess.

Soon the sky began to turn a starlit lavender. Many looked up and admired it, for it was often said that when you are no longer moved by the last stages of dusk in the Mexican desert, it is time to shake the hand of your Maker. It lasted for ten full minutes, the sky suddenly a depthless black dotted by a million silver shimmers. Piñon torches were lit, and a restorative breeze, originating from the tips of the Sierra Madres, animated the milling crowd.

The Marias departed first: it was almost nine o'clock, and soon there would be a notable increase in the number of Texans coming over the border for an evening of mescal quaffing and carnality. The village poor hung around a bit longer than most, understandably reluctant to return to the sweltering tin-roofed hovels of the ejido. The curandera, on the other hand, seemed to vanish — one second she was there and a second later the overturned crate that had supported her was abandoned in the dust. This, of course, did nothing to counteract the popularly held suspicion among Corazón's elderly residents that she dabbled in the black arts, and had sacrificed more than one baby goat in honour of Satan.

It was around this time that Francisco Ramirez escorted Violeta Cruz back to her place of residence. The couple walked along Avenida Cinco de Mayo, turning south when they reached Violeta's street. She stopped when she reached the door of her house, where she was momentarily caught in a beam of starlight, causing her flowing black hair to turn a colour in keeping with her name. Her eyes were a depthless Mayan jade. Her skin, as was the case with some norteñas, was the pale white of rice pudding. Francisco felt an exhilaration that bordered on the vertiginous; as he stood gazing at her, he experienced a sudden and profound understanding of what people meant by the grace of God. Yet just as his spirit began to soar, she looked up at him, her eyes doleful.

— Francisco, she said.

— Sí, Violeta?

— I have to talk to you.

— All right.

— I . . . I'm not sure about this.

— Not sure about what, Violeta?

— *This*. You, me, spending time together . . . Francisco, I just don't know.

— What is it?

She lowered her eyes and looked embarrassed. — Francisco . . . there's a problem. If we are to formally see one another, you must ask my mother's permission. It is only right. I will not sneak around behind her back. It isn't proper, and she would not permit it.

Francisco suddenly felt a mild sense of unease, as though he were about to enter a terrain where nothing, not even the solidity of the earth beneath his feet, could be trusted. As every young man in Corazón de la Fuente knew too well, Malfil Cruz considered her daughter too much of a prize for the simple, dust-caked boys of the town. It did not reduce

Francisco's feelings of despondency that Malfil Cruz was probably right.

— You would like me to have a meeting with your mother?

— Francisco, she said witheringly. — It is not a matter of what I want or do not want. It's a matter of what needs to be.

{3}

AS HE TRUDGED HOME, FRANCISCO RAMIREZ SKIRTED
the west face of the plaza, his thoughts so ravaged by worry
and desire that he failed to notice that there were still four
men left in the village square, their faces lit by torchlight.

Though the town had no official hierarchy, there was a
sort of ersatz leadership in place, a quartet of hombres whose
relationship with Corazón de la Fuente was almost parental
in both affection and degree of responsibility. The semi-
crippled mayor, Miguel Orozco, lived in a one-room house
near the town hall. Corazón's wealthiest resident, a handsome
Spaniard named Antonio Garcia, owned a ruined hacienda
just east of town, and for this reason was ordinarily referred
to as the hacendero. Carlos Hernandez, a lean-faced local
with a moustache the size of a chihuahua, operated Corazón
de la Fuente's only drinking establishment, and this designa-
tion had afforded him a moniker as well. The town priest, a
man known as Father Alvarez, dressed just like every other
hombre in town: in boots, Levi's, a denim shirt worn so tight

that the material stretched at the buttons, and, to hide his bald pate, a slender cowboy hat. They were all around forty years old, the closeness of their ages uniting them as surely as their loyalty towards the town of Corazón de la Fuente.

— Compadres, the hacendero said in his gravelly voice. — I must be off.

The mayor, the cantina owner, and Father Alvarez all struggled not to grin.

— But why leave so early? the mayor asked in a voice that feigned innocence. — We're all going to the cantina. Why not join us?

— Sí, said the cantina owner. — I have some real Jaliscan tequila. It came in just the other day. Good for the more discriminating among us.

— It's tempting, said the hacendero. — But I'm busy these days. I think I told you I'm about to take delivery of a new horse?

— Sí, said the mayor. — We heard.

— Then I'll say buenas noches.

— Buenas, said the others. — And be careful with that horse of yours.

The remaining men stood in the plaza, all three smiling as they listened to the fall of the hacendero's lizard-skin boots.

— That hacendero, snorted Father Alvarez. — It's not a horse he's interested in riding, am I right, amigos?

— We should wait here a bit, said the cantina owner, — and catch him doubling back to visit Madam Félix.

— Come on, primos, said the mayor. — We all have our peccadilloes. We all have our little fictions. Can you blame him for wanting a little company? After what the revolution did to that hacienda of his?

The others nodded and conceded that the mayor had a point.

— Speaking of love, said the cantina owner, — did you see who was with Francisco Ramirez?

— Ay sí, said the mayor. — Violeta Cruz. My God, she's a beauty. It takes the breath away. Do you think Francisco's the one who'll finally snag her? I always thought she'd marry away.

— You never know, said Father Alvarez. — No woman is made of stone. Still, my guess is that Francisco is one muchacho who's bitten off more than he can chew.

The three men all chortled sympathetically, each having suffered the brutality of unrequited love in the past.

— Come on, said the cantina owner. — Let's go for that drink.

The three walked towards the north end of the plaza, moving slowly so that the mayor could keep up. At Avenida Hidalgo they turned west, their conversation interrupted by the far-off braying of coydogs.

The town's lone watering hole was nothing more than a refurbished adobe house, no bigger or smaller than the other addresses along the street. The cantina owner pushed open the heavy knotted door, which had remained unlocked since the day that a thirsty commandante in the northern army had shot the padlock off with a Smith & Wesson the size of a rolling pin. The mayor and Father Alvarez stepped into the hot gloom and waited while the cantina owner lit an oil lamp and placed it in the middle of one of the tables. He then retreated to the mesquite-wood bar, which still bore splinters and perforations gained during the northern army's visit. He lit a second oil lamp and returned with four glasses and the bottle of tequila. After filling all four, he lifted his own glass.

— To lucha! he proposed.

The men laughed and then tipped their glasses, enjoying the spread of warmth across the back of their throats. Soon after, they heard a knocking at the rear of the saloon. The cantina owner stood and walked towards the back door, which opened onto a sewage gulley and, beyond that, an eternity of ink-black scrub. An ejido-dweller, looking obsequious and parched, was waiting. Carlos filled the man's cup with a frothy, malodorous pulque, the favoured beverage of those who had migrated up from the south. He then accepted a few pesos in return; it was a transaction that had become, over the years, the lion's share of his business. He sat back down, poured a second round of tequilas, and said to the mayor: — Tell us some more about the radio tower, Miguel.

— Ay, Carlos. What do you want to know?

— Is this Dr. Brinkley really going to build it?

— It's starting to look that way.

— And will it really be the most powerful transmitter in the world?

— One million watts. At least that's what Brinkley says he's aiming for. Course he *is* a gringo, and what he says and what he means could be two different things.

The mayor leaned forward. — Still. He says you'll be able to hear the signal in Alaska. In *Russia* even, when the weather's right.

— Imagine, said Father Alvarez. — Tiny Corazón de la Fuente, reaching all those people. It's about time we did something right.

The men paused. It was almost too much to believe. A year earlier there had been nothing, *nothing* to live for in Corazón de la Fuente. The revolution had taken everything from them: their pride, their sense of purpose, the belief that the future existed for all people and not just the lucky few who happened to be related to whatever thug-led government was in power that year.

— So, come on, said Alvarez. — Tell us, is this Brinkley an honourable man?

Miguel Orozco took a slow, savouring taste of his second tequila. — I'm just the mayor. All I know is that if this tower goes up, the ejido dwellers are going to get jobs helping to build the damn thing, and if those poor bastards are occupied that's good enough for me.

— But you didn't answer the question, said the cantina owner. — What's this Brinkley *like*?

The mayor thought. — Full of big ideas. Generous. He speaks Spanish, though I'm not sure where he picked it up. He wears tortoiseshell eyeglasses and a ruby tie clip. And I tell you, he's wealthy enough.

— He'd better be. The last thing this town needs is a half-built radio tower rusting in the hot sun.

— He has a mansion with a private zoo and sixteen Cadillacs. You be the judge.

— And all of it from that crazy medical procedure of his, Father Alvarez said witheringly. — I bet it doesn't even work.

— They say it does, answered the mayor.

— Really? said the cantina owner. — Using the gonads of a *goat*?

— I wouldn't care if he used the testicles of an ostrich. If he wants a radio station to promote his business, it won't be me who gets in his way. God knows this town could use a kick-start. The people need something like this, something to stop them from brooding over the value of the peso and the loved ones they've lost. Something to give them the ability to believe again.

They all pondered the wistful truthfulness of this statement.

— They have a joke about Brinkley on the American side, added the mayor.

— Sí? said the father.

— What's the fastest thing in Del Rio, Texas?

— Tell us.

— A goat passing Dr. Brinkley's clinic!

Even Father Alvarez chuckled. — Those crazy gringos, he said sourly. — I tell you, nothing they do surprises me anymore. They say that in Villa Acuña there's a doctor who cures cancer with an extract made from armadillo livers, and in Ciudad Juarez there's a medic who reverses aging with a concentrate of vulture saliva and ground Gila-monster stomachs.

— And I suppose, said the cantina owner, — they all want radio towers to advertise their businesses as well.

— There's talk.

— Bah, said the cantina owner. — I'm skeptical.

— I am too, said the father.

The mayor looked affronted. — All I know is that Brinkley showed me letters from satisfied customers, all swearing that the goat-gland operation made them as frisky as a vole in heat. He has cabinets full of them.

The cantina owner's eyes widened, and a spark came into his voice. — He has *letters*?

— Hundreds. Drawer after drawer full. I saw them when I visited his practice in Del Rio.

— I don't believe it, said the cantina owner. — Sewing the cojones of a billy goat inside a man? It can't work. It wouldn't work.

— Then don't believe it.

— Don't worry. I won't.

The mayor and Father Alvarez both looked at the cantina owner, surprised by his sudden prickliness; usually such gloomy presentiments came from Father Alvarez, who was known for his taciturn disposition. The cantina owner drained his tequila, slammed his glass against the table, and looked towards a place that was neither close nor far.

— Ay no, he reiterated, nervously fiddling with the tips of his enormous moustache. — I don't believe it for a moment.

The trio stayed up late that night, talking about the things that most concerned Mexicanos of their age: fútbol, government corruption, food, and, of course, the capriciousness of the fairer sex. These were topics demanding exhaustive attention, and the men spent longer than normal in each other's company. As the hours passed, the cantina filled and then emptied. Their conversation, though beset by lulls that were in no way uncomfortable, continued until the sky outside the shuttered windows began to brighten. Seeing spears of dusty light penetrate the cantina, the three men stood and bid each other adiós. They all stepped into the street. Here they took deep breaths and enjoyed the way that the pale morning light made the roofs of the houses seep orange.

They parted. The cantina owner walked behind his bar and entered the room he shared with his sullen wife, Margarita. Father Alvarez had only to walk a few doors west, where he lived in a dusty room littered with books, newspapers, and laundry. The mayor had the longest walk of the three, for he had to hobble all the way back to the plaza and then cross it to reach his abode on the eastern edge of the square, where the good people of Corazón de la Fuente had given him a room when he became mayor all those years ago. Given his bad foot and the disequilibrium caused by a night of tequila drinking, this walk took some time. The mayor didn't mind. In the early hours the village exuded a peaceful knowingness that made him feel content with the way in which his life was passing. He reached the plaza and paused before the town hall, where his office was located. From there he looked along Avenida Cinco de Mayo, beyond Madam Félix's brothel, to the field where the gringo Brinkley would, if fate chose to smile upon them, build his radio tower.

He grinned briefly and moved on. Fatigue gripped him as decisively as the onset of a sore throat. The smack of his boot heels echoed off the façades of the houses, and it became easy to pretend that an unseen presence, wearing the same leather boots and suffering from the same laboured gait, was limping along beside him, offering him a sort of ghostly company.

{4}

THE FOLLOWING MORNING, FRANCISCO RAMIREZ
awoke, as always, to the crow of roosters. He rose, scrubbed
his face till it was as pink as a mongrel's nose, shaved with
a straight razor his father had given him on his thirteenth
birthday, and tamped down his thick dark hair with a tonic
made from diluted palm tree resin. He then choked down a
breakfast of tortilla and guava juice, his appetite victimized
by nerves.

Returning to his room, he donned the suit his father had
once worn to Sunday morning services. Francisco was pleased
to see that he had grown into the garment: the cuffs fell just
to the tops of his boots, and the sleeves lightly graced the base
of his big, creased hands. He regarded himself in his great-
great-grandfather's mirror, subtracted the greenish hue, and,
for a moment, felt bolstered by his appearance, his slightly
rearranged nose notwithstanding.

Francisco straightened his shoulders and emerged from
the room. His father was seated at a table with Francisco's

little brothers, both of whom looked up with a smear of warm oatmeal around their mouths. Also seated at the table was Francisco's abuela, Doña Susana, who grinned at her eldest grandchild, recalling the awkwardness of her own first exercises in romance. Francisco's brothers, meanwhile, sensed that something of uncomfortable importance was about to occur, and though they had no idea what it was, they nonetheless giggled.

Francisco's father rose and approached his eldest son. — Mijo, he said. — You are a fine young man. Malfil Cruz will see this.

— Sí, echoed Francisco's grandmother. — Don't worry.

— I'll try.

— And always remember, said Francisco's father. — Determination and an honesty of intent will get you just about anything in this world.

— I know, Papi. You have told me this a million times.

— It is something worth saying a million times.

Francisco then enacted a ritual performed every time he left the house. He walked over to the windowsill and picked up the picture of his mother, immortalized forever in a chipped plastic frame. He kissed her image, reliving the warmth he had once felt in her arms. He then replaced the photo and set out, careful to walk slowly so that he didn't raise too much dust from the avenue; in this way he maintained the polish he'd given his boots the night before. He discreetly crossed himself as he passed the doorway of the town's ravaged church, at which point he realized that what he really needed was a quick, fortifying visit to Father Alvarez. He doubled back through the plaza and reached the house of the

man who'd both presided over Francisco's Communion and
blessed his arrival on this earth.

He knocked. A moment later Alvarez was peering at him,
a sliver of light reflecting off his naked scalp.

— So, he grunted. — Francisco Ramirez. Is there a funeral
today nobody told me about?

— No, Father, said Francisco.

— Well then, what is it? My head's killing me.

— I'm going to the house of Malfil Cruz. There I will ask
for permission to spend time with her daughter.

— And you'd like a blessing to up your odds?

— If I could, Father.

— Francisco, you know this isn't a matchmaking service.
Besides, I got kicked out of the business, remember?

Francisco nodded in sympathy. Thanks to the communist theory that had spawned the revolution in the first place, it
was still a punishable offence to practise religion in public, to
wear religious garb outside one's home, to publicly swear allegiance to Jesus, to hail Mary within earshot of a neighbour, to
hang any sort of cross above a residence doorway . . . The list
was so long and thorough it was doubtful that the country's
latest president had memorized it himself. What was certain
is that a brigade called the Red Shirts still rode around trying
to enforce the country's anti-religionist laws, its principal tar-
gets being priests, nuns, seminary students, and any person
sufficiently impertinent to be seen in public on bended knees.

Consequently, Father Alvarez no longer gave Sunday lectures, did not hear confession, and dressed in the manner of
an ordinary norteño male. Yet it was equally true that, during
moments of extreme personal crisis, Alvarez could be urged

to re-don his ecclesiastical cap, if only metaphorically, and stealthily grant a blessing or two.

— Por favor, Francisco said in a lowered voice. — I need all the help I can get.

Alvarez took a long, exasperated breath. — Then again, our existence as a race does depend on procreation. I suppose you might as well come in.

Francisco followed Alvarez into his small, dark abode. As in most houses, a hammock stretched along one wall and the kitchen extended into the open air from the back of the house, where it was topped by a lattice of huizache branches. Francisco watched as Alvarez opened the top drawer of a large oak desk beneath the room's northern window. He retrieved a small glass bottle, walked back across the room, and stood before Francisco.

— If you succeed in your intentions, will you be respectful and kind towards Violeta?

— Sí, Father.

— And will you treat her with the degree of courtesy with which you would treat a daughter of your own?

— Sí.

— In that case, I hereby sanctify your mission.

Father Alvarez pulled the tiny cork from the bottle. He then splashed clear liquid on Francisco's shoulders, not bothering to tell the young man that it was nothing more than water collected from his cistern after a rare Coahuilan rainstorm, and no holier than the acts committed at the House of Gentlemanly Pleasures.

— All right, you're ready. Go fulfil your destiny. Just do me a favour . . .

— Sí?

— Don't blame me if Malfil Cruz gives you a kick in the seat of your pants.

Forewarned, Francisco knocked on the door of Violeta Cruz's row house. From inside he heard stirring. A dog or two howled from the alley next door. The door creaked open.

Malfil Cruz was a tall, lean woman with frizzled hair who, Francisco never failed to notice, did not in any way share her daughter's ethereal beauty. She worked as a laundress, her little house permanently infused with the scent of lye. Her hands, Francisco noticed, were pink and raw-looking.

— Hola, Francisco.

— Hola, señora.

He entered. The living room was dimly lit to fend off the heat of the day. Two high-backed chairs, which would have looked ratty in proper light, were set in the middle of the room, facing each other. Between them was a small, unadorned table. From the back of the house Francisco could hear rustling and the clinking of spoons; he surmised that Violeta was preparing a pot of coffee.

— Por favor, said Violeta's mother. — Have a seat.

Francisco hesitated before sitting, fearing he might take the favoured spot of Señora Cruz. But it was hot, and the room's dense, soapy odour made him feel slightly weakened. Malfil again gestured towards one of the chairs, and this time Francisco obeyed. Violeta's mother took the seat opposite him and regarded him for a moment, her expression one of scrutinizing concern. Just then Violeta emerged from the rear of the tiny home, carrying a tray bearing two cups and a small pot. As she lowered the tray to the table between them, the pot jiggled and a small amount of coffee spilled.

— Careful, Malfil hissed at her daughter.

As Violeta straightened, Francisco could swear he caught her rolling her eyes.

Malfil leaned towards him. — Coffee?

— Sí, gracias.

Malfil Cruz poured two cups and handed one to Francisco. He took a sip, his mouth filling with a rich, black-earth deliciousness. He felt himself calm slightly. Again the two sat in silence, Francisco understanding that it would be impertinent for him to speak first. Violeta's mother, meanwhile, sat looking at her cup and saucer as though disinclined to regard her guest. She took a sip and reflexively licked away the drops clinging to her flaking lips. Finally she looked at him.

— Violeta says you would like to have a word with me.

— Señora Cruz, he started, — it's true.

— Well, out with it, mijo. I have work to do.

Francisco glanced at Violeta, who lowered her eyes. He then cleared his throat and said: — I'm afraid I've fallen for Violeta. With your permission, I was hoping she might accept me as her boyfriend.

Malfil took a deep breath, straightened her shoulders, and looked at Francisco as though she were inspecting a mule. And then, suddenly, Francisco saw it: a slight softening of her carriage, a barely perceptible melting of the iron posture with which Malfil Cruz ordinarily met the world. Her eyes softened and seemed to mute slightly in colour and intensity.

— Francisco, as you well know, it is my feeling that Violeta is not yet old enough to consort with the muchachos of this town. By the same token, you are neither as callow nor as superficial as most. For this reason, I'm willing to make you an offer.

Malfil Cruz hung her head and for a few seconds said nothing. She now looked unalterably sad.

— Francisco, she started. — Though you were young at the time, you may still recall the day on which a division of Villa's army rode into Corazón and set fire to the cantina and pointed a gun at Carlos Hernandez.

— Ay, señora. I was quite young but I've heard stories.

— Pues . . . you may or may not know that Violeta has an older brother. His name is Pablo.

— Sí, said Francisco. — The one who went away.

— Villa's henchmen came here that night. Looking for whatever they could take. Of course, Violeta and I were in the desert, hiding with all the other women. But we had neighbours who saw the whole thing. When the Villistas saw that we owned nothing of value, they shot at the ceiling — go ahead, look up, you can still see the splinters — and then they took away my husband and my beloved Pablito. They were last seen on the backs of horses, blindfolded, their hands fastened by yucca twine.

Francisco said nothing. Señora Cruz rose and walked over to a battered cupboard that stood in the corner. She opened the drawer and removed something. When she turned, Francisco could see it was a photograph. Malfil Cruz crossed the room and, eyes damp, stood beside the chair on which Francisco was sitting.

— My husband was killed in a fight near Chihuahua City, may God rest his soul. My son, however, disappeared.

She leaned over and held the photograph before Francisco.

— You see, Francisco? He looks a little like you.

Francisco looked at the photograph.

— I am a woman, Francisco. I cannot wander off whenever I feel like it, asking questions of anyone I care to. It would not be proper. But *you* . . . you are a young man. You are a free man. Take this picture. I want you to try to find out what happened to him. They rode in the direction of Piedras Negras. It was years ago. This is all I know.

Francisco took the photograph. Pablo was standing in the sun, his arm around his mother, a cowboy hat shading his eyes. It was true that he bore some similarity to Francisco, in that he was broad-shouldered and thick-armed and, at the age of sixteen, could pass for fully a grown man.

— If you could find out what happened to him, I would be eternally grateful. The rest would be up to Violeta. Do we understand each other?

Francisco continued staring at the photograph in his hand. It was so crinkled and worn it felt coarse, like the finest grade of sandpaper. Although the young man's eyes were shaded by his hat, Francisco could still see the mischief flaring within them. This contrasted with the solemn, almost exhausted look in Malfil's eyes. Suddenly, Francisco realized something. Pablo had been a handful. Looking at the photo, Francisco wondered if perhaps mother and son had quarrelled before his disappearance. Could it be that Malfil's continuing torment was fuelled as much by guilt as by maternal love?

— Sí, Francisco finally said. — We do, señora. My final exam takes place in the middle of June, and then my days will be mine.

— Gracias, Francisco, Malfil responded. — Trust me when I tell you that I would not grant just anyone this task.

The rest of the meeting was filled with polite conversation, most of it concerning the coming of the tower. On this topic Malfil Cruz was exuberant: the project was filling the entire town with a sense of possibility, and for this reason she had felt a rekindling of her desire — ay no, of her *need* — to discover what had happened to her only son. When the coffee was finished and a respectful amount of time had expired, Francisco Ramirez stood and thanked Malfil Cruz for entertaining him. After bowing slightly to both Malfil and Violeta, he excused himself and walked towards the door. Yet just before leaving, he turned and said something that had the resonance of the prophetic.

Don't worry, señora. I'll find your son. Or I will die trying.

{5}

JUST BEYOND THE NORTHEAST CORNER OF TOWN
was the rickety wood-planked bridge separating México from
Los Estados Unidos. At most hours of the day customs guards
sat on either end of the little bridge. The American guard had
a small cabin in which he kept a radio, a fan, a stack of pulp
novels, back issues of the *Saturday Evening Post*, and a small
icebox in which he stored his lunch, a roster of snack items,
and a variety of soft drinks. His Mexican counterpart had
nothing more than a hat to keep the sun off his head and a
three-legged kitchen chair he'd salvaged from the municipal
dump, an operation that had exposed him to odour and crow
attack. While both guards were theoretically in place to control the flow of commerce and immigration between the two
countries, they functioned mostly to collect bribes from those
powerless enough to feel intimidated by their presence. Most
of Corazón's residents, when needing to visit los Estados, simply chose to swim for it.

Exactly two weeks after the Reyes brothers' lucha night,

the dusty stultification that so characterized life in Corazón de la Fuente was fractured by the rumble of three Model T pickup trucks crossing the bridge at precise twenty-metre intervals. All three vehicles turned right at the sandy impression that was Avenida Cinco de Mayo. The drivers then motored west, past the ejido, the remains of Antonio Garcia's once-grand hacienda, the central plaza, and the long, jacal-style lodge that was Madam Félix's House of Gentlemanly Pleasures. With the entire town excitedly watching — noses pressed against windowpanes, mothers calling for their children to come see, men opening celebratory bottles of cerveza — the gringo drivers pulled up at an expanse of flat desert scrub. Here a half-dozen men got out, all dressed in dungarees, workboots, and hard hats. To those townsfolk who were perplexedly looking on, it was as though the men feared a vulture might suddenly expire from a heart attack, plummet through the broiling air, and clunk them on the head.

The men started walking around the area's perimeter. Occasionally they stopped to point, arm-sweep, or gesticulate, actions that were often accompanied by raised voices. One of them kept unrolling construction plans, which he would hold vertically, and then horizontally, and then vertically, before his own flummoxed expression. The gringo trucks came again the next day, and the day after. Then, in the following week, the only visitors to the work site were voles and the occasional deer wandering into town to feed on scraps missed by the town's stray-dog population. A gloomy quiet descended upon the lot, causing some townsfolk to wonder whether the project had fallen through. But then, one morning, Holt tractors equipped with dozing blades could be seen approaching the river. Ignoring the Mexican border guard, whose chair collapsed from the resultant vibrations, the drivers chugged across the shaking bridge and turned right. Upon reaching town, they rattled walls and cracked windowpanes and shook wooden dentures from the mouths of the town's elderly.

They stopped at the work site. In true gringo fashion the men got right to work, no cigarettes or chit-chat or cups of warm chocolate (fortified, more often than not, with a little fermented agave). They immediately began pushing around mounds of the thin, tan, wormless soil, stopping only to drink Coca-Cola and eat a quick canned-meat sandwich at noon. After lunch they worked for the whole of the afternoon, never once stopping to nap or sip pulque or sneak off for a quick visit with a mistress. All of this was a source of fascination for the people of Corazón de la Fuente, who, having little better to do, gathered and spent the day watching. Some of the more enterprising set up food stands from which they sold organ-meat tacos and warm beer, only to pack up when it became obvious that the gringos were interested only in the bland-looking lunches they'd brought from home. When the sun was low in the sky and starting to turn the colour of marmalade, the tractors chugged back through town, fracturing whatever windows they had failed to crack on their way in that morning.

Within three days, a four-hectare field of bramble, mesquite, and prickly pear had turned into a mound of light brown soil. Suddenly, the coming of the tower seemed more than a vague possibility: all you had to do was close your eyes and you could imagine it, reaching towards the relentless sun, risen magically from the moistureless earth. The following day, Mayor Orozco went to welcome the project foreman. It was a short greeting: though the mayor's English was rudimentary, it was accomplished in comparison to the foreman's Spanish. They shook hands and grinned at one another.

— Welcome, said Miguel.

— Ain't nothin', said the foreman.

— If joo needing any assistance, please just inform me.

The foreman nodded and resumed hollering instructions at the bulldozer operators. His actions, at least in the eyes of those watching the proceedings, were brusque and lacking in courtesy, and a small minority of townsfolk felt that he should have been rebuked by the town's kindly, if indecisive, mayor. By the end of the day the work team was gone.

The field sat quiet for the next nine days. Just when the townsfolk began to suspect that a serious delay had occurred, the same vehicles came rumbling back through town, though this time they were fitted with grading blades. Throughout the day, the mounds of dead Coahuilan earth were spread out, scooped up, churned, spread out, scooped up . . . On and on it went until the field was more or less as flat as it had been before the project started. The difference, of course, was the glaring absence of agave, huizache, mesquite, scrub grass, succulent plants, vole mounds, scrap metal, broken bottles, spent artillery shells, and all manner of flowering cacti. The adults of the town looked at the field, struggling to keep rein on their soaring feelings of hope. To the town's children, the field was now as tempting as an actual sports field; the foreman soon posted security guards to keep dirty-faced little ones from playing on the site, their makeshift balls fashioned from inflated goat udders. At the end of the day, the tractors rumbled towards the American side of the border, again caus-ing damage too petty to complain about, given the notices that were appearing throughout town, posted on walls, fence posts, and palm trees. In a faultless Spanish they read:

¡Attention One and All!

To the good and fair people of Corazón de la Fuente, I do hereby invite you to attend a job fair that I, John Romulus Brinkley, will be sponsoring in the central plaza of your charming town next Saturday morning. Refreshments and a light lunch will be served, and I do hereby guarantee that all those who are not afraid of a little hard work, and who meet some basic job requirements, will leave with gainful employ-ment. So come one, come all, to a morning of productive, good-hearted fun.

Sometime later that week, the strangulating heat that had gripped northern Coahuila for a month finally broke, a cool breeze descending from the north like a susurration of hope. The townsfolk, used to waking early in baking temperatures, now awoke for a more pleasant reason: they were too excited to sleep. Wrapped in woollen ponchos, eyes crusty with sleep, gripping cups of hot coffee or the chocolate beverage known as atole, they drifted out of adobe homes and tin-roofed hov-els alike. Clustering in the central plaza, they chatted and smoked cheap punche cigarettes and kept glancing furtively towards the bridge separating nations.

A truck pulled up, the crowd parting to make room. In the cab were three men: the project foreman, a sub-foreman, and a translator named Geraldo who was obviously not from the north, as he had the distracting habit of addressing everyone as *chango,* a southern expression used in place of *primo* or *compadre.* As Geraldo began advising the crowd to form a single, orderly line, the two gringos set up a table in the middle of the bandstand where the Reyes brothers had put on their wrestling display. Geraldo also tacked a large handwritten sign to one of the square's dying palo verdes. On this sign were the rules: no women, no one under eighteen or over sixty-five, no one without the usual complement of arms and legs, no one with a criminal record. The line soon extended through the plaza, along Avenida Cinco de Mayo and past Antonio Garcia's hacienda, only to peter out somewhere in the smoky, festering depths of the ejido.

As the two gringos began taking down the names of the eligible, another truck showed up. Within minutes, a pair of smiling women from the other side of the river, each with a gingham apron and upper arms as wobbly as gelatin, began giving free cups of lemonade and pieces of tepid southern-fried chicken to those who cared to join a second queue. By the end of the morning, everyone who qualified was informed that he had a job; this included Francisco's delighted father, who had not worked since the middle days of the revolution, when a misdirected government shell had destroyed the tannery where he was employed.

— Okay, changos, Geraldo began to yell, his arms waving in the air. — Time to go home, party's over, the chicken is all gone, when we need you you'll be the first to know . . .

❖ ❖ ❖

Again there was a period of maddening inactivity. Days turned to weeks, and an agonizing ennui set in. The boredom, the relentless sun, the gruesome memories of the war, the monotonous diet of rice and beans and cereal — all of it now seemed unbearable when weighed against the promise of employment. As those weeks turned into a full month, the day of the job fair began to seem like something imagined, as though it had existed only in the columns of wavering air that rose from the streets at high noon.

But then, one morning, a convoy of diesel-engine flatbeds, all carrying metal I-beams, began rolling through the narrow, dusty lanes of Corazón de la Fuente. Given their loads, it was difficult to negotiate the turn encountered at the plaza: the eldest palm tree on the square was repeatedly assaulted, and the house with the misfortune of being located at the junction was scraped by the protruding girders. Upon reaching the work site, each driver dumped his bundle of I-beams before returning to the American side and fetching another. This went on for a full day. The damaged palm tree keeled over, taking another one with it, and the façade of the scraped house grew so thin it became permeable to the hot, dense air.

The following afternoon, a little blue Ford automobile with a speaker mounted on its roof cruised through Corazón de la Fuente. Ears perked at the sound of Geraldo's crackling, distorted voice: *Listen up, changos, good news, tomorrow's the big day, report to the site tomorrow, good news, good news, it's all starting tomorrow, seven a.m., don't be late, tomorrow's the big day* . . . This went on for the better part of an hour. The Ford careered along Avenida Cinco de Mayo and Avenida Hidalgo, around both the central plaza and the second, smaller plaza, and through the wider pathways of the ejido, causing many of its impoverished residents to believe they were being evicted.

The following morning, 127 men, a few dozen of whom actually lived in the neighbouring village of Rosita, congregated in the work field. Each wore a cowboy hat, patched Levi's, and huaraches fashioned from tire shards and lengths of old string. In short order they were given shovels, riveting gloves, and second-hand steel-toe boots. This was followed by a five-minute lecture on safety, which was translated, perhaps too concisely, by Geraldo:

— These gringos were too cheap to get you helmets, and if a beam falls on your head it'll squash like a plum. So for the love of Christ, be careful.

The assembled workers all nodded and went to work. Their efforts were directed by the sub-foreman, who, in typical gringo fashion, lacked both patience and foreign-language skills. There was excessive yelling, confusion, and swearing in both Spanish and Kickapoo, one of the Native languages spoken in northern Coahuila. Still, by nine o'clock even the most obtuse of workers had gleaned enough to know that his job was to dig one of three large craters in which the foundations of the tower would be placed. A trio of huddles formed, the backs of the men facing the depthless white sky, the rays of the sun piercing work shirts thinned by repeated washings. Owing to the dictates of machismo, the workers didn't stop often enough to drink water, such that within an hour their tongues began to swell, their lips began to crack and sting, and their skin began to show the first rubbery signs of dehydration.

At ten-thirty there came the clanging of a large metal cowbell. This puzzled the workers until it was explained that they were now allowed to break from their labours. They stood, groaning, hands on their lower backs, and proceeded to smoke hand-rolled cigarettes and drink cups of real coffee provided by the building company. A second ringing indicated that their break — which couldn't have been more than fifteen minutes — had expired. Shocked, the men returned to work.

At lunch they were given ham-and-cheese sandwiches and Coca-Cola. During their afternoon break they smoked and drank coffee and complained that the muscles in their shoulders were starting to ache as badly as the muscles in their lower backs. At four o'clock the bell rang again, signifying that their workday had ended. The workers hung around for a while, looking at the immense depression they had created in the soil. They then trudged off to their homes, where repasts of bean and tortilla were already being warmed over low, smouldering fires.

The workers returned the next day, and the day after. In the middle of the fourth day of digging, the cowbell sounded at a time that was neither their lunch nor one of their breaks. The men stood and looked curiously at each other, muttering *Qué pasa?* Within minutes, Geraldo was pacing from one group to another, informing them that they were done, the holes were big enough, any further and they'd hit mud. Not knowing what to do, the workers mostly plopped themselves down on the soil and pensively smoked, those with flasks of pulque considerately passing them around. Dutiful wives, many of whom had watched all day from the sidelines, saw the work stoppage and rushed to give their husbands quesadillas flavoured with pickled chili.

Within the hour, trucks piled with bags of concrete mix began pulling up to the site, and it now became the men's job to offload them next to the three caverns in the ground. The men worked late that day, apparently earning something that Geraldo described with the English word *overtime*. They went home past sundown, their way guided by torches. The next day the men were divided into three groups. There were those who dumped the concrete mix into wheelbarrows, there were those who mixed the heavy substance, and there were those who began filling the first of the foundation pits. Midway through the following morning, a cantilevered crane arrived on a flatbed. A group of men were borrowed from concrete duty to help offload the crane, and by mid-afternoon the workers were helping guide the first of the foundation girders into the damp concrete. By the end of the day a beam protruded diagonally from the first hole, its tip gamely tilted towards the imagined summit of the tower. For the people of Corazón de la Fuente, that single rigid beam had a symbolic value: it was the town, reaching towards the promise of the sky.

This was achieved late on a Friday afternoon. The men lined up to be paid, each receiving a packet containing as many pesos as they typically earned in a year. Around five o'clock in the afternoon an impromptu performance was given by Los Inconsolables del Norte (who had been practising and who no longer played with quite such a wheezing, anemic quality). Someone's abuela, a sturdily built little woman with eyebrows as thick as caterpillars, initiated the dancing. She was followed by laughing children, a few off-duty Marias, and a coterie of señoras in snug, brightly patterned dresses. As always, the last to join in were the men, who looked stiff-backed and worried about scuffing their boots on the twists of discarded metal that lay about everywhere. This sparked a wholesome, familial riotousness, without any of the fistfights and pistol firings that so commonly mar Mexican festivities.

Someone started a bonfire, and a grinning local arrived with a deer that he had shot, skinned, and gutted that very week. Dinner was impaled on a spit and placed over the flames, the buck seeming to gain an expression of mildly indignant surprise. When it was cooked through, shreds of meat were sprinkled with salt and lime, wrapped in flour tortillas, and served to anyone who was hungry. Francisco and Violeta ate together, their faces reflecting the light of the fire, while everyone around them drank and laughed and danced. Soon after, children were dispatched to kitchens and cellars to fetch buckets of fermented agave punch, most of which was as potent — and about as flavourful — as nitroglycerine. Liberal servings were passed around in the traditional gourd-shaped glasses known as jícaras.

The faces of the townsfolk, caught in the low flames still warming the deer's underbelly, turned speckled and orange, like something glimpsed in dreams. Everything wavered. Children ran in excited circles, like ricocheting points of energy. Men hung arms over shoulders and sang wheezing corridos about lost love and survived battles and the luscious torment that was life in México. A pistol, and then another, came out, the owners passing them around while boasting about the damage they had caused during the revolution.

There was a surfeit of firing into the air, all of which was accompanied by pronouncements of love to the moon and the stars and the sand and every one of the women in their sad, miraculous country.

{6}

IT TOOK A WEEK AND A HALF FOR THE BASE OF DR.
Brinkley's tower to peek out of all three corners of the foundation. Yet once it did, it grew exponentially, the three sections
of the structure tapering towards one another not unlike
a famous tower that, the workers were told, had recently
been erected in some distant European city called Paris.
The more fearless of the workers — meaning the Kickapoo
Natives — began earning additional wages by fitting and
bolting beams, their bodies looking small and vulnerable
from down below. Much of the work on the ground was now
done by men with their chins pointed upwards, their round
faces flushed by the restoration of their dignity.

Accordingly, the worry so firmly etched into the faces
of the townspeople eased, making room for expressions of
gaiety. Music, produced by accordions or wind-up Victrolas,
could now be heard coming from windows in the early evenings. With full bellies, the residents took to walking the plaza
after dinner, a profoundly Mexican pastime that had been

lost during the revolution, when roving bands of psychopaths were a chronic preoccupation. Carlos Hernandez's cantina was now so busy in the evenings he had to import homemade liquor from other towns to keep his customers satisfied and his pulque buckets full. The town store, which was operated by a hirsute individual named Fajardo Jiminez, did a roaring trade in tortillas, toothpaste, soap, salsa, dried cornmeal . . . in all of the staples that, in times of deprivation, the poor spent hours each day making for themselves. Soon the residents of Corazón de la Fuente grew used to sounds that had all but disappeared over the past decade: the sound of happy chatter, of accordion music being played by jubilant fingers, of boots tapping the dust in impromptu waltzes, of children excited by the end of the school year, of men bragging about things they'd done when young and strong and filled with bravado, of women gracefully burping away the indigestion caused by heavy meals, of couples celebrating in the way that couples always will — in the early hours, their children asleep, their hammocks swaying with movements inspired by merriment and love.

For Francisco Ramirez, the coming of summer had definite, if unintended, consequences. In his final exam of the school year he was too distracted by the promise he had made to Malfil Cruz: maybe he could ask to borrow one of Antonio Garcia's horses to use in his search for Violeta's brother. Francisco considered the notion some more, growing so excited that he botched a series of questions regarding the Pythagorean theorem. The more he thought about it, the more he felt it would succeed. The hacendero was nothing if not an honourable man, a lover of women and horses, a believer in tradition, a student of México and all its glorious conceits. Above all else, he was a subscriber to the time-honoured code that exists among gentlemen, and it was for this reason that Francisco visited the hacendero the very next morning, his disastrous mathematics exam already a trivial memory.

He found him right where he knew he would find him: in the small paddock siding his artillery-ravaged mansion, happily brushing the stallion he had recently purchased from a fellow rancher who lived near the border of Chihuahua. It was good to see the hacendero looking so content; while everyone in town had suffered personal losses during the revolution, nobody had lost as much financially as Señor Garcia. Before the start of the fighting, he had owned a body of land whose head lay just shy of Piedras Negras, whose feet lay close to Sabinas, and whose belly was sufficiently concave to allow for the existence of Corazón de la Fuente. Likewise, the hacendero's horses had enjoyed the run of a ten-hectare enclosure, and they were kept at night in an enormous ventilated barn constructed by members of a Mennonite community who farmed wheat southeast of Chihuahua City. Then came the series of violent coups that comprised the revolution.

Porfirio Díaz had fled like a frightened preschooler, and the army of Francisco Madero was the first to requisition some of the hacendero's land, which was put to use as a campground for revolutionary forces. This requisitioning happened again under Carranza, and again under Huerta, and again under Obregón. With time, the various revolutionary governments sold off most of the hacendero's land and converted what little was left into the communally owned ejido, the beneficiaries of which were mostly tubercular peasants from the south. Each day, it seemed, another family arrived and another tin-roofed hovel, reeking of sweat and smouldering coal, was erected on land that had been lovingly tended by generations of Garcias. Scattered in and amongst the shantytown was the farming equipment donated by one of the provisional governments. Most of it was never touched, the peasants having neither the knowledge nor the inclination to use it. As a consequence, it was mostly left to rust in the harsh northern weather, its principal function now to give lockjaw to shoeless children, who regularly cut themselves while playing war games with old scythes and tillers.

— Francisco! exclaimed the hacendero. — How are you? Have you met Diamante, my new caballo?

Francisco reached out to touch the horse on his muzzle, only to have Diamante snort haughtily and retreat a few steps.

— Careful, primo, cautioned the hacendero. — He's got a bit of a temper.

Though Francisco did not own a horse and was not from a family of horsemen, he was nonetheless a norteño, born with an appreciation of things equine as surely as he had been born with feet and hands.

— Ay sí, said Francisco. — He is magnificent. You're one lucky hombre.

The two chit-chatted for a few minutes, mostly about the hacendero's new horse, the heat, and, naturally enough, Dr. Brinkley's tower. When there was a natural pause in the conversation, Francisco finally cleared his throat and announced his purpose.

— Señor Garcia, I came here today because I need to ask you a favour.

— And what would that be?

— I was wondering if . . . pues . . . I was wondering if I could borrow one of your horses.

— And what do you plan to do with it?

Francisco hesitated, cleared his throat, and spoke. — I am searching for the son of Malfil Cruz.

The hacendero paused, forcing himself not to grin. — Well, then, he said. — When a woman requires our help, we must do what we can. How long will you be gone?

— I don't know. As long as is required.

— And you do realize that there is bus service in northern México now?

— I do.

— Yet you want to feel the wind in your hair, and hear the drum of hooves on hard-packed earth. You want to be free, and not bound by bus schedules and clanking diesel engines. I understand this, Francisco. Diamante, of course, is out of the question, as he would kill you within the hour. You can take one of the grullos.

Francisco followed the hacendero towards the corner of his once-great paddock, where a pair of ancient mares were gumming a lunch of hay stalks. Each regarded Francisco with a dull, unblinking gaze.

— Estrella's on the left, said the hacendero. — Beatriz is on the right. Take your pick.

— Which one do you recommend?

— It doesn't matter, mijo. They're both slow as molasses, but as dependable as the rise and fall of the sun. Either one will get you there.

Estrella released a foul cloud of undigested carrot, which

Francisco chose to interpret as a gesture of assent. — That one, he said.

Siding the paddock was a creaky old barn that, thanks to revolutionary cannon fire, was missing a goodly portion of its rear wall. The hacendero walked towards it whistling, and when he returned he was carrying an old saddle and bit. He stopped before Francisco and blew on the saddle, disturbing a layer of settled dust. They both entered the corral.

Despite the fact that Estrella hadn't been ridden in years, she didn't whinny, try to move away, or in any way complain when the hacendero placed the saddle on her topside. In fact, as the hacendero cinched the straps beneath her low, sagging belly, Francisco began to wonder if the old horse had fallen asleep. Only when the hacendero reached into a pocket and produced an apple did Estrella turn her head and accept it with a snort.

The hacendero led her out of the paddock and walked her towards the heat-deadened avenue. He handed Francisco the reins.

— Don't worry, joven. She's a good horse, even if she's a little long in the tooth. Give her lots of water and feed her whatever you can. Road grass will do; she's not particular. Be nice to her and tell her she's pretty. Tickle her behind the ears and tell her what a good caballo she is. Once upon a time she meant a lot to my family, and my only request is that you be kind and respectful and don't punish her without good reason.

— I understand.

— Adiós, Francisco.

— Adiós, Señor Garcia. And gracias.

❖ ❖ ❖

Before leaving town, Francisco led Estrella towards the village store and tied her to one of the hitching posts erected outside. Once inside, he called the name of the store's owner, who was originally from a little village in Zacatecas where a genetic disorder called hypertrichosis caused many of its residents to be covered, head to toe, in thick whorls of hair. The trapdoor leading to the cellar opened, its rusting hinges producing a muffled creak. Fajardo emerged, a row of pearl-white teeth showing through his mat of coarse copper fur.

— Hola, Francisco. I was just downstairs. I got a shipment of calabazas today.

— Hola, Señor Jimenez.

— I heard you are taking a trip.

— Sí.

— Well, let's get you stocked up then.

Francisco bought deer jerky, apples, a jute cloth filled with flour tortillas, and a bottle of drinking water. After thanking Fajardo, he walked Estrella diagonally across the town's central plaza, the clopping of hooves resounding off the crumbling pink façade of the town hall. He walked Estrella past Violeta's house, past the Callejón of Slumbering Bitches, past the House of Gentlemanly Pleasures, and, finally, past the ascending radio tower of John Romulus Brinkley, which had reached a height of about fifty metres, the three sides of the tower now having met like a touching of vines. Francisco stopped, craned his neck upwards, and watched Kickapoo workers shooting rivets into the upstanding girders, the whole time marvelling at the way in which this tower, this lofty assembly of lug nuts and steel, was gradually altering his conception of what was and was not possible. It, Francisco realized with a start, was the reason he felt he would succeed in his mission.

Francisco put a boot into Estrella's stirrup and threw a leg over, the horse's only reaction being to sag noticeably in the midsection. After getting his bearings, he ordered *Vamanos* and made an encouraging noise by sucking air through the teeth on the right side of his mouth. Estrella stared forward. Francisco called louder — Vámonos, vámonos — and made a rocking motion with his pelvis that, under any other circumstances, would have been considered lascivious. When Estrella did nothing more than belch loudly, Francisco lightly touched his spurs against the horse's flank.

Estrella responded by whinnying and shedding a portion of dead skin from her sides. She then ambled in the direction of Francisco's destiny, her head hanging low, a cloud of poorly digested feed grass wafting along behind them.

{7}

AS PREPOSTEROUS AS IT MAY HAVE SEEMED, THERE were people in town who disliked that Dr. Brinkley had chosen Corazón de la Fuente as the recipient of his tower. Foremost among these was the curandera, the bristle-faced old witch who lived in a shack out in the desert. Her real name was Azula Mampajo, and it was becoming more and more common to see her patrolling the perimeter of the work site, waving bunches of smouldering herbs while simultaneously moaning. This unnerved the Kickapoo Indians labouring on the tower, all of whom followed the same belief system as the curandera. The accident rate at the building site — which had not been low to begin with — increased. One unlucky indigenous, upon hearing the curandera's incantations, lost his balance and fell from the second tier of the tower, breaking an arm and a smattering of ribs.

The next day, one of the sub-foremen, accompanied by Geraldo the translator, confronted the woman, who was performing a fitful jig while waving around bunches of stinkweed. She stopped and regarded them through eyes that, over the years, had grown milky and weak.

— Lady, said the foreman. — Y'all cain't be distractin' my workers like that.

The curandera turned to the translator, who interpreted the sub-foreman's request as follows: — He said to fuck off back to hell, you malodorous witch. If you don't, we'll drown you in the river.

She withdrew, muttering, kept to herself for a few days, and was then seen off in the distance, performing spooky rituals by herself. Over the next week or so she inched towards the work site, until the day came when the workers again started misfiring their riveting guns and walking off crossbeams. One of the sub-foremen was again dispatched to talk to her, and again she was told to fuck off by Geraldo, who this time emphasized the sentiment by pushing her into the dirt. Nothing if not resilient, the old woman picked herself up and directed the less filmy of her eyes towards Geraldo.

— This tower, she pronounced, — is the work of the devil.

She then punctuated this sentiment by kicking Geraldo in the shin. He leapt around on one foot, swearing as only a Mexicano can swear, while the old woman walked off snickering.

Yet the person who most resented the project was the man who, ironically enough, benefited the most from all of the new wealth in town. For this reason, the cantina owner, Carlos Hernandez, had to suffer in silence. He had to fake joyfulness every time someone commented on how the project was increasing the amount of money the workers were spending in his cantina. He had to feign high spirits whenever a customer said *I bet you love this tower!* over a cup of frothing pulque. He had to chuckle sincerely every time someone ordered a cerveza and offered the following opinion: *This tower is like a gift from heaven for you, sí, Carlito?*

This, the cantina owner found, was difficult. It was the way the structure was growing — so unbending, so powerfully bolted, so incorrigibly rigid. It was the way in which it was beginning to penetrate the white-blue sky. It was the way in which, every weekday, it grew bigger, mightier, more prominent, a development that mocked both the cantina owner and the problem that plagued not only his every waking moment but many of his sleeping ones as well. Even in his dreams, he was hounded by images of drooping water hoses, of wilting flowers, of finding a fine young mare in the desert and, no matter how hard he spurred her flank, not being able to make her gallop.

He could remember how it started — in those terrible times when cannons rumbled and the peso was suddenly no good and reports of slaughter, at the hands of Villistas and federales alike, were blowing into town like gusts of bad weather. It was an afternoon on a sleepy Tuesday. The town was just coming alive after its customary siesta; the cantina owner, having enjoyed a plate of tacos al pastor, an amorous interlude with his wife, Margarita, and a nap in which his dreams had been pleasant, was reopening his cantina for those clients who needed something stronger than coffee to arouse them after their midday repose.

Suddenly he heard a commotion. From outside there came alarmed cries and dogs barking and footfalls scurrying through the dusty streets and warnings called out by frantic mothers. He opened the cantina shutters and stood on the stoop, and sure enough, people were running in every direction, most particularly the womenfolk, who were being chased into the desert by their frightened, round-faced grandmothers. When the cantina owner stopped one of his neighbours, a flushed tannery worker with ruined hands and a spider-web complexion, the man blurted *Listen, Carlos, listen!* Standing on his stoop, the cantina owner filtered out the sounds of people running and dogs howling and grandmothers yelling *Hurry, hurry!* That's when he heard the percussive beat of horse hooves against the desert floor.

Ten minutes later they were riding through the streets of Corazón de la Fuente, whooping and firing off rounds and frightening children and wearing the gold shirts of those with a zealous loyalty to Pancho Villa. They headed straight to the House of Gentlemanly Pleasures, only to find it abandoned in the dusty heat of midday. With nothing else to do, they headed for the town's only watering hole. There must have been twenty of them, all with sombreros, bandoliers, and moustaches as bushy as fox tails. Their Levi's were dirtied with road dust and their fingernails were stained with the oil that sweated from the grips of their pistols. They sat, and started banging their fists against the tabletops.

The cantina owner raced to serve them cervezas and tequila and mescal and even the pulque he normally gave only to the poor ejido dwellers. As the revolutionaries got drunker and drunker they got uglier and uglier, their stubbled faces growing flushed and goblin-like. As the cantina owner worked behind the bar, cleaning glasses and pretending he was deaf, he listened to them badmouth the town and its people. And then one of the rebels loudly surmised that the fairer sex had been rounded up and carted off into the desert and so there were no women under the age of sixty to keep them company, and that this surely indicated that this place, this Corazón de Whatever, was a town that supported the federales. Why else, he opined, would they be so hostile to the army of the north, which was only fighting for their liberation? Why else, he snarled, would they be so niggardly with their damn women? Enraged, the Villistas all started yelling and howling and firing their pistols into the cantina's ceiling beams. Sensing their mood, the cantina owner retreated to the room behind the saloon, emerging only to serve them.

In short order the rebels had drunk the cantina owner dry, save for a case of special añejo tequila that he kept in his basement. When the soldiers next started clamouring for drinks, the cantina owner waved his arms in the air and said *We're finished, we're done, no hay más*. At first the revolutionaries thought he was joking. They all laughed, and more than one of them slurred a variation of *Come on, hombrecito, don't be like that*. The cantina owner repeated his lie — *Compadres, what can I do about it?* — until they finally realized he was serious. They quieted, and reflexively looked to a guy sitting in the corner, a homely and dirt-streaked hijo de puta whom they all called the capitano. He just sat there, the back of his chair leaning against the cool adobe wall, considering the news with a foul, consternated expression. He rose slowly, all eyes watching. When he reached the cantina owner, he pulled out a pistol the size of a baby's arm and he pressed it against the cantina owner's sweat-drenched temple. From that close,

Carlos could see that the man's right eye was made of glass, and that it had become scratched and cloudy with wear. The capitano grinned, his teeth a smear of tartar and the stringy remains of something he'd eaten.

— So, the rebel growled. — You are sure you have run out? Maybe you have forgotten a bottle or two of tequila, tucked away for special guests?

— No, said the cantina owner. — There's nothing.

The capitano cocked the enormous trigger, the resulting noise screaming in the cantina owner's ears. — Are you *sure*, cabrón?

The cantina owner swallowed. — Sorry, he gulped. — I made a mistake. There may be some in the basement. — Qué bueno! exclaimed the officer as he re-holstered his weapon. — This mujer says there's more in the basement.

And then they were in his root cellar, overturning baskets of potatoes and beets and cabbage, and he knew when they'd found the tequila for a cheer went up and pistol fire aerated the floorboards. The visitors resumed drinking. The red-faced cantina owner, watching from the corner, felt himself shrink, his body becoming that of a child frightened by the coming of night. One of the revolutionaries, a greasy mongrel with missing fingers, was about to open the very last bottle with his teeth when the capitano ordered him to stop. He was passed the bottle. The capitano stood on his chair and looked across the room.

— Before we go, I just wanted to thank the owner of this establishment for all his kind hospitality.

He then poured the contents of the tequila bottle over the aging wooden table and lit it with a match. As the men walked laughing from the cantina, Carlos rushed to his bedroom and grabbed the embroidered bedspread given to him by his in-laws on his wedding day. He used this to beat back the flames. When he was finished, he sat alone in his smoke-filled bar and shivered. He could not control it. His teeth shook and his nose ran and his heart fluttered and his fingers would not stop trembling. It was if he were sitting in the coldest place on earth, not a bar in the middle of a small Coahuilan border town.

A week passed. A week in which he felt ashamed to look his wife in her lovely blue-black eyes. On the night that his problem first presented itself, the cantina owner had been tired, and he concluded later that this was likely the problem. He retired to his bed, where Margarita was waiting with open arms and a suggestive, mirthful smirk. He kissed her, and when it came to the point at which man and woman melt together like heated wax, he suddenly found himself assaulted by a vivid memory of that Villista capitano, all bad teeth and halitosis, firing away at the floorboards, wood chips leaping into the air, the other rebels shrieking with laughter.

He squeezed his eyes shut and tried to think only of Margarita's comely tetas and the lovely curve of her fleshy coffee-toned thighs. When this didn't work, he thought of the curve of her ballooning hips, and when this didn't work, he pictured the hunger that radiated at such moments from her luscious red-painted lips. He felt nothing but the re-ignition of his shame.

— Not tonight, he told her. — I'm tired.

— Ay, pobrecito, she responded with an understanding smile. — You work too hard.

The following night he was interrupted once more by the memory of his humiliating encounter. Margarita, naturally, pretended it didn't bother her: to do so would have been an insult to her husband's machismo. This did not help. With time, Margarita stopped dabbing the hollows of her neck with agua de rosa and took pains to be asleep by the time her husband came to bed. The cantina owner, for his part, perpetuated the charade by retiring later, and by no longer coming up behind her when she was bent over their sink doing dishes, which he had once done so often, and with such giggling abandon. He spent more and more time in the cantina, sitting alone and smoking. She, in turn, repressed her affections towards her once manly husband and redirected them towards a private relationship with Jesús. She turned pious, and dour. Their marriage, once a torrent of colour, turned into something chilly and grey.

The cantina owner tried everything. He drank a little tequila before congress, thinking this might relax him, and when that didn't work, he tried giving up beer and liquor altogether, in case they might have been dimming his energies. Thinking his blood might be a little thin, he switched to a diet consisting solely of beef necks and goat's milk; this played havoc with his digestive system and caused him to smell like an abattoir. He went on long walks to energize his system with fresh air and exercise. He forced himself to fantasize all day about the pleasures of the flesh, which in the end only served to frustrate him. In his dirt-floored cellar he secretly prayed before a statuette of San Judas Tadeo, the patron saint of lost causes, and received only sore knees in return. He even thought about visiting Madam Félix's House of Gentlemanly

Pleasures, thinking that the Marias might know of some wicked measure to restart his motor. There was only one problem: the Marias functioned within the gringo economy, and like all residents of Corazón de la Fuente (with the possible exception of the hacendero), he couldn't afford even Maria de los Sueños, a pudgy Chiapan girl who, it was rumoured, wore a halo of furry moles on her left buttock.

The night came in which the cantina owner, feeling as desperate as it is possible to feel, lay in bed waiting, his eyes cast upwards at the dark ceramic ceiling. At around two in the morning he rose. He slipped out the kitchen door and made his way along a dark mud alley behind his neighbours' houses. Creeping from shadow to shadow, he reached the southwest tip of the pueblo, at which point he more or less broke into a jog: the moon was a blaze of illuminating silver, and he worried that someone out for a late walk might see him. As he trotted, he heard crickets and wind and the soprano howl of coydogs.

Panting, he knocked at the door of Azula Mampajo, the town's curandera. It opened. She peered up at him, her head turned slightly to favour the less milky of her eyes.

— Señora, he said. — Please, I . . .

— I know what is wrong. I can see it on your face, you poor bastard. Come in. I will help you.

The cantina owner left her fetid home with a paste consisting of mashed huizache leaves, dried piglet bladders, and water blessed by an epileptic seer who lived in the desert near Acuña. For the next fourteen days he mixed a few spoonfuls with simmering water and then swallowed it under the light of the desert moon. On the fifteenth night he returned to his wife's open arms and found that his marital life was in no way revived, their lovemaking still akin to jimmying a padlock with an oyster. And so he gave up. It was easier, in a way, to just accept his new reality. He spent more time in the cantina, and he depended on his closest male friends to satisfy the need for human companionship. In this way he settled into a life of silent, barely tolerable angst, his only consolation being that many people had similarly flavoured lives in the sad, bereaved years of the revolution.

But *now*, every time he passed the tower, he was reminded that there was something else he could try, some new and expensive mortification he could subject himself to. Having worked so hard to accept his post-concupiscent life, he resented that he was being asked to rattle the very principles of his insufficiency. By the same token, there was also a part of him, however repressed, that still remembered what it was like to lie beside his wife with more than a tormented, paper-thin sleep to look forward to. There was a part of him that still remembered what his lips felt like when pressed against hers, and there was yet another part of him that remembered, with an almost painful clarity, how it felt to tear open the blouse of a woman whose sultry, black-eyed gaze was encouraging of a beast-like comportment.

One evening around dusk, he stood on the stoop of his saloon and gazed at the nearly completed tower. All around him was activity: school had finished for the year, and the streets ran with children, all excited to be free of spelling primers, chalkboards, and the regular experience of having their knuckles rapped with a wooden ruler. A fury grew within the cantina owner. He couldn't stand it that, for the rest of the town, this phallic monstrosity symbolized good fortune and promise, while for him it mocked his most shameful of inadequacies. He seethed. He brooded. He fantasized about what he might have done had he been carrying a pistol the night those Villistas set his saloon on fire.

It was at this moment — staring up at the tower, hands clenching at his sides, frustration welling inside him — that he suddenly turned. He stormed through his place of business and marched through the room where he slept with Margarita. A few seconds later he was in the desert, striding towards a substantial mound of scrub. On the other side of the mound was a large stand of mesquite trees. Beyond that, entirely hidden from view, he began digging beneath the large, flat leaves of a prickly pear. Every few seconds he paused and looked in every direction, ensuring that he wasn't being watched. After a few minutes he uncovered a plain metal box, in which he kept the money he was accumulating from the increased business that had come to his saloon. Huddled over, he began to count. Through a series of stealthily placed inquiries, he had learned that Brinkley's goat-gland treatment cost two hundred gringo dollars, an amount significantly higher than the average Mexicano's yearly salary. A curious chill rose from a subterranean pocket of cold, sifted up through the desert floor, and entered the very core of his being. Though the day was broiling hot, he felt a shiver run through him.

Though he didn't yet have the money, he would, soon enough.

{8}

AS FRANCISCO RAMIREZ RODE ATOP THE HACEN-
dero's old grullo, the sounds of the village faded into the
background. After another twenty minutes, rider and horse
reached the main roadway running along México's northern
border, the sun beating down on Francisco's head and shoulders. He looked up, and for the next minute he rode with
spheres of red flaming against the packed-earth roadway.
They were heading west. Every few minutes a truck filled
with building equipment filched from the construction site
in Corazón raised dust into Francisco's throat and eyes as it
headed towards the interior. When they were farther away
from the town, there came a silence so profound that banks
of sound created by Francisco's excited mind spilled over the
plains, turning the desert into a place where thoughts were
louder than the rustling of wind, the call of hawks, or the
clopping of an old nag's hooves.

An hour passed, and then another. Stretching before him
in all directions were cholla and brambles and pale earth and

prickly pear and huizache and blossoming mesquite trees. Beneath him was a scramble of scorpions and small lizards. The sky was a blue bleached pale by the brutalizing sun. Far away, at the very edge of his vision, the desert turned into a series of undulating ridges, an illusion created by the heat. Above him vultures flew in lazy, ominous circles.

When he got thirsty, he drank. When he got hungry, he pulled the knapsack off his shoulders and helped himself to a chew of deer jerky. Every time he reached a fork in the road, he selected the one heading more or less in the direction of Piedras Negras. As the day wore on, all motion that he had previously detected in the desert — snakes, scuffling voles, the drifting of sand — ceased, and suddenly Francisco felt completely alone. He looked in all directions and could see only scrub and the dwindling, needle-thin roadway — even the huizache and mesquite trees had abandoned him. The vultures, which had been drifting above him all morning, so high they looked like winged black insects, had gone somewhere as well. Without their presence to add perspective, the sky was rendered limitless and, oddly enough, suffocating.

He made a calculation. It was noon, and he hadn't yet reached the tiny outpost called Rosita, which was more or less halfway to Piedras. This concerned him; with each passing hour it seemed that Estrella's gait was becoming more lumbering and rheumatic. At this rate it would be a full day before they reached their first destination, and Fajardo Jimenez had packed only enough provisions to see him to mid-afternoon at best.

Just then Francisco heard a protracted, distressed whinny coming from Estrella. He dismounted and looked into the horse's dull eyes. Patting Estrella's muzzle, he tried to soothe her with words softly spoken. Still, her breathing sounded laboured, as though her old lungs contained liquid.

— What is it? Is my pretty horse thirsty?

Again Francisco looked around, and as he did he struggled to banish any thoughts of his predicament from his mind. His only choice was to walk her through the brambles separating the roadway from the banks of the Río Grande.

— Come on, Estrella, he said, taking her lead.

He stepped into the desert and pulled her along slowly, giving her plenty of time to step her old feet around stones and small rocks and animal burrows. After a hundred metres or so, he heard a sneeze.

— What is it? he asked her in a voice intended to calm.
— You managed to catch a cold in this heat?

The horse shuddered, and that's when Francisco saw the projection of blood, looking like paint shot from a rifle, on the desert floor.

— Oh, Estrella, he said, again struggling against the panic welling inside him. He took one or two more steps towards the river and heard a strangulated whinny come from the hacendero's old horse. Francisco took a deep breath and stepped back towards her. Patting the softness between the horse's sad eyes, he kept saying *Oh, I know, señorita, we're in a bit of a jam, it's true, good thing we're both young and strong.* It was in the middle of this attempt at consolation that Estrella trembled and then slowly lowered herself to the desert floor, her legs folding beneath her like a day-old fawn's.

Francisco did the only thing he could do: he walked to the roadway and waited, hoping that some form of help might come by. As the heat rose wavering and light blue from the highway, he found his thoughts turning to places he had never seen and things he had never done. After ten minutes or so, he walked back to the tawny mound that was Estrella, only to find that she had lowered her head, apparently unbothered by the intense heat transmitting from the sand. He stroked the fringe of dusty hair hanging over her eyes and said *If you could just hang on a little longer, mi bonita,* at which point he trudged back to the roadway, where he again waited, his eyes reddening from both strong emotion and the reflection of sun off chipped asphalt. When he went back the third time, there was a murky foam on the hot sand in front of Estrella, her eyes motionless against a buzzing of flies.

Francisco sat on the earth and stroked the poor animal and told her she had done well, that it was his fault for expecting so much from her, and he hoped she could find it in her heart to forgive him. As he spoke, he noticed something so odd as to be impossible: despite the horse's weight, she barely made an impression in the earth. *Estrella,* thought Francisco, *without the heaviness of our souls we'd all be able to take flight, am I right?* He choked, a rise of emotion that he would not permit; later, when he'd figured a way out of this mess, there would be time for regret and feelings of loss. Instead he hardened himself, unbuckled the straps of the saddle, and pulled it away from the horse's weathered midsection. He then carried it back to the roadway and put it down and sat on it and waited with a heaviness of heart compounded with feelings of intense worry.

Francisco looked in every direction. As he did, he forced himself to breathe slowly and take stock of his situation. He had nothing at his disposal but a little water and a sack half-filled with tortillas, and he had no idea how long he'd have to ration these items. To deal with this decision, he forced himself to pretend he had nothing. He cleared his mind and thought of Violeta and the village, and as the midday sun began its daily scorching of the earth, he swore he could hear the voices of those familiar to him — male and female, young and old — echoing in the sky's infinite white.

Francisco waited, the brim of his hat pulled down over his eyes. He had heard of cases in which people trapped in the desert had temporarily gone blind in the harsh, relentless glare, only to be found crawling towards some imagined source of water, a hand waving ahead of them like a beetle's antenna. Others, he knew, succumbed to madness, only to be found ecstatically muttering psalms through cracked, bleeding lips. As he sat, Francisco fought to banish such fearful thoughts, only to find that it was difficult; in times of crisis, he was discovering, the mind darkens, becoming more of an enemy than the situation itself. He breathed slowly and deeply. The voices in his head drifted into silence, replaced by a mounting thirst. In response he took only the tiniest sips of water, sips that barely served to dampen his tongue and cool the flameless blaze at the back of his throat.

He heard a distant, indistinct noise, a sort of soft clicking. He turned his head and saw something that, in the blistering heat, looked watery and black, not unlike ink marks on cotton parchment. Francisco watched it shimmer, hoping upon hope that it wasn't some sort of hopeful mirage. After a minute or so he concluded that it *was* coming closer, and that the quavering vision was an old buggy drawn by a pair of mules. It took forever to reach him. The skin on his face and hands felt scorched.

The rear of the wagon was covered by a heavy woven tarpaulin. In the front seat were two men, both of whom wore cowboy hats and chambray shirts and Villa-style moustaches. As the cart pulled up, Francisco noticed the hands of the driver, which were covered with scars and small nicks and streaks of oil.

— Qué onda? asked the passenger.

The man was grinning, and Francisco noticed he was missing a pair of teeth, leaving an indecorous part in the middle of his smile.

— No mucho.

The two men looked appraisingly at Francisco. The driver spoke. — Looks like you've had a bad day, primo.

— Sí.

— That your saddle? asked the passenger.

— I'm just using it.

— It's a nice saddle.

— It's old.

— I wouldn't mind having me a saddle like that, said the driver. — And the stirrups, I think they're silver. And look at the stitching. It's like a rodeo star would have. You a rodeo star?

— No.

— Then why you got a rodeo saddle?

— It's borrowed.

— The horse too?

— Sí.

Both men started laughing. The driver slapped the top of his right leg. — Whoever you borrowed it from ain't gonna be happy when he sees what you did to his horse!

Francisco looked up and down the desolate, baking roadway. He returned his gaze to the two and asked: — Where are you going, señores?

— Uhhh . . . Rosita, said the driver.

A few seconds transpired. The two men looked at each other, and then the driver stepped down and said: — So. You need a ride or not?

Francisco narrowed his eyes; he knew that the men were contrabandistas, shuttling liquor into the United States. His choice was clear. He could either accept a ride from these suspicious characters or he could face the prospect of spending a night in the desert, where, in addition to a ravaging thirst, he'd fall prey to hunger and falling temperatures and every manner of scorpion and stinging spider.

He rode between the two men, both of whom smelled of sweat and liquor and stale, settled-in smoke. The saddle was between his feet. Behind him, beneath the tarpaulin, he could hear bottles rattling. When the driver turned off the roadway onto a tiny dirt track that headed in the general direction of the river, Francisco realized that they were no longer heading to Rosita, if in fact they ever had been.

— Stop the cart, he said.

— What for? asked the driver.

— Just stop the damn thing and let me walk.

This prompted both men to chuckle and the driver to say: — You ain't goin' nowhere.

A few seconds later, as the wagon slowed to manoeuvre

around a boulder, Francisco put his right fist into his left hand and drove his right elbow into the face of the bandido on the passenger side. The man fell into brambles, holding his spurting nose. Abandoning the saddle, Francisco leapt from the cart and began to run towards the roadway. When he heard the cock of a pistol and the driver saying *Hold up, pendejo, or I'll shoot you in the back*, Francisco instinctively stopped and slowly turned. The driver came around the cart with his pistol pointed at Francisco's head; when he reached a point where a blind man wouldn't have missed, he squeezed the trigger.

— Hijo de puta!

— What happened? said the passenger as he picked himself off the dirt.

— The gun jammed, cheap piece of shit.

— Try it again.

He spun the chamber and again aimed the gun at Francisco's forehead. Again it refused to shoot.

— It won't work. Let's go.

— Try again, pendejo. I think he broke my goddamned nose.

— I said forget it, let's go.

A minute later Francisco was alone in the middle of an endless Coahuilan scrub. He stood motionless, the emotions within him so intense that his body refused to accept them as his own. This state of grace did not last long: he began to shake so violently that he fell to his knees and vomited a translucent slime, after which he rolled over and closed his eyes against the white sun, panting so fiercely his ribs hurt.

When he caught his breath he turned over and, for no good reason, began pawing at the earth like an enraged dog, till his fingertips were ragged and his nose ran and his lungs felt heavy with dust. He stayed there, on hands and knees, panting. When he finally regained his breath, he rose because he had to, and rummaged through his knapsack. He drank the small amount of water left in his bottle, which somehow only magnified his thirst. Commanding himself to think, he looked down the twisting, bleached track that had led his would-be killers to this spot: it was little more than a pair of ruts in the sun-baked earth. One option was to walk back along the path towards the roadway and hope that the cool temperatures of night might bring out a few travellers. He turned, squinted his eyes in the opposite direction, and spotted what looked like a thin, mud-red interruption in the relentless desert. This, he concluded, was the Río Grande. He devised a new plan, this one motivated primarily by thirst. He would find the river, and there he would drink muddy water, refill his water bottle, and return in the direction from which he'd come, hopefully flagging a ride with some travellers who might, if all went well, refrain from murdering him. If it turned out that he had to spend a night curled up in the desert, he'd find himself a sandy lee and do just that.

He put his head down and trudged. With only the barest hint of a path, he had to veer around every manner of agave and yucca and low, spiny cactus. He kept thinking of Violeta — of her green eyes and wavy black hair and her soft, graceful manner. After a half-hour of delirious marching, the sound of the river grew into an actual stirring, the thin, mud-red line a slowly moving banner. He pressed on, his gaze focused just ahead of his tired feet. With time, his thoughts deadened and his actions became robotic. His tongue swelled, and he could think of nothing but the baking, tuberous presence in his mouth. His thoughts of Violeta dwindled, and the sounds of the desert no longer came to his tired, sunburned ears. Even the fear for his own survival — a fear that had propelled him in this direction in the first place — disappeared, and when Francisco finally stumbled upon the gently sloped banks of the river, his first reaction was to stop and peer curiously at the rush of grey water, as if he had no idea what it was or how he had found himself here.

It all came back: the river, the desert, the horse, and the saddle with the nice embroidery and how he had nearly got himself killed over it. Then he was running towards the river while simultaneously pulling off his clothing and making weak, strangulated yelps. He jumped in and splashed madly and tasted metal in the cool, delicious water. When he finally crawled out, he reached his hands towards the sky and, eyes clamped, let his naked body dry in the sun.

Eventually he opened his eyes and dressed and, shortly after, noticed he was not the first person to have graced this spot. A few metres away were the blackened remains of a firepit, along with a jumble of paper bags, half-eaten tortillas, torn bedrolls, cooking utensils, and old clothes. In the middle of the firepit was a rusted old coffeepot that bore a large dent on one side. A bit farther on, someone had nailed two mesquite branches into the shape of a cross and pushed it into the beach. Francisco was considering his next move when he heard rustling. Before he could react, he looked up at the top of the bank and watched as a lone hombre emerged.

The man was dark and had a compressed mestizo nose. He was shorter than Francisco, though just as stocky. He was maybe twenty-five years of age.

— You are crossing? asked the man in a thick southern accent.

— No, señor.

— Then why are you here?

— A pair of criminals left me here.

— Criminals? Really?

— Contrabandistas, actually. They stole my saddle and would have shot me had their gun not jammed. Then they left me out here.

— Dios mío.

Seconds passed. Francisco asked: — Where are you from?

— Chiapas.

— You're a long way from home.

— I have relatives in Texas. What about you?

— I'm going to try to walk back to the main road and get a lift to Piedras.

— Ay, that road. I was out there for hours before I got a lift. And even then it was in a donkey cart. I've been travelling all day just to get here from Sabinas. It's the heat. By the way, was that your dead horse I passed? There were so many flies I had to put my hand over my mouth.

— Sí.

— Jesús, hombre. Talk about luck. You want to eat?

The man opened his backpack and took out a bundle wrapped in brown paper. They both sat on a fallen mesquite branch and shared tortillas and jerky and water. *Gracias*, Francisco kept saying, between bites. *Muchas gracias, señor*. As the sun began to dip and turn a deep, spectral orange, the man started a fire with the half-burnt wood left in the pit.

— Looks like we're here tonight.

Francisco tightened his collar over his throat and prepared for the cold of the desert. Meanwhile the man stared into the flames, his face flickering with tones of red and yellow and blue. He fetched two potatoes out of his knapsack and edged them into the ash. After a few minutes of pushing them around with a stick, he stopped and looked at Francisco.

— You know what you should do? Swim with me in the morning. There's a good, newly paved road on the gringo side, and you'll catch a ride into Eagle's Pass in no time. They have actual cars over there, not just wagons pulled by burros. There you can cross back over into Piedras.

— I'd get caught.

— Even better. Let immigration drive you there themselves.

— Won't they beat the mierda out of me?

— If they took the time to beat up every wetback they found they'd never get any work done. Sometimes they even give you a sandwich.

Francisco thought about this. — You want me to swim to los Estados and let the immigration people take me back to Piedras?

The man shrugged. — It's what I'd do.

He slept curled like a baby, his right side resting on scrub and his head on his knapsack. It was cold that night, his sleep thin and shivering. Well before daylight, he felt a cold hand touch his shoulder. Francisco stretched and rubbed his eyes as the Chiapan collected his things in the moon's low shimmer. Once his possessions were packed, the stranger put his backpack over his shoulder, walked to the water, and said *I'll see you on the other side* before slipping quietly into the river. Francisco rushed to the edge and watched him swim towards the far bank.

Francisco crossed himself and then slipped into the water. As he struggled towards the far bank he thanked God that the current happened to be running in his favour — like most Coahuilans he was a perfunctory swimmer at best. He emerged at a spot on the bank about thirty metres west of where his travel companion had climbed out and gone on without him. As Francisco walked towards the roadway running along the gringo side of the border, the first scarlet rays of morning fell from the east. He reached a wire fence denoting the existence of a ranch. When Francisco began to climb it, his foot slipped and he tore his shirt. Upon inspecting the damage, he shouted curse words that faded slowly in the chilly, vaporous air.

He walked a little bit farther, reaching the two-lane border highway just as the sun cleared the horizon. It was still cool, and in his dripping-wet clothes he had to shuffle on the spot to stay warm. Fittingly, a black and white sedan was the first car to pull over.

One of the policemen had latino features. He, naturally, did the speaking.

— Buenas días, joven.

— Buenas, señor.

— Did you swim across the Río Grande this morning?

— Sí.

— I take it you are not a resident of los Estados Unidos?

— No, señor. I'm sorry.

— Well, in that case, I think we're all going to take a little ride.

An hour later, Francisco found himself in a locked room with about two dozen other illegal immigrants, all of whom had wet clothes and frightened expressions and an air of inextinguishable fatigue. Around nine o'clock they were given fried-egg sandwiches wrapped in wax paper. At ten o'clock they were packed into a small bus with doors that locked only from the outside; as it wound its way through Eagle's Pass, Francisco peered at real yankee barbershops and real yankee saloons and real yankee grocery stores and he marvelled at how healthy everybody looked and how clean and new their hats were. In the bus there were not just Mexicanos but Guatemaltecos and Salvadoreños as well. They were all dropped off at the border. As they were under the authority of the police, they were saved the indignity of having to pay a small bribe to enter their own country. This irony caused Francisco to grin for the first time since he'd left Corazón.

Once on Mexican soil, Francisco took off his still-damp knapsack and hunted for the picture of Violeta's brother, which was creased and moist and had torn diagonally from the lower left corner to the centre. Again he grinned, albeit bleakly. He had yet to ask a single person whether the muchacho in the picture looked familiar, and already he had survived the death of Antonio Garcia's horse, a murder attempt, a night spent shivering in cold desert scrub, a swim across el Río Grande, and an arrest by the authorities. He was bone-tired and filthy and longed only for the comforts of home.

With some emergency pesos he had sewn into the bottom of his knapsack, he bought himself an order of tacos de menudo and a one-way ticket on a rickety, belching bus that had the words *Jesús Es El Numero Uno* written in blue paint across the sides and front. It took him three and a half hours to return from Piedras Negras, as opposed to the traumatizing thirty-six hours he'd needed to get there. Throughout, he sat between a nun and a Kickapoo Indian who snored like a small breed of dog, his head resting on Francisco's aching shoulder.

Around noon he was dropped on the roadway outside of Corazón de la Fuente, at which point Francisco lowered his gaze, cursed his own failure, and trudged home in the unrelenting sun.

{9}

IN THE MIDDLE OF THE LITTLE PLAZA FACING THE
home of Roberto Pántelas was an old stone well that had provided the original mission-dwellers with water. Spanning the
sides of the well was an arch made from hand-cut stone. When
building it, the Franciscans had used no mortar or dowelling
of any kind: only an exact proportion of weight to height had
kept it up through centuries of wind, rain, war, and locust
assault. Along the side of the arch was an inscription that, it
seemed, had been chiselled by a mason with a paucity of fore-
thought: *God is a fountain, and that fountain is the heart of joy,
and that joy is our reminder of the grace of God, and the grace of God
is our guiding light in our battle against heathenry and . . .*

The lettering, which had grown so puny that squinting
was required to read it, ended there. Still, it was speculated
that this inscription had inspired the town's name — Heart
of the Fountain — it being patently obvious that there was no
other fountain within the municipal limits. There was also no
geyser, stream, creek, or reliable puddle — only the distant

gurgle of the Río Grande. For centuries the people of Corazón had relied on the well for water, only to watch their supply turn silty, and then sludgy, and then muddy, until the day came when the famed well of Corazón de la Fuente offered only worms, beetle husks, and the occasional lifeless vole. The rope that serviced it frayed, then broke. Fifty years on, everyone in Corazón (save for Madam Félix, whose brothel benefited from rudimentary plumbing) got their water from a rusty, clanking pump installed north of the village.

The well was now used for a different and, some would say, curious purpose. Residents would stare into its inky depths and reveal their secrets. No one knew quite how this tradition had started, though everyone was in agreement that the Pozo de Confesiones, as it had come to be known, had tranquilizing powers, and that talking to its echoing bottom somehow left one feeling calmed. Francisco Ramirez, as one example, visited the well immediately after returning from his failed search for Violeta Cruz's lost brother. He hung his head into its mushroom-scented depths and confessed that, had he been armed, those two contrabandistas would now be lying dead on the desert floor, their foreheads graced by a bloody third eye, their organs grazed on by buzzards, their eyes plucked out by scavenging beetles, their skin broiled by the relentless heat, their testicles gnawed on by ravenous sidewinders . . .

Inside his little home, the molinero listened, and grinned. Given the proximity of his living room window to the Pozo, coupled with the way in which the elderly disappear in front of those not beset with old age themselves, he was always the first to hear fresh gossip in town. He was the first to know

that the cantina owner suffered nightmares stemming from
the day in which a unit of Villa's army had shot up his cantina and then set it alight after dousing the furniture with
prize tequila. He was the first to discover that the hacendero
was in love with Madam Félix, and yet could never marry
a woman with such a disreputable profession. He was also
the first to know whenever one of the Marias got pregnant
and had to pay a midnight visit to the curandera, where the
unwanted child would be delivered to heaven upon a carpet
of magical utterances.

Fortunately, he was a gentleman above all else. It was one
of the reasons he had always been so popular with women.
He never betrayed secrets or used overheard admissions to
gain advantage. It was a pledge that he had made to himself:
he would never, ever act upon knowledge gained because of
his proximity to the well. It was also a pledge that, after decades of adherence, he would finally disobey.

That evening, one of the town's señoritas, a girl named
Laura Velasquez, came to the well. It was a clear night, and
the packed white dust of the plazita looked auburn under the
desert moon. The molinero watched as she stopped before
the well's aperture and, after a moment, began to tremble.
A second after that, he could hear her weeping softly. This
surprised him. Yes, it was true that physical beauty had not
graced Laurita the way it had graced some (well, most) of
the town's other señoritas, and that, at the age of twenty-
one, she had been a spinster for so long her marrying years
were generally considered behind her. It was also true that
her teeth were, by any definition, unconventional, and that
the mild discomfort they caused her while chewing had

affected her eating habits, rendering her somewhat less than curvaceous.

By the same token, she had always struck the molinero as happy, as the sort of person for whom simple pleasures were sufficient. She was remarkably kind, and the molinero figured that this was the source of her contentment — she was always running errands for the sickly and delivering food to shut-ins and knitting bonnets for newly arrived babies. In the eyes of the old molinero, she was the sort of woman who might have joined a convent and led a life whose rewards included quiet contemplation and a profound connection with God.

And yet here she was, hair lit by moonlight, shoulders shaking with grief, tears dripping down her long, thin nose. It was a sight the molinero could barely stand to witness: in the workings of a small town, the satisfaction of a person like Laura Velasquez functioned as a sort of inspiration for those who were far luckier but who nevertheless considered themselves to be having a bad day. Her inner peacefulness, the molinero understood, functioned as a source of illumination, particularly in difficult times, and the last thing Corazón de la Fuente needed was for this light to be extinguished. Oh no — the pueblo could survive poverty, bloody upheaval, and whatever other ludicrous, blood-soaked indignity Mexican history would dream up next. But he wasn't sure it could survive a dampening of Laura Velasquez's spirits.

In a thin, croaking voice, she asked: — O Jesús, please tell me. Why couldn't I have been pretty?

This was too much for the old Casanova to bear. He stood up from his old, dusty chair — a movement that resulted in cramping, grunts, and shin pain. After feeling for his cane, he shuffled as quickly as he could towards his bedroom. Sitting on his old, creaking bed, he tucked his nightshirt into a pair of worn, soil-encrusted dungarees. Realizing that Laura could leave at any minute, and that the ability to do anything with rapidity had deserted him sometime during the reign of Benito Juárez, the molinero hurried to pull on his boots. This resulted in the spasming of a muscle in his lower left flank, right where it intersected with his spindly, liver-spotted hip. He swore, rubbed himself, cursed the invention of old age, stabbed the floor with his cane tip, swore again, and then struggled more successfully to his feet. He limped through his small house, checked his snow-white moustache in a dust-coated mirror, and stepped into the street.

Laura Velasquez turned. Her face looked hot.

— Señor Pántelas, she gasped. — I'm sorry I woke . . .

— Shhh, mija, he responded. — There's no need.

He lowered his head and made towards her. His knees, which hurt him at the best of times, now had a companion in his hip, which was issuing an electric pain through his entire left side. When he reached her he stopped. She sniffled, and once again spoke a few words of apology. He waved them away.

— Señorita Velasquez, he said. — As you can see, I am an old, old man. My eyes are filmy and my knuckles are the size of plums and I have been known to fall asleep in the middle of conversations. Yet I was not always this way. When I was young and muscled and a town could not survive without the contribution of a strong-armed molinero, women would blush when I passed by. On Saturdays I wore a rodeo suit and sang songs about men who saved women from pistoleros and drag-ons. I was good with words and horses and games requiring might. I was a man who understood what secrets lurked in the feminine heart, and I understood what words soothed the secret fears of women. Most importantly, I recognized the characteristics of *real* beauty, not the sort of beauty that can do nothing but stare back insipidly from the surface of a mirror.

The molinero stopped to catch his breath. When he next spoke, his voice was a gurgle.

— Do you understand what I am saying? I have watched you since you were a little girl still playing with dolls and tea sets. I have watched the way you treat people, and I have observed you during tranquil moments when you thought no one was looking.

He gestured towards her, his finger pointing to a spot that might have been considered inappropriate on a woman with more bosomy architecture. — *You,* he opined — are by far the most beautiful woman in Corazón de la Fuente.

The next day, around eleven o'clock, the old molinero was in his kitchen, eating stale oatcakes and a jam made from pomegranate seeds. He heard a knock. He rose, crossed his living room, and used his shoulder to push open the door, which had a habit of sticking in all but the driest weather. There stood Laura Velasquez. She was sporting a mild, restrained smile that both conveyed the gentle nature of her soul and concealed the rickety misshapenness of her teeth. In her right hand was a bucket filled with brushes and cloths and bottles. In her left hand was a broom.

The molinero stared at her, blinking. Her smile deepened, and he reflexively backed away from the door. She entered and looked around, her gaze travelling from wall to wall, from floor to sagging ceiling, from corner to cobwebby corner. Most would have sighed or made some sort of deprecating joke: his was an abode that had clearly not benefited from a feminine touch for many years. Every square centimetre was covered with dust, old newspapers, unwashed glasses, plates crusted with food, and unlaundered clothing. In one corner, near the doorway to his grease-stained outdoor kitchen, was a pile of rusting metal parts that had fallen from the mill itself, which occupied a shed behind the house.

— I'm going to tidy a little, she said. — Está bien?

Already she was lining up her brushes and bottles on his table, in much the same way that a general might arrange a collection of pistols. The molinero was tired that morning, and for some reason his gums hurt. Though his understanding of decorum told him that he shouldn't allow her to do this, he didn't quite have the energy to stop her.

She went to work, humming. Within five minutes she had risen so much dust that the molinero's eyes stung, his oatcakes tasted gritty, and his coffee was swimming with the very flecks of dirt that Laura was, at that moment, banging free from the ceiling with the end of her broom. Between tampings, she said: — Perhaps you would like to take a walk, señor? That way I won't bother you.

It was a typical day in north Coahuila, the sky thickened by sun and the air smelling faintly of creosote. The molinero suddenly felt good to be alive, and those who noticed him ambling towards the plaza remarked that the old man was whistling, and that his gait wasn't quite as halting or as stiff as usual. He sat on a wrought-iron bench opposite the church and looked up at the marvel that was Brinkley's tower. With its fuselage complete — only the antenna needed to be attached — the tower had already reached a magnificent eighty-five metres, a height so extreme that the molinero could barely make out where the tower ended and the rest of the sky began. As a man who had worked around machinery all of his life, the molinero couldn't help but marvel at the polish of its girders, at the precision of its construction, at its stateliness. Moreover, the tower broadcasted an almost lordly reassurance: Brinkley wouldn't have built it were another war even a remote possibility. People in town felt safer with the tower now hovering above them. He could see it in their faces, in the way they walked, in the ease with which they now smiled.

Lost to feelings of immense contentment, the molinero heard a shuffling *clip-clop*. He looked over, and there was Miguel Orozco limping towards him. Again the molinero grinned. It was just after one in the afternoon, and it was clear that the mayor was already knocking off for the day.

— Qué onda, Roberto?

— No mucho, Miguel.

— Can I join you?

— Claro, said the molinero. — Claro que sí.

— Smoke?

— Sí. Gracias.

The two men lit cigarillos and gazed up at the tower, which considerately blocked the sun from their eyes. They sat puffing, the atmosphere so heavy and still that the smoke hung in the air like dense blue webs. As the heat of the day climbed, both men cultivated a thin film of perspiration on their brows, on their upper lips, and in the creases of their necks.

— Do you know Laura Velasquez? asked the molinero.

— Of course.

— She's cleaning my house.

— She's an angel. She really is.

— Ay sí, said the molinero. — But you know what they say about angels. They always have at least a little devil lurking deep inside.

Both men chuckled at the molinero's witticism. Later, when they had finished smoking, they both rose to their feet, a laborious production given the molinero's age and the mayor's bad foot, the latter acquired during one of the more disturbed phases of the revolution. Predictably, the mayor limped off to the cantina. The molinero, meanwhile, shuffled back to his home. Inside, he found Laura packing up.

— Do you like what I've done? she asked.

He looked around his little cottage. She had collected all the laundry, dirty dishes, and old newspapers, and then swept the space she'd created. The room looked bigger, it smelled of flowers, and the sun coming in through his window wasn't thick with dust motes. It was no longer, he realized with a start, the home of an old man.

— Sí, mucho. Gracias.

— I'll return tomorrow. I didn't have time for the kitchen.

— No, por favor, you don't have to.

— I know that, Señor Pántelas.

Laura Velasquez shyly grinned.

— But I want to.

The next day, as promised, Laura again came with her cleaning utensils and her bashful, tight-lipped grin. This time, however, the molinero had awoken earlier, giving himself time to bathe and shave his grizzled features, his eyes sufficiently dim that he failed to notice the halo of fine cuts and gouges he'd distributed over his jawline. When he opened the door and presented himself, Laura smiled so freely that he saw, for just a moment, the tips of her broken, misshapen teeth.

As the molinero sat in the plaza, smoking once again with Miguel Orozco, Laura finished the job she had started the day before, chiselling away at years of grease and smoke and the resin produced by cooking over smouldering green branches. When the molinero returned, he stood gaping, his eyes welling with the sort of tears caused by fond memories: he was remembering his own mother, in this very kitchen, cooking stews made from vaca tail and nopales. As he looked around, he had the hopeful thought that maybe, just maybe, this kitchen might play host to the creation of pleasing memories once more.

She was at his door at eleven o'clock the very next day, wearing the same skirt and white cotton shirt that, the molinero was starting to notice, had a tendency to tighten against her body whenever she reached for something, revealing a feminine litheness that the old man had not previously associated with Laura Velasquez. This time she was carrying a large, round wicker basket. After nodding hello and refusing an offer of coffee, she headed towards the bureau in the corner, where she had stuffed all the clothing she had picked up over the past two days. When she opened the top drawer, her nose wrinkled slightly at the odour that puffed, cloud-like, into the room. This embarrassed the molinero, who turned to leave.

— No, she called brightly. — You don't have to leave. Not unless you want to.

A minute later she left the molinero, her basket filled with every stitch of clothing he owned, save for the shirt and dungarees he was wearing. He spent a quiet morning reading his newspaper with a magnifying glass and mulling over the strange, ancient sensation that was building inside him — a sensation that made the area behind his knees feel vaguely weakened and that left his thoughts a miasmic swirl. *Jesús*, he thought with a grin. *I'm as badly off as that poor cabrón Francisco Ramirez.*

She came back late in the afternoon and left her basket in the middle of his table: in it were his trousers, shirts, socks, and underwear, all of which had been beaten against the rocky bank of the Río Grande, rinsed in water scented with clematis, and left to bleach in the relentless Coahuilan sunshine. His socks, he noticed, had been mended, and the more shredded denizens of his underwear drawer had been scissored into neat, square handkerchiefs.

— Do you like? she asked, her grin revealing a smile that, to the molinero, was both tragic and sublime.

— Laura . . . Tomorrow, I don't want you to clean or work or help me with anything. Instead, I'd like you to come have tea with an old man who, for some reason, no longer feels quite so old.

A moment passed.

— Está bien, she said.

Thus came the day that, given the profusion of curious eyes and ears in Corazón de la Fuente, would pass into local history as the one in which a twenty-one-year-old girl fell in love with a stooped and rickety senior citizen who, it was true, knew women as intimately as a chef knows his knives. With a pot of jicama tea steeping in his outdoor kitchen, the molinero opened the door. He was wearing pressed trousers, a chambray shirt, a gabardine donkey jacket, and a homburg. His facial cuts from the previous day's shave had healed considerably, such that they now looked no worse than a sprinkling of paprika. He had trimmed the few hairs still clinging to his speckled, leathery scalp, and he had splashed himself with a cologne that wasn't nearly as pungent or vinegary as it could have been, given its vintage. He smiled. He watched as her eyes brightened. They stepped towards each other, and, as will happen with two people who were together in a past life, flowed into each other's arms, all skin and muscle and bone disappearing, leaving only a shimmer of blissful, radiant energy.

A few days later, Roberto Pántelas and Laura Velasquez were walking together around the plaza. Far above the town, Kickapoo Indians were helping to place the tower's antenna with the aid of a crane so vertiginously high it defied imagination; naturally, a crowd had gathered to watch, and to toast the completion of the tower with glasses filled with everything from iced tea to mescal. And yet, as the two walked by, the crowd collectively turned and took in Corazón's latest, and unlikeliest, couple.

— Everyone knows, said Laura.

— Claro, said the molinero. — They are happy for us. As you know, this is a town of good people.

After that, the molinero and his much younger sweetheart walked hand in hand when out together, and it was said that whenever Laura Velasquez left the old man's house, her cheeks shone with a redness caused by one thing and one thing only. Meanwhile, even the poorest ejido dwellers had stopped using the services of a molinero; they had money now, and they preferred to buy their cocoa and corn preground in the store of Fajardo Jimenez. The molinero didn't care — a bit of lost revenue mattered little when compared to the smiles of his fellow citizens. Besides, he had worked hard all his life, and he deserved to dedicate as many hours as possible to his new-found happiness.

There was, of course, another reason why he didn't care. For about a year, the molinero had been growing a lump, right in the middle of his sternum. Recently it had begun to issue a pain through the bones and muscles surrounding it. With a certainty possessed only by the aged, he knew that this protuberance would prove to be his end. Again, he didn't care, or at least he didn't care greatly. Few grew to be a man of his age, particularly in such tumultuous times, and his life had been rich with joyfulness and romance. In fact, he grew dizzy with gratitude every time he thought of the sweet, soft-voiced gift that the Lord had sent him in his waning years.

Now that his final days were upon him, he experienced an intensity of emotion that, while wonderful, would have been impossible to live with had he known it throughout the whole of his life. Every time he saw a buzzard circling in the cloudless white sky, he would stop and watch it, his neck crooked with awe. Whenever he spotted a child, he was overcome with a tearful desire to rush over and pick the little creature up, the absence of children in his life being his one true regret. Every time he placed a forkful of fajita meat in his mouth, it was as though the Creator himself were strumming what was left of his taste buds. Each time he passed Dr. Brinkley's tower, he felt as though the town was being rewarded for having displayed such resilience during the revolution. While walking he would suddenly feel amazed that his feet, which had grown so leathery and sparrow-sized with age, had carried him without complaint for the better part of a century. For all of these gifts he felt grateful and humbled.

One day Laura visited with a lunch of tortilla, avocado, and grilled tripe. As she sat slowly eating, each bite causing her upper and lower teeth to uncomfortably collide, the molinero could only stare at her, beaming, his food untouched. Slowly she grew self-conscious. Her hand lifted to her mouth, reflexively hiding the source of her homeliness.

— Roberto, she finally peeped. — Qué pasa?

He swallowed and continued beaming at her. He couldn't say it. To do so would be an end to the anticipation incurred by this moment, and he was enjoying this more than he'd ever enjoyed anything.

— Laura, he finally said. — You have given an old man a final taste of life. For this, I adore you with the entirety of my soul.

He paused to breathe. — And I want to give you a present.

— A present?

— Sí, preciosa. A testament to my undying love.

She looked at him, blinking.

— Laurita, he said, savouring the moment, — I am going to have your teeth fixed.

{10}

VIOLETA CRUZ WAS IN HER TINY HOUSE, LYING IN the hammock her mother ordinarily used, which was suspended between a pair of roughly hewn mesquite poles that offered the added benefit of preventing the roof from caving in. As she brooded, she gnawed at the tiny sliver of nail still existing on the ring finger of her left hand. She proceeded to gnash it into a mushy non-existence, at which point she began gnawing on the cherry-pink cuticle that resided underneath.

Francisco. *He* was the problem. Before he entered her life, her attitude towards the young men of Corazón de la Fuente had been simple, liberating, and so easy to maintain. It had all started around the age of twelve, when members of the opposite sex had begun sniffing around her like ants to a spilling of sugar. Their demands were relentless — to go for walks, to have some ice cream, to attend a fiesta. Her response, meanwhile, was always swift and unambivalent: *No, I can't, I have schoolwork to do.* It finally reached the point where the male youths of the town, their egos collectively bruised, decided that Violeta either had to be a nun in training or a woman in name only, and not worthy of their virile attention.

It was the way the local men dressed, with those skin-tight dungarees and denim shirts stretching at the buttons. She hated the way they hung around in semi-feral clumps, hissing *Mamacita!* at every señorita who happened to walk by, as if this single word were clever enough to win a young woman's attention. She hated the way they continually cut classes — she would never do that, education being a means to a future — and she detested that they seemed to have no goals other than playing football in the scrubby fields surrounding the mission. Even more so, she hated the way they obviously spent a significant portion of their morning before their own reflections, combing their pomaded hair into stiff, sheeny concoctions.

And then, one month ago, Francisco Ramirez knocked on her door and respectfully asked to accompany her to the Reyes brothers' lucha night, a courtesy so lacking in precedent she became flustered and, after a moment of awkwardness, assented. Since that night, she'd brooded continually over whether she'd made a mistake or opened an interesting new door in her life. Yes, he was a handsome young man, his misaligned nose only adding to his appeal. Yet it was equally true that he was the sort of muchacho whose appearance seemed beside the point, his real attributes residing in a place not reflected by a mirror. Apparently he did well enough in school, spoke a fair bit of English, and was an intimidating presence on the football pitch, achievements you would never have heard about from Francisco himself. Unlike the boastful young men in town, Francisco was an hombre of few words, with most of his thoughts being communicated by the limpid clarity of his light brown eyes. It was this quality of his — this air of sad, contemplative knowing — that had crept up on her that night, igniting the first, hesitant sparks of interest.

But if Violeta became seriously attached to him — and she was at an age when the other chicas in town were taking husbands and starting families — her future would be clear. She would quite likely stay rooted in Corazón, an eventuality she would not permit for herself. Since she was a young girl, she had dreamt of a man who could take her and her mother away from the insecurities of México, with its constant threat of violence and deprivation, and she worried that Francisco, who had no professional ambitions that she was aware of, would not be that man. For as long as she could remember, she had pictured herself marrying a man who might furnish her with some of the better things in life — a decent house, perhaps, and a good education for her children — and she believed that Francisco would never be able to do this for her. Since she was a niña in ribbons and a pinafore, she had imagined herself with a man of privilege, and she knew that *privilege* was a word she would never associate with the family Ramirez. And yet . . . *Ay, ay, Francisco, how is it that when I am near you, my heart beats erratically and I have to fight the impulse to giggle like an amused child? How is it that my stomach feels light, and the area behind my kneecaps uncomfortable? How dare you do that to me, Francisco Ramirez? How dare you complicate things so?*

She heard a knock on their heavy wooden door. Sighing, she disentangled herself from the hammock just as her mother ran in from the small kitchen backing the house and threw open the door. As though summoned by her thoughts,

Francisco was standing in the dusty street, hat twisting in his large, strong hands. He was dressed in clean clothes, and a lock of his hair had fallen over his forehead, where it curled into a sort of question mark. His face was covered with small cuts and bruises, and she knew that these had been acquired during his quest to find her brother. In fact, according to rumours that had been circulating through town, there had been moments in which Francisco had had to exhibit real courage — something about a dead horse and a stolen saddle and a pistol aimed at the middle of his face. Violeta closed her eyes and struggled to banish these thoughts. The idea that Francisco might have risked his life for her caused her to feel slightly vertiginous, as if she'd contracted a mild flu.

— Francisco! exclaimed her mother. — Por favor, come in! Violeta! Where *are* you? Francisco's here . . .

Francisco nodded and entered. Violeta went back to the kitchen and poured some acrid, half-warm coffee left over from breakfast into a carafe. She then put the carafe and two cups onto a tray and brought them into the living room, where her mother and Francisco were already sitting opposite one another. She put the coffee on the low mesquite table.

— Would you like a coffee? asked Violeta's mother.

— Sí, said Francisco. — Gracias.

Violeta poured him a serving. She filled a second cup and handed it to her mother. Without asking permission, Violeta sat, gaining an impatient glance from her mother. When Malfil spoke, her voice was quavering with emotion.

— You have had an adventure, mijo.

— Sí, said Francisco.

— I heard that your trip was very difficult.

A silence followed. Violeta's mother was staring at a point on the floor halfway between her feet and the little table; Violeta could tell she was both frightened and anxious to hear what Francisco had to say. Francisco, meanwhile, sipped his coffee and looked miserable. Violeta heard her mother sniffle, and she realized Malfil was struggling not to cry.

— Francisco, Malfil Cruz finally said, — you found out what happened to my Pablito?

— Sí, Francisco said.

— Then tell me, joven.

Francisco was looking at his hands, which were clamped so hard in his lap they had drained of colour. — He is alive.

Violeta's mother cried out so loudly that the old men passing time in the plaza all stifled their conversations and turned their heads in the direction of the outcry.

— Dios mío, I knew it, Francisco! I knew it, I knew it all along! I could feel him . . . out there . . . A mother can tell these things . . . Ay, Francisco, gracias, gracias, gracias . . . Now tell me where he is!

— In the jungles of the south, señora. He had a falling out with one of Villa's generals and he went down there to fight with Emiliano Zapata. After Zapata's assassination he moved on. Now he's in a small town in Chiapas, helping to feed poor Indians. He's so far from civilization that he can't even get to a cable office. Plus, the roads barely function in the sierras. It takes a full month of hiking to get where he is, and that's just from San Cristóbal, which is nearly impossible to get to itself. You'd need a good year to visit, and chances are you would come down with malaria. Plus, his days are filled with helping others grow cocoa and plátano. He has saved many people from starvation, señora. Many, many people. It's doubtful he would ever leave.

— But how do you know this?

— I talked to some men. Older ones, in a cantina called Garibaldi's. They remembered him, and referred to him as el Honorable. When they spoke of him, they did so with admiration in their voices and pride in their bearing. I could tell they were pleased to be from the same state as Pablo Cruz. I wouldn't say he was a hero of the revolution, not quite, but it is nonetheless true that his noble reputation exists far beyond the confines of this little village of ours.

Violeta watched as her mother, sobbing loudly, hugged Francisco. She then ran to Violeta's room, where moans of happiness soon drifted past opened shutters. This awoke the dogs in the adjoining alley, all of whom lifted their heads and joined her in a concerted emotional wail.

Violeta peered at Francisco, who looked slightly ashamed.

— Francisco, she said. — Come with me outside.

They stepped into the street. With her arms crossed over her stomach, Violeta turned and looked up at Francisco.

— I can't decide whether you have been unspeakably kind or unspeakably cruel. I am pretty sure, however, that it was one or the other.

— My only fear is that now she'll try to reach him.

— She won't. Deep down, she knows he's dead. Deep down, she knows my brother was another victim of the revolution, and the furthest thing from a hero. Your story has given her something to tell herself. She won't attempt to confirm it.

— I wanted to make her happy.

— I know, Francisco Ramirez. I know.

There was a long silence. Finally, Violeta cleared her throat and spoke.

— Tonight the radio station goes on the air. Do you want to go to the celebrations with me?

Francisco paused, and then smiled.

— Sí, Violeta, he said. — Mucho.

{11}

LATER THAT DAY, VIOLETA TOOK A LONG BATH IN water fragranced with aloe leaves. When she finally emerged, she rubbed her hands and feet with a cream made principally from milk foam, and she anointed her wavy, ink-black hair with a tonic scented with jasmine. She stood before a mirror, wondering what it was that all men saw in her. Try as she might, she could never find it; the only thing that reliably stared back at her was a lingering melancholy.

After dressing in a long skirt and a formless white cotton blouse, she grudgingly put on a hint of eye shadow and a lip stain made from ground beetle shells. She turned and left her room. Her mother, hearing Violeta's footsteps, rose from her chair.

— Ay, mija, she sputtered. — Whatever you do, be careful.

— Careful, mami?

— With Francisco. He is just a young man. There are many like him.

— Mami. What are you trying to say?

— I was your age when I became pregnant with your

brother. You know I'll be furious if you make the same mistake I did.

— *Mami!*

— I'm just saying . . .

There was a knocking at the door. It was Francisco, who bid Malfil a good evening. Violeta then kissed her mother goodnight, and the couple stepped into the dusty street.

They walked slowly, neither speaking. It was as if they both knew that something momentous might happen that evening, and that any talk would feel banal, if not silly, in comparison. Violeta, for one, felt the nervousness experienced when one's outlook on life threatens to falter and perhaps even crumble. Francisco, meanwhile, felt as though he was on the cusp of a great ascendency, one that left him dizzy and a little short of breath. At Avenida Cinco de Mayo they turned east and found themselves amongst townsfolk and ejido dwellers and hordes of children, all of whom were walking towards the site of the radio tower. As they neared it, Violeta could see that a crowd had already gathered.

There were clowns making balloon animals for the children and there were braziers piled with sizzling meat and there were cauldrons filled with water for maize and there were tables mounded high with tortillas and refrescos and jugs of horchata and there was a table where little ones were happily cutting shapes from bands of crepe paper and there were incandescent lights rigged up around the perimeter of the field. As the sun sank further, everything acquired a purplish, electric glow that only added to the excitement of the evening. Los Inconsolables del Norte were playing their brand of wheezing polka on an elevated stage that had been erected to one side. In response, cowboys and señoras and beaming grandmothers and a dozen or so tower workers with fifths of mescal tucked into their back pockets were whooping and kicking up dirt, and every time the band stopped playing they hollered for more until the music resumed and they could all start expressing their joy once again. Even the town's mayor, with his bum foot and egregious sense of rhythm, was dancing with a group of grimy ejido children, all of whom were clapping and squealing and jumping up and down.

Meanwhile, women were coming up and saying *Violeta, you look so beautiful.* The menfolk, most of whom had liquor on their breath, kept throwing knowing glances at poor Francisco, glances that clearly said *I hope you know the lay of the land, cabrón.* Off to one side, the brothers Reyes were practising their high kicks. Beyond them were a few of the Marias, who were grabbing a moment between clients to watch the festivities from afar. The old molinero was shuffling with his fiancée, Laura, and the cantina owner was promenading with his wife. Even Father Alvarez, normally so burdened, was laughing at the crowd's collective merriment. The air was thick with the smoke of salchichas and fajitas and frog-sized cucarachas, the latter sprinkled with lime juice and salt and then roasted until their shells popped like corn. Meanwhile, people danced and talked and laughed, and as more tower workers arrived with flasks in their back pockets, the air was flavoured by yet another scent, this one the most Mexican of all: tequila mixed with the hot, hot breath of those who were happy.

Ay, Dios, Violeta caught herself thinking. *Is there anyone, anywhere, who enjoys a fiesta more than a Mexicano?* On that glorious night in Corazón de la Fuente, with the whole world smelling of grilled meat and agave and her nose filling with the dust kicked up by laughing black-eyed children, and Los Inconsolables del Norte playing the same numbers over and over, and everyone's belly stuffed with carne and tortilla and frijoles and nopales and pulque and machaca and menudo and birria and refresco de naranja — Violeta Cruz knew this was not possible.

At the base of the tower was a makeshift stage, and in the middle of this structure was a huge ornamental power switch. Around half past nine, during a pause between songs, a cowboy at the edge of the festivities started waving his arms and yelling for people to be quiet. The revellers humoured him, and then everyone heard the sound of a motor, coming from the direction of the bridge separating Corazón de la Fuente from Del Rio, Texas. While the rattle of an engine was no longer a rarity in Corazón, this sound was nothing like the deep, throaty rumble of the trucks that came and went from the work site, jarring windows and leaving irreparable ruts in the streets. This motor was quieter and had an airy, restful quality — it whooshed, rather than grumbled — and some of the more imaginative townsfolk wondered if the vehicle it powered might actually be gliding.

The sound grew. A pair of headlights topping an ornate grille and bumper came into view. This was followed by a long, polished hood and an open-air coach the size of a typical Corazón home. The vehicle passed the plaza and Madam Félix's House of Gentlemanly Pleasures, the lights growing in size until they resembled a pair of full moons, albeit slung close to the earth. Whispered suppositions circulated through the crowd, and when everybody realized that they were right, that they really *were* being visited by the esteemed doctor himself, children clapped and men felt pleased and women placed their hands over their mouths, as though in the presence of someone regal.

The car's chauffeur stopped at a respectful distance from the gathering and continued to stare impassively ahead. Behind the driver was the doctor himself, resplendent in a white summer-weight suit made by a Savile Row tailor. His hair was swept back from his narrow forehead, and his eyeglass frames looked to be fashioned from the shell of a tortoise. He wore a Vandyke that, judging by its pristine appearance, had been trimmed and treated with tonic that very day. Though he couldn't have been more than forty years of age, his hands rested upon a walking stick that was topped by a diamond the size of a walnut shell.

The chauffeur, still unsmiling, stepped out of the good doctor's Duesenberg and opened the doors belonging to each of his passengers. Brinkley stepped out onto the work site and looked up to regard his radio tower, which shone like an immense diamond in the artificial lights. When he turned to face the people, he was smiling, and his narrow, dark eyes were twinkling. Though a small man, the doctor nevertheless seemed to take up a lot of space — it was as though his benevolence produced an aura that had its own weight and volume. Not knowing how to show their gratitude, the citizens of Corazón de la Fuente merely gawked. John Romulus Brinkley hesitated before this worshipful gaze, and then he raised one of his hands and gave a pivoting, self-conscious wave.

When he spoke, his Spanish was all but flawless, with the slightest of accents.

— Hello, everybody, he called. — What a wonderful evening!

This broke the ice. There was applause and cheers and whistles and, on the part of those women who'd been widowed during the war and had gone years without the attention of a husband, flirtatious glances. When his welcome finally subsided, Brinkley joined Mayor Orozco on the stage. The entire town looked on. Noisy children were silenced by their parents, and drunkards were hushed by those responding more appropriately to the moment. The night turned silent, save for the chirping of crickets and river frogs.

The mayor cleared his throat and looked over the crowd.

— Ladies and gentlemen, he announced.

He coughed into his hand, took a deep breath, and smiled at his own attempt to sound official. This inspired a ripple of amusement in the crowd, and when he continued, it was in a tone that everyone recognized as his own.

— Today is a big day, and I will keep my comments brief. Our town, our beloved Corazón de la Fuente, has known many hard times. These have been long years, years of deprivation and difficulty, years of locusts and bad weather and turmoil.

There was a pause. When he resumed speaking, his voice had turned almost confessional. Everybody strained to hear, and the elderly in the crowd began turning to each other and muttering *What is Miguelito saying?*

— There have been so many times in which I have observed your strength and your resolve and your warm good humour, and have been proud to call myself your mayor.

There was a moment of silence, followed by hooting and whistling and, predictably, the unsafe discharge of handguns. Miguel lifted his palms and gestured, as if to say *Enough, por favor.*

— Compadres, I would like to take this opportunity to thank Dr. John Romulus Brinkley for his interest in our humble pueblo, and I would like to do so by offering him the key to the city. Everybody, please join me in welcoming Dr. Brinkley to the stage.

The mayor took a step back as Brinkley stepped forward, assuming a spot beside the giant switch. When the applause finally died down, Miguel Orozco reached into the pocket of his jacket and pulled out a key to the town hall. It was the size of a wolf's forepaw and looked to have been forged out of rusted metal.

— Dr. Brinkley, may I present to you . . . the key to our fair village.

Brinkley held up the key, his eyes beaming behind tortoiseshell frames. It was a full minute before the applause finally dwindled. The doctor stepped forward to speak.

— Ladies and gentlemen, he announced. — My name is John Brinkley and I am a medical doctor.

He paused, enjoying the quiet that had descended upon the crowd. — But I was not always this way. The slight drawl you detect in my voice is Appalachian in origin. Oh yes, like many of you, I was born poor. I grew up without shoes, and the only meat I was fortunate enough to consume was Sunday-night possum. I shivered through the winters and perspired rivers during the summers. I know what it is like to be without clothing or adequate nourishment, and I know what it is like to go to school with holes in my clothing. Oh yes, I know the indignity, I know the shame. I know the way it can leave you feeling exhausted and hopeless. Oh yes, my people, I *know*.

Again he paused, his eyes casting over the crowd.

— Of all my achievements . . . and I've had a few, I won't deny that . . . of all my achievements, my proudest to date is helping to bring some measure of prosperity to the fine, fine people of Corazón de la Fuente.

The applause bordered on the apoplectic. It was only when it finally petered out, a process that took minutes and minutes, that a croaky voice rang out from the rear of the crowd.

— *Stop!*

Everyone turned to see that Azula Mampajo, the village curandera, was standing on an overturned potato crate waving a bony arm in the air, looking even more disturbed and witch-like than normal.

— Stop! she yelled again. — Can't you people *see*? This man is a liar. This man is a peddler of myths and false hope. He's just playing with you! You're an amusement to him and nothing more. You're a new suit of clothes, and one he'll wear out quickly. I can't believe you think he really cares about you. Believe me, I've seen the future, and by the time he gets through with you, there'll be nothing left of your town but smouldering debris!

This outburst spawned a rabid response from the people of Corazón de la Fuente, many of whom wanted to step up and shoot the old witch and be done with her forever. It was the hacendero, Antonio Garcia, who arrived at a more level-headed solution: he marched towards her and grabbed her around the midsection.

Wrinkling his nose at her bovine odour, he said: — That's just about enough out of you, old woman.

He then dragged her kicking and howling out of the glow cast by the generator-fed lights. Meanwhile, everyone laughed at this spectacle. *She is worried about losing patients to the doctor!* someone loudly opined, and this caused those assembled to laugh all the harder. Up onstage, the mayor grinned bashfully at Brinkley.

— I'm sorry, doctor.

— Ah, there is no reason to apologize! Everywhere I go and everywhere I speak, there are those who object to the march of progress. It is a cross men of science are born to bear. If you want to know the real truth, I enjoy such moments, for if people like that good woman are so threatened by my work, it means I am truly getting somewhere.

Everyone applauded, including the mayor, who also lifted his chin and laughed. In the midst of this merriment, the good doctor looked at his watch, a movement that caused a majority of the crowd to do the same, even though most of them were not wearing timepieces.

— I see, announced Brinkley, — that the time is upon us!

He paused, mouth open, while continuing to look at his watch.

— All right, he said slowly. — All . . . right . . . just a few more seconds . . . Here we go: ten . . . nine . . .

The crowd joined in.

— eight . . . seven . . . six . . .

Violeta, who found herself swept away by the drama of the moment, began counting as well.

— five . . . four . . . three . . .

And even the very young and the very old, both of whom had lost the gist of what exactly was happening, counted while making chopping noises in the humid night air.

— two . . . one . . . Ladies and gentlemen, I give you XER, the Sunshine Station from Between the Nations!

The doctor then gestured excitedly at the mayor, who reached up, grabbed the enormous switch, and pulled. The crowd hushed. A second passed, just long enough for a look of worry to pass over Brinkley's features. It disappeared when, seemingly from nowhere, the nasal tones of a popular gringo hymn came from a radio that had been set up on the stage.

> Will the circle be unbroken
> By and by, Lord, by and by?
> There's a better home awaiting
> In the sky, Lord, in the sky . . .

A second after that, the people of Corazón de la Fuente looked up, their mouths open, their eyes widening with disbelief. A collective gasp passed from the lips of those assembled. A hundred metres above them, the tip of the tower glowed. A second later, the sky erupted with a shimmering frog-green corona, the result of high-powered radio frequencies ricocheting between clouds and the floor of a desert. For those who were watching this sudden dance of light, it was a moment that redefined their concept of beauty, amazement, and what existed within the realm of the possible.

After regarding the light for a few seconds, Violeta turned away, understanding full well that its brilliance was unlocking a part of her that for too long had remained buried under layers of studiousness and grief. She looked at the crowd of green-tinted faces around her and felt a joyousness that she did not in any way trust, and that made her feel more than a little uncomfortable. She then turned to Francisco and said *Forgive me* with such a confusing mixture of joy and gravity that it all but spoiled what happened next.

Violeta Cruz seized Francisco Ramirez by the shoulders, pulled him towards her, and kissed him full on the mouth.

{DOS}

{12}

AS THAT TORRID SUMMER WORE ON, CHANGE CAME
with a rapidity that no one without the benefit of clairvoy-
ance could have predicted. The streets of Corazón de la
Fuente, once so quiet that you could sit for hours on a plaza
bench and hear nothing but the hum of your own cogitations,
were now occupied most hours of the day and night, and not
always by the most temperate of characters. The reason was
simple. Money had come to the residents of the ejido, most
of whom had originated in unfathomably poor states like
Oaxaca, Michoacán, and Chiapas, and who had grown up
trading corn, cocoa beans, squash, potatoes, or handicrafts
woven by single-toothed grandmothers. This was the problem. You didn't save squash left over after a good growing
season, as it simply grew mould. You didn't save whatever
potatoes weren't consumed by your family: they turned
mushy and gave off a sweet, alcoholic scent that attracted
wasps. Likewise, you did not save money you earned simply
because an impulsive gringo doctor decided he needed a radio

tower. There could be yet another coup, and then all of the pesos spilling out of your pockets, mattresses, and furniture cushions would be as worthless as Coahuilan dust.

Now that they were rich, and no longer busy with the tower, the men of Corazón de la Fuente filed into Carlos Hernandez's cantina like penitents before a cross. By the afternoon of any given day, dark, squat-shouldered drunks were reeling along the town's two main avenues, singing melancholy songs about life in poor Sierra Madre villages. In the mornings, those who hadn't made it back to the ejido would awake sprawled against curbs or lying face down on plaza benches, their mouths as dry as sand. It was rumoured that one lucky drunkard awoke sprawled over the lip of the Pozo de Confesiones. Had he shifted his weight during the night, he'd have likely snapped his neck in the resulting plummet.

Whereas the residents of Corazón de la Fuente had once awoken to the crowing of roosters, they now woke to the rough sound of drunkards, who would groan, rhetorically ask *Where in the chingada am I?* and then throw up on their huaraches. Whereas mothers once let their children play in the streets at all hours of the day and night, they were now careful to pull them in by the time the sun was lowering and the first wave of mescal drinkers was staggering out of Carlos's saloon. Mostly, the townsfolk accepted this as one of the drawbacks of progress.

Two hundred kilometres west, the town of Piedras Negras suffered from the same undesirable elements. There they had given rise to an industry of people selling late-night quesadillas and tripe stew from street carts, a practice that was already in its nascence in Corazón de la Fuente. The cantina owner now employed a bartender named Ernesto to keep up with business, and Fajardo Jimenez needed counter help now that his shop stayed open until the wee hours. Prosperity, it seemed, really had come to town, the long-time residents of Corazón reasoning that it was only a matter of time before the ejido dwellers ran out of money. In the meantime, they would have to be fools not to help relieve them of it.

Local drunks, their veins coursing with cerveza and ancient native wisdom, weren't the only ones taking to the streets of Corazón. Over the river in Del Rio, Dr. John Romulus Brinkley was offering reduced rates at the Roswell Hotel for any out-of-state resident who came to have his Compound Operation. Afflicted gringos responded in droves, all of them having heard of the procedure — as well as the hope it presented — on Radio XER. This proved to be a boon for at least one scarab-ring-wearing businessperson in Corazón de La Fuente. Brinkley's clients would rest up at the Roswell, waiting for the post-operative throbbing to be replaced by a different, more pleasant brand of pulsation. Eager to find out whether their money had been well spent, they would cross over to Corazón de la Fuente, their way lit by flashing green skies, their hands gripped tight around one of the bills that Madam Félix had posted all over Del Rio. Showing an understanding of both euphemism and the limits of the law, she described her business as a place where a massage, a hot bath, a decent cigar, and other prompters of relaxation could be procured.

The townsfolk of Corazón de la Fuente soon grew accustomed to the sight of a lineup leading from Madam Félix's door and extending along Avenida Cinco de Mayo. A cottage industry of vendors arose, who sold these men everything from tacos to Chiclets to hair combs to tiny glasses filled with murky home-distilled mescal. Beggars from all over Coahuila, many of whom were blind and/or suffering from stunting genetic disorders, also made their way to Corazón, knowing full well that men about to partake of sin often redeem themselves with a little almsgiving. Others came from the southern half of the country, having incorrectly heard that there was still work to be had at the tower site. During the day these wretches shared the streets with drunken ejido-dwellers, converting the plazas and side streets into makeshift sleeping places.

A taxi industry sprouted, seemingly overnight. Anyone with a burro, cart, or bicycle with commodious handlebars would now wait at the bridge for the procession of men who crossed every night, looking simultaneously bashful and ravenous as unfed coyotes. Upon crossing the border, Madam's clients were always willing to pay for some form of guide, having been told time and time again that México was a foul, lawless snakepit where the sun burned holes in your retinas, the ground crawled with scorpions, and every manner of degenerate was waiting to prey upon you. As a result, even those Mexicanos with nothing more to offer than a trustworthy disposition would, for a commensurately lower fee, offer to guide visitors on foot to the House of Gentlemanly Pleasures, which was beginning to gain a reputation as one of the finest bordellos in northern México. Upon reaching Madam's, the gringos tended to tip their porters well, if only to express their relief at not having been murdered along the way.

Soon there were so many taxistas in Corazón that a tertiary industry arose. Those with a knowledge of English — or the ability to fake a knowledge of English — began selling lessons to the taxistas, so that they in turn could put their clients at ease with such disarming phrases as *Is a bery bootiful ebening, señor,* and *You liking some hoochy-coochy, meester?*

One such tutor was Francisco Ramirez, who put a sign to this effect on the wall of his family home, advertising that he was offering English lessons on Saturday mornings. Francisco's English was passable at best, but he benefited from his reputation as a young man who had somehow vanquished an entire posse of bazooka-wielding psychopaths in the middle of a scorching-hot desert. Soon admiring students started knocking on the family's mesquite-plank door, holding out a handful of pesos and asking if this was enough for a lesson. Mostly they were indigenous folk who'd come north during the revolution, having grown up without the benefit of a bilingual border culture. They were uniformly swarthy and doe-eyed and had a guileless habit of blinking when nervous or confused.

— Now repeat after me, Francisco would say. — *I am very pleased to meet you.*

— I am bery pliss to mit joo.

— Not quite, Francisco would explain in Spanish. — You're saying *b* instead of *v* and you're making your long vowels short. Try again.

— I am bery pliss to mit joo.

— Remember last week? When we studied the difference between the *b* and *v* sounds?

— Sí, Francisco. (blink)

— Then let's give it another go.

— I am bery plissed to mit joo.

Though this was frustrating, Francisco benefited from a high level of motivation: he had a sweetheart now. And while it was true that Violeta did not ask him for things, as most of the other chicas in town would have, it was still nice to bring her flowers purchased from Indio vendors who spent their days combing the desert for cactus blooms, or to buy her the occasional soft drink from the store of Fajardo Jimenez. They would then go walking through town, Francisco conscious of the leering, resentful glances being cast in his direction. He didn't care, for each afternoon the time would inevitably come when the day began to weaken over the western plains. At such moments it was as though the peaks of the distant sierras were lancing the sun, causing it to bleed molten colour across the skies.

In this passionate light, Francisco and Violeta would walk along a goat path forged during the revolution by women escaping the satanic demands of men with guns and no one to answer to. It meandered south past the old Spanish mission and continued well into the desert. After a kilometre or so, the path finally came over a rise and terminated in a long, sandy lee that, on a night when the clouds were full and the corona was operating at peak illumination, offered a brilliant kelp-green vista of the Coahuilan desert. It was a place of undeniable wonderment, the howls of roving coydogs providing an atmospheric soundtrack.

Since the end of the revolution, the spot had served a different, much more pleasing, purpose. It was here that the young of the town met for romantic assignations, away from protective fathers and mothers worried that their daughters were about to make the same mistakes they had made at that age. Often, upon reaching the lee, Francisco and Violeta could see as many as a dozen couples, stretched along at ten-metre intervals, all embracing in the tarragon-hued starlight.

Francisco would then escort Violeta to an unoccupied spot well away from the others, and there they would loll amid sandy brambles and press against one another, a heated connectivity occurring between lips and mouths and hands and skin and hips and the sort of words spoken when only the present tense is relevant and desire is made tangible and matter converts to a fluid, glowing energy and the whole of the universe becomes simple and glorious and intended for the benefit of young people only.

Love, in other words, was in the air. There was something about the existence of the tower, its mammoth tip throb-bing red, that enriched the blood, tantalized the flesh, and caused the hammocks of Corazón de la Fuente to bounce with a ferocity that had not been known during the libido-draining years of the revolution. The aging molinero, in love with Laura Velasquez, felt a sprightliness invade his body: there were times when he had to remind himself that he was eighty-eight years of age and not an infatuated teenager. The hacendero, too, found himself newly enraptured with his paramour, Madam Félix, so much so that at times he con-templated telling the whole village of their love. It was also known that Consuela Reyes, mother of Alfonso and Luis, had caught the eye of a carpenter from Rosita, who had visited on the night that Radio XER went on the air and the skies began to shimmer with green light.

Even the cantina owner, Carlos Hernandez, long denied the physical expression of love, felt inspired by the town's collective ardour. Late one night he walked into the desert, his way lit by the rippling corona. There he extracted the money he kept in his safety box, which had grown exponentially since the explosion of gringo traffic to the town. He stuffed his savings into his jeans, returned to his home, and slept that night with his earnings hidden in his pillowcase. Margarita, who respected the invisible line between them, was none the wiser.

The following afternoon he saddled a neighbour's burro and headed towards the bridge, his pockets bulging with pesos and dollars. To anyone who asked, he claimed that he was heading to Del Río to investigate the possibility of buying a saloon mirror unmarred by pistol fire and the yellowing caused by time's passage. He passed the guard on the Mexican side of the border, who was dozing against the first post of the bridge railing, his hat pulled down over his brow. At the other side, a diminutive border guard in dark glasses emerged from his cabaña, only to begin a routine familiar to every Corazónite who needed to cross into America with dry clothing. The guard asked to see a passport. The cantina owner apologized and, in workable English, admitted that he did not have one. The guard said that was a problem. The cantina owner said he hoped it wasn't too big a problem. The guard said maybe there was something he could do. The cantina owner said it would be most appreciated. The guard offered to sell him a transit visa, though it would cost ten dollars.

Carlos countered that he was just a poor cantina owner. The exchange went on and on. Though both men were bored by the charade, neither knew any mechanism to avoid its time-honoured practice. In the end, the cantina owner successfully crossed into los Estados Unidos, his pocket lightened by exactly one dollar. The transit visa never manifested itself.

He rode towards the main street of Del Rio, Texas, which lay about a half-mile west of the international bridge. After leaving his burro tied to a hitching post next to a row of automobiles, he entered the town's department store, promptly left through the rear entrance, and doubled back until he reached the Stonewall Hotel, a plain, five-storey grey-brick building that was known for having the first and only elevator in the town of Del Rio. The building was fronted by a large rectangular lawn dotted with acacia shrubs. It was here that Dr. Brinkley's clinic operated from the top two floors. Out back, Carlos could hear the bleating of penned Toggenburg goats.

After a series of quick side-to-side glances, the cantina owner stepped into the elevator, his apprehension overcome by the novelty of this experience. He debarked on the fourth floor and found a door marked *Reception*. He removed his hat and entered a roomful of men hiding behind magazine covers. He then approached a receptionist seated at a desk towards one end of the room. She wore a denim shirt with a galaxy of stitching.

— Hello! she chirped.

— Hello, he answered, his *h* so overly compensated it sounded like a rushing of breath.

— Would you like to see one of the doctors?

The cantina owner nodded.

— Lovely, the woman said. — Now, what is your name?

— Carlos Hernandez.

She wrote this down. — As you can see, we're very busy today. Just take a seat, and one of our attendants will be with you in a moment.

The cantina owner squeezed between a fat, sweating man in a bowler hat and a skinny man wearing farmer's overalls. Neither so much as glanced at him, and the fat man refused to relinquish any of the armrest. The cantina owner sat with his arms tight to his body and surveyed the room, catching glimpses of stony, discomfited expressions, all peering at him above copies of the *Del Río Herald* or the *San Antonio Express-News*. He stood and picked up a tattered edition of the the *Houston Chronicle* from an end table, squeezed back into his seat, and, like the rest of the men in the room, pretended to read.

Time passed with an excruciating slowness. *Ay, caray*, he thought, *I'll develop a craving for tin cans and boot soles. In the morning I'll wake my neighbours with my bleating.* He grinned, albeit briefly, and then watched his thoughts grow suspicious and dark. *What do you think, pendejo? That they'll give you the best surgeon in the place? That you'll get Brinkley himself? Oh no, a poor Mexicano like you, with burro shit on your boots and a moustache worthy of Pancho Villa, you'll get the cutter with shaky hands and a hangover and a known antipathy towards those with bronze skin . . .*

The more his thoughts swirled, the more uncomfortable he grew, till the moment came when he decided he was going to march out, fetch his neighbour's burro, and flee. He was just about to stand when a sobering hallucination alighted on the pages of his paper. It was the face of his Margarita, and in this vision he saw something he had to confront each and every day: her depleted opinion of him, an opinion that seemed to diminish further with each week of matrimonial deprivation. It glistened in her newsprint eyes and oozed from every grey newspaper pore.

— Señor Hernandez?

The cantina owner's thoughts were vacuumed up through space and time. He closed the magazine on the disgruntled features of his wife. A young man wearing a green surgical gown was standing in the doorway. The cantina owner stood and followed the man down a hallway and into a small room. They sat.

— Bienvenido, said the attendant while reaching for a clipboard. — I'm going to ask you few questions.

— Sí.

— How long have you been suffering from impotence?

The cantina owner lowered his gaze. In México you would never ask a man to reveal something so disgraceful. — It has been a while, he confessed.

— And you are married?

— Sí.

— And for how long have you been married?

— Eleven years.

— So you haven't always had this problem?

Of course not, you offensive hijo de puta, the cantina owner yearned to say. Instead he just shook his head, *no*.

— Do you have children?

Again he hung his head. There had been a time when he and Margarita had spent entire days in their large, feather-mattressed bed, both of them laughing as the towns-folk pounded the locked doors of the cantina, yelling for chilled cerveza. Back then it had seemed as inevitable as the setting of the sun that they would have four, five, maybe even a half-dozen children.

— No, he answered. — We wanted to, but it never happened.

— I see. Tell me, was there some event that, mmm, triggered your impotence?

— I no understand.

— Was there . . . something that seemed to cause your problem?

The cantina owner thought of the leering, horrific face of the capitano, the contents of his stomach beginning to writhe. — No. It just started happening.

The young man wrote this down. — Tell me, Señor Hernandez, are you suffering from fatigue? From feeling tired all the time?

Finally, the cantina owner thought, a question that did not embarrass him. He nodded.

The young man smiled. — Of course, of course. I could have answered this question myself. And are there times when you find it difficult to go to the bathroom?

— Hmm, not . . .

— Of course there are. And I bet I don't even need to ask the next question. Are there times when you feel pain in the lower abdomen?

I am from México, Carlos was tempted to answer. *I have lived through revolution, through famine, through locust plagues and drought. I feel pain everywhere, at all times, in places you don't know about.* Instead, he just said: — Sí.

The young man scribbled. — I am happy to say, Señor Hernandez, that you have a very simple problem, one experienced by many, many men, particularly during times of stress, and one that is completely treated by our Compound Operation. Do you know what this involves?

— I think so.

— It's very simple, the incision very small. All we do is take a culture made of extracted goat . . .

— Sí, sí, I know. When I can have it?

The man blinked at him as though surprised.

When? Señor Hernandez, didn't you know? We pride ourselves on offering same-day service. With so many clients from out of town, we really have to, don't you think?

With that the attendant summoned a tiny Asiatic nurse with glasses so thick they rendered her eyes the size of avocado stones. The woman led the cantina owner down the hall, entering what was clearly a former hotel suite, a surgical cot in place of an actual bed. She instructed the cantina owner to lie down, lower his trousers to his knees, and pull his shirt up to the middle of his chest. Carlos relinquished the last shreds of his dignity, and when he next looked at the nurse, she was bearing a syringe. The cantina owner stiffened with fear, then felt a prick just above his pelvic bone.

— There you go, said the nurse. — Now you just wait here.

Again the cantina owner obliged, his genital region turning so numb that, after ten minutes or so, he could no longer feel it; it was as though the terrain existing between his upper thighs and navel had disappeared. As he waited, he looked around the room, a decision he immediately regretted. The wallpaper was peeling, the light fixture attached to the ceiling directly above him was filled with dead flies, and the carpet had been mended in spots with electrical tape. He closed his eyes and shuddered, and was about to call off the whole operation when Dr. Brinkley himself came bursting into the room, his eyes shining behind his tortoiseshell frames.

— So it's true! he exclaimed in Spanish. — One of the nurses mentioned that one of Corazón's own was here for treatment, and I just had to come and see for myself. It's Señor Hernandez, is it?

— Sí, Francisco said, his face blooming into a grateful smile.

— Well, in that case, welcome! You are officially the first person of Mexican residence to have my world-famous Compound Operation. Not only am I going to do the procedure myself, I'll knock ten percent off the bill. In fact, you can tell your compadres over the border that the offer is open to any resident of Corazón de la Fuente. It's the least I can do for that town of yours. In fact, lately I've been thinking of doing something nice for your whole village, some sort of civic event . . . It must have been a real inconvenience, putting up with all that construction. All in good time, of course.

The doctor stopped, caught his breath, and extracted a scalpel from a tray that was teetering on the arm of a battered old sofa.

— Well, then, let's get started. My advice is that you close your eyes and think pleasant thoughts. In a few minutes, it'll all be over.

The cantina owner left that afternoon with two things: a fútbol-sized wadding of gauze spanning his inner thighs, and a prescription for what the doctor referred to as *post-operative medicinals*. In the Del Río pharmacy, Carlos purchased three containers marked simply *#4*, *#18*, and *#26*, each of which bore a picture of a smiling Dr. Brinkley. Number 4 was a minuscule red pill that to the cantina owner looked a little bit like an engorged chigger. Number 18 was a green and white vial. Number 26 was a chalky-textured pill the size of a quail egg that, as the prescription label suggested, was best ingested with an ample accompaniment of liquid. Number 4 came in a vial, number 18 in a small brown glass bottle, and number 26 in a jar the size of a cow's udder. He was to take one of each every morning and evening, as well as an extra dose of number 18 every time he experienced what the label referred to as *a noticeable smarting of the prostate*. This last instruction left the cantina owner a little unsettled, as he was not exactly sure what the prostate was, what function it performed, or where he would feel discomfort if and/or when it started to smart.

Nonetheless, he gingerly mounted his burro, rode to the bridge, entered into banal negotiations with the American guard, passed the still-sleeping Mexican guard, and wrinkled his nose as he passed the reeking slum that engulfed Antonio Garcia's bombarded hacienda. He then rode smiling into Corazón de la Fuente, causing many of the townsfolk to comment that the owner of the town cantina must have located a saloon mirror to his liking.

{13}

AS SHE DID MOST NIGHTS, MADAM FÉLIX LAY IN BED
with her not-so-secret lover, the Spanish hacendero Antonio
Garcia. It was around three o'clock in the morning, and
yowls of delight (along with the squeak of rusty bedsprings)
were still emanating from the rooms where the Marias
plied their trade. This didn't bother the hacendero, who was
pleasantly exhausted after a day spent astride his new horse
and, after that, his woman. The same could not be said for
Madam Félix, who was being kept awake by the best kind of
business worries.

— I tell you, Antonio. I don't know what I'm going to do.
The Marias, they are all tired to the bone. They are working
around the clock. Maria de las Rosas, she has bags under her
eyes the colour of a crow's wing. And Maria de los Flores,
her hair is starting to thin, which always happens when she
is stressed. None of them are eating or sleeping properly,
and they're all complaining about clients having bandages in
weird places. The other day, Maria de la Mañana told me that

she had a client who, when his clap of lightning came, started bleating! And Maria de la Noche — already she's doubled her rates and still they're lined up out the door. It can't go on like this. Mind you, the Marias are all making a fortune. They'll all be madams themselves in five years. Maria de la Noche could afford her own House *now*. Still, I worry about them.

The hacendero rolled over to face her. His face looked soft with the coming of sleep.

— You could try closing once in a while.

— It's not so simple. If I turn away business, the Juans might go somewhere else. Piedras, maybe, or Villa Acuña.

She held up her left hand, admiring it in the moonlight creeping through her heavy velvet curtains. Her new ring, which she wore on a finger two over from the finger bearing the scarab in glass, was fashioned from a ruby the size of a plum stone.

— Still, she said,   being busy has its advantages.

— So expand.

— Expand?

— Find more Marias.

— I was thinking about that . . .

So do it, amor, and let me get a little sleep.

The next afternoon, as the Marias began to rise, the house filled with yawns and groggy chatter and the cook began heating a cast-iron pan for tortillas. Once coffee had been served, Madam called Maria de las Rosas, a pretty girl with bronze skin and hair that cascaded halfway down her back, into the small office that the madam maintained in the room next to her boudoir. Here she informed Maria that she looked exhausted, that she couldn't afford to have a Maria with bags under her eyes, and that she was sending her home to her village in Oaxaca for a well-earned vacation.

— But, Madam! Maria protested. — I need the money!

The madam had expected this, and calmed Maria with a matronly *shhh*. — I know, preciosa, I know. Don't worry, I'll pay for your trip. It's just that I can't stand to see any of my Marias looking sad or tired.

She leaned close to Maria de las Rosas, as if to say something conspiratorial.

— Besides, I think that you and I could come up with a small arrangement that might be, mmm, beneficial to us both.

Maria de las Rosas blinked. Over the years, Madam Félix had employed many smart Marias and many dumb Marias. While their intelligence generally didn't affect their work one way or the other, the madam always found that she tended to establish friendships with the smarter ones and maternal relationships with the dumber ones. With Maria de las Rosas, she could easily have tucked her into bed at night after giving her a snack of wheat biscuits and honey.

— I don't understand, Madam.

— Maria, we are short-staffed here. I need more Marias . . . two at least.

Maria blinked several times; Madam had to control the instinct to roll her eyes.

— Let me put it to you this way. Do you think there might be some young women in your hometown, pretty and ambitious like yourself, who might like to take up a profession similar to yours?

— You mean . . . become putas?

Madam Félix sighed. She did not like to hear abrasive language from the mouths of her Marias, and she particularly did not like her profession spoken of in such denigrating terms. Still, given the delicacy of the situation, she elected not to castigate poor Maria de las Rosas.

— Sí. I'm looking for a few girls to work here as Marias. Of course, I would give you a finder's fee that would more than make up for any, mmm, lost-opportunity costs you incur while on vacation. Do you think you could do this for me, Maria?

Again Maria stared at her blankly. But then, slowly, a wave of comprehension came over her. She clapped her hands and smiled like a child who has just been given ice cream.

— You want me to find you fresh whores!

Madam rubbed her eyes. — Sí, Maria. Can you do this?

— Madam, I come from a poor village in Oaxaca. There is nothing there but sadness. People say they mean and problems. The children run around bare-bottomed and snack on the paint peeling from walls. The only question is, how many Marias do you need?

— Two, said Madam. — Maybe three. And make sure they're eighteen.

The next day, Madam Félix escorted Maria de las Rosas to the main highway, where Maria would catch a bus for Piedras Negras and destinations beyond. As they waited for the bus to come, Madam Félix gazed towards her tiny village. She had to smile. From this distance, the buildings of Corazón de la

Fuente looked like penitents gathered at the feet of Brinkley's mighty, all-seeing radio tower. A few minutes later, Maria boarded a rickety pale blue bus named *El Campeón del Cielo* and, with a tear in her eye, was gone.

The madam promptly hired a group of ejido-dwellers to erect a small extension to the south side of her brothel to accommodate the new Marias. They set to work with alacrity, using tools and materials they'd had the foresight to pilfer from the tower site. Meanwhile, business carried on as usual in the main part of Madam's House of Gentlemanly Pleasures. Though the other Marias had to shoulder Maria de las Rosas' workload, they were all buoyed by the promise of new troops, lunch hours to themselves, and more than three hours a night of rest.

A week and a half later, in the middle of an afternoon that was hot even by Coahuilan standards, a buggy pulled up in front of Madam's. In the front seat, next to a driver hired in Piedras Negras, was Maria de las Rosas. In the back seat were a pair of trembling little beauties, each with eyes the size of silver dollars. Madam Félix hustled out, paid the driver, and helped her new Marias down from the buggy. Neither, she would have bet, was a day over sixteen.

— Buenas días, she said.

Both the girls looked at the packed dust of the roadway.

— Buenas, one of them peeped.

They really were pretty: doe-eyed and high-cheeked and with just the right amount of Indian to make them look exotic. They both wore peasant dresses that, Madam noticed, had been mended in two or three spots. She touched one of them on the shoulder.

— You are Maria del Día. Do you understand?

— Sí, señora.

— Por favor, preciosa, here I am called Madam or Madam Félix.

— Sí, Madam.

Madam Félix turned to the other.

— You will be called Maria del Maíz.

— Sí. Gracias.

— You are now both attendants in my House of Gentlemanly Pleasures. Here you will practise the world's oldest profession. It is an honourable profession, and one that you will perform with pride and with dignity. You will dress in the finest clothes and you will always be treated with respect. Your days here will be busy and content. You will learn to walk with your head up, your back straight, and your eyes alive with knowing. If you work hard and do not send too much of your money home, you will retire by the age of thirty and not have to work another day in your life.

— Gracias, they both peeped.

— Bueno, said Madam Félix. — You both must feel hungry, and in need of a long, hot bath.

Over the next week, Madam Félix let her paperwork pile up so as to attend to her new charges. It was a big job. First she escorted them to Piedras Negras. In a shop tucked within the tight, sunless passages of the Zaragoza Market, she had a pair of cinched-waist dresses made for both of them. She also bought them French leather walking shoes. As they had grown up barefoot, or wearing only the flimsiest of huaraches, she had to teach the new Marias how to lace them (*above and under, above and under — sí, sí, eso es*), how to walk in them (*lift your feet, mijas, lift your feet*), and how to keep them supple with rendered goat fat. She also took her new waifs to a salon and had their dark tresses trimmed and pinned in a waterfall arrangement that not only showed off their eyes, neck, and cheekbones, but lent them an aristocratic air.

Halfway through the day, Maria del Maíz became sniffly and admitted she was homesick. As Maria del Día looked on, struggling not to shed a tear of her own, Madam wrapped her arms around the weeping Maria and purred *I know, mija, I know. Now dry your eyes. We'll go have a pastelito.*

After Madam had fed them cake and tea sweetened with piloncillo, they travelled back to Corazón, each of the new Marias now looking like a princess and behaving, of course, like an illiterate campesina. Over the next week, Madam showed them how to walk without slouching, how to look a gentleman in the eye when speaking, how to use euphemisms when referring to acts that were physical in nature. She taught them how to bathe, properly and thoroughly, and she instructed them where to dab rosewater for maximum stimulating effect. She taught them how to prevent pregnancy by using a mixture of vinegar, sotol resin, and mashed beetle shell (it was a recipe Madam had purchased, naturally enough, from Azula Mampajo, the town curandera). She taught them how to pronounce the final letter of each word, such that a phrase such as *tres horas* no longer came out sounding like *tray hora*, and she slowly rid their language of the galaxy of swear words that uneducated Mexicanos use three times per sentence. She trained them not to end each sentence with the interrogative *verdad?* (*You are a Maria now, you don't need to ask whether you are correct*) and she extinguished their Mexican habit of starting every sentence with the imperative *oye* or *mire* (*The sound of your lovely voice, my darlings, will command sufficient attention*). She taught them how to apply makeup, and how to feign interest in political opinion. She taught them English phrases (*Hello, how are you? My name is Maria*) and the fundamentals of wine, cigars, horses, and any digestif not distilled from the pith of a maguey plant. Above all else, she taught them to appreciate themselves, mostly by standing them before a mirror in a room illuminated by candles.

— Look at yourself, Marias. Look at your eyes, your hair, the contours of your lips. You are beautiful, you are poised, you are Marias. Do you see it?

— No, Madam, peeped Maria del Día.

— I'm sorry, echoed Maria del Maíz. — My mother, she always said I was plain.

— Your *mother*, countered Madam, — was jealous.

Their tutoring continued. She taught them how to hold a coffee cup (pinky finger extended), how to smoke a ciga-rillo (in a tapered black holder as long as a zucchini), and how to toast a gentleman's health (respectfully, subtly, voice cascading with nuance). Four days later, after a morning les-son devoted to the Mexican War of Independence, she again placed her new charges before a candlelit mirror.

— Look at yourself, she said once more. — Look at your eyes, your hair, your . . .

She stopped. A tear was slipping down Maria del Día's cheek. Maria del Maíz's lips were parted, and she looked as though nothing short of a hurricane could tear her eyes away from her flame-hued reflection.

— You see it now, Madam said.

— Sí, they each said with a sniffle.

The next morning she turned them over to Maria de la Noche, who tutored them in the myriad ways of pleasure: how to hurry a gentleman when there's a lineup at the door, how to slow a gentleman on a quiet night when you want a big tip, how to bolster a gentleman who no longer feels he has a place in the world outside of Madam's house. She taught them how to behave like a woman whose heart is bursting, like a woman distracted by ravenous desire, like a woman who knows nothing of men and wants nothing more than a kindly instructor. She taught them how to behave peevishly, imperiously, submissively, innocently, wantonly, and/or primly. Most importantly, she taught them how to tailor their composure to the unspoken, perhaps even unrealized, needs of each gentleman.

Finally, on a night when a cool wind was blowing in from the north and the air was fragranced with creosote, and coyotes howled in distant choirs, and the stars were so bright they fought with the sea-green corona for galactic prominence, Madam slipped Maria del Día and Maria del Maíz onto her roster of Marias. The girls, despite their rural ignorance, had learned well. Their gentlemen emerged from their respective bedrooms with expressions of almost sublime contentment, coupled with a profound reluctance to leave. Each, Madam noticed, stayed to enjoy a cigar and a jigger of cheap Venezuelan spirits, poured, quite naturally, from a bottle of Tennessee's finest.

{14}

ONE SATURDAY MORNING, FOLLOWING A NIGHT DUR-
ing which Francisco and Violeta had kissed until their lips
turned as pale and rubbery as the belly of a frog, Francisco
awoke and dressed for his weekly tutoring job. He had stopped
giving lessons in his home, a consequence of his grandmother's
complaint that his pupils smelled of woodsmoke (they did)
and that the people of the south were somehow heretical in
nature (a popular opinion among elderly northerners, who
could not fathom the worship that the dark-skinned Virgin of
Guadalupe attracted in other parts of the country). To avoid
upsetting the old woman, Francisco started giving his lessons
in the depths of the ejido, where entire poverty-wracked families now crowded around him, listening to him conjugate
irregular verbs. His payments, as the tower workers' money
depleted, grew less and less regular. Often at the end of his
sessions, he was presented with a bowl of goat stew or a batch
of homemade tortillas, or, as happened one noon hour, the
recitation of a blessing that protected against epidermal boils.

Francisco's father soon suggested that his son quit — often the remunerative soups suffered from bits of bone and gristle, not to mention ingredients that were obviously reptilian in nature. Yet Francisco couldn't. It was the delighted look on his students' round, bronze-tinted faces every time he arrived. In him they saw the knowledge that they hoped would one day lead them out of the ejido, and Francisco didn't have it in him to extinguish that hope.

After a breakfast of porridge and juice, Francisco left the house whistling, a habit he'd acquired since being visited by the sumptuous anointment that is love. Upon reaching the central plaza, however, he pulled up short: most of the vagrants who now lived in the square were milling around the blue wooden doors of the town hall. Francisco approached, his nose wrinkling at the scent of unwashed clothing, and tapped the shoulder of one old-timer who, upon turning, revealed himself to be missing an eye. The remaining eye, meanwhile, fell upon Francisco like the sight of a rifle.

Francisco swallowed and fought the inclination to recoil.

— Excuse me, señor, he said, — but . . . what is happening?

— Don't you know, joven? Sometime in the middle of the night, a huge truck showed up in the plaza. Two gringos opened the back and carried out a huge glass sphere that looked like it was filled with, of all things, balls of gum.

— Qué raro, said Francisco.

— Ay sí. They had a key to the town hall. They opened the doors and carried the thing inside. Then they locked up and drove away. One old bum had his foot run over.

— What can it all mean? Francisco asked rhetorically, a question that was running through the heads of every person in Corazón de la Fuente. This included the mayor, Miguel Orozco, who had arrived about twenty minutes earlier and was now the lone person inside the hall. Slowly he limped around the huge transparent ball, feeling puzzled. The only people who possessed a key to the building were himself and the governor of Coahuila, a reputedly flatulent hombre who had not shown his face in Corazón during Miguel's entire decade as mayor, and who had also not responded to any of the mayor's numerous letters requesting funding for roads, running water, electricity, reliable telephone lines, and the hiring of a dog catcher.

Yet upon finishing his second circuit around the sphere, the mayor realized with a start that there was one other hombre who had a key. In fact, Miguel had given him the key himself. This excited the mayor, and he looked around at the chipped yellow walls of the foyer, seeking confirmation. Though there was nothing save for an old revolutionary poster announcing that the peso was no longer the currency of México, it didn't matter: only one person could have done this. The mayor limped up the steps to his second-floor office, where one of the village's few telephones was slowly coming away from its spot on the peeling wall. After several attempts (the phone lines of México being what they were) he reached the Roswell Hotel, where he spoke to one of the doctor's many assistants. In this manner he learned everything.

The mayor spent the rest of the morning in a more typical fashion: reading the newspaper and daydreaming. At noon, his secretary — an old village woman who worked about ten minutes each day — brought him a lunch of tortilla and machaca. When he was finished, he drank a cup of coffee and smoked a punche cigarette while waiting for the clamour beneath him to die down.

When the last of the townsfolk finally got bored and wandered off, the mayor rose, limped down to the foyer, and stood grinning at the sight of the immense gumball machine; the truth was, he'd never realized that Brinkley was quite so eccentric. Thankfully, his were the sort of eccentricities that were a pleasure to accommodate. He clomped over to Carlos Hernandez's cantina, ordered a cerveza, and sat with the cantina owner and Father Alvarez.

— Goddamn it, Alvarez said. — Out with it, primo.

— Out with what?

— Why is all that gum in your office?

The mayor leaned close to his two old friends. Though he had pledged not to reveal Brinkley's surprise, he had done so before being faced with an afternoon of drinking with his closest amigos. — Can you keep a secret?

— No, said the father. — Tell us anyway, you cagey pendejo.

The mayor rolled his eyes at the father's cantankerousness. — This Saturday, after the lucha show, Dr. Brinkley is going to bring the machine onto the bandstand for a contest. Whoever comes closest to guessing how many gumballs are inside it will win a hundred American dollars.

— A hundred dollars! exclaimed the cantina owner.

— He may be a bit loco but he is generous, said the mayor. — He wants to help us celebrate our Día de la Independencia.

— Bah, spouted Father Alvarez. — A hundred dollars is a day's worth of piss for a cabrón like him.

— Father, said the cantina owner. — Maybe you'd like a lemonade for the next round.

— And maybe you'd like to go to heaven. It doesn't mean it's going to happen. And by the way, why do you keep wriggling? You look like you've got a marmot in your pants.

The cantina owner reddened. — I played fútbol yesterday, and I'm a little sore.

— Gentlemen, interrupted the mayor. — Por *favor*. After the contest, Brinkley is going to smash the thing open with a mallet and let the kids of the town have all the gumballs they can carry away.

— That, joked the cantina owner, — could be one lucha fight worth seeing.

By the time Saturday night had rolled around, there wasn't a soul in all of Corazón — as well as the neighbouring towns of Rosita and Piedras Negras — who didn't know that the world-famous goat-gland doctor was going to give out a hundred dollars and a hoard of free candy on México's Independence Day. Unlike the past several Saturdays, when attendance at the Reyes brothers' lucha displays had dwindled to Consuela Reyes, her recently acquired suitor, and a few teenaged fans of Los Inconsolables del Norte, the entire plaza slowly filled. Francisco arrived early to save a good seat for himself and Violeta. The mayor escorted the ancient molinero and his sweetheart, Laura, who was excited about her upcoming trip to a dentist in Saltillo; they sat in reserved seats along with the cantina owner, the hacendero, and Father Alvarez. A breeze was wafting down from the sierras, taking away just enough of the day's humidity to make the evening enjoyable.

The last two seats were reserved for Dr. Brinkley and his wife, a woman who had yet to grace the town of Corazón de la Fuente. Time and time again the mayor had to inform others that the seats were off-limits, a sentiment the molinero reinforced by holding his piñon-wood cane across the chairs and asking the uninformed parties to *go to the back, por favor.* Meanwhile the plaza kept filling with poor strangers arriving from parts east, west, and south. Soon there were spectators squatting on roofs, perched in the denuded palo verde trees, and jostling in the avenues leading away from the plaza. Most, the mayor noticed, were dressed in tatters.

The lucha show proceeded pretty much as usual. After circumnavigating the stage, Consuela Reyes clanged her cast-iron pan with a fritter spoon. Her oversized sons began circling one another, their arms making slow circling motions in the air. Two minutes later, Alfonso was holding his bleeding nose and Luis was running around the ring, distraught with feelings of guilt.

After the boys were led away by their mother, Los Inconsolables del Norte played for ten minutes, inspiring guffaws from those who had come from neighbouring villages and had no allegiance to the band members or their families. This angered those who had grown up with the group members, and soon came the arguments and shoving that are usually a precursor to fisticuffs. Pistols were seconds away from being drawn when, thankfully, los Inconsolables stopped playing. From their elevated position on the bandstand, the musicians had noticed that the doors to the hall were opening.

The loud ensuing creak silenced the crowd, which parted to make room for the arc of the doors.

Three large Texans, each wearing the nervous expression that gringos inevitably acquired when surrounded by Mexicanos, carried the giant gumball machine to the centre of the stage. A long minute followed, during which a mixture of confusion and anticipation rippled through the crowd. Dr. Brinkley appeared in the doorway of the hall; he was wearing white pants, a blue-striped donkey jacket, and a straw boater bearing the colours of the Mexican flag. Slowly he walked to the bandstand, pausing occasionally to wave at the crowd, kiss an infant, or fold a coin into the hand of a small, dark-eyed child.

The doctor stopped next to the sphere. Motioning with his hands, he peered in every direction through his tortoise-shell glasses. His hair was so lacquered with pomade that it reflected the green light rippling through the sky above him, giving the impression that his head was made from kelp. After a practised dramatic pause, he lifted his arms and began to speak.

— Ladies and gentlemen, he announced in his exemplary Spanish. — It has been three months since the first broadcast of Radio XER, the Sunshine Station from Between the Nations. I am here today to thank each and every one of you for your hospitality, your welcome encouragement, and, perhaps most significantly, the opportunity to spend some time in this glorious little town called Corazón de la Fuente.

He paused for a moment of applause.

— It's no secret that, in the short period in which I have become associated with your town, I have come to hold you all in only the deepest of regard, and I would like to do everything in my power to aid your restoration. As my Appalachian mother used to say, *If you're gonna sit, might as well pick a nice chair.*

This time he paused for polite chortling.

— Anyhow, the other day I was dining with the good missus, and I said to her *Minnie, I want to do something for the people of Corazón de la Fuente on the day of their independence.* Well, to make a long story short, she pondered and then said *John Romulus, do you know what people enjoy?*

He paused dramatically, looking in all directions, his eyes squinting with glee.

— *People enjoy a contest*, she said. *People* love *a contest.* Well, I thought about this for a moment and I said to myself *When the woman is right, the woman is right.* A half-hour later and there I was, on the phone with a representative of the Acme Gumball Machine factory of Alton, Illinois, who was only too pleased to fabricate a customized dispensary for this evening's festivities. And so, my good people, I am left with a single question, which I will put to you right now.

He paused, looking in every direction, his face a mask of mock seriousness. — Which of you would like to win some *money*?

There was an eruption of yelling and jostling and the shoving aside of old people and the stepping on of children, for though John Romulus Brinkley considered himself a man of humble origins, having been born in a tarpaper shack in the Ozark Mountains, he really wasn't, not by Mexican standards. He had no idea what it was like to live through a decade of bloody revolution or to feed his children maguey worms in a vain attempt to get a little protein into their blood, only to watch them grow up with the vacant smiles and stunted language unknown to the adequately fed. Despite being a man who felt for others and who believed he really had the capacity to help people, he had no idea what it was like to dress his children in coffee sacks with holes cut for the arms and huaraches fashioned from old bits of tire rubber. As the crowd pushed tighter and tighter against the stage, the doctor's pleased expression faltered, and over the roar of the crowd he could be heard yelling at his assistants *For the love of God, pick a few contestants!* His Texans, big-armed farm boys who towered over the Mexicans, waded in and grabbed anyone who didn't look dangerous and dragged them to the stage. By the time they were finished, Brinkley was standing amongst a half-dozen contestants, all of whom looked on with mild terror as the equally terrified farm boys struggled to keep the rest of the crowd off the stage.

Slowly the crowd simmered down. Brinkley swept a fallen lock of hair off his forehead and struggled to regain his breath. Beside him stood a couple of ejido dwellers, somebody's grandmother, and an excited vagrant with a stump for a left hand. Finally there was Violeta Cruz, who was attracting whistles and catcalls from those men in the audience who were strangers, and didn't understand that here, in Corazón de la Fuente, the daughters of the village were treated with courtesy and respect. Again there was hostile shoving. Francisco, his hands shaped into fists, waded towards the source of the catcalls, only partially relieved when they died down of their own volition.

— All right, said the doctor. — I am going to ask each of these fine contestants to guess how many gumballs there are in the sphere, and the one who comes closest to the correct answer, which I have ably stored in my noggin, will win one hundred dollars. I'd like to now let the contestants have a long, hard look.

The contestants all turned and started studying the immense ball. Some of them moved their lips as though attempting to count, and some were jabbing a pointed fore-finger into the air, as though operating an imaginary adding machine. Violeta, meanwhile, gazed at it intently, her glori-ous eyes darting, her faultless teeth gnawing on the tip of her left ring finger.

— Now, take your time, said Brinkley. — This isn't a race . . .

He waited another minute and then announced that he would begin. He went to the first contestant, an impoverished youngster suffering from psoriasis and inflamed elbow joints.

— A thousand? said the boy.

— One thousand! said Brinkley. — An admirable guess, my boy . . .

He proceeded to the second in line, a toothless labourer who, having lost his job on the completed tower, had been drinking heavily for ninety full days, behaviour that had both estranged him from his wife and children and given rise to a piney body odour.

— Six hundred, he muttered.

— Six hundred it is! said Brinkley, who was clearly begin-ning to enjoy himself again. He moved to the third contestant, an old woman who lived in town and was known for knitting booties for the newborn. Realizing it was her turn, she hesi-tated, then said: — Ay, Dr. Brinkley, I can't imagine . . .

— Well, take a guess, my fine lady.

She lifted a shaking hand to her mouth and stared at the sphere through small, milky eyes. — Hmmm . . . one thousand five hundred?

— Fifteen hundred it is!

The doctor moved on to the next two contestants, whose bids were 632 and 1,140 respectively. He then stopped in front of the last participant. Violeta Cruz looked up at him with her immense jade orbs. Brinkley stared at the young woman as if noticing her for the first time. For the longest time he was silent; this inspired a ripple of confusion among the townsfolk, who had come to know Brinkley as a man never at a loss for words. Violeta, meanwhile, folded her hands behind her back, an instinctive attempt to hide her badly chewed fingernails.

— Señorita? he finally managed.

Violeta continued looking up at him. Her eyes narrowed, and she cocked her head, ever so slightly, to the left — Mmm, twelve hundred?

John Romulus Brinkley could do nothing but stare into Violeta's depthless eyes, his mouth parted ever so slightly, colour drained from his features. A moment passed, and then another. Suddenly the good doctor was possessed by an enormous, beatific smile. He straightened and turned, his arms outstretched, blood rushing back into his high, egg-shaped cheekbones.

— SEÑORES AND SEÑORAS! he boomed. — WE HAVE OURSELVES A WINNER!!!

This announcement so aroused a gang of inebriated delinquents from Rosita that they stormed the stage with planks removed from a nearby livestock pen and took it upon themselves to smash the sphere to bits. This, in turn, exacerbated the long-time antagonism that existed between the two towns — an antipathy that, legend had it, was born during a disputed call at a fútbol game several decades earlier. As the gumballs spilled over the bandstand, the young men of Corazón similarly armed themselves, and the two sides started swinging. Everyone else either raced for home or took cover in alcoves, the lone exceptions being Francisco and Violeta, who fled towards the desert lee, soon discovering that they had it to themselves that night.

Back in town, the ensuing riot lasted a good fifteen minutes, during which dozens of people suffered broken noses, blackened eyes, and lacerations so severe they would later require poultices made from a mixture of chicken fat and butter. The plaza's wrought-iron benches, forged by Galician ironmongers three centuries earlier, were uprooted and toppled — only their extreme weight stopped them from being thrown through the windows of the town hall. It wasn't long before chagrined Corazónites had run home to arm themselves and pistol shots echoed through the streets. The offending visitors scrambled towards the outskirts of the village, though not without yelling over their shoulders that the people of Corazón de la Fuente were all hijos de putas and that they enjoyed fornicating with burros.

As for the gum, most of it was collected by starving Indians, who sold it to the very children who had been supposed to get it in the first place.

{15}

VIOLETA'S EYES POPPED OPEN. IT WAS MORNING, and the light creeping in through the shutters on her bedroom window was a pale creamy white. She rolled out of her hammock and, despite her windfall of the night before, felt like crying — how she longed to live in a place where a simple contest didn't turn into a showcase for violent degeneracy.

Yet there was another, more urgent reason for her melancholy. Upon reaching the desert with Francisco, she'd felt herself overwhelmed with excitement — it was a mixture of her big win, the danger in the air, and the attention paid to her by the rich foreign gringo. Feeling desirable all over, she chose that night to finally let Francisco Ramirez unfasten the buttons of her blouse, slip the garment off her shoulders, and deposit it upon the sands of the desert, where it glowed a faint rosemary colour under the shimmering skies. Guiding Francisco's hands, she'd all but commanded him to release the clasp of her lace brassiere, such that it too fell to the granular sand. That's when it happened. Suddenly, she found herself thinking of Francisco not as an entire human, but as a collection of parts — of strong arms, of broad shoulders, of muscular thighs, of those sad, illuminating eyes. The moment this disassembly occurred, something inside of her flared, something ruthless and unbidden and wild. She tore at poor Francisco, leaving scratches on his chest and tooth marks on his shoulders, directing his fingertips to a portion of herself that she'd always pledged would be first touched by whatever gallant, worldly hombre carried her away from the deserts of Coahuila.

Yet no sooner had he dampened the tips of his first and second fingers than a macabre vision formed before her eyes, a vision of a life spent following in her mother's footsteps, her forearms corroding in baths of lye, her frock hem tugged at by dirty-faced children while her belly swelled and ached with yet another, her beloved husband lost to whatever historical outrage her country had most recently devised. The desert air seemed to turn frigid and damp. A shiver ran through her body, and for a moment she felt unable to breathe. Finally she succeeded in gulping a draught of air, which allowed her to blurt *Qué haces, Francisco!* while slapping him across the face. He stopped. They both sat up, faces burning. Francisco, placing a hand against his smarting cheek, caused her heart to momentarily ache. She pushed this sensation away, quickly dressed, and said, by way of explanation, *Francisco, I'm sorry. It won't happen before I'm married.* For the next few moments she watched his jaws gnash and his eyes narrow and his gaze drift far off along the kelp-hued desert floor.

As she did every morning, Violeta started a fire beneath

the cast-iron grate that she and Malfil used to cook their meals. She then patted flour into their morning tortillas, all the while contending with a painful constriction in her throat — her feelings for Francisco were so writhing and contradictory she felt they might succeed in choking the life from her. As the room filled with smoking oil, she set about making coffee. When it was brewed, she brought a cup to her mother, who was just beginning to stir.

— A hundred dollars! Malfil exclaimed. — What will we do with it all? Is there anything you particularly need?

Violeta shook her head. — We'll save it for my schooling, mami.

— Bah! I tell you what. After I get dressed I'll go down to Fajardo's and buy some meat. What would you say to that? And not goat or armadillo, either. I feel like *real* fajitas for dinner. Would you like that?

Violeta went to the window of their living room and leaned into the street. Even on Violeta's small street, which was well down from the plaza, there was a surfeit of garbage: spent bullet casings, empty mescal bottles, soiled goatskin prophylactics. From the Callejón of Sleeping Curs she could hear a low, steady whimpering.

Her mother dressed and the two of them had breakfast. When they were finished, her mother kissed her on the head and left their little house with its cracked foundation. Violeta swept the floor, did some of her homework, and generally brooded about the inhuman temptation that was Francisco Ramirez. Her mother returned, whistling and carrying a bag filled with vegetables, sugar, granos de café, and the neck meat of a bull. Side by side, the two began preparing a real

Mexican lunch, though after a while Malfil Cruz noticed her daughter's suppressed mood.

— Mija, she said. — Why so quiet?

— It's nothing, mami.

The two continued chopping onions.

— Did you and Francisco have a fight?

— No.

— Then what is it, mija? You won a hundred dollars last night. You should be singing.

— I suppose I'm just tired, mama.

— Well, I guess *so*. It was late when you came home.

— Claro.

— Really, I should punish you. Francisco hasn't tried anything, hmm, ungentlemanly?

— No, mami!

— Good. Keep it that way. The last thing you need is a little Paquito running around. The last thing you need is a little *anybody* running around. It would ruin your future.

— I know, mami. You've told me a million times.

— Good. I'll stop when I've told you ten million times. There is nothing more important than your future.

There came the sound of cawing ravens and the restless shifting of hot, sandy air that was a constant aural backdrop in Corazón de la Fuente. The alleyway dogs, after a night of being frightened by pistol shots, were beginning to collectively snore. Oddly, Violeta could also hear what sounded like the idle of a motor. A few minutes later, as if to prove her suspicions correct, a knocking came at the door.

— Híjole! said her mother. — Who could it be?

Malfil Cruz crossed the floor, making sure to avoid spots

where the boards were splintering and dust was sifting through. Violeta kept chopping, though she looked up when she heard her mother's exclamation of *Dios mío!*

— Dr. Brinkley! Malfil gushed as she moved to one side. — Please, please, come in!

— Good morning, said Brinkley as he stepped into their small home. — I hope I am not disturbing you.

Violeta saw the room through the eyes of the visitor: a broken floor, a single table pushed against the wall, and the hammock where her mother slept. There were only two chairs, one of which noticeably teetered. She suddenly felt embarrassed by the meagreness of their life in México, as if she herself had some hand in causing it.

Her mother grabbed the good chair and placed it before the doctor. In response, he beamed and said: — No, no, señora, it's not necessary. I have to sit all day. I have a tendency to walk when I speak, anyway. A nervous habit, I'm afraid, but one that nonetheless afflicts me. *Ants in the pants* is what we called it when I was a boy.

The doctor laughed, his small eyes turning to slits behind his tortoiseshell glasses.

Violeta's mother chuckled as well.

— Doctor, she said, — where did you learn to speak Spanish so well?

— I spent some time in South America. Exploring, really. The most wonderful time of my life, I have to say. Unburdened, free, a young man on the loose.

— How wonderful! Malfil gushed.

— Yes, said the doctor. — We should all have such a time in our lives.

Malfil turned towards her daughter. — Violeta, what are you doing? Get the doctor some coffee!

— No, no, please, Brinkley interjected. — It is not my wish to burden you this morning.

— But doctor, it's already made.

— No, please, I reiterate, don't go to any bother. Besides, I drink nothing but distilled water.

— We have rainwater. Would that do?

The doctor looked delighted. — Why, yes! That would be most delectable.

Violeta stepped into the little open-air kitchen extending from the rear of the abode. Using a ladle, she filled a glass with the water they collected during Coahuilan rainstorms, which happened for only a few minutes each month, albeit with an intensity that routinely collapsed rooftops and inspired nightmares in children. After re-entering the house, she handed the glass to Brinkley. He took a sip and smiled broadly.

— Aaaaah, he said. — There is nothing more salubrious than a glass of fresh, pure, clean, uncontaminated water. I always say that if you drink five of these a day you'll live to be a hundred, and you'll enjoy good health during each and every one of those years.

— Dr. Brinkley, said Malfil Cruz. — Muchas gracias for last night.

Brinkley's face turned sour. He put down his water glass. — Ah, he said. — Last night. I don't know what got into my head. I seriously underestimated the desperation of . . . Well, best not to speak of it, except to say that it was an experiment I will not soon repeat. I merely wanted to show the town of Corazón some appreciation for all its hospitality, and for any inconveniences it may have suffered as a result of the tower. I do that, you know. Take a local interest. Try to involve myself in communities. Suffice it to say I have people on the streets right now, cleaning up any and all damage, and I've decided to build a playground next to the school as a way of apologizing. I feel terrible about the whole thing.

There was an awkward silence. As usual, it was hot and dark in the Cruz home. While this ordinarily didn't bother Violeta, on this morning, with a well-dressed gringo visitor wiping his brow with a monogrammed handkerchief, it was all but unbearable.

— Señora Cruz, the doctor said. — There's something I would like to speak to you about. Something I'd like to speak to you both about.

He glanced at Violeta, who felt her heart start to pound. Malfil Cruz smiled and sat on the teetering chair. Violeta backed up and sat in the middle of her mother's hammock, obliging the doctor to sit on the one good chair. After a moment's hesitation, he reluctantly did so and began speaking.

— Last night, Violeta guessed the exact number of gumballs in that glass sphere. Well, not quite the exact number, but pretty darn close.

— Sí? said Violeta's mother.

— It really was most remarkable. In fact, it made me wonder if . . . *Well* . . . This is most awkward, as it sounds rather eccentric, I'm afraid. But it made me wonder if Violeta has abilities that not all of us have. Abilities of a . . . how do I put this? . . . a psychic variety.

Malfil Cruz giggled. — Oh no, doctor, you are . . .

— Sí, Violeta interrupted. — I do.

— *Qué?* asked Malfil.

— Sí, Violeta said again, not believing the words coming from her mouth. — Often, I get a feeling about things that are going to happen. Sometimes I'll be thinking of nothing at all and I'll get a . . . a . . .

— A tingling? Brinkley interjected.

— Sí. I get a tingling.

Brinkley laughed. — I thought that might be the case. Tell me, Violeta, do you speak English?

Her mother answered for her daughter. — Of course she does. Violeta is a very good student. She speaks English very, very well.

— In that case, I have a proposition. One of the more popular forms of entertainment these days are radio mediums. Do you know what a medium is?

Violeta and her mother shared a glance.

— No, said Malfil.

— It's a person, usually a woman, who has psychic abilities, not unlike Violeta. Through a marvellous new technology, something involving patch lines or trunk lines or the like, believe me when I say that electronics has never been my forte, listeners can actually call in and describe their problems on the air. The medium then does her best to help. As I say, it's getting very, very popular. XEX in Villa Acuña has one, as does XED in Juárez, and they are both doing very, very well. In fact, during their medium hours, I practically have to pay people to listen to my station.

The doctor grinned at his own witticism and looked at both women. — Do you understand what I am proposing?

— Not really, said Violeta's mother.

— I would like to hire Violeta to be XER's medium. She would broadcast every Saturday afternoon, from five to six o'clock. I think it would be a very positive experience for her.

Violeta's heart raced. She glanced at her mother, who for some reason looked fatigued by the request.

— Señor Brinkley, uttered Malfil. — I don't know . . . She is still a young girl, and she has a lot of homework and chores, and without a man in the house it's hard enough already for me to get things done.

— Señora Cruz?

— Sí, doctor?

— You'd be able to *hire* someone to do her chores.

Malfil Cruz looked at him, her face trembling with incomprehension. — You mean . . . you'd pay her?

— I would pay her seventy-five silver dollars per month. Not paper. Silver.

Violeta's madre took a deep, shuddering breath. Her eyes turned glassy with tears.

— Doctor, she said tearfully.   This is the answer to all of our prayers.

— No, señora, he said with a satisfied grin. — It's simply a business proposition, one that will hopefully prove beneficial to both parties.

{16}

JUST AS THE GOOD DOCTOR WAS BEING DRIVEN BACK across the splintering bridge between nations, Father Alvarez emerged from his one-room casa. He walked along the avenida, waving away every homeless beggar asking him for a few pesos, his only intention to reach the cantina and spend a tolerable afternoon quaffing cerveza with his amigos. Yet just as the father reached the side street upon which the town saloon was located, the cantina owner's wife, Margarita Hernandez, emerged from an alleyway and spotted him. She headed his way, her face flushed, a corner of her white blouse revealingly untucked, her bountiful dark hair in a telltale disarray. She held a forefinger in the air, as if testing the direction of the Coahuilan breeze.

— Father! she called. — I need to talk to you.

— Please, Margarita, he answered. — You know the law. I am Father no longer. Just call me Alvarez.

Margarita was the sort of person who ceased taking in information when excited about something, and this was such a moment. Ignoring his request, she began to babble.

— The radio station, Father. Have you listened to it?

— A little, he answered.

By this he meant that he was pretty sure he'd heard XER playing in the background the last time he'd been in the cantina. As far as he could remember, Brinkley's station seemed inoffensive enough, little more than the tedious drone of "Will the Circle Be Unbroken" interspersed with lectures regarding health and good welfare, all of which promoted Hinkley's clinic in Del Rio. Mind you, the father had never really listened, if only because the station broadcast entirely in English, a language he had to concentrate to understand. When others had the option of studying the gringo tongue in high school, he'd been conjugating Latin verbs in a México City seminary.

— So then you know!

— Know what, Margarita?

She leaned towards him. — The programming, Father. Much of it is . . . is . . . salacious in nature.

— Salacious?

— Sí.

— Margarita, por favor.

— I was listening last night. The language, Father. Particularly during the health report.

Father Alvarez sighed. — As long as parents don't let their children listen at certain hours I don't see what the problem is.

— But that's not all! Much of the content is religious.

— What I used to do is religious, Margarita. We can hardly blame John Brinkley for living in a country that hasn't yet lost its soul.

— But, Father! Have you listened closely? Have you heard the sermonizing? It starts most nights around seven . . .

— Seven o'clock is my dinnertime, Margarita.

— So then you *don't* know! Father Alvarez . . . the ministers on the radio station . . . they're Baptists! There's one who is a . . . *Pentecostal*. They're demons, Father, snake-handling degenerates. And they go on for hours!

Alvarez felt a stab of revulsion and loathing. He commanded himself to breathe deeply, and reminded himself that the revolution had taken away his vocation, a situation he could do nothing to remedy, and that it was none of his business what tripe Brinkley chose to air on that ostentatious radio station of his. Margarita, meanwhile, was oblivious to the colour draining from Alvarez's face.

— The Pentecostal . . . he speaks in tongues! He has a segment in which people telephone the station and he puts them on air and they're howling like monkeys or roaring like lions or — she took a deep, shuddering breath — *speaking dead languages*. The other day a child called up and afterward they said he'd been speaking Sumerian. In México, of all places! I'm asking you, Father. What are we going to do?

Again he did not respond: the ground was swaying a little beneath his feet, and he found he needed all of his energies just to maintain his equilibrium.

— I'll tell you what *I* think we should do, Margarita continued. — I think we should talk to Miguel Orozco. He is the mayor, after all. It's his town. He should be able to talk to Dr. Brinkley and demand that all religious programming of an unsuitable nature be banned from any radio station on our soil.

— Miguel? Alvarez said weakly. — You want to talk to Miguel?

— If it were up to me, I'd have the whole station taken off the air. It's disgraceful, all this talk of men's problems and goat glands and . . . Dios mío! . . . *the vitality of the reproductive organs.* Can you believe that, Father? That they're talking about these things on a radio station broadcasting from our good town?

Margarita sped off, the father now succumbing to a wave of frustration and despair. It was simply too much, this fresh knowledge that Pentecostals — practitioners of a faith that was guttural, adolescent, and completely lacking in nuance — had access to a radio station whose signal apparently reached all the way to Russia, while *he*, a father in the Roman Catholic Church, had had his profession thrown into the sewer like a spoiled armadillo carcass. He strode to the saloon and flung open its doors, startling the cantina owner and the mayor, both of whom were enjoying their second glass of cerveza while discussing whether or not they might indulge in a jigger of tequila.

— Father, said the mayor. — Qué onda?

Alvarez ignored him and marched up to the cantina owner. — Carlos, I need to borrow your radio.

The cantina owner looked at him quizzically.

— I need it, repeated the father.

— Okay, okay. Take it, it's behind the bar. The battery, though, is a little low. Do you want a cerveza too?

Alvarez claimed the radio and, instead of joining his friends for a drink, headed towards the swinging wooden doors. He stepped into the laneway, where he was bathed by white sun, and walked along Avenida Hidalgo until he reached the sagging one-room adobe row house where he lived. It was neat as a pin, solely because young village daughters now came once a week and cleaned up. While the Father appreciated this, the arrangement also meant he could never find anything. His newspaper, his reading spectacles, his wallet, the slippers he wore in the early morning and late evening . . . they all seemed to disappear into the wasteland of orderliness that the muchachas left behind every time they visited.

As with many homes in Corazón, a hammock stretched along one wall. Alvarez climbed in, the motion causing the ceiling beams to groan. He came to rest and pressed a few buttons on the radio. A weak light appeared on the tuning dial. This was accompanied by a man's voice, speaking in English. Alvarez had to listen intently, for the light on the dial kept fading and the voice kept rising and falling in volume. And though Alvarez couldn't understand all that was being said, it seemed there was nothing distasteful reaching his ears beyond the nasal pitch of a farmer discussing soybean prices. The voice faded in and out for another minute, at which point the dwindling light coming from the dial ceased being a light at all. Father Alvarez shook the radio, causing nothing more than brief snippets of sound to come from the infernal box.

He sighed, climbed out of his hammock, and surveyed the room, his eyes scanning each clean surface, each uncluttered stretch of floor, and each dust-free piece of furniture. Finding his wallet was no simple matter; it required a degree of concentration that he had once reserved for spiritual questions. First of all, he had to remember which señorita had come yesterday — they all had their own methods of cleaning and their own spots for hiding away his possessions. He could barely picture her; he seemed to recall black hair and a halo of freckles across the nose. Of course, this described pretty much every young female in the town of Corazón de la Fuente. To be truthful, whenever he gazed upon a girl poised to become a woman, it was her youth and nothing but her youth that made an impression — it trumped eye colour, skin tone, distinguishing birthmarks, or whatever particular loveliness the girl happened to possess.

Finally it came to him — it was the girl who had a lisp, the one they called the Little Spaniard. He could hear her, clear as a bell: *Buenath tardeth, Father.* Her real name was Rosita (or Rosana or Rosaura or Rosalita), and she was the one who never failed to put his wallet and reading spectacles in the little hutch that greeted visitors as they stepped inside the front door. He rushed towards it, opened the squeaky hinged door and, gracias a Dios, saw his wallet sitting atop his slippers and an unfinished tripe sandwich he'd told her not to throw away. A second later he was out the door, his wallet in one hand and the cantina owner's radio in the other, heading for the store run by the hirsute Zacatecan.

A bell chimed when Father Alvarez walked into the dark, crowded store. Fajardo came out from the back and greeted him. A stand of tomatoes, avocados, jalapeños, cilantro, and onions separated the two men.

— Father, said Fajardo. — Can I help you with something?

— I need a battery.

— What type?

— Whatever type this damn thing takes.

The father held up the radio. Fajardo nodded; he knew the model for the simple reason that he had sold it to the cantina owner in the first place. He ducked behind the counter. Upon surfacing, he passed over a heavy battery.

Father Alvarez paid and shook the store owner's hand, a moment of contact that would have given him pause a few years earlier but that he didn't think about now. Like most residents of Corazón de la Fuente, he had long ago decided what Fajardo looked like beneath his insulating layer. Now his eyes automatically subtracted the fur, revealing a wiry Mexican man who worked hard, lived with his condition with grace, and contributed greatly to his community.

The father retraced his steps through Corazón. At home he lay in his hammock and put the radio on his stomach. He switched it on. The voice of an announcer filled the room. Though he was fairly sure it was Dr. Brinkley speaking, he wasn't certain. Any characteristics of Brinkley's voice — the quiet self-confidence mixed with his quaint Appalachian slang — were lost behind the barrier of a foreign language. Alvarez listened intently, and in so doing he extracted many words and phrases that were more or less the same in Spanish, including *impotencia* and *la función de la próstata* and, of all things, *los secretos del bedroom*. Despite the grim amusement these words caused him, he soon grew bored with listening, if for no other reason than the words between these phrases formed an indistinguishable blur. He put the radio on the floor next to him, concluding that Margarita must have been exaggerating.

At the top of the hour, the talking ended. Father Alvarez yawned, climbed out of the hammock, and searched for the

spot where Rosita (or Rosaura or Rosana or Rosalita) might
have left his newspaper. Meanwhile, his small house was filling with twangy American music, all violins and washtub
basses and atonal vocals. The father found his paper, read a
bit, drifted off, woke up, helped himself to a draught of goat
leche he kept in a green plastic bucket on the cool ceramic
kitchen floor, read a bit more, drifted off a second time, and
then made himself a simple dinner of machaca, tortilla, and
beans seasoned with epazote sprigs. On the far side of the
room, the father folded his newspaper and thought about his
evening plans. Probably he would spend his night reading.

That's when it occurred to him that the music on the radio
had stopped and had again been replaced by talking. This
time his ears perked. His face flushed. *Today*, he heard, *we'll be
talking about the end of days and how it's almost upon us . . .*

Alvarez stood and drew closer to the radio. He did so cau-
tiously, as though approaching a poisonous snake. *For the good
Lord told us in the Book of Revelation that, one day, each and every
one of us would endure a reckoning . . .* Alvarez swallowed, his
throat suddenly dry. Though he didn't totally understand
what the announcer was saying, he did know that these
weren't the sage ramblings of a radio doctor but the fire-and-
brimstone language of a country preacher.

He went closer to the radio, the glow of its dial now something demonic, its very operation a taunt from the world
of darkness . . . *For those lucky few who have devoted their lives
to Christ, there will come a rapture . . .* and with each step, the
fact that this signal was being heard in Alaska — ay, ay, in
Russia — further enraged the father. He stopped about a
metre from the radio and stared. What little English he did

know was religious in nature, and certain terms kept leaping out at him: *day of judgement . . . signs and wonders . . . the Lord's limitless fury . . . number six-six-six.* He felt himself growing nauseated. This was the verbiage of philistines, of simpletons. And yet *it* was reaching the ears of Eskimo fur trappers, and not the poetic nuance of Catholicism.

Trembling with umbrage, he took another half-step closer to the radio. The voice — he could make out a heavy Southern drawl — stopped and was replaced by a different voice. Judging by the sudden presence of static, the father concluded that it was a phone-in caller. It took him another moment or two to realize that the caller — a highly agitated woman — was not speaking in English and *was* speaking in Latin. He listened closely, trying to pick out individual words, and couldn't — the voice was racing, desperate, crazy, inflamed. And yet this poor caller's Latin was a hundred times more intelligible than her next choice of dialect. For as the father stood rooted to the floor, his face burning with enmity, the caller suddenly stopped talking, made a sound resembling an indigestive growl, and began squawking like a chicken.

The radio host's voice returned. Because the father's mind was sharpened by rage and disgust, he more or less understood what the preacher said. — Glory be to God, he boomed, — we got ourselves a durned soothsayer!

Father Alvarez stormed out of his house, trudged towards the cantina, flung open the wooden doors, and marched over to the bar. The cantina owner's mouth hung open when he saw the state of his old amigo.

— Mescal, Alvarez ordered. — And for the love of Dios, leave the bottle.

{17}

A LIMOUSINE DRIVEN BY ONE OF BRINKLEY'S CHAUF-
feurs stopped in front of the home belonging to Malfil and
Violeta Cruz. Though the car was incrementally smaller than
Brinkley's Duesenberg and was made by a manufacturer
called Mercedes, it was similar in that the initials *JRB* appeared
on the dashboard, on all four wheel hubs, on the front and
rear bumpers, on the polished mahogany running boards, on
each of the sun visors, and on all of the Corinthian leather
seats. The driver stepped out and was immediately attacked
by a team of ravenous curs emanating from the alleyway.
He jumped back in the car and began swinging a rolled-up
newspaper at the dog closest to his window. In response, the
animals barked with rabid intensity and vindictively doused
all four tires with pheremonal spray.

Violeta and her mother heard the ruckus. Over the past
hour they'd washed each other's hair and put on the only nice
clothes they possessed. In the case of the younger Cruz, it was
the blouse and white skirt that she had worn to her fiesta de

quinceañera. In the case of the older Cruz — who was still only thirty-three years of age, though neither as high-cheek-boned nor as raven-haired as her daughter — it was the pale blue dress she had worn to church in the days when Father Alvarez was still considered a man of the cloth. They stepped into the laneway and nodded respectfully at the driver, who was too intimidated to step out of the car and open the rear door for them. Instead he nodded his greetings and gesticulated at the seat behind him. Violeta climbed in and gazed out the window as the driver put the car into gear.

As the limousine was too large to turn around in the narrow streets, the driver had no choice but to drive west along Avenida de Cinco de Mayo, past the House of Gentlemanly Pleasures. A few hundred metres beyond the radio tower, the street curved and linked with Avenida Hidalgo, which ran along the bottom of the pueblo. Well off in the distance, Violeta could see a thin spiral of smoke drifting skyward from the hilltop shack belonging to the curandera.

The front of the car came around in a slow arc, a tiresome manoeuvre in that many of the homeless who had flocked to newly rich Corazón de la Fuente had turned the area flanking this intersection into a squatter's camp. The Mercedes' tires bumped over sleeping rolls, cooking logs, tent pegs, mescal bottles, pulque gourds, and old, dented pots. This angered the squatters, who chased after the car throwing rocks, old shoes, and lumps of bark soap, all the while yelling the vilest of profanities at the tops of their smoke-damaged lungs.

Soon the limousine passed the cantina and entered the plaza, which was filled with vagrants, tortilla vendors, and toothless, emaciated prostitutes who had been refused employment by Madam Félix. Heads turned as the car circled past the town hall, the church, and the store operated by Fajardo Jimenez. It then exited at the northeast corner of the plaza, again turning onto Avenida Cinco de Mayo. The road meandered for several blocks before arcing around the ejido and Antonio Garcia's hacienda and heading towards the bridge separating an obscenely rich nation from an incorrigibly poor one.

The driver crossed without having to pay the usual assortment of bribes, and then travelled along the main street of Del Río before stopping in front of the Roswell Hotel. He opened Violeta's door and wished her a good day.

— Gracias, she said to the chauffeur, who tipped his driver's cap and smiled professionally.

Violeta and her mother entered the lobby of the hotel, which in truth was a hotel no longer, in that every suite was now taken up by Brinkley's medical facility or his radio station or his growing pharmaceutical enterprise. Naturally, he'd kept on the hotel's staff to clean, make beds, deliver sandwiches, and bring coffee in the middle of the night.

Violeta looked around, admiring the chandeliers and fine wool carpets, and was about to comment on the opulence of the hotel when a paunchy, middle-aged man dressed in a brown suit came up to them.

— Greetings, he announced in English. — I am Dale Stollins, the manager of Radio XER, or, as we like to call it, the Sunshine Station from Between the Nations. You must be Malfil and Violeta Cruz, am I correct?

— Jess, said Malfil.

— In that case, welcome.

He thrust a beefy pink hand towards Violeta's mother. The older woman took it while smiling graciously. He then offered his hand to Violeta; her palm came away damp, and she had to fight the urge to wipe it against the fabric of her skirt.

The two women followed him to a door marked *Exit*. He pushed it open with his shoulder and they followed him down a cement staircase. At the bottom of the steps he pushed through another door, this one bearing three white letters — XER — surrounded by a squadron of lightning bolts. They entered a carpeted, tomb-like quiet. The lights were low, and when Stollins told them that Dr. Brinkley was still doing his *Happy Health Hour*, he did so in a voice that was practically a whisper. This pleased Violeta, as silence had a way of calming her mind and stilling the worries that galloped through her head at all hours of the day and night. Stollins led them through the empty lounge — there was a sofa, stuffed chairs, thick orange carpeting, and a chalkboard running along the length of one wall. As they walked along a hallway lined with closed doors, Violeta could hear the sound of voices speaking into telephones, though these voices were muted as well, and she wondered if perhaps the offices had been soundproofed.

Stollins reached a window and stopped. His face was illuminated slightly, making his flesh look almost orange. He then motioned with an index finger and whispered *the broadcast booth*. Violeta looked inside. Brinkley was sitting before a microphone, looking as dapper as always in his tortoiseshell glasses and three-piece Savile Row suit. His tie clip was a diamond-studded lightning bolt, configured in the same style as the station logo.

On the wall next to the booth's window was a mounted loudspeaker. Beneath it was a red plastic button. Stollins pushed it, causing Violeta to start as Brinkley's voice broadcast through the passageway: *Have you ever, my dear listeners, noted the difference between a stallion and a gelding? The stallion stands erect, neck arched, mane flowing, champing at the bit, stomping the ground, seeking the female, while the gelding stands around half asleep, going into action only when goaded, cowardly, listless, with no interest in anything. Men, don't let this happen to you — remember, a man is only as old as his glands, and sometimes even the most hale among us need an injection of . . .*

Stollins turned it off, smiled, and led Violeta and her blushing mother back to the lounge. The women sat in cushioned chairs and declined offers of coffee, tea, refrescos, and distilled water. They waited, fidgeting, and when Malfil Cruz leaned over to ask *How do you feel?* Violeta responded by saying *Good, mami, good*. Meanwhile, Violeta looked around. The walls were a pale blue. Her mother was flipping through an American newspaper, and Violeta could see her lips move when she stumbled upon words she was unsure of. Minutes passed, during which Violeta enjoyed the comfort of the chair, the clean scent in the air, and the flowers on the coffee table before her. Here the problems of northern México were as distant as the South Seas.

Brinkley appeared in the doorway of the lounge, smiling. He approached and spoke in the same low voice that his manager had used.

— Ahhh, Señora Cruz. *Violeta*. I'm so happy you both came.

He shook both their hands. His palms were cool, dry, and rendered supple through twice-daily applications of an aloe-based cream. — Please, he said. — Come with me.

Once again the two women walked along the hallway. When they passed the broadcast booth they saw that Brinkley had been replaced by an older man wearing overalls and a red flannel shirt.

— That's Farmer Jeb, Brinkley said over his shoulder. — He does a show called *Farm Report*. It's very popular amongst our listeners. Radio XER caters to a primarily rural audience, you see.

He stopped before a door at the very end of the hallway. They all stepped inside and took seats at a small round table.

— You ladies have been offered something to drink, I trust?

— Claro, said Malfil.

Brinkley picked up the receiver and, switching to English, said: — We're here, Annabel.

A minute later a young woman in a tight-fitting skirt arrived with a tray bearing a pitcher of water and a trio of glasses. She set it on the table in front of Brinkley and left. After filling all three glasses, he took a long draught from one of them and smiled.

— All right, he said, — let's get down to business. We have a bit of work ahead of us.

He looked straight at Violeta. — I want you to say something for me. And remember, from now on we're using English.

— All right, responded Violeta.

— I want you to say *You are listening to Rose Dawn, high priestess of the Sacred Order of the Maya*.

Violeta nodded, and said: — Joo are leestenin' to Rose Dawn, high priestess of the Sacred Order of the Maya.

Brinkley grinned and Violeta dropped her gaze to the top of the table. She felt ashamed of her inflected vowels, her mispronounced consonants, her overly compensated *h*'s.

— Perfect, he said. — Delightful.

— No, doctor, I am sorry. I will work on my accent . . .

— No! Don't change a thing! We'll practise a little more tomorrow, all right?

The next day, and the day after that, Brinkley's limousine driver fought the same growling dogs, the same tight laneways, and the same embittered street dwellers, all in an effort to usher Violeta Cruz to the Sunshine Station from Between the Nations. Once there, she waited for Brinkley to finish his daily *Health Talk*. Then, for the next hour or so, he trained her in the fine art of radio broadcasting. He taught her which light meant that she was on the air (*The red one, señorita*) and he taught her how to speak into a microphone without distorting her voice (*Your mouth should always be about four inches away*). He taught her to keep her lips moistened (*It stops them from popping*) and he trained her to remain completely still while the broadcast light was on (*Trust me, the microphone picks up everything*). He taught her how to make her voice sound distant and impassive (*As though, my dear Violeta, you have come from another place and time*) and he taught her how to tell which caller had promise and which should be ignored (*It's called pain, my dear — if it's not there, move on to the next caller*).

Working together, the two of them also created a life story for her character. Rose Dawn, it seemed, governed a mystical order in Guatemala, communicated telepathically with eagles, had astral-travelled to most parts of the earthly plane, was married to the spirit of a highland wolf, viewed time as an artificial construct, had made peace with the dark side of humanity, and enjoyed keen memories of each of her past lives, which, at this point in her rebirth cycle, numbered in the several hundreds. Many, it seemed, had coincided with the age of the pharaohs.

— The most important thing, Brinkley told her, — is that you never give Rose Dawn's life story in one whole chunk. Commit it to memory, and let little bits and pieces of it come out with time. You'll entrance your audience that way. With time, they won't be able to get enough of you.

— Dr. Brinkley?

— Yes?

— How do you know all of this?

Brinkley threw back his head and laughed. His eyes turned to slits and they sparkled with light. — Ah, Violeta. I have worked hard, I have applied myself, I have lived purely, and I have seen results. I do prize industry above all else, you know. That is all. There is no mystery, Violeta.

— You have been so kind to me and my mother, Dr. Brinkley. And to my town also.

That's when she saw it: his grin abandoned his features, leaving behind a man who looked, if only for one second, flustered and self-conscious.

— Please, was his response. — Call me John.

The following Saturday, at two minutes to five o'clock in the afternoon, Violeta Cruz found herself sitting in broadcast booth number two of Radio XER, listening to the tail end of Dr. Brinkley's health lecture over a small, crackly speaker

mounted on one wall. On Saturdays her show would replace
Farmer Jeb's daily agricultural report. There was a table in
front of her, and on that table was a microphone. She wore a
pair of headphones. Meanwhile, across the river in Corazón,
every man, woman, and child had heard that one of their
own was going to be on the air. Each and every one had, in
turn, managed to place themselves within earshot of a working radio. Some, like the hacendero Antonio Garcia, were
doing so alone, in the privacy of their own homes. Some, like
the lowly residents of the ejido, were gathered by the dozens
around barely working hand-cranked radios. At least one, a
village ex-priest named Alvarez, was dead drunk and spitting
invective, his shirt front messed with spilled liquor.

Violeta listened to Brinkley sign off — *May the Good Lord
put wind in your wheat and lead in your pencil* — followed by
some fiddle music that slowly faded to static. She then heard
Dr. Brinkley's voice again.

— Now today, my good listeners, ol' Dr. Brinkley is proud
to announce a new feature on the Sunshine Station from
Between the Nations, a feature you are sure to find most edi-
fying and entertaining. Rose Dawn is the high priestess of the
Sacred Order of the Maya, a mystical order from the Petén
province of Guatemala. Thanks to the miracle of modern
travel, every Saturday at five o'clock she will be right here, in
our Roswell Hotel studios, offering spiritual counsel to those
who most need it.

Violeta heard a swell of organ music accompanied by a
sound made by waving an unfolded coat hanger in the air.
This went on for a half-minute, and when it faded the doctor
said: — Good day, Rose.

— Buenos días, Dr. Brinkley.

— I trust your journey to the lovely town of Del Rio, Texas, occurred without incident?

— It did, sir. It was most comfortable.

— And I trust your empathetic powers are at their sharpest . . .

— Ay sí, doctor.

— Well, in that case, Miss Dawn, we have our first caller, a Sam Wesler of Stillwater, Oklahoma, on the line.

A strange voice came through her headphones. It belonged to an older man, and it quavered with emotional pain.

— Miss Dawn?

— Sí, said Violeta. — How I can help joo?

— Well, said the voice, — it's just that, well, two years ago, my wife of forty years, she died of heart problems.

— I see.

— And now, out here on the farm, I often feel as though she's . . . jeez, Miss Dawn, I can barely say it, I feel so foolish . . . but I often feel as though she's with me. I can't explain it any better than that, except to say that sometimes, when I'm out milking the cows, I think I can hear her voice, speaking in the breeze. And at night, when I'm reading my paper, I'll feel a presence in the room, coming from where my missus always sat to do her knitting. Other times I hear footsteps coming from upstairs, and occasionally at night I'm woken by the creaking of doors opening and closing. Could you tell me . . . is my wife still with me or am I just a crazy old man?

Violeta paused for two or three seconds, feeling not at all guilty about what she was about to do: Dr. Brinkley had taught her that hope was a rare thing, and blessed was the person selfless enough to grant it to others. She lowered the pitch of her voice and spoke without reflection or intonation.

— Meester Wesler, I haff conferred telepathically with the other priestesses of the order, and with spirits who are existing in places we can no understand. Among us, we have reached a conclusion.

She paused for three or four beats.

— *Joo*, I am happy to say, are no alone.

{18}

THE HACENDERO GALLOPED THROUGH SCRUBLAND and plains and full-blown desert, where the wind blew sand over his tracks and the only way to keep his bearings was to watch the position of the sun, the moon, and the stars. Perched atop Diamante, he galloped in blazing, untempered heat and in the shadow thrown by the sierra. He followed arroyos till they trickled to nothing, and he slept in a bedroll under the stars, missing neither Corazón de la Fuente nor the insecurities that plagued him in his old, molested mansion. In this way he rediscovered his love for all things Mexican and his reasons for never having returned to España, even during the horrible throes of the revolution.

He marvelled at buttes and crags, and he washed himself in small clear-water cascades. He rode so far south that the land gave way to pine trees and walnut groves, and he journeyed so far west, in the direction of Sonora, that the land he knew — a land of palo verde, mesquite, and prickly pear — turned into a world of saguaro and cholla and barrel-shaped cacti. Another time, after a week of near solid galloping towards the eastern horizon, he and Diamante made it all the way to the Gulf of México. Here the hacendero dipped his boot heel in the salt water and then turned around. They spent that night camped in the desert and returned home via a slow, winding depression that took them through Mexican villages, Mormon communities, and Kickapoo settlements composed of nothing but animal-hide tepees and mangy, teat-swollen dogs.

The hacendero had never been happier. His mind had cleared and his muscles felt young. He smelled aloe and creosote and jojoba and, coming upon an iguana that had expired under a rich red sun, the stench of meat turning putrid. He saw desert turtles, mountain bear, wild boars, wolves, raccoons, pumas, beavers, bell vipers, sidewinders, armadillos, scorpions, tarantulas, dwarfed guacamayas, enough voles to fill a canyon, and buzzards so inquisitive they would trail the hacendero for hours on end, providing shade for his sunburnt, reddened neck. One night, with a single shot from his Smith & Wesson, he dropped an old buck with a rack the size of a wood stove. He spent that whole afternoon making jerky over a low, smouldering Indian fire. He would have spent a good deal more time at it had Diamante not started to snort and glare at the hacendero and stamp the earth with his front hooves. It was, the hacendero knew, his way of saying *Dios mío, I'm a horse. You going to ride me or not?*

Early one evening he returned to his hacienda after riding Diamante through the valleys and chasms that crisscrossed the Sierra del Burro. It had been a good day. The mountains had been full of eagles, and he had seen a wild ram leaping from one pillar of rock to another. Diamante, meanwhile, had ridden on the verge of wildness; as usual, the hacendero's arm muscles hurt from reining in his stallion whenever the terrain turned too steep or pebbly. They were about twenty metres from the paddock's wire gate when Diamante, for no reason that the hacendero could discern, pulled up to a standstill.

— What is it, caballo? he asked while patting his animal on the flank.

Diamante whinnied, fought the bit, and tiptoed backwards. In response, the hacendero lightly spurred his horse. Diamante sprinted forward a few dozen steps and then veered to the side before stopping once again.

— *Diamante!* the hacendero shouted, and this time when he spurred the stallion's sides, the horse snorted and fought his bit and turned in circles. The hacendero dismounted and took Diamante by the muzzle and stroked him between the eyes. *Eso es,* he kept saying. *Eso es, mi caballo.* Eventually, Diamante's breathing calmed and the lather on his coat dissipated into the tawny dusk.

The hacendero was truly puzzled. He looked in every direction, and saw nothing that might have spooked his horse. Yet every time he drew Diamante towards the opened paddock, the horse would take three steps, whinny, and try to shake free from the hacendero's gloved hand. This went on and on, until finally he managed to get the horse in through the wire gate. Suddenly Diamante broke from his owner's grip and darted towards the rear of the paddock, where he stood in the lee formed by the back of the hacendero's home.

Antonio approached his horse and asked: — Did you see something you didn't like in the desert? Maybe I should give you a few days off. That's it . . . you're the type of horse who doesn't know when to quit. Still, you always look so happy when I saddle you in the mornings . . .

For the next three days, the hacendero lavished his stallion with attention. He brushed him thoroughly, using a special gnat-trapping comb he'd ordered from a livery in Houston. He fed Diamante his favourite oat-and-molasses cookies, and he personally inspected Diamante's hooves for cockleburs, cactus needles, and bits of glass or nails. He found nothing, which didn't surprise the hacendero, as he was extraordinarily careful with his horse whenever the terrain was littered or rocky. He then tried mucking out the enclosure himself, thinking that his horse would be soothed by being near the person who cared most for him. He also hoped that all this extra attention would cause his stallion to forget whatever it was that had alarmed him.

Instead, he achieved the opposite. On the second day of not riding out, the hacendero noticed that Diamante rarely ventured away from the wooden rear wall of the paddock. Whenever he did, he stayed in the exact centre of the yard, as though afraid of the front and sides of his enclosure, both of which were formed by metal fencing topped with barbed wire. His condition worsened. In the middle of his third day away from riding, Diamante erupted, charging in circles around the paddock. Just as suddenly, he stopped, raked his head against the earth, and galloped towards the corner of the paddock where Beatriz spent her days, mindlessly chewing. Without the slightest provocation, Diamante nipped the bereaved old mare in the haunch. Beatriz screamed, and by the time the hacendero had raced out of his home, it was Beatriz who was charging around the ring, her eyes wide with fear. — *Diamante!* the hacendero yelled as he ran after Beatriz. — What have you done?

That afternoon the hacendero hired the Reyes twins, Alfonso and Luis, to build a small wooden enclosure within the paddock, where Beatriz could be protected from Diamante's electric disposition. For wood, the hacendero instructed the boys to tear up floorboards from the hacienda's great room, which had been partially de-walled by misdirected artillery fire during the revolution and was now partitioned off with old bedsheets. The Reyes brothers went right to work, their strong backs useful when it came to the more stubborn planks. Unfortunately, what Luis and Alfonso possessed in the way of muscle was counteracted by their lack of building skills: Beatriz's enclosure turned out rickety, vaguely lopsided, and marred by several large holes. Still, it did the job. Beatriz entered willingly, pleased to have a place to take refuge. When the hacendero followed his not-so-secret path to Madam Félix's House of Gentlemanly Pleasures that night, he did so with the knowledge that his aging mare would probably still be alive when he returned the next morning.

When the hacendero next attended to Diamante, he found his horse standing as still as a figure cast in marble. He called the horse's name, unnerved when Diamante did nothing but gaze bitterly towards the horizon. Then, when the hacendero approached and took Diamante by his halter, he noticed that the horse had been rubbing himself against the rear wall of the enclosure, and his left flank was now pinkish and raw. For the first time the hacendero felt genuine annoyance with his prize stallion.

— What is it, caballo? What in the name of God is the problem?

Again he looked around, struggling to see what might be spooking his horse. It was as if there were ghosts, unseen and ferocious, tormenting the poor animal. The hacendero's heart was beating hard, and he was short of breath. He turned back to his horse.

— That's it, he said. — We're going for a ride.

The hacendero marched through the yard and opened the padlock that hung on the door to his small adjoining tack room. He picked up his favourite saddle — the one with embroidered silk string roses — and carried it into the paddock. He put it on Diamante, the horse snorting and whinnying as his owner tightened the straps. He then took Diamante by the bridle and tried to lead him to the wire fence that separated the paddock from the wilds of the Coahuilan desert. Diamante took two or three steps and then planted his forelegs. The hacendero swore and jerked hard on the bit, a movement designed to bring pain to Diamante's mouth. The stallion jerked his head so fiercely that the bridle slipped out of the hacendero's gloved hand. In the same instant the horse whipped his head back around and bit the hacendero's still raised forearm. Thankfully the hacendero had withdrawn his arm just enough that Diamante's mouth was filled only with a length of riding jacket.

The stallion spat out the cloth and reared, almost striking the hacendero on the head with a hoof. Diamante landed and then reared even higher, this time producing an

equine shriek so loud it was heard in every nook and corner of Corazón de la Fuente. The hacendero took another,
alarmed step backwards. A depthless, weighty silence descended — gone were the cawing of ravens, the crackle of
cooking fires, the call of hungry children. The hacendero
was breathing hard, his back against the wire fence of the
enclosure. Diamante glared at him through eyes born in
hell. In that awful moment the hacendero faced the possibility that his horse — always so high-spirited, always so sensitive — had turned rogue altogether.

A second later, the hacendero discerned a tinny, barely
perceptible music. The moment he heard it, he realized he'd
been hearing it all along; the only difference was that, in the
intensity of the moment, he had finally started to perceive
it. He listened harder and made out the squeak of violins,
the thrum of a washtub bass, and the ear-repulsing yodel of
a gringo country-and-western singer. He dug a forefinger
into each ear and experienced a diminishment of the win-
cing, ghostly sound; this proved it wasn't a product of his
own frantic mind. He then looked in either direction, trying
to determine its source. He saw nothing, and for a moment
he wondered whether he had somehow developed the same
madness as his horse.

Then he realized what was happening. Dropping to one
knee, he placed his ear against the wire surrounding his
paddock, and finally he heard what had been tormenting
his animal.

Will the circle be unbroken
By and by, Lord, by and by?

There's a better home awaiting
In the sky, Lord, in the sky . . .

{19}

VIOLETA SAT IN LOW LIGHT, AT A ROUND WOODEN table marred by coffee-cup rings. Her headphones were in place. In front of her were a glass of water, a vase filled with several dozen white roses, and a microphone resembling a dinner plate. Across from her was a large rectangular window; manning the switches and levers on the other side was a controller named George Peters, who had taken over from Brinkley after the first week's program.

Violeta felt exhausted. That afternoon she had advised callers suffering from job loss, ailing children, malignant growths, palsies, missing pets, chronic indigestion, cheating spouses, arthritic parents, and truant children. She had to wonder whether all Americans led such tragic lives, or whether it was just the people who called her radio program. Either way, it made her feel a little sad about the human condition — if people as fortunate as the gringos couldn't be happy, then who in the name of Jesús could?

— Miss Rose, Peters said. — We have a Mrs. Jane B of

Baton Rouge, Louisiana, on the line.

— Hola, Violeta said. She heard the usual nervous shifting and throat-clearing. Then there was silence. — Missus B? she asked.

— I am here.

— How I can help joo today?

— Oh, Miss Dawn. It's my . . . it's my father.

— Go on.

— It's just that . . . well, Miss Dawn . . . my father worked hard his entire life. His entire *life*, Miss Dawn. He had great plans to travel with my mother. They were going to go to Oregon to visit my aunt, and they were even thinking of crossing the border to Canada and do some fishing. They had so many plans, Miss Dawn. My father retired last year, and it seemed that the very next day he came down with a nasty cough. He went to see his doctor, and discovered he had cancer in his lungs. He was a heavy smoker, you see. Within three months he died.

Violeta felt her throat constrict.

— And now I can't help but feel . . . oh, Miss Dawn, I can barely even say it . . . but I feel bitter with the Lord for letting a man work so hard his entire life, only to take that life away when the man finally had some time to enjoy it. I can't sleep, and sometimes I find myself crying for no reason, as if the frustration of it all is about to swallow me whole. Do you understand, Miss Dawn?

— Jess, Violeta said, her voice trembling. — I understand.

— I love listening to your show and I trust your advice and I wondered if there was anything you could recommend.

Violeta paused and bit one of her nails. Her eyes were moist.

— Missus B? Close your eyes. Now try picture your father's favourite place. Did he have one?

— He did, Miss Dawn. I don't know if I mentioned this, but he loved to fish, and there was a little watering hole just down the lane from his house.

— Tell me, Missus B.

— Well, there was a live oak tree and he'd sit on one of the lower branches that hung over the creek. And there was a break in the trees, and sun would pour in through that break around two o'clock and he would sit there feeling all right with the world. Right where he sat there was a little eddy, and he said that the catfish loved to pool in that eddy because there was no current and the water was warm and it was as though they were waiting for him. That's what he told me, they practically jumped out of the water. And sometimes, when I was little, my ma and I would go there and picnic with him, eating sandwiches next to him on that branch of the live oak tree, and above us the sky was a deep, rich blue and the ground was the dark green of a forest, and I don't think I ever saw him looking so content. And I swear, I *swear*, the three of us always came back singing.

— Missus B?

Violeta paused.

— Please trust me. He is there now.

The program ended with a field recording of nocturnal tree frogs that Dr. Brinkley had made during a foray up the Amazon. It was a trip, he'd told Violeta, during which he'd

consumed snake blood for sustenance, learned how to hunt
with blow darts, and contracted a malarial fever so brutal
he'd begun speaking in the voice of his forefathers. As she
walked towards the XER lounge, Violeta's theme music gave
way to the accordion music that signalled the hour hosted by
Mrs. Fay Parker, a Del Río native and author of the locally
available cookbook *Victuals for Visitors*. Violeta took a seat,
closed her eyes, and attempted to calm herself.

The station manager came into the room.

— Miss Dawn, he said.

— Hola, Dale.

— Dr. Brinkley would like to have a word with you.

Violeta gulped. — What does he want?

— I'm not sure, Miss Dawn.

Violeta combatted a strong sense of foreboding. She'd been
on the air for a full month, and the show probably wasn't getting any listeners. She stood, attempted to console herself with
the knowledge that at least she'd tried her best, and followed
Stollins up the stairs towards the medical clinic. They walked
along the third floor of the Roswell Hotel, down a hallway pad-
ded with thick maroon carpeting. All sound was muted, and
the light thrown by the sconces seemed purposefully restful.
They stopped at the end of the hall, before a door bearing gold
lettering that read *John Romulus Brinkley*. The manager tapped
and looked expectantly at the grain of the wood.

— Yes? said a voice from inside.

The station manager opened the door just a little. He
poked his head inside and said: — Miss Dawn is here, sir.

— Well for Pete's sake, Dale, don't just stand there. Show
the young lady in!

Stollins grinned and backed away from the entrance. Violeta stepped inside Brinkley's office, trying to not look awed. This was difficult. A pair of crystal chandeliers descended from the ceiling, a sofa upholstered in zebra hide stretched along the far wall, and the walls were lined from floor to ceiling in dark, smooth wood. But what most drew Violeta's attention was the better part of a rhinoceros's forequarters, affixed to the wall over Brinkley's left shoulder.

— Ah, said the doctor. — The rhinoceros. Do you notice anything different about it?

— No, she muttered.

— Look closely . . .

He was speaking in Spanish, and she followed suit. — I'm sorry, doctor. I'm afraid I'm not an expert.

— The horns, señorita! There are three of them! Do you see?

He sprung from his chair, and touched a knobby black protuberance between the horns that Violeta had assumed was an overgrown wart. — *This*, the doctor proclaimed, — is a South American rhino. From the Paraguayan lowlands, no less. I bagged it in a marsh during a respite from my medical studies. An impressive specimen, you must agree. Not too many people even know that *Rhinoceros sondaicus* so much as exists in South America. Most people think they come only from Africa.

— Sí, doctor. I thought this as well.

— You wouldn't believe what they have in the jungles of Paraguay. A lion that looks a little like the sphinx. A small, spotted tiger. A toucan with a hornbill the size of a mariachi trumpet. I'm no expert, but I'd say they have variations of everything but elephants and the odd marsupial. Oh yes, it's a hunter's paradise. You should go someday.

— I can't tell you how much I would like to travel, doctor.

He stood smiling at her. — I suppose you're wondering why I requested the honour of your presence.

— Sí.

— Come now, Miss Rose, no need to be coy. You must have *some* idea.

— Is it about the show?

The doctor threw back his head and laughed. When he again looked at her, his eyes had narrowed into gleaming slits. — I suppose it is, Violeta, I suppose it is! I'd very much like to show you something . . .

The doctor rose and crossed the floor of his office, a manoeuvre that necessitated a quick dodge around a statue of a cherub whose skin was the teal green of an agave frond. He reached a door that, Violeta assumed, belonged to a closet.

— Ready?

He pulled open the door, revealing a small room stuffed to the ceiling with letters, postcards, boxes, and parcels, all of which immediately tumbled onto the polished wooden floor. This cascade took half a minute, and when it finally ended, Brinkley beamed and said: — Have you ever laid eyes on such an outpouring of public approbation?

— No, sir.

Brinkley whooped. — Oh, Violeta, your modesty is astounding. You really don't understand, do you? Violeta, the popularity of a radio personality is judged by how much mail he or she receives.

He paused for effect. — *You*, my dear, are by far the biggest mail-puller at Radio XER.

Violeta looked again at the spill of mail, which had tumbled all the way to the tips of Brinkley's fine leather shoes. She grinned bashfully. Brinkley reached down, picked up an armful of letters, and threw them in the air.

— All that mail, Violeta asked. — It's really for me?

— Yes! exclaimed Brinkley. — Yes, yes, a thousand times *yes*! Not only are you the biggest mail-puller at XER, but my sources tell me that you're out-pulling Miss Rosalita Dusk at Radio XEX in Villa Acuña and Miss Rosaurita Day at Radio XED in Ciudad Juárez. My sources tell me, Violeta, that you're out-pulling more than the two of them *put together*. Listen to me, Miss Dawn. Sales of my goat-gland operation and my patented Dr. Brinkley post-operative tonics have risen by thirty percent since you've gone on the air. By *thirty percent*! At this rate I'll have to build another clinic. I'm thinking of New Mexico . . . Oh, I almost forgot! The other day I received an invitation, and a most pressing one at that, to attend to the reproductive ills of an Indochinese emperor, and by gum, I might just go. The remuneration, of course, will be substantial. As my papa always said, *Son, you gotta make hay while the sun shines.*

Violeta lowered her gaze and felt a blush coming to her cheeks. — I'm just glad I could help, she said.

— You know what I think it is? It's your *way*, Miss Dawn. When you speak, you do so with this sort of . . . how do I put it? . . . empathy. Yes, that's it. There's a *caring* there. The other mediums, when they speak, they sound mendacious by comparison. Miss Dusk, with her smoky voice and Germanic vowels — she sounds like she's running a two-bit con, all the way. And Miss Day, with all that swooning and crying — too obvious, every second of it. But *you* . . . when you tell them their cancer is going to go away, or their husbands are bound to quit the bottle, or their lives will be better in the new house, you sound as if you really hope this will happen. You sound as though you've had your own share of pain in this world, and can understand exactly how they are feeling.

Brinkley rose and peered at Violeta with a look of self-satisfaction. He tucked his thumbs in the pockets of his vest and rocked on the heels of his oxfords. — Tell me, Miss Dawn. How much am I paying you?

— Seventy-five dollars a month, doctor.

— In that case, let's raise it to one hundred. You deserve it, Miss Dawn. You deserve every penny.

Violeta smiled broadly. — Oh, Dr. Brinkley, I can't accept . . .

— Oh yes, you can, my dear. And by gum you *will*.

Violeta went home that night with an ermine stole — a bonus gift from Brinkley — wrapped around her. Though it was far too warm for the border and raised a blotchy, unattractive heat rash on her shoulders, she wore it to bed that night, and then she hid it under her bed the next day, afraid it would be pilfered by one of the consumptive thieves who were now as common as houseflies in Corazón de la Fuente. The day after that, Violeta returned from school to find her mother in a state of advanced excitement.

— Look! Malfil said, while hopping from foot to foot. — One of Dr. Brinkley's drivers delivered *this*.

She handed Violeta a single white envelope bearing the words *Señorita Dawn*. Violeta accepted the envelope and admired it for a moment. It was bordered in gold leaf and, if she wasn't mistaken, scented with an essence of rose petals.

— Open it! Open it, mija!

— All *right*, mami.

Violeta carefully inserted a nail into a tiny break in the seal and tore it open in a slow, steady line. Inside was a single bleached-white card. Her lips moved as her eyes roamed the surface.

— What is it?

Violeta gazed at her madre, a look of disbelief in her eyes. — It's Dr. Brinkley. He wants me to . . . he wants me to join him and his wife for dinner after the show next week!

That week, Malfil and Violeta Cruz travelled to nearby Nava, their moods so enlivened they argued only once, in the middle of the trip, when Malfil suggested with a smirk that the good doctor looked at Violeta with more than professional respect in his eyes. In response, Violeta challenged her mother by saying *Mami, he is a married man*. Malfil in turn accused Violeta of suffering from either the naivety of youth or sheer stupidity, at which point Violeta accused her mother of being filthy-minded and rude. For the next ten minutes they both sat stiffly, gazing from their respective sides of the bus.

In Nava they looked up a locally famous seamstress who was rumoured to make gowns for the wife of the Coahuilan governor. By the end of the week Señora Veracruz had produced a sea-blue dress with ruffles running around the neckline, a tapering bodice, and a ballooning of fabric at the hips.

— Mija, Malfil said, with tears in her eyes. — You look like a goddess.

On the morning of Violeta's invitation, her mother took her to Corazón's newest business establishment: two and a half weeks earlier, a peluquería had opened on one of the side streets connecting avenidas Hidalgo and Cinco de Mayo in the east end of the pueblo. There a middle-aged woman named Tabita rinsed Violeta's sumptuous dark hair with rosewater and then piled it atop her head in a decorative fall of pins, ribbons, and barrettes. When she was done, Violeta looked five years older, and her piercing jade eyes seemed as big as plums. Her walk home was accompanied by frank stares, repeated calls of *Mamacita!* and at least one proposal of marriage.

Once at home, Malfil treated what little was left of her daughter's fingernails with a paste made from crushed beetle shells, which tasted so bitterly poisonous that Violeta wouldn't be tempted to succumb to her favourite nervous habit in front of the Brinkleys. That afternoon the two waited together, Malfil turning to her daughter at one point and saying: — You are my whole world. You know this, don't you, mija?

— Sí, mami, answered her daughter. — I know this.

— If anything ever happened to you I would die.

— Mami, said Violeta. — Please.

Her limousine arrived at five o'clock. In evening slippers last worn by her mother at her own wedding, Violeta barely survived the dusty, uneven laneway separating her house from the open door of the vehicle. She arrived at the station at half-past and, as always, lubricated her vocal cords with a cup of hot water flavoured with lemon. She was behind her microphone precisely at six o'clock, at which time the Rose Dawn theme filled the station.

It was a draining show. Violeta found that she couldn't concentrate on the stories told by her listeners, and several times she had to ask them to repeat themselves, which she got away with by pleading that she had accidentally fallen into a regressive trance. At two minutes past seven o'clock, the broadcast booth relinquished to Fay Parker, the portly host of *Victuals for Visitors*, Violeta took a seat in the XER lounge. Her thin hands gripped her kneecaps. At five minutes past seven, Dale Stollins arrived. He looked at her.

— Why, Miss Dawn, you do look lovely today.

He led her outside and helped her into the limousine. As they drove, the driver kept sneaking glances at her in the rear-view mirror. Violeta, meanwhile, gazed out the back-seat window, savouring the soft, buttery leather beneath her. The town of Del Río thinned as they drove. The houses grew farther and farther apart, until they were replaced altogether by neatly furrowed grape fields, old wooden barns, and pastureland. They passed beneath immense weeping cypress trees that hung over the roadway and tickled the top of the limousine. Violeta opened her window and felt the warm breeze on her face; she could hear the chirrup of crickets, the soft purr of the car's motor, and the throaty bedspring wheeze made by bullfrogs. They passed a swamp, and for a half-minute or so she could smell putrid water. When they finally stopped, the sun was just starting to drop, turning the sky a dusky purplish colour.

— We're here, the driver said.

He got out and opened her door. Violeta stepped out before

a huge pink-stucco mansion with turrets and fountains and rose gardens and tennis courts and marble Roman columns and a swimming pool the size of a Corazón de la Fuente city block. There was also a miniature zoo stocked with dozens of Texan deer and antelope, all of which, upon hearing the closing of the car door, gawked at Violeta while vacuously chewing. The driver pushed open tall wrought-iron gates bearing the initials *JRB*.

— Follow me, he said, and they walked along a path leading through a topiary garden. The bushes, Violeta noticed, had all been groomed to resemble animals that Brinkley had reportedly seen in the jungles of South America: tigers, rhinoceros, various monkeys, anaconda snakes. They arrived at a pair of arched oak doors that had been stained the same light pink as the rest of the house.

The driver knocked. The door was opened by an elderly Mexican gentleman in a butler's uniform. Everybody smiled, and the driver said he would wait in the car. He then disappeared behind a magnolia pruned to resemble a hippopotamus.

— Buenas noches, said the butler. — I am Ricardo. This way, por favor.

He led her towards a room so lofty that Violeta's immediate reaction was to crane her neck and gaze at the distant ceiling, which had been decorated with a fresco of chubby, trumpeting angels. Ricardo gestured towards a high-backed chair and said *Por favor, señorita*. Violeta continued to gape; neither her eyes nor her mind was sufficiently trained to absorb the opulence before her. The chandeliers, the leaded etched windows, the gleaming floors, the antique furniture, the grand piano — all of it melded, producing a single, overwhelming impression.

The butler left and Violeta waited in the cool, cavernous room. She sat with her back straight, hands folded in her lap, wondering what sort of dinner might be served in a house like this. Probably something that came under a dome of glass, like she'd seen in movies detailing the life of México's aristocracy.

The doctor entered, beaming.

— So there you are, he said in Spanish. — How kind of you to join me.

— You have a beautiful house, doctor.

— Oh, it's nothing. Would you like some champagne?

— Sí, Violeta said, as though champagne were something she enjoyed most weekends.

Brinkley turned. Violeta listened to his footsteps dwindle in volume until they stopped being sounds altogether. The doctor returned with Ricardo trailing along behind. Grim-faced, the butler was carrying a silver tray bearing two shallow, wide-brimmed glasses. He lowered the tray before Violeta. She took a glass. Brinkley took the other. When he made no motion to sit down, Violeta hopped to her feet, accidentally spilling a few sticky drops on her dress.

The doctor held up his glass, looked her in the eye, and said: — To Rose Dawn, high priestess of the Sacred Order of the Maya.

They touched glasses, and Violeta let her first exposure to alcohol pass over her lips. — It's delicious, she said.

— I'm glad you like it. Later, if it would please you, I could show you my wine cellar. I say, you must be famished.

— No, she said. — Well . . . I suppose I am a little hungry.

— Good! Come. I'll show you to the dining room.

They set off, along hallways and beneath archways, passing a succession of grand rooms. Violeta peered in each one, feeling simultaneously dazed and oddly at home. The first was stocked, from floor to ceiling, with books; Violeta wished she could go in there and read them all, thinking this would then give her the knowledge and the sophistication of the doctor himself. The next room was filled with animal heads, each mounted on the wall and looking expressionless; this room unnerved Violeta, and she was glad to pass it. The third room was the strangest of all, in that it contained a huge table covered in green felt that had, around its edges, six holes the size of apples. It occurred to her, as it had in the past, that gringos were a different breed, with mores and customs that never ceased to mystify her.

They came to a chandelier-lit room housing a long, narrow table that could have sat about three dozen dinner guests. At the far end of the table, next to a bay window overlooking the estate's zoo, were two place settings and the opened champagne bottle, submersed in a bucket of ice.

— But, doctor, there are only settings for two.

Brinkley glanced towards the end of the table, as though this news surprised him as well. He turned to her, looking so unaccountably regretful that Violeta worried she might have said something wrong.

— Ah, he said. — My wife.

He paused long enough that Violeta began to wonder whether this was the only explanation he would offer.

— Violeta, he said sheepishly. — Back home in North Carolina, we have a thing called a shotgun wedding. Might you know what that is?

— No, doctor. I'm afraid that I don't.

— It's when the father of a young woman decides that her relationship with her young man demands the sanctification of God. That is where the shotgun comes in. The young man, I'm afraid, has little to say in the matter.

— I think I understand.

— It was a long, long time ago. We were scarcely older than you are now, my dear. My marriage, I confess, has been a charade for some time now. She has gone to live with her dear old mother in Richmond.

— You mean . . . you are preparing to divorce?

— Yes, Violeta. That is the long and the short of it. But please, we have a wonderful meal to look forward to. Let's talk no longer of unhappy subjects. Please, have some more champagne. There's vichyssoise on the way.

Vichyssoise turned out to be a cool potato soup that both refreshed Violeta and left her tongue feeling enlivened. She drank a little more champagne, such that by the time their salad arrived — a mixture of clover and a seedless dark purple fruit she was pretty sure didn't grow in the northern hemisphere — she had found the courage to ask the doctor the thing that most intrigued her.

— Dr. Brinkley?

— Sí, Violeta.

— I was just wondering about your . . . your Compound Operation. I was just wondering if it, you know, is like Rose Dawn, or whether it actually . . .

The doctor chortled so exuberantly that a morsel of violet fruit emitted from his mouth, arced through the air, and landed on the surface of a medieval oil painting.

— If it really *works*? Ah, my dear Violeta, you really are a delight. And don't worry . . . that is exactly the question that surfaces with the greatest regularity. And I must admit it is a fair question, efficacy being the concern foremost in both the mind of the public and the mind of a responsible physician. Well, I'm here to tell you, young lady, that the proof is in the pudding. I myself have had the full Compound Operation four times, and I am proud to say that I have the vigour of a man half my age. I'd also like to add that only the goats in question suffered any deleterious side effects.

Brinkley beamed in a such a pronounced manner that Violeta couldn't help but follow suit.

— You see, Violeta, the male reproductive system and the female reproductive system are like . . .

He gazed out the window towards his zoo, which had turned a pale indigo under the moon.

— They are like deer and antelope. They are related, and yet completely different, animals. Without the full and able functioning of the reproductive system, the male of the species withers and dies. This is a medical fact. Without the able functioning of the prostate, the male suffers a diminishment of the secretions responsible for energy, for acute mental functioning . . . even the ability to experience joy. It has been scientifically proven that only the surgical implantation of a billy goat's reproductive apparatus will remedy this. In fact, I am now indicating the Compound Operation for all men past the age of forty-five, not just the ones suffering from marital impediments. What I tell people is this: you can't be a stallion when age has turned you into a gelding. Do you understand, Violeta?

— Sí, she said, shocked at some of the things he had just told her. At the same time, she felt mildly thrilled. In México men did not talk of such things with women, particularly with women who were only nearing adulthood. Struggling not to blush, she already felt as though she was a long, long way from her ravaged little village on the wrong side of the Río Grande.

— Why, said Brinkley, — I have patients who are on their fifth and even sixth Compound Operation. Would they do that if their needs weren't being satisfied?

Brinkley's face then fell, and he looked at the surface of the table with the rueful expression of someone who had travelled a great distance and had not found what he was seeking.

— But I'll tell you, my dear. They say that America is the land of freedom, of laissez-faire, of capitalism unbound. Well, that's true if you're a Rockefeller. But if you're from a poor mining town in North Carolina, there are forces to keep you at your station. There is a structure that wants to keep you there. The hounding that I get . . . Just this morning I received a letter from the Internal Revenue Service in which they asked for a most unfair settlement. One that would severely compromise myself, and the foundations I support, were I to follow its recommendations to the letter. And don't get me started on the American Medical Association, who'd rather run me out of town than acknowledge my success. Do you know why, Violeta? Because my achievements upset the apple cart. My accomplishments, they believe, take too big a slice of the pie. Am I making any sense?

— Sí, she said. — I think so.

Suddenly Brinkley's smile returned. — But enough with

that! It was dreary of me to bring it up. Please forgive me. We are here, after all, to celebrate your success. Should we have some more champagne?

The doctor had another glass while Violeta only pretended to sip at hers — she'd begun to feel a little light-headed, and she realized she would get drunk if she continued imbibing in earnest. With the tenderloin in morel jus that followed, the doctor served a red wine he referred to as claret. Though it was delicious, she took only a few prudent sips.

Meanwhile the good doctor asked her questions about herself. She told him about her schooling, about growing up in a poor Mexican town on the border, about her desires for the future. She even found herself opening up about the losses that the revolution had brought to her family, an admission that brought her to the verge of tears yet at the same time left her feeling unburdened. By the end of dessert, a jiggling white substance called blancmange, she found that she was taking notice of the doctor's features. For some reason she had never noticed how high his cheekbones were, or how soft his skin was, or how his eyes were a mysterious shade of bluish grey; her father's eyes, she suddenly realized, had not been dissimilar. She felt her skin flush. When she thought of all that Brinkley, a campesino from an apparently poor place called North Carolina, had accomplished, she felt as though anything was possible for her own life. This possibility made her feel emotional, and sufficiently vertiginous that she swayed a little in her chair.

Brinkley noticed this. — Is everything all right, my dear?

— Sí, she said.

— You look a little . . .

— No, no, doctor. I feel wonderful. It's just that I've had a long day, and I think the big meal has made me a little tired.

A look of deepest sincerity passed over the doctor's features.

— I wonder if we should call it an evening.

— Sí, she said, her regret perhaps too expressively written on her lovely features. The doctor escorted her to the door himself, and said goodnight with a handshake and yet another expression of gratitude. She was then placed in the limousine that had brought her there and returned to the home of her mother, who naturally had waited up for her daughter so as to pepper her with questions about Brinkley, his wife, and their lavish American lifestyle across the river. Violeta answered some of the questions truthfully, some of them falsely, and some in accordance with the grey area that exists between the two.

The following week, when she accepted another invitation to dine with the doctor in his mansion — *The place is so big and lonely, Violeta, and I find you to be such wonderful company* — Violeta told her mother that the doctor was now hosting dinner parties every Saturday night for the staff of XER. At the end of that evening she was again delivered back into the arms of her mother, only to return to the doctor's mansion the following week.

That evening, having acquired a fondness for the taste of champagne, she imbibed far more than a single glass, only to discover that the beverage had a magical quality: it somehow conjured feelings of elation along with a bemused acceptance of the world and its foibles. At the end of the night Violeta found herself discussing art with the doctor, something she would never, ever have attempted with the loutish, ignorant males of Corazón de la Fuente (even Francisco, though undeniably clever, wouldn't know a da Vinci from a Raphael).

— To see Diego Rivera's mural in the National Preparatory School! she told him. — What I would give!

The doctor smiled and leaned across the candlelit table. — Would you like to know something?

— Sí, claro.

— I own a Rivera. It's a minor work, I admit, painted when he was unknown and his art wasn't so burdened with revolutionary themes. Nonetheless I could show it to you.

— Oh, Dr. Brinkley, I would love to see it.

— It is upstairs, Violeta. In one of the chambers. Would you like to follow me?

She peered at him, heat rushing to her cheeks. On the one hand she was conscious of the dictates regarding the propriety of women and the thousand and one lectures that her mother had given her regarding the satyr-like desires of men. On the other hand was the unaccountable fact that the empty, mournful feeling that assailed her at all times mysteriously lessened when she was in the presence of this courtly foreign, and significantly older, doctor. She closed her eyes and listened to the peacefulness of her heart; in this way she prolonged the tortured delight that was this moment.

Finally she opened her eyes. Just as she had suspected, the doctor was still there. Beneath the table, she pinched the fleshy part of her right leg. When she failed to awaken, she smiled bashfully and said: — Ay sí, doctor. Of course.

{20}

TWO NIGHTS LATER, FOLLOWING A DINNER OF PORK
stew with rice, Francisco Ramirez went out. He headed
towards Violeta's, a task that involved navigating around
entire dirt-smudged families that seemed to be camped out
in every space sufficiently large to host a flattened cardboard
box. Francisco, with graver matters on his mind, was more
or less oblivious. Over the past week or so he had sensed a
change in his relationship with Violeta, a slight cooling that
could very well be a product of his imagination. Her face
did not brighten·upon seeing him the way it used to. More
often than not she looked a little sheepish, an already gnawed
fingernail travelling to her mouth, her eyes flitting from left
to right. She now seemed impatient with his invitations to
have a euphemistic walk in the desert, and the last time she
had assented, her kisses seemed as though they were coming
from someplace other than her broiling latina soul.

Yet as he approached Violeta's door — an approach accompanied by the howling of feral dogs — he also knew that

Violeta's reticence could all be a conjuring of his imagination. Having had a boyhood that coincided with a decade of revolution, it was true that he sensed darkness hiding around every corner. He knocked on the door, and suffered an eternity of waiting. Malfil Cruz answered.

— Ay, Francisco! she exclaimed. — How *are* you?

— I am fine, Señora Cruz.

— And is it me you're here to see, or is it my lovely daughter? Francisco grinned and looked at his boot tips.

— I might have known, Malfil jibed. — No time for an old woman? Wait here. I'll fetch her.

Malfil stepped back into the gloom of the house. Francisco listened to her footfalls grow fainter and then cease altogether. These sound effects were followed by a pair of deliberately lowered voices. Malfil returned.

— I hate to tell you this, Francisco, but Violeta has a big test tomorrow.

— She does?

— I'm afraid so. She needs to study. She's so busy these days, the poor thing barely has time for her schoolwork.

— She wouldn't be free for a minute?

— She doesn't want to lose her train of thought . . . Don't worry, Francisco, just come by this time tomorrow.

Francisco left, his disappointment flavoured with an emotion that he didn't understand at first, but that he came to realize was a disorienting fearfulness: it felt as though the packed-earth street might not be there to catch his next step, or that the sky above were losing patience with the sun and on the verge of telling it to go warm some other planet. With a shake of his head he dismissed this sensation, attributing it to an excitability that seemed to be the primary side effect of infatuation. The following night, at the exact time prescribed by Malfil Cruz, he arrived at Violeta's door. Again Malfil answered, and again she retreated into the lye-scented shadows in order to summon Violeta. This time he heard her having a low, impatient conversation with her daughter, a discussion that terminated with Malfil spitting *Está bien, Violeta!* Then, just as he heard Malfil begin her return to the entranceway, Francisco noticed something of a disturbing nature resting on their dinner table. Hurriedly — for Malfil was a woman who bolted, as if forever late for a train — Francisco focused his eyes so as to pierce the low light, and realized he was looking at a bouquet of scarlet roses that must have numbered in the dozens.

Only one man, he thought, *could have sent those flowers.* His mouth immediately went dry, his hands clammy. When Malfil informed him that Violeta wasn't feeling well, alluding to a discomfort not experienced by males, it was as though she were speaking from several hundred metres in the distance.

Francisco thanked her and walked off, his movements now accompanied by a plummeting of spirits so profound it threatened to affect his balance. His stomach churned and his temples pulsed with discomfort. The sensation worsened. Upon reaching home, he expelled his dinner into the beige porcelain bowl in which his grandmother had once bathed him, a lie about questionable vendor tripe coming up between retches. When he was done, his father gave him a cold compress and suggested he take to his bed.

He waited two and a half days before attempting to see Violeta again. It was a calculated gambit, Francisco betting that, with the passage of time, Violeta would begin to miss the passion he knew he'd inspired the night she'd won the gumball contest. The next sixty hours passed like mud through an hourglass. Lengthy periods transpired in which its passage ceased altogether, only to suddenly loosen and resume its murky slump downward. Seconds passed as minutes, minutes impersonated hours, hours mimicked days. At school, Francisco conducted himself as though in a dream. In his history class he was hectored by an unfeeling professor after bungling a question involving the War of Independence. That afternoon, playing fútbol in the field out by the old Spanish mission, Francisco collided with another player, knocking him so hard to the ground that the youth looked up with momentary dismay in his eyes. Though the fallen player laughed it off a few seconds later — *A todo madre, Francisco, what's gotten into you?* — Francisco couldn't help be bothered by the way in which his frustration had escaped so suddenly, and with such malevolent results.

Saturday morning arrived, with Francisco brusquely conducting his lessons in the ejido. He stayed for one hour only, and then announced his departure so abruptly that many of his students feared he had developed a dislike for them and might not reappear the following week. Brushing off entreaties to stay and enjoy a rice dish made with squirrel meat and yucca, Francisco tromped off, returned home, bathed, dressed in clean Levi's and a white shirt, and proceeded to the store operated by Fajardo Jimenez. There he bought a packet of tortillas, some carne seca herbed with oregano and garlic, a tin of peaches packed in syrup, and some chocolate biscuits that had come all the way from Guatemala. After thanking Fajardo, he packed his knapsack and reached the house of Violeta Cruz just before the lunch hour.

He knocked. Predictably, Malfil answered, evincing the same delight she always generated when laying eyes on Francisco. But this time when he asked to see Violeta, her expression faltered. She retreated, Francisco soon hearing the hissed voices of two people struggling to maintain an argument in confidence. There was a long stretch of silence, and then Violeta was at the door, saying only *Hola, primo*.

He knew. He knew by the way she had not primped in any way, her long tresses a tangle, her blouse a miasma of wrinkles, her feet bare against the floorboards. He knew by the way in which she kept glancing in either direction, up and down the street, her gaze refusing to meet his own. He knew by the way in which her arms were crossed at the elbow, revealing the fingernails she chewed so ravenously. He knew by the way her left heel bounced, as though enlivened by a nervous disorder. He knew by the way in which she, cruelty of cruelties, had referred to him as *primo*. Not *querido*, not *amor*, not *guapo* . . . but *primo*. He was a cousin to her now, a platonic entity.

He also knew that the conversation they were about to have would be a formality at best.

— Hola, Violeta, qué onda?

— No mucho, Francisco.

— You look like you slept late.

— I'm so busy these days, Francisco.

— I heard that.

— My job at the radio station . . . I can barely keep up with the other areas of my life.

— Sí, sí. Your madre told me this was the case.

There came a long, awkward moment in which the only sound was the rustling of curs in the laneway.

— Violeta, I bought some things to have for a picnic. I thought we could go down to the river for a change.

— You know I'd love to. It's just that . . . I've got my homework to do, and then I have to help with the cleaning, and then I have to cross the border to the station. Perhaps some other time?

Francisco refused to let his emotions see the light of day, reasoning that the one thing left to him was dignity.

— Cómo no, he said. — Some other time.

He then turned and trudged away, refusing to turn and take a last look at Violeta. In so doing, he missed a sad, unalterable truth: Violeta watched him walk all the way to the end of the block, her teeth so badly assaulting the nail of her left thumb that her tongue was soon visited by the tang of seeping blood.

Francisco, meanwhile, reached the expanse of the town's central plaza. He stopped, looked up at Brinkley's monolithic tower, and gestured obscenely while spitting *Your madre takes it in the culo, cabrón.* He then walked up to a family of grubby peasants camping in the shade thrown by the town hall and offered them every morsel of the food he had purchased for his picnic with Violeta. At first they reacted suspiciously; a tension had developed between the old-time residents of Corazón and the new arrivals, and the peasants' first reaction was that the package must somehow be tainted. Convincing them that this was not the case required a considerable amount of gesturing, for Francisco did not know how to speak the native language of rural Oaxaca, and the family's knowledge of Spanish was limited to a few common pleasant-ries. Assured, the squatters finally took the treats, their faces beaming as they dipped their stubby, earth-crusted fingers into peach syrup.

Refusing to be defeated, Francisco decided to visit the per-son whom he trusted most when it came to matters of the heart. He crossed the plaza and, as always, found his elderly friend sitting on the bench outside his house, facing the Pozo de Confesiones. Inside, Francisco could hear Laura Velasquez humming delightedly.

— Hola, Francisco, said the molinero, his voice sounding stronger than it had in years.

— Hola, señor.

Sit, sit.

Gracias.

For a minute or two neither said a thing. Francisco knew that he didn't have to explain; the molinero would have seen it in the heaviness of Francisco's gait and in the sadness of his expression.

Finally, Francisco spoke.

— Tell me, Señor Pántelas. Have you ever been spurned?

The molinero chortled. — Have I ever been spurned? Listen to me, my young friend. I have been spurned by as many women as have accepted me into their hearts. The point is this: just because a woman rejects you once doesn't mean she will continue to reject you. Do you understand me, joven?

— I don't think I do, Señor Pántelas.

— Women are capricious, wilful, unsure of what is contained in the recesses of their own desire. They are not single-minded creatures as we are, Francisco. They are multifaceted, perpetually careering like a storm let loose in the desert. It's what makes them so wonderful. It's what makes them worth fighting for.

— Now I really don't understand.

— Do you love Violeta Cruz?

— Sí.

— I know you do. I can see the pain in your eyes. I'll ask you another question. In your heart of hearts, do you think she still has feelings for you?

Francisco hung his head as though ashamed, and said: — Sí, molinero. I do.

— I think she does too. Something is stopping her from acting on those feelings, and you must free her from its chains. Do you understand? You must not roll over and give up. You must fight to win her back.

— But how do I do this?

— Ay, said the molinero. — That's the trick, isn't it? I tell you, Francisco, if love wasn't such a difficult game, winning wouldn't be so much fun.

Again the two lapsed into silence. Francisco thought about the molinero's counsel. How could he, a penniless villager, take on a wealthy, famous doctor like Brinkley? How would this be possible? The more he thought about it, the more he became angered by the unevenness of the playing field upon which he competed. Yet as he grew angry, his thoughts sharpened, and he felt a vengeful strength fomenting inside him.

Somehow he would get that runty, four-eyed hijo de puta. The only question left in his stirring mind was how.

— Now let me be, said the molinero. — Laura and I are leaving for Saltillo on Monday morning, and at my age I'll need at least a day and a half to rest up. Oh. And one other thing.

— What's that, Señor Pántelas?

— You are young. You have a heart that works. You have legs that carry you without complaint.

— So?

— Be happy, joven. Be happy.

For once, Francisco didn't listen to the old man's advice. He was halfway to his home when he stopped suddenly, his mind a blaze of inspiration, his body humming with a suspicion that could easily be turned into action. Taking an energizing breath, he turned and marched all the way to the bridge separating Corazón de la Fuente from los Estados Unidos, a tuft of risen dust hanging behind him. As he stepped onto the bridge's old wooden slats, the Mexican border guard noted Francisco's narrowed eyes and bristling gait and concluded that this might not be the day to ask the solidly built young man for the usual bribe.

The gringo border guard, a small man whose sensitivity to the sun demanded that he spend all day in his well-appointed cabin, was not as astute.

— Hey there! he called as Francisco strode past him. — You need a durned transit visa!

Francisco stopped and slowly turned, his features as tight as piano wire.

— That may be true, he said. — But it's also true I am much bigger than you are, pendejo. It's also true I'm in no mood for you and your hijo de puta transit visa. Ask me again, and I throw you in the river.

The border guard considered this for the briefest of moments. — Have a nice stay, he said, and waved Francisco through.

{21}

TRUE TO HIS WORD, THE MOLINERO SPENT ALL OF
Sunday harnessing his energies, despite Laura's winking suggestion that the best rest was acquired after carnal exertion.
The following morning, just after the sun's fulminating rise,
the pair caught a lift with a muchacho who delivered fruit to
the store of Fajardo Jimenez. They rode to Piedras Negras in
a camioneta smelling of guava and plantain. Throughout, the
molinero chatted with the driver, who seemed interested to
hear that this gracious old man with the thick white hair was
taking this girl — his granddaughter, probably — to Saltillo to
have some sort of metal restraining device placed on her teeth.
As they continued chewing the fat, the molinero talked about
life in Corazón de la Fuente, specifically how the town had
grown so much richer, and so much more difficult to live in,
since its windfall.

— You know what they say, commented the driver.
— There's no such thing as a free lunch, verdad?

The hombre dropped them at the Piedras bus depot, and

refused the pesos the molinero offered him.

— No, no, he said. — Buy your granddaughter some tooth-paste on me.

He then drove off before the molinero had a chance to correct him.

Then came the difficult part of the journey: six hours in a rickety old diesel bus named *La Concepción Inmaculada*, in which they were stuffed into a row of seats already filled with a pair of Kickapoo Indians, a trio of schoolchildren, a doz-ing grandmother, and a hobbled chicken that periodically shat on the molinero's pant leg. Seeing this, Laura laughed till tears formed in her mirthful dark eyes. For the molinero, her delight was almost worth having his trousers soiled.

As the day progressed, the air inside the bumping tin vehicle became thin and broiling, as if the heat from the sun were using up the oxygen. Too hot to doze, the passengers turned quiet and still; during the middle hours of the day they mostly stared at the desert scrub extending forever on either side of the bus. It was dusk when they finally pulled into Saltillo, the right side of the bus an ember in the failing sun. The tired couple found a small hotel off the central plaza and went to sleep early. As a result they awoke before dawn and admired a sky lit only by stars. They made their way to the market and, in the cool of morning, ate a breakfast of cheese, coffee, and fresh strawberries at the stand of a vendor who kept breathing on his hands to keep them warm.

Slowly the street came alive with cleaners and stray dogs and men hawking trinkets. Laura and her molinero watched for the longest time, feeling pleased to be amidst the bustle of an actual city. Around nine o'clock they found their ultimate destination on a side-street home to ironmongers and clothes-lines. The couple stepped out of smeary daylight and climbed up a dark stairway to the sound of hammers striking metal. At the top of the stairs, towards the end of a grimy hallway in which a brother and sister were playing jacks while dressed only in underpants, the couple found a door marked *Dentista*. They pushed it open and found an hombre in a white smock sitting in a large chair, drinking a glass of strong, aromatic coffee. He jumped out of the chair and smiled.

— You must be Laura Velasquez, he said.

— Sí, said Laura.

— And you, sir? he said, extending his hand towards the molinero. — You're Roberto Pántelas? The one who sent me the cable, sí? The cable about helping your . . . Is she your granddaughter?

— No, said the molinero with an agreeable smile. — She's my fiancée.

This information stymied the dentist, who blinked in the manner of a man with dust in his eyes. The molinero occupied these awkward moments by looking around the office, noticing how its impeccable cleanliness was at odds with its location. The dentist, having recovered, gestured towards the chair in which he'd just been sitting.

— Bueno, let's get started. Laura, would you please take a seat . . . Señor Pántelas, you could go for a walk, or you're welcome to stay and watch. It's your choice.

The molinero looked over at Laura, who understandably seemed a little ill at ease.

— I'll stay, he said.

There was a row of plain high-backed chairs against the

wall of the office. The molinero sat in the one closest to the action and watched as Laura was fitted with a clanking copper-and-steel contraption that would have resembled a fox trap were it not for all the wires, bands, and hooks that dangled from it. As the dentist crammed the device into Laura's gaping mouth — it was a procedure that involved nitrous oxide and more than a little forearm strength — the molinero found himself falling even more deeply in love. It must have hurt like a real hijo de puta, and yet she didn't complain, wince, or reflexively push away the dentist's muscled hands. Watching the procedure, the old man realized he was seeing Laura's soul writ large and, by extension, the soul of the Mexican woman: it was that equal mixture of acquiescence and bravery, that sublime contradiction of vulnerability and strength. It was no wonder he had loved so many women in his long, long life, and every single one of them Mexicana (with maybe the odd Guatemalteca and an occasional Hondureña thrown in for good measure).

A long hour passed. With the apparatus wedged in place, the dentist began tightening it with a series of screwdrivers, ratchets, and needle-nosed pliers.

— Almost done, he said, and proceeded to equip Laura with a leather headdress that looked like the helmets worn by American football players, albeit with a metal coil that wrapped around the lower half of Laura's face. Again the molinero felt himself sink a little deeper into the wondrous tailspin called love.

When the dentist held a mirror for his patient, Laura turned her head to both sides and, in a voice warmed by gratitude, said: — Gracias, doctor. Muchas, muchas gracias.

— It's the birth of ortodoncia, commented the dentist. — Trust me, it will help many, many people.

They ate at a taquería around the corner, the dentist having left a small aperture in the front of the apparatus, through which Laura fed herself tortilla stuffed with calf brains and a white salted cheese. During the bumpy ride back to Piedras Negras there was a gradual shifting of bodies, so that by the time the bus passed the city of Monclova, the seat in front of Laura was filled with dark-eyed children, all of whom stared at her while picking their noses. By the time the bus was rattling through Sabinas, however, she had disarmed them with games of patty cake, peek-a-boo, and spotting animal shapes in the cacti; the molinero doubted they even noticed her dental contraption any longer. In Piedras the couple managed to get a ride in a small, fume-spewing lorry headed east. Shortly before they turned onto the roadway leading into Corazón, the truck engulfed by white blue sky, Laura turned and asked — Do you hear that?

— Hear what?

— Music.

— Music?

— I can barely make it out. It's like it's very close and far, far away at the same time.

— Qué raro, offered the molinero. — There must be a radio somewhere. But with my hearing, it could be blaring in my ear and I'd barely notice it.

Laura shrugged and closed her eyes. She was on the sunny side of the lorry, her face bathed in dusty light. The driver left them at the edge of town, well beyond the ejido, claiming that he was running low on time. After a few minutes they hitched a ride with a rag dealer who had rigged a cart to a burro. By the time they reached the centre of town, they were being followed by a half-dozen excited children, all of whom were yelling *Laura, Laura, show us your braces!* or *Laura, Laura, did you bring us all something?* Sure enough, Laura climbed down from the donkey cart and started handing out goat-milk candies she'd purchased in the Saltillo market. When all of the children had one, she made her rounds to the elderly. From the stoop of his little house the molinero heard her being greeted, over and over, by those whose adult children had been murdered by the revolution.

Laura stayed busy for the rest of the day, though the molinero noticed that she kept rubbing her jaw and temples. Yet whenever he asked her if she was bothered by the braces, she would say *No, it's nothing* and then smile weakly beneath the layers of copper, steel, and cloth. That night, when her long day was finally finished and a relative quiet had fallen over the village, she lay down beside the molinero. After tossing and turning for a few minutes, she said: — There it is again.

— The music?

— No. You can't hear it? This time it's a man talking in English. I think . . . I think it's Dr. Brinkley.

— How could that be?

— I don't know. It comes and goes. I don't understand it. I think maybe it's my imagination.

The next day Laura awoke, fixed the molinero his breakfast, and immediately went to do her errands. And while she presented a happy face to the townsfolk, all of whom asked her questions about Saltillo and her trip to the dentist, there were many times when the molinero observed her in quiet moments rubbing her ears and looking as though she was suffering from a low, constant pain. Meanwhile he visited each of his neighbours, a process that involved a full day and several cups of bitter, burnt-tasting coffee. His intent was to ask if any of them listened to Brinkley's station, and they all told him the same thing: unless Malfil Cruz's daughter was on, the last thing they'd listen to was those infernal hillbilly jingles that Brinkley always played.

The next day was even worse. Laura began to look haggard with lack of sleep, and she no longer smiled when dealing with the senior citizens under her care. Several times during the day the molinero caught her placing a damp cloth on her forehead, and he noticed that she had taken to sighing, often and loudly. Shortly after lunch, the molinero came to the rare decision that he needed a drink. He put on his hat and boots and ambled across town to Carlos Hernandez's cantina. As he made his way across the plaza, he was stopped by an old, old man named Jaime de la Roya, who waved from his perch on a wrought iron bench. Though Señor de la Roya was actually younger than the molinero, he was not blessed with the older man's health or vigour: his hands shook, his stomach didn't work properly, his eyes were failing, and he needed help to do most things. As such, he was one of the village elderly that Laura made a habit of visiting.

— Qué onda, primo? asked the molinero.

Jaime didn't answer. Instead he raised an arm as gnarled as a tree branch. — Your fiancée, compadre. I need to see her.

Again Don Miguel felt as though unseen hands had dumped ice water over him. Laura never, ever missed her rounds. — I'll tell her, he said.

— Gracias, amigo. It's not pressing, it's just that I haven't had food in my larder for a few days, and the laundry is piling up around my ears . . .

The molinero walked to the cantina. There he joined the mayor, the hacendero, and Father Alvarez, all of whom seemed preoccupied. The mayor was expressing concern about the changes that had come to the town, the hacendero was worried about his horse, and Father Alvarez . . . well, he was the worst, noisily obsessing over the death of the Church and the attendant rise of dastardly forces.

— By the way, said the molinero, — Where is Carlos?

— Where else? snapped Father Alvarez, who was slurring his words just a little. — In the back with Margarita. I tell you, I don't know what's got into those two. You can't even order a drink around here anymore without pounding on their bedroom door.

— Ordering another drink, the hacendero observed, — is the last thing *you* need to be doing, Alvarez.

— And maybe you need to be minding your own business, Antonio.

— Gentlemen, implored the mayor. — Por favor. We are all friends here.

He stood and limped over to the bar himself, where he poured the molinero a respectful tequila. The old man let the drink warm his belly.

— Do you want another? asked the mayor. — It's good for what ails you.

— Ay no, Miguel. A second mescalito and I'd fall over and hurt myself. Besides, nothing is ailing me these days.

Just then the cantina owner entered the saloon from his room at the back, a shirt tail hanging over his belt, his sizeable moustache topping an equally sizeable grin. The others rolled their eyes as he rushed over to offer his arm to their elderly guest. In this way the molinero was able to rise from his seat.

— Adiós, compadres, he said. — I'll see you all soon.

Slowly the molinero shuffled home, sticking to the shade thrown by blue and pink adobe walls, his head lost in hard thought and worry. When he reached his little house, he opened the door and stood in the entranceway, his heart breaking. The person he loved most in the world was weeping.

— Roberto, she cried. — Come, come.

He moved towards her and struggled to his knees. She had stuffed her ears with strips of cloth and was holding her head.

— Ay, pobrecita. Is there anything I can do?

— It's not even in my ears. The noise . . . it's in my jaw, in my cheekbones, in my forehead. That horrible racket is *inside* me.

The molinero wrapped his thin, blue-veined arms around her wracking shoulders. In so doing, his ear brushed against the thin metal wire that wrapped around her mouth, and he finally determined what was tormenting his Laurita. He recoiled, and then leaned in close again, only to hear the most popular song in los Estados Unidos, a song that, to the residents of Corazón de la Fuente, was about as pleasing as an assault of locusts.

> *Will the circle be unbroken*
> *By and by, Lord, by and by?*
> *There's a better home awaiting*
> *In the sky, Lord, in the sky . . .*

{22}

MIGUEL OROZCO, THE MAYOR OF CORAZÓN DE LA
Fuente, stood at his window in the town hall, gazing out over
the plaza, feeling the pangs of loneliness that are often experienced by those who are liked by everyone and truly loved by
no one.

He sighed. The previous night, thieves had broken into
his office. As a consequence of this invasion, the mescal bottle
he kept in his lower right-hand drawer was gone, the town's
only existing map of Corazón lay in a mound of shreds, and
the framed sepia photo of his Oaxacan parents that he kept on
his desktop had been snapped in half, presumably over somebody's knee. Again he shook his head and thought fondly
of the days before the tower. Back then, when his morning
obligations had proven excessively strenuous and Carlos
Hernandez had not yet opened his cantina, Miguel would
often take his business to the plaza and sit in the shade of a
palo verde. Thus ensconced, he would stretch out his legs and
look up at the roofless church, recalling his own little village

down south. A cool wind would ruffle his hair, and a feeling
of contentment would settle over him like a woollen blanket.

And *now*.

Look at it, thought the mayor. *Just* look *at it*. Every bench
occupied by a campesino with nowhere to go. Every square
inch of patio covered by the bedding of vagrants. The town's
beautiful wrought-iron bandstand hung with bedsheets. Bare
palo verde branches festooned with drying brassieres, work
shirts, and underpants. Litter everywhere. Empty bottles.
Dirty, pockmarked infants. Every day, it seemed, more of
the country's poor arrived; the rumour that there was still
work to be had at the tower site apparently refused to per-
ish. Others came because they'd heard of all the money
attracted by Madam Félix's House of Gentlemanly Pleasures.
Naturally, many of these were petty robbers, who carried dull
homemade knives in their pockets. Others were roasted-corn
vendors, who fought each other for locations closest to the
brothel. He couldn't even blame them. By three o'clock in the
afternoon the lineup from Madam's house extended all the
way to the plaza, where it blocked the arched doors of the
town hall. To leave his office, the mayor often had to shoulder
his way through a line of nervous, unspeaking gringos, all
with their hats pulled down over their eyes.

Again the mayor sighed. He limped back to his desk and
sat. It was late morning and already he was exhausted; sleep
hadn't been coming easily of late, and when it did it was
fractured and shallow. He rested his forehead on crossed
arms and brooded about past times and hardship. Soon his
thoughts grew disordered and oddly textured, his dreams flavoured with memories of the revolution, when he had served

as an indentured cook for Pancho Villa's army of the north, an experience that had left him with three missing toes and a hatred for conflict in all its festering variations.

He came awake to the sound of boots angrily striking the steps leading up to his office. They grew louder and louder, culminating in the hacendero's presence in his doorway. Judging by the red tint of his complexion and the stiffness of his carriage, he was not paying a pleasure call.

— Miguel, said the hacendero. — It's this damn tower.

The mayor sighed. — What about it, Antonio?

— The signal is so strong it's broadcasting through anything metal. Fencing wire, wrought iron, anything. I was walking past the cemetery the other day and voices started talking to me from the cross topping a gravestone. I thought the dead had come alive.

— I know. It's an unforeseen bother.

— Well, it's driving my horse crazy. Do you have any idea how much I paid for Diamante? Do you have any idea how much Diamante is *worth*?

— What can I do about it?

The hacendero approached the mayor's desk and planted his knuckles on the surface that ordinarily supported the mayor's coffee cup and newspaper.

— You can talk to your amigo Brinkley and tell him to turn the thing down.

— Antonio, he's hardly a friend.

— You know him better than anyone in this town.

— That's not true, there's Violeta . . .

— Miguel! Don't dodge the issue.

The hacendero strode off, his lizard-skin boots striking

the floorboards as noisily as they had on the way in. The mayor thought about knocking off early and heading to the cantina, where, with any luck, he'd locate peace, quiet, and a frothy mug of cerveza. He was just about to leave when, once again, he heard footfalls on the steps leading up to his office. A few seconds later, Francisco Ramirez was standing in his doorway, looking aggrieved and more than a little dusty.

— Hola, Señor Orozco.

— Hola, Francisco. What can I do for you?

— Earlier today I went to the other side.

— Really? This is getting to be a strange habit of yours. Crossing the bridge, only to come back in a couple of hours? Most people stay awhile. What took you there this time?

— The Del Río library, Don Miguel. I have something to show you.

Had Francisco not been wearing such a bitter expression, Miguel might have laughed out loud — Dios mío, primo. You really do march to your own drummer. You went to the Del Río library? I didn't even know they had one. I thought the closest one was in San Antonio.

Francisco ignored the mayor's facetiousness.

— I had a hunch about something.

— All right, joven. Let's hear it.

Francisco stepped towards the mayor's desk and reached into the inner pocket of his jacket. He extracted a folded piece of paper.

— It's all right here, said Francisco.

— What is, joven?

— *This*, said Francisco, methodically unfolding the paper and placing it on Miguel's desk.

— It's from the *Fort Worth Chronicle*. I waited until a fat man coughed, and then I tore it out.

The mayor regarded the sheet. Surrounded by an ad for an upcoming rodeo was a photograph of none other than John Romulus Brinkley. Miguel read haltingly. Though the bulk of the vocabulary was beyond him, he understood that the write-up was less than favourable.

— Ay, Francisco, you teach English, not me. Could you give me the gist?

— It's an editorial complaining about medicine in Texas. It's saying that the State of Texas should join the American Medical Association to keep out all the cheats and frauds. It's an article, Don Miguel, in which the writer uses *this* man as proof of his argument.

Francisco leaned over and poked Brinkley's forehead, the sweat of his fingertip causing the ink in the photograph to smudge slightly. Francisco was now breathing hard with indignation.

— People are complaining over there. They're saying his operation is a fake. The tax people are looking into him too . . .

The mayor felt a sudden foreboding. For some reason he'd never noticed how odd Brinkley's smile was, an irritating blend of cheerfulness and utter pomposity.

— All right, Francisco. All right. I'll see what I can do.

— Do you promise, Don Miguel?

— Hijo, said the mayor. — I might not know much, but I do know enough to never make promises.

Francisco turned and left, expressing his frustration by pounding the floorboards so hard that an old framed portrait

of Benito Juárez fell off the wall, the glass shattering all over
a quarter of the mayor's office. Miguel sighed, waited a few
minutes, and was again readying to call it a day when, once
more, he heard footsteps. Unlike the previous footfalls, however, these were laboured and irregular, as if their owner was
pausing occasionally to rest. After minutes of stop-and-start
progress, Roberto Pántelas, the aging molinero, came shuffling
into the mayor's office. The mayor hurried to take his forearm.

— Ay, primo, said the molinero. — Gracias, gracias. Help
an old man take a seat. And if it's not a bother, perhaps you
have a little water?

The mayor grabbed the earthenware pitcher he kept
on his filing cabinet. He handed the molinero a glass and
said: — Roberto. You shouldn't be climbing those stairs. If
you needed to talk to me, you could have just caught up with
me on the square.

The molinero took the first in a series of deep, restorative
breaths. When his lungs had finally calmed, he said: Miguel,
how long have you been the mayor here?

— Five years.

— And how many times have I bothered you with a
complaint?

— Never.

— Then this time, indulge an old man. That radio signal is broadcasting through Laura's braces. It's making her
crazy. You and I both know if there's any girl in this town that
deserves happiness, it's her.

— Can't you just have them taken off?

— I spent all the money I had in the world to have them
put *on*. You know how much she needs them.

The mayor nodded. — I know, amigo.

— So do one thing for me, Miguel.

— Sí?

— Get that gringo to turn that thing off, and save me the trouble of crossing the river and putting a bullet in his head myself. And don't think I'm joking. I'm eighty-eight years old, so a life sentence isn't much of a deterrent. Now help me up. You don't want to get between a crusty old man and his nap time.

After helping the molinero to the front door of the town hall, the mayor returned to his desk and put his head in his hands. Clearly he had to do something. Unfortunately, he hadn't the faintest idea what that thing might be. Then it occurred to him. If nothing else, the revolution had turned México into a democracy. A democracy with only one party, it was true, and where its rivals tended to disappear just before election day, but a democracy nonetheless. Strictly speaking, a mayor's job was to represent the interests of his constituency, and he decided that he would devote the remainder of his day to discovering exactly what those interests might be.

His first stop was the store owned by the hirsute Zacatecan, Fajardo Jimenez.

— Hola, Miguel, said Fajardo.

The mayor, dispensing with niceties, asked him straight out.

— Fajardo, what do you think of this radio tower?

— The tower? Are you kidding me? Business has never been better. I'm thinking of applying for membership at the Del Río Golf and Country Club. And if they let me in, I'm going to fight for the inclusion of other Mexicanos. Ay sí, the radio station is the best thing that has ever happened to Corazón de la Fuente.

— But what about . . .

— The *best* thing, Miguel.

The mayor left and hobbled along Avenida Hidalgo towards the cantina. There he found Carlos Hernandez cleaning glasses and whistling happily. A few former tower workers were already asleep on the tabletops, snoring into pools of spilled cerveza.

The cantina owner came over to the mayor's table with a bottle. He set it down, a ring of condensation immediately forming around the base. He sat and poured two measures in glasses that could have used a wash.

— This radio station, said the mayor. — You think that maybe . . .

— Maybe? Maybe what, primo? It's the best thing that ever happened to this place.

— But what about all the filth? All the vagrants crowding the plaza?

— You're worried about a few bums on the streets?

— There's more than a few.

— I know some people. Friends of friends with pistols. Throw a few dollars their way and the streets could be clean by nightfall.

— Por favor, Carlos. Too many problems are solved that way already.

— Of course you're right, Miguel. Do you need anything else?

— Not right now.

— Well, if that changes just talk to Ernesto. In the meantime, I've got to go. I think, er, Margarita needs me . . . .

The mayor smiled and ordered a bowl of birria flavoured with drops of habanero salsa from the cantina's new bartender. He was just about to tuck in, the rich aroma of braised goat exciting his senses, when Father Alvarez marched in and sat beside the mayor. As usual, the father was in a deep gloom.

— What is it? asked the mayor, his appetite retreating.

— What is it? I'll *tell* you what it is. I was walking down the street when a weathervane topping one of the houses started talking to me. Don't smile, Miguel. It was one of those religious shows that Brinkley plays. All six-six-six and the number of the beast. I tell you, Miguel, the philistines have won. The moneylenders have conquered the temple.

The mayor sighed, his appetite now completely vanished.

— Miguel and Roberto want me to do something about the tower as well.

— Did I say I wanted you to do something about it? *Did* I? The truth is I don't care what you do, cabrón. The only thing I know is that I'm going to order a bottle of something strong from that hombre behind the counter, I'm going to take that bottle to my ugly little room, and I'm going to drink until I'm no longer conscious. Have a good day, Miguel.

Father Alvarez did just what he'd promised, and left. The mayor, beginning to sulk a little himself, ordered the first of several cervezas. Over the following two hours he talked to everyone who came by about the radio tower. Public opinion, he found, was pretty much split in half. Those who benefited from the tower wanted it to stay, while those who didn't benefit from the tower wanted it gone. *And what about you?*

the mayor asked himself once his third cerveza had started to make him feel reflective. *Why are you the only one who can see both sides of the story? Why is it you're the one who always has to sit on the proverbial fence?*

He finally stood and headed for the swinging doors. There was no way around it: he was going to have to petition Corazón's most important businessperson. He took a deep breath, shook some feeling into the less effective of his two feet, and clomped down a side street filled with dogs and gold-toothed crooks and saggy-breasted putas and toothless old women selling bunches of dried epazote. He emerged on Avenida Cinco de Mayo, turned left, and walked past the queue that now extended at all hours of the day and night from the front doors of Madam Félix's.

The mayor shouldered his way along. As he approached the front door, the men at the front of the line began to worry that he was trying to butt in.

— I'm the mayor! Miguel protested. — And I must speak with Madam Félix!

— No speeky the Spanish, said a large gringo at the front of the line. — Go back to México . . .

— I *am* in México, said the mayor in English. — And you're in *my* country, pendejo.

The gringo's face turned the light red of a dwindling sun. Having remembered that he really was in México, he resented having been made a fool of by the limping foreigner standing before him. He shoved the mayor hard on both shoulders. Miguel landed in earth muddied by a thousand pairs of snake-leather boots and lay looking up at the white-blue sky, wondering what in the name of Jesús he had done to deserve this.

Just then a pair of Marias emerged from the house to take a breath of fresh air. Upon seeing the downed mayor, they screamed and ran towards him.

— Get away! they both yelled. — Get away from heem! Anyone who touching heem no getting in the casa!

The men backed away, fearful they'd be sent to the back of the line. The two Marias kneeled and looked into the mayor's beleaguered eyes. He, in turn, looked up into theirs. Though it was difficult to keep all of the Marias straight — it seemed that new ones were arriving every day — he was relatively sure that his rescuers were Maria del Mar and Maria de la Mañana. Both, he thought, were the most beautiful creatures he had ever seen.

— I'm fine, he assured them.

They each took an arm and lifted him to his feet. The client who had knocked down Miguel now bent over and picked up the mayor's hat. Sheepishly, he handed it to Maria del Mar, and then backed submissively into line.

— Why are you here? asked Maria del Mar. — Are you feeling lonely? I could attend to you myself, if you'd like . . .

— Ay no, said Miguel. — From a Maria as lovely as you, I couldn't afford a handshake. But thank you anyway. I need to speak with Madam. Would you happen to know if she is free?

— For you I'm sure she will take a break from whatever she is doing. Come in. Por favor, come in, it's this way.

He followed the two Marias around the side of the house and entered via a door at the back of the brothel. The mayor stepped into a velvety, red-tinged gloom. He could smell strong tobacco and lanolin. As he moved along a hallway lit by red lamplight he felt a strong transgressive thrill — despite having known Madam Félix for years, he had never actually set foot in her House of Gentlemanly Pleasures. He heard moans, and the percussive sound made by thin brown hands slapping flesh. From beyond a beaded curtain he heard a gringo client call out *Maria, I love you, my wife doesn't understand me* . . .

Maria del Mar and Maria de la Mañana stopped before an imposing mesquite door. Maria del Mar rapped lightly with one knuckle. She waited a few seconds and then rapped again.

— Qué? was the response.

— Madam! Maria del Mar called through the door. — I have the mayor here.

There was a moment of silence. — Miguel? Miguel Orozco is here?

— Sí, Madam.

— Ay, qué bueno! What a surprise! Just give me a second.

Maria del Mar smiled at the mayor and rocked on her feet. A half-minute passed before the door opened. Madam was wearing a long jade-coloured silk gown. Her feet were in lamé slippers and her hair was gathered atop her head and held in place by a tiara that, the mayor suspected, sparkled with actual diamonds. As always, she looked resplendent.

— Miguel! she said, cupping his right hand in both of hers. — What a pleasure!

She motioned him towards the heavy wooden chair opposite her desk. As the mayor took a seat she regained her position behind her massive oak desk. Madam then lit a cigarillo and offered one to her guest, who gladly accepted. The smoke tasted of almonds, and it was about as harsh as chiffon cake.

— It's delicious, he said. — Gracias.

— So. To what do I owe this pleasure?

He paused, searching for the right words. — It's the town, Madam. Obviously you have noticed. The plaza crowded with the homeless, the skies lighting up green all night long, petty crime on the rise. And it is true that you can't get away from the signal. People are complaining. They are saying it's unnatural, music coming from their cutlery drawers. They want me to . . . they want me to talk to the doctor. They want me to ask him to lower the wattage. Some want me to kick him out altogether.

— You could do this?

— I suppose I could try.

Madam smoked and looked thoughtful.

— Let me explain something, Miguel. Since the radio station started advertising Dr. Brinkley's procedure, my business has gone up three hundred percent. Yes, you heard me right. Already I've had to hire five new Marias, and I've got another two on the way. This means that there are seven more families living in Oaxaca and Chiapas and Michoacán who now have enough to eat, who can now afford school fees for their children, and who now wear actual clothes instead of old cut-open malva sacks. You're originally from the south, so you understand that this is no small thing. Just the other day, Maria del Alma told me that with all the money Maria has sent her, her mother has opened a beauty salon. Before, the woman spent all day worrying about survival. Now she spends her days cutting hair and filing nails. Plus, she now gives most of the money Maria sends her to her brother in San Luis Potosí. Now his family is eating and wearing real clothes, and his children can afford such luxuries as pencils and notepaper. What the radio station has done is provide a step-up for families all over México, and that step-up in turn provides for other families. The gringos call this economics. You must think of this before you talk to Dr. Brinkley.

— But what about the disorder that has come with it, Madam? Our town is no longer safe. There are reports of ornaments being stolen off graves in our cemetery. Last night thieves broke into my office . . .

— It's temporary. A necessary evil. You can use our business taxes to start a police force.

— But we don't collect business taxes. We don't collect taxes of any kind. It never seemed worth the trouble.

— So *start*, countered Madam. — I can afford it, as can the cantina owner. And that hairy Zacatecan who runs the town store is practically a millionaire. With all the money in Corazón, other businesses will start up soon enough, and then you can collect taxes from them as well. I've heard that a restaurant is going to open next month near the Pozo de Confesiones, and I've heard talk of a muchacho who wants to set up a barber shop right on the plaza.

— I've heard the talk as well.

— *Miguel*. It's called free enterprise. Pretty soon you'll be able to pay yourself a good salary, and nobody deserves it more than you. Let me put it this way. Yes, I am prospering, thanks to Brinkley's station. And as I expand, I'll need to buy furniture, and mattresses, and red light bulbs, and brandy, and pretty soon I won't have to travel to los Estados Unidos to do it. I'll be able to buy them all here, in Corazón de la Fuente. *That*, Miguel, is progress.

The mayor left feeling buoyed, if only because Madam had convinced him that the best thing he could do was adopt a wait-and-see attitude. It was a sensation that abated the moment he stepped into the street. At five in the afternoon it was so loud with barking curs and arguing putas and lolling drunkards and caterwauling babies that he could barely hear himself think. Brinkley's tower, once such a pristine architectural marvel, now loomed over several dozen homeless families living beneath it, its girders stained with charcoal smoke, its three mighty legs spanned by dirty laundry. As he passed the lineup leading to Madam Félix's door, one of her prospective clients called out *Hey, look at the crippled wetback*, a comment that neatly exemplified the vulgarity that had settled on his poor, humble town on the border.

{23}

SADLY, THE SEVENTEENTH BIRTHDAY OF FRANCISCO
Ramirez coincided with the arrival of a rumour. It seemed
that a certain young muchacha, known equally for her studiousness and her beauty, was spending an unusual amount of
time with a certain wealthy doctor, who of course would also
remain nameless, and that this particular muchacha had been
spotted coming back across the bridge in the small hours, by
chauffeured limousine no less, and this late return had caused
friction between this nameless young woman and her anxious, lye-scented mother, their shouting having caused the
stray dogs in the neighbouring alleyway to start howling like
pin-stuck banshees.

Though no one was cruel enough to pass these rumours
directly to Francisco, the town was small, and some of the
older gossips were hard of hearing and had a tendency to raise
their voices when speaking. Even if Francisco hadn't heard
the news reverberating off pale blue adobe walls, it wouldn't
have mattered. He had known far in advance of the inevitable

suppositions, had known just from the guilt-marred gleam in Violeta's eyes. To make matters worse, it was clear to him that the mayor was going to do nothing, not one thing, about Brinkley's presence in their once peaceful town. This frustrated him so badly that he now spent much of his sleepless nights trying to concoct a way to ruin Brinkley and not spend the rest of his life behind gringo bars.

And so, on his birthday, Francisco made one request and one request only. He was in no mood for celebration. If the family could keep the festivities to a bare minimum he would appreciate it.

He did not get this wish. Francisco's nearsighted grandmother believed that he needed a diversion, so she took it upon herself to create his favourite meal: pimientos stuffed with ground beef and raisins, served with a salsa blanca, a salsa roja, and a salsa verde (the dish, originally created to commemorate México's ejection of the Spanish, recreated the colours of the country's flag). To accompany this she made pot beans dressed with epazote and cheese, and a rice whose grains had been left to roast over a low pinewood flame before the addition of stock. To stimulate the appetite she made tacos al pastor, and for dessert she made a chocolate birthday cake seasoned with chiles and a dusting of ground sugared pumpkin seeds. As with most traditional Mexican meals, it was nothing if not labour-intensive. She was up with the dawn, toasting the almonds for the salsa blanca, and was hard at work until dusk, at which point she began complaining that her bunions were sore.

With his heart so heavy that it compressed his stomach, Francisco could barely eat. Every mouthful tasted like paste, and no matter how much he chewed each bite, the food aggravated the lump he now carried at all times in the centre of his throat. Though the antics of his brothers saved the fiesta from being a completely solemn affair, the birthday boy nonetheless grew despairing during the presentation of the chocolate cake, which was accompanied by the requisite singing of "Feliz Cumpleaños." On that day the lyrics of the song seemed cruelly ironic, it being obvious to Francisco that, without Violeta's love, he could very well go through the whole of his life without ever again knowing what happiness felt like.

When the meal was over and the dishes cleared away, Francisco noted that his father was peering at him with a mixture of pride, empathy, and, if Francisco wasn't mistaken, impishness.

— Ready, mijo?

— Ready?

— Sí. Get your jacket.

Father and son walked through the streets of Corazón de la Fuente. Each had a tall, sturdy frame and a deliberate stride, and it was obvious to anyone who didn't know them that the two men shared the same lineage. All around were families cooking meals over low, smouldering fires, and as they walked they were approached by a dozen beggars, all trying to sell them Chiclets. Francisco the elder bought a few packets and then waved the rest away.

— Francisco, he said to his boy. — I would like to talk to you about Violeta.

Francisco sighed.

— Mijo. I know that you love her because, like you, she

has a certain solitary, pensive nature. Of course, there is also her extreme beauty.

— Sí, papi.

— Yet she also has an unattainable quality. Did it ever occur to you that maybe it is precisely this quality that you find irresistible?

— I don't understand.

— Francisco. Your mother died of typhus when you were ten years of age.

The two men walked in silence for a few strides. When Francisco Senior again spoke, his voice was rendered shaky by sadness. — I wonder if your concept of love for a woman is a love that cannot be returned. Could it be that you yearn for the type of love that you have for Violeta because it feels like something you know too well already? Because it feels like something you've known since you were a boy?

The two men stopped and faced one another.

— Mijo, added the older Francisco. — We Ramirezes are faithful men. Loyalty runs through our veins as surely as blood. Once our affections are stirred, nothing will dim them. That is the reason I have yet to so much as glance at another woman. It is both our curse and our noblest feature.

Francisco now saw that his father had led him to the door of Carlos Hernandez's cantina. Confused, he returned his gaze to his father's slender face.

— Hijo. Today you have reached seventeen years of age. It is my greatest wish that you have a drink of tequila with me.

Francisco was hit by a wave of emotion so fierce that, had it not been for the rules governing the behaviour of men, he might have permitted his eyes to mist. Instead he straightened, appreciating what his father had managed to do: momentarily replace his heartache with a moment far more significant.

— Of course, he managed.

Things were slow in the cantina. Now that the locals had run out of tower money, most of Carlos Hernandez's business was conducted via the back door, through which he sold measures of pulque to anyone with a few centavos and a valorous liver. Hearing the saloon door swing open, the cantina owner, who was reading a newspaper at the bar, looked up.

— Well, look at that, he said. — A pair of Franciscos! To what do I owe the pleasure?

— Hola, Carlos, said Francisco Senior. — I believe you know my son.

— Of course. Hola, Francisco.

— What you may not know is that it is his seventeenth birthday today, and I would like to commemorate the occasion with the finest tequila that you have in the house.

— Be careful when you say that! I have a few very good bottles that I keep on hand for when the hacendero comes in. And as you know, he has expensive tastes.

— I understand that, primo. I have been preparing for this day for quite a while.

— Well, in that case, welcome.

The cantina owner reached below the bar and fumbled around for a few seconds. When he straightened, he held a bottle half-filled with amber liquid.

— One hundred percent agave, and the best that the grand state of Jalisco has to offer. I tell you what, Francisco. I'm in the mood for a drink myself. If you will tolerate my company, we'll call it my gift to the young man.

During the ensuing ten-minute discussion, in which Carlos Hernandez and Francisco Ramirez Senior argued over who would pay for the tequila, Francisco looked around, noting the ways in which the room matched the one he'd conjured a thousand times in his imagination: the rings on the tabletops, the bullet holes in the ceiling, the dull, settled-in scent of smoke. There were still charred marks on the wide-planked floor, a souvenir from the night in which a unit of Villistas had set the place on fire. As with all Mexican cantinas that served only men, the pissoir was in the main room, attached to the west-facing wall. Even Carlos's wife, the previously cheerless Margarita Hernandez, was said to enter the family business only during times of extreme necessity.

A compromise was eventually reached. Francisco the elder would pay for the first round, the cantina owner for the second. Carlos poured the tequila into three large snifters. When Francisco went to take a sip, his father tapped his arm and said: — Not so fast. This isn't the rotgut you and your amigos swill up at the mission. First, hold the glass up to the light and admire the colour.

Francisco lifted his glass so that it was directly between his nose and one of the kerosene lamps.

— Look closely, interjected Carlos. — Whereas you probably first thought it was simply the colour of honey, you will notice a tone of buttercup yellow around the edges, suggesting that this tequila has been aged patiently, under the most tender conditions, rendering it a colour closer to spun gold.

— Sí, said Francisco. — You're right.

— Now, said Francisco's father. — Smell it.

Expecting his nose to be singed by alcohol fumes, Francisco gave the beverage a cautious sniff.

— Ay no, said the cantina owner. — Don't be shy. It won't bite. Stick your nose right inside your glass and let its scent do the work.

Francisco did as he was told, his eyes widening with surprise. — Dios mío, he exclaimed.

— Exactamente! Now, exactly what do you smell?

Francisco sniffed again and thought hard. — Straw, he said. — And avocado.

— Cómo no? said the cantina owner.

— And cactus blossoms.

— Anything else?

— Mesquite, suggested Francisco's father. — And oregano.

— And creosote, said the cantina owner. — With a whiff of cilantro.

— And one other thing, said Francisco's father, taking another deep sniff. — Something I can't quite place.

— Sí, said Francisco. — I smell it too.

— May I give you gentlemen a hint?

— I think you might have to, Carlos.

— Perhaps a little . . . dulce de leche?

— Sí! father and son exclaimed simultaneously. — Dulce de leche!

All three lifted their glasses, taking the most reverential of sips. For Francisco, the taste was as gentle as the cool, woodsy breezes that follow a Coahuilan downpour . . . breezes that, for a short time, make you forget that México is a place of dust and hot weather.

— Mijo, said the cantina owner, contentedly twiddling his moustache. — Do you like it?

— Sí, said Francisco. — I do.

— Of course you do. It is the taste of México, captured in a glass.

Father and son stayed in the cantina for a good long time, and several more rounds of tequila. This was unfortunate. After the elating effect of the first two tequilas began to wane, Francisco Senior, hardly a drinker by nature, made an age-old mistake: he attempted to resurrect it with a third tequila, and then a fourth. By the time they were midway through their fifth, Francisco's father had begun to pine terribly for his wife. Songs she'd liked began running through his head, and he imagined he could smell her perfume mixed in with the other smells in the bar.

But the more affected was Francisco Junior, who was beginning to make an elementary discovery about amor. Just because you may understand why you love a person doesn't make that love any less potent. If anything, insight only strengthens the infatuation, as it gives it shape, a reason for being, and proof of its existence. It was a little like seeing a phantasm for the first time: what used to be an ephemeral belief is transformed into fact. He began to recall the feel of Violeta's lips on his own, and the way his heart thrummed every time he was in her presence. Simultaneously the room began to rotate, inspiring a turbulence in his stomach that was not at all pleasant.

Francisco excused himself. Walking unsteadily, he went

outside and found a path to the desert behind the cantina, where the sound of his retching soon mixed with the whir of car engines. It was a Saturday night, and even as Francisco lost the birthday meal he hadn't wanted in the first place, gringos were streaming across the narrow bridge between nations, following the brilliant green corona as determinedly as bees in a quest for honey.

One of these was a Texan named Edward Phillips, who had driven over that night in a Chevrolet the size of a small yacht. He had undergone the Compound Operation four days earlier and was eager to test the efficacy of the procedure. Following a team of grubby-faced children to the House of Gentlemanly Pleasures, he left his vehicle in the car park that Madam now operated in a stretch of desert west of the radio tower. He tipped the children, paused to admire the green hues rippling through the sky, and joined the lineup of men leading to the brothel's door. In the queue, Edward Phillips steadied his nerves by drinking cans of Moctezuma beer, purchased from a campesino who referred to him as *meester*.

Finally he gained entrance to Madam Félix's infamous bordello. He was shown to the waiting room, where he drank a pair of tequilas in quick succession and smoked an above-average Cohiba. He was then invited to the room of Maria del Alma, who attended to him in such a way that his fingertips blazed and his heart palpitated and his mind erupted with colour. After, he was shown back to the waiting room, where he decided to toast the success of the Compound Operation with another tequila. With his blood thus enriched, he asked for another go, and was ushered this time to the chamber of Maria de la Noche, who introduced him to pleasures so profoundly diabolical he decided, in mid-act no less, to devote the rest of his life to hedonistic pursuits.

This was no small moment in the life of Edward Phillips. Until that moment he had made his living as a small-town pastor, and had dedicated his life to a certain austerity of the flesh. To celebrate his decision to spend eternity in hell, he elected to enjoy yet another tequila before getting behind the wheel of his car, his level of inebriation such that he forgot to turn on his headlights. He swerved through the darkened streets of Corazón de la Fuente, his side mirror casually glancing against adobe facings. After a minute or two he realized that he was lost. He responded by using the Lord's name in vain, laughing giddily at his own heresy, and speeding up. In so doing, he unwittingly cruised away from the bridge leading to his own country, instead of towards it. This mistake inspired a small degree of panic.

By the time he reached the plaza containing the Pozo de Confesiones, he was moving at forty-five miles per hour. Furthermore, he was still badly distracted by thoughts of carnality and sin and the new life he had pledged to pursue. Or, failing that, he figured he would indulge his newly debauched self whenever he was on Mexican soil, a strategy employed by legions of family men who had confessed their sins to him over the years. Edward Phillips chortled. *If you can't beat 'em*, he thought, *you might as well join 'em*, for truth be told there were things about his life on the other side that he wouldn't mind hanging on to, foremost among them being his wife's peach melba, decent golf courses, and the shining faces of his children.

Unfortunately, he was so preoccupied by the theological debate now raging within him (asceticism versus experience;

contemplative pleasures versus pleasures of the flesh; knowledge of things godly versus a surrender to things earthly)
that he didn't notice that a thin young girl with a twisting of
metal in her mouth was, at that exact moment, stepping into
the lane in front of him. He also didn't know that her name
was Laura Velasquez, that she was engaged to an eighty-
eight-year-old molinero named Roberto Pántelas, or that
she'd decided that a walk might take her mind off the fiddle
music ceaselessly transmitting through her braces. As his
headlights were off, he also couldn't see that the poor girl was
caressing both temples, and had entered the sort of dismayed,
self-contained world often caused by low-grade suffering. He
did, however, spot her at the very last moment, her face lit by
fear, her hands held aloft in useless defence, at which point he
was upon her.

There was a scream, though what followed was far more
chilling   the sudden cessation of that scream. Phillips, wanting only to escape the Mexican police, sped away. Those within
earshot came running from their homes dressed in night-
clothes and slippers. Among them was the molinero, who,
given the slowness with which he moved, was among the last
to reach the scene. But once he did, the crowd parted to let him
through. He approached his beloved and slowly worked his
way to his knees. He embraced her rag-doll body. Upon hearing her attempt to speak, he put his ear to her mouth.

— Mi amor, she whispered. — Forgive me.

— Forgive you? he whispered.

— I should have been more careful . . .

Laura took a final, shuddering breath and, in that weighted
moment, quit the terrain of the living. The molinero opened

his mouth to moan, his anguish preventing the issuance of sound. Tears flowed from his old eyes, forming twin streams over snow-white stubble, until one rolled off his chin and landed on Laura's reddening blouse. He buried his face in her neck, his rickety spine arched against chambray. *Oh, my Laurita*, he finally managed, *not you. Not you, not you not you not you.*

His words came in the same rhythm as the rocking of his body, a sight so disturbingly sad that many of the onlookers began to weep themselves, for they all understood that they had just witnessed the termination of not one life, but two.

{24}

TWO DAYS LATER, FRANCISCO AWOKE IN HIS SHARED
bedroom. The last residue of his hangover was finally gone,
his distress now emotional rather than physical. He dressed in
the same formal outfit in which he'd first visited Malfil Cruz,
and he ate breakfast with his father and grandmother, both of
whom were also dressed for Laura Velasquez's funeral. They
ate in silence, the only sound the scraping of cutlery against
metal plates.

When they were finished with their hotcakes, Francisco's
father said to his son: — Would you like me to come with
you?

— No, papi.

— Pues . . . if you need any help, just come and get me.

Francisco pulled his hat over his eyes and stepped into
the laneway fronting his house. As he walked towards the
molinero's, he watched the homeless arise, stretch, kiss their
children awake, and make low twig fires. The streets were
redolent with the smell of tortilla and burning wood. Chatter

spilled from doors opened to the day's rising heat, the topic of conversation always the same: the tower had taken the life of Laura Velasquez.

Francisco was just approaching the town's smaller plaza when he heard an odd sound. He stopped, listened carefully, and heard it again: it was a little like the noise made by air escaping from a punctured tire. This time, the sound persisted long enough that he was able to identify the direction from which it came. He turned and faced the darkened entranceway of a small home that had been abandoned during the revolution and left to become the domicile of a family of bats.

Pssst he heard yet again.

The curandera, looking as wrinkled as an avocado left too long in the sun, was standing on a doorstep messy with guano and sawdust. She was perhaps five feet tall, had unclipped hairs sprouting from her chin, and wore a Kickapoo amulet around her neck. She was peering at Francisco so unnaturally that he instinctively started, even though he considered the rumours regarding the woman's satanic abilities to be the fodder of nitwits.

He cleared his throat. — Hola, señora, he said.

The curandera coughed and continued to peer at Francisco through the eye not entirely coated in a milky film. — You're Francisco Ramirez.

— I am, he answered.

— That's good, she croaked. — That's good.

— What's good, señora?

— I was hoping it would be someone I could trust. I was hoping it would be someone who could get the job done.

Francisco was surprised to find that his heart was beating irregularly and that his palms suddenly felt clammy, as though he had just wrapped them around a length of cool pipe.

— I promise you, he said. — I haven't got a clue what you're talking about.

She chortled, revealing peggy, yellowing teeth separated by dark spaces.

— *You*, she said. — It's going to be *you*. Yesterday I saw your face. Lifting in the smoke of my fire. That's how I knew. That's how I *know*.

Francisco swallowed dryly and struggled to contain his breathing.

— You're speaking in riddles, señora. And I can't say I like it.

The old woman said nothing, preferring to gaze at Francisco with a delight that seemed mildly fiendish. Finally, she cleared her throat and spat so forcefully into the street that a puff of dust rose towards her shins.

— Good day, Francisco Ramirez. You know where to find me.

She ducked into the gloom of the ruined house, melting into the shadow of its interior. A second after that, he could hear only the flapping of bat wings and his own speeding thoughts.

Francisco straightened and continued walking towards the house of the molinero. He forced himself to chuckle. Clearly, the old woman was unbalanced, and capable of only the most deluded gibberish. A moment later his mirth evaporated and a chill ran through him. He remembered that on the day when Radio XER had gone on the air, the curandera had stepped forward and proclaimed that this Dr. Brinkley was a fraud, and would harm the town. Though Francisco had jeered along with everyone else, it was also true that the fleetest of thoughts had run through his mind. It had been an uncomfortable thought, and Francisco had naturally chased it away before it could take root and spur action. Yet now, walking towards his heartbroken old friend, that thought returned to him. This time it refused to be banished so easily.

The old woman knows something.

Combatting the onset of a headache, Francisco Ramirez reached the plazita containing the old well. The confusion caused by the curandera's appearance was replaced by anger. He shook his head in disgust. Broken bottles were strewn around the plazita, and the gutters were clogged with every sort of refuse. A spent and razored brassiere hung from a denuded palo verde. Worse, the Pozo de Confesiones was now clearly being used as a toilet by those living rough on the streets, such that its clammy depths could no longer offer succour to those feeling guilty in thought or action.

He knocked on the molinero's wood-plank door. When there was no answer, he checked to see if the door was unlocked. He walked in and found the old man seated, shirtless, on the edge of his bed. Francisco's first observation was how slight the molinero had grown with age; Francisco was old enough to remember the days when Roberto Pántelas, still in his seventies, had been as big around the chest as the hacendero. Now Francisco could count each one of the molinero's ribs, protruding through papery, bluish skin. With each breath, the old man wheezed.

Francisco sat beside his ancient friend, the straw mattress rustling and growing thin beneath his weight. He waited, saying nothing, wishing to touch the molinero but not feeling it was his place. The only thing he could give the molinero on this terrible morning was his nearness.

— Joven, the old man finally said, his voice so weak that Francisco had to struggle to hear it.

— Sí?

— Why is it that you and I are such close amigos, do you think?

— I don't know.

— I do. You have an old soul, whereas I am simply old. This gives us a lot to talk about.

Under any other circumstances, Francisco would have chuckled.

— Señor Pántelas, if you are feeling poorly I can tell the others that you . . .

— No, said the molinero. — No.

Francisco helped comb the old man's hair. He helped him brush his teeth with baking soda, and he applied a polish made from beeswax and lard to his creased leather boots. As he did so, Francisco felt a crushing sadness for his old compadre. Overnight, it seemed, grief had caused the years to catch up with the molinero, rendering him shaky and weak. Francisco went to the molinero's closet, which was neatly arranged, thanks to Laura, and pulled out a suit for him to wear. It was only when he was helping the molinero button his shirt that he noticed the hard, veinless lump in the middle of his chest.

— Señor, said Francisco. — What is that?

— It's nothing, the old man answered with an exhausted wave. — I've had it for years. Besides, who cares anyway? Now let's go.

Francisco held the old man's forearm as they walked along Avenida Hidalgo towards the town cemetery, which had the distinction of being the burial place of the infant grand-niece of Venustíano Carranza, the revolution's second interim president — her little coffin, it was said, had been no bigger than a hat box. They walked along a dusty path that wound through the gravestones, the molinero growing shakier and shakier as they approached the newly dug grave.

Francisco refused to let go of him, saying: — It's all right, my old friend. If you fall I will catch you.

Much of the town had turned out, the mourners including the mayor, the hacendero, and the hirsute store owner, Fajardo Jimenez. The cantina owner and his wife were there as well, though those with keen powers of observation noted that a tension seemed to have re-arisen between the two, for the couple were neither speaking nor holding hands. Meanwhile, the victim's parents were learning of the savage, incoherent pain caused by outliving one's child.

The molinero too was beginning to look as though he'd been transported to a world of eternal punishment. His eyes, having drained themselves a hundred times over in the past thirty-six hours, refused to produce tears, causing them to redden and burn. He began to tremble and to whimper piteously. Francisco firmed his grip on the old man's arm. The hacendero saw this and came over to take the other arm. In this way the molinero managed to remain on his feet.

Malfil and Violeta Cruz were there as well, though Francisco forced himself not to look in Violeta's direction, for fear that his anger and frustration might choose that inopportune moment to erupt. Madam Félix, meanwhile, looked resplendent in Castilian funeral garb — even her unused handkerchief was fashioned from black cotton lace. All of the Marias were in attendance as well, none crying more vociferously than Maria del Mampo, whose prominent larynx bobbed like a yo-yo as she wept. The curandera stood far off, beneath the speckled shade of a mesquite tree; there she muttered to herself while performing some sort of twisting motion with a handful of fireweed. Francisco commanded himself not to look in her direction either, as he was still feeling unnerved by their encounter.

They all waited. From somewhere nearby, the signal of Brinkley's damnable radio station could be heard, and they all knew that silencing it would involve far more than searching for whatever radio had been accidentally left on. There were a few uncomfortable coughs, and above, the wafting of vultures. The spear like shadow thrown by the radio tower mocked them.

When the citizens of Corazón de la Fuente heard boot steps they looked up, thankful that Father Alvarez, after much pleading by the village faithful, had agreed to preside over Laura's funeral. He was, however, still dressed in secular garb, his hands notably — some would say bitterly — free of Bible, cross, or rosary.

The sky was bleached white. There was a dry, unpleasant wind. The whole world smelled of corn husks and wood. The Father's voice wavered with a sorrow not in any way feigned.

— Ashes to ashes, polvo al polvo . . .

As Alvarez spoke, the hacendero kept taking quick, flitting glances at Madam Félix. Even in mourning, he thought, she was as proud and noble as any woman he had ever known. *Life is so, so short*, he thought. *I've been a fool to have kept my feelings a secret for so long.* He lowered his eyes to Laura Velasquez's grave; the poor girl was in a closed plank coffin with a cross carved into the top. Though her death was tragic, it was a sobering reality that every person here would one day share Laurita's fate. The only difference would be in the details.

The hacendero returned his attention to the outdoor service, which was coming to a close.

— And so we say to you, O Lord, may your child Laura Velasquez slumber in peace, for she sleeps in the eternal grace of your kingdom.

There was a long, melancholy pause, during which the circular nature of life became, for just a few moments, poignant and obvious. After a while four campesinos appeared with rusting shovels, which they used to shovel dirt into the grave. When the first clod of dirt hit Laura's casket, her mother wailed and fell to her knees, clawing the earth like a madwoman. After a few minutes, a few local women, including the cantina owner's wife, pulled her away.

Just then the mayor, the cantina owner, and Father Alvarez moved into the hacendero's field of vision.

— We're going for a drink, said the cantina owner. — You will join us?

— Maybe. I don't know.

They nodded and grimly walked off. Malfil and Violeta Cruz drifted back towards the town, though they did so with a noticeable distance between them. The molinero stood at the edge of the newly filled grave, his lower lip trembling, refusing to let Francisco Ramirez take him home. Seeing this, the hacendero felt his heart thud with both the wonder and the pain that come from being alive. He turned and noticed that Madam Félix was still in attendance. The hacendero filled his lungs and, in full view of those left, walked up to his amor.

— Hello, señora.

— Señor Garcia, she said, with practised formality.

— I was wondering if I may have the pleasure of escorting you back to your place of business.

The ensuing silence was total. The town's crows stopped cawing, the wind stopped rustling branches, the cries of Laura Velasquez's mother were muted. Madam peered up at him, amazed by this public proposal. — Claro que sí, she said in a quavering voice.

The hacendero held out his arm and she took it. He then walked with her along the path connecting the cemetery with the rest of the town.

— I have missed you, he said. — With everything that's been going on, I've been too busy to visit.

— I've missed you too. How is Diamante?

— I hired the Reyes brothers to replace his metal fence with one made of wood. It's about as straight as a drunkard's path but at least it's built. Time will tell. I am hopeful. I have to be.

— It's all so sad. Poor Laura.

— Poor molinero.

They reached Avenida Hidalgo. Heads turned, though not as many as once would have — there were so many newcomers who knew nothing of the not-so-secret history between the town's hacendero and the town's brothel owner. Again the hacendero felt stupid. Imagine, hiding his feelings for all these years. And why? Madam's profession? His reputation as an aristocrat? *Ay, cabrón,* he thought. *This isn't España. Here, different things matter. Here, different rules apply.*

He could feel the warmth of her hand transmit into his elbow. They reached Avenida de Cinco de Mayo, where the lineup to the House of Gentlemanly Pleasures was already halfway down the block. Madam unlocked the rear door and led the hacendero to her boudoir, where they made the sort of slow, gentle amor that arises only from the experience of sorrow — while not deliriously pleasurable, it leaves in its wake a gratifying comfort, and a strengthening of one's ability to tolerate the immense profundity that is life. They both lay on their backs and lit thin, fragrant cigarillos. Coils of blue-green smoke drifted towards the ceiling. A long time passed, during which they linked fingers and felt tired.

Finally the hacendero spoke. — I was talking to Miguel before the funeral. He assured me he's going to speak to the gringo tomorrow.

Madam took a long, luxurious puff. — Which gringo?

— Well, Brinkley, of course.

— Brinkley? The mayor's going to talk to Brinkley?

— Sí.

The madam lifted herself to her elbows and then turned on her side. The hacendero continued to lie in a state of half-sleep, his eyes closed, his breathing heavy. For a moment she said nothing, instead admiring the handsomeness of his features — those high cheekbones, that prominent jawline, his long, boyish lashes. She ran a finger over his lips, causing him to smile gently.

— Hmmm, she said. — I told him not to. I'll have. to remind him.

The hacendero's eyes slowly opened and he looked dreamily at the woman who was no longer his secret love.

— It's funny, he said, — but I thought I heard you just say that you were going to stop the mayor from talking to Brinkley.

Her voice was still smoky with the delight caused by the intimacy between a man and a woman. — I did say that, silly.

The hacendero raised himself to his elbows, bringing him to the same level as Madam. As she played with the thicket of hair on his chest, he looked at her, not quite understanding what he was hearing.

— Mi amor, you have to agree that the tower has to go. You have to agree that this was the last straw.

She stopped running her fingertip over the hacendero's chest, and a slight sharpness invaded her voice. — Has to go? I have five more Marias coming in from the countryside. That's five more campesino families who are depending on me. I *need* that station, to create more customers.

— You want *more* customers?

— Of course I do. I am in business. Why wouldn't I?

The hacendero blinked and felt his mouth turn dry. — I'd just assumed, given what happened to Laura Valasquez, that you'd changed your mind.

— Well, I'm afraid you assumed wrong, guapo.

— But even you can see the changes that have come to this town.

Madam sat up straight. — I see some growing pains that the mayor, if he wasn't so ineffectual, could deal with easily. And what, by the way, do you mean by *even you*? Eh, hacendero?

— I simply meant that . . .

— Oh no, out with it, cabrón. What exactly did you mean?

The hacendero noticed that he was breathing hard and that the sides of his face felt warm. He couldn't believe it. The town was now so united in its hatred for the radio tower that he'd naturally assumed Madam had changed her position as well. This continuing support was madness, plain and simple. And yet, if he was honest with himself, the thing that bothered him most was the discomfiting fact that Madam Félix, his mujer, was daring to disagree so totally and unashamedly with him, an hombre. When he next spoke, his words were no longer informed by reason or intelligence, but instead by the flames of an ancient machismo.

— I meant that you are acting like a puta.

Madam screamed and buried her face in her hands, where her tears mixed with mascara and ran down her cheeks like thin, muddy blood. The hacendero got out of bed. He was attempting to pull on his trousers just as Madam grabbed the heavy onyx ashtray from the table next to her. He was just getting his second leg into his pants when she hurled it with the might of six men. It clipped the hacendero on the side of the face. He fell, kicking, and the next thing he knew she was on top of him, weeping and slapping at him and calling him an hijo de puta and saying, over and over *I knew it would come out! I knew all along what you really thought of me! I knew it I knew it I knew it!*

He grabbed her by the upper arms and threw her off. She fell, weeping hysterically, not just for the hacendero but for other severe torments she'd known in her life, all of which were choosing that moment to spring upon her. The hacendero finished pulling on his boots, shirt, and waistcoat and stormed out of the bedroom. As he charged down the hallway, he saw pair after pair of decorated eyes peering from partially opened doors. It was only when he reached the street and was met by dozens of frank stares that he realized his right eye was beginning to swell, and that he was bleeding from the spot where the ashtray had made contact with his cheekbone. He lowered his hat so that his broad face was more or less covered by the brim, and hurried along the street. When he reached his house, he was breathing heavily and feeling desperate; a minute later, his stomach was warmed by a tumbler's worth of brandy. He poured another and drank it as well. He then paced the floors of his ruined house, until he noticed that he was mumbling like a madman.

He paused before a large gilt-edged mirror that, thanks to a Villista rifleman, bore a crack running along the diagonal. He approached the mirror and looked at himself. The blood from his wound had stopped trickling and was beginning to harden against the side of his face. His right eye, he knew too well, would soon turn the indigo of a panther's coat and swell so badly that when he placed a hand over his left eye, the world would come to him in the shape of a slit.

He went to his quarters and for the next two days remained in bed, nursing himself with cigars, brandy, and the knowledge that, if worse came to worst, he still had money to buy passage back to Spain.

{25}

OVER THE NEXT FEW WEEKS, WORD SPREAD AMONG
Corazón de la Fuente's long-time residents that Madam Félix
was the only person in town who still supported the presence of Radio XER, the Sunshine Station from Between the
Nations. Word also spread that Madam and the hacendero
had not only severed their long-standing love affair, but had
chosen to do so less than an hour after finally admitting to the
rest of the village that it actually existed. Rumour also had it
that the couple had separated because of differing opinions
regarding the tower. This meant one thing: the radio tower,
having ruined the public spaces of Corazón de la Fuente, was
now reaching into the lives, the hearts, and, perhaps most significantly, the bedrooms of its people.

Madam had lived side by side with the other townsfolk
for more than a decade, and in that time she had always been
treated with respect, courtesy, and gratitude. In return, she
had always helped out wherever possible. Each September
she bought pencils and notebooks for the students of the

primary school, and it was widely known that her money was also responsible for the juice and tortillas given to children who came to school without a lunch. Because of these acts, small talk in the streets and plazas of Corazón de la Fuente had never included pronouncements on the morality of Madam's business. Madam's coterie of Marias was shown a similar respect. When one of them went out for a stroll, she did so with the happy knowledge that men would tip their hats and women would wish them a pleasant afternoon, and that more than one child would run up and offer a squeaky-voiced *Hola, señorita*.

All that changed with a rapidity that even the most pessimistic of Mexicanos couldn't have predicted. In the cantina run by Carlos Hernandez, the local men began to complain that they had always been denied the fleshly treats offered by the Marias, for the simple reason that they'd never had the gringo dollars necessary to sample them. Though this complaint had never been previously voiced in his cantina, it seemed that the frustration must have existed for years, in a place where sentiments fester and turn rank. One afternoon, while passing a table of drinkers, he heard one of them say *Ay, cabrones, what I wouldn't give to stick my parado in one of those Marias . . .*

The cantina owner stopped, turned, and looked down at the man, who was so drunk he was swaying from side to side. — Get out, he ordered. — I won't allow such talk here.

The next day, when he overheard a comment similar in its vulgarity, he did the same, this time sparking ugly glances and the possibility of trouble. By the third time, the cantina owner was overcome with raw fatigue. He sighed, and did nothing more than throw the offensive hombre a sour glance; by the end of the week his cantina echoed with every sort of slur regarding the brothel at the end of town.

The women of Corazón de la Fuente were arguably worse. With their men drinking in the cantina, they would gather in the plaza and, under parasols woven from palm fronds, chat about the weather, their children, and how much they'd always hated those sluttish, eye-batting Marias. As with the hombres, their true feelings had never before been spoken aloud, and for this reason had acquired the odour of rot.

Ay, was the refrain. *How can I get my husband interested in me when those whorish Marias are constantly on his mind?*

Or: *Amigas, you would not believe what my husband asked me to do to him the other night, and it's all because of the filthy thoughts those Marias put in his head.*

Or: *Ay, primas, those Marias, walking around in broad daylight dressed like common putas . . . there ought to be a law.*

At this last accusation they all nodded in solemn agreement, even though it was not in the slightest bit true. Madam always insisted that her Marias dress primly when in town, an edict involving long skirts, high-collared blouses, and only the most rudimentary of makeup.

Soon the Marias could not take a walk without being subjected to hostile glances and whispered insults. Madam was treated this way as well. One day she walked into the store operated by Fajardo Jimenez to buy a quart of juice. The store was full, mostly with local women buying what little they could afford, given the drinking habits of their husbands. As soon as Madam entered, they all stopped speaking and stared straight ahead; this created a tension in the store that angered

Madam, and further strengthened her resolve to support the radio station. She barged through them, head up, and placed her order with the Zacatecan, who smiled and, unlike the others, treated her with the cordiality he felt all of his customers were due. She left, though not before confronting one of the women with a bitter *What are you looking at, bruja?*

The next day, around noon, when the Marias were in the process of waking up and making coffee and performing their morning ablutions, a sibilant crash came from the direction of the parlour. All of the Marias went running, and stopped at the doorway: in the middle of the madam's Persian rug was a halo of broken glass, along with a brick wrapped in a sheet of paper. Madam, wearing her long red satin dressing gown, pushed through her Marias and paused in the doorway as well. Then, with a disgusted *humph*, she tightened her robe around her neck and approached the mess. She bent over and picked up the package, careful not to tear the paper as she removed it. Naturally, the note was covered with the sort of disgusting, animalistic comments that self-hating men have always made towards women. But what made Madam gasp, a bejewelled hand covering her mouth, was the fact that the handwriting looked decidedly feminine.

— What's so interesting? she barked at the Marias — Get back to what you were doing. And somebody clean up this mess.

Other slights were made in town, some of which were accompanied by a little pushing and grabbing. Then, one night, around two o'clock in the morning, Maria de los Flores was tending to a client when she thought she smelled something. She ceased her cantering, sniffed the air more thoroughly, and immediately felt a registering of panic. She dismounted, her gringo yelling *Whattya think yer doing?* as she raced to the back of the house. Flames were just beginning to crawl up the wooden jacal-style rear wall. She screamed, ran inside, and alerted the other Marias, whose customers were soon growling their objections as well. Within minutes all of the Marias were out back, beating down the nascent fire with potato sacks, worn-out robes, and unlaundered sheets. This stemmed the blaze, and morning revealed a large, black burn on the rear of the house, which from a distance looked like the entrance to a cave.

— Imagine, Madam spat. — Too stupid to start a decent fire. All they had to do was douse the wall in gasoline and the house would've gone up like a pile of dried leaves.

This was hardly a source of consolation for the Marias, and one night, when Madam was having a bath in water softened with lechuguilla milk, they all met in the corral backing the house. The meeting was necessarily brief. Their gringo clients, as always, were lined up around the block, every one of them as amorous as a jailed felon.

— These are dangerous times, noted Maria del Alma.

— I don't think, said Maria de la Noche, — that any of us should go out after dark.

— No, said Maria de la Mañana. — It hardly matters anyway, given how busy we are once the sun sets.

— And, said Maria del Sol, — when we go out during the day, I think we should always be with someone.

This proposition was met with silence, as most of the Marias counted on a daily constitutional to clear their heads and find some degree of solitude.

— Sí, sighed Maria de las Montañas. — I think Maria is right. We should always go out with a partner. Even in broad daylight.

Again there was a brief silence, during which the suggestion hung in the air with the resonance of a bell. Then Maria de la Noche spoke.

— After a while, when things cool down, we can go back to normal. But not now. There's a real bad feeling in town.

As Maria de la Noche was the most influential of the Marias, they all nodded and then hurried back to their jobs.

From then on, the Marias travelled in packs of three and four. Sometimes they responded to the taunts and insults that inevitably came their way — Maria de la Noche was particularly known for the sharpness of her tongue — though usually they walked straight ahead, stony-faced and non-responsive, wondering why they should be so pilloried for simply wanting a touch of exercise. In this way they remained safe. There was the odd piece of tossed fruit, and one morning some malcontent on a rooftop attempted to douse them with a bucket's worth of slop water. Fortunately, his aim was poor, and only Maria de los Flores suffered a slightly dampened calf.

There was one Maria, however, who neglected to follow the new safety procedures. Maria del Mampo came from a town in Oaxaca that was known for producing males who lived in the guise of a female. Though she wore makeup, high-heeled shoes, and a corset laced so tightly her cheeks looked continually flushed, it was nonetheless true that she was the size of a large hombre, shaved three times a day to avoid a shadow, and had a muscularity consistent with a childhood spent toiling in coffee fields. *She*, she believed, could handle anything dished up by the short-statured louts of Corazón de la Fuente. Besides, as the only Maria who could satisfy the more outré desires of Madam's clientele, she rivalled Maria de la Noche as the house's top earner. This gave her a false sense of security. Her knowledge of the ways of sin, she believed, was like a shield, protecting her from both enmity and bad fortune. Of course, there was another reason for Maria del Mampo's cockiness. She carried a knife as long as a rolling pin tucked into her garter.

Maria del Mampo continued to leave the House of Gentlemanly Pleasures whenever she wanted to. If there were other Marias who needed shampoo or cigarettes or a can of sugar-cane juice — qué bueno, she had company. If there weren't, she went out alone, be it early morning or mid-afternoon or the dead of night. This alarmed her fellow Marias.

Ay, Maria, they would say, *you can't act this way!* In response, Maria would laugh and femininely place a hand across her chest, as if to say *Behave what way, amigas?*

But Maria, they would warn, *the streets are very dangerous.* To this she would cackle — her voice had the pitch of an older woman who smoked too much — and say *Dangerous? The streets of this one-horse town? I'm the one they should be afraid of.*

One evening, just before midnight, Maria del Mampo decided she needed a cigarette. Though she could easily have had one inside, in the interval between customers, it was a beautiful, clear night; a walk in the cool air, she felt, would do her good. Before stepping onto Avenida Cinco del Mayo, she wrapped herself in a heavy woollen shawl that made her look a little like a war widow. She lit a cigarette and stood for a moment, trying to decide whether she wanted to turn left, towards the drunkard-filled plaza, or right, which would take her out past the radio tower. From the plaza she could hear whooping and fistfights and loud hollered arguments. Under skies lit green and flashing, she turned right and tottered along the hard-packed dust. Gradually, the avenida tapered down to one lane, and the light thrown from windows grew sparse and irregular. Maria walked through pockets of dark, her head filled with memories of her village in Oaxaca. There were so many things she missed from the south: real mole, corn tortillas, decent pulque, her family. With things as crazy as they were in Corazón, she had noticed herself thinking about a return.

And yet.

What was she supposed to do? Crawl back with her parado taped between her legs? Go back to living like a . . . *campesina*? She liked having enough money for lipstick, silky under-things, and perfume. She had grown accustomed to smoking real tobacco, not lowly punche. She even liked her work, except when she was tired or when the client was boorish or unwashed, at which time her job was still less onerous than sweating in a field of coffee beans. Most of all, she enjoyed not having to worry about whether she would have enough to eat each day. This in itself was worth fighting for.

She heard boot heels behind her, falling upon hard earth — by her reckoning there were three pairs. Her heart quickened, even though she knew they were probably just clients of Madam, out for a smoke and a stroll. She kept walking, and the steps continued to follow, a tripled echo of her own hurrying steps. When she stopped, they stopped as well, only to resume the moment she continued walking.

— Hey. Puta.

So, she thought, some stupid locals, drunk and probably getting away from their fat, hectoring wives. No wonder they were foul-tempered.

— Hey, another voice said. — *Putita*. Turn around and show us something.

— Yeah. Take off your shawl. Show us your tetas. We won't hurt you.

Maria walked more quickly, though at the same time she refused to let herself be frightened. She would turn back towards town where Cinco de Mayo rounded to meet Avenida Hidalgo, and lose these stupid pendejos. Behind her she heard their collective breath quickening and turning shallow.

— Puta, she heard again. — Stop, we just want to talk to you!

She felt herself anger, for in her mind she could picture them: stoop-shouldered, flat-nosed, a head shorter than herself, and so drunk they could barely stand. She had nothing to be afraid of. *She* was half-male and half-female in a country of machos, and had faced far, far worse. She stopped, suddenly, and was not at all surprised when the men behind her did likewise. She turned. As she suspected, they were vagrants, losers, chump-change morons in tight shirts and jeans stained with diesel and red earth, their feet adorned in the most worn of huaraches. She eyed them with a dead-eyed glare.

— What do you want?

They all bore the slight semicircular sway of drunkards. To her right was a tiny lane filled with metal scraps and old tires. To her left were scrub and low cacti.

— Come on, she said. — I haven't got all day. What in the chingada do you want?

One of them grinned, revealing metal and black spaces. There was something in the slow, lingering way he did it that frightened Maria, and made her think, for the first time, that she should have listened to her sisters and not gone out walking by herself. The hombre in the middle, a fierce-looking little brute with tattoos on his hands and face, grinned as well. Yet Maria found that she was now most unnerved by the one on the left, who looked solemn and preoccupied, as though thinking hard about something. Her heart sped. Her breathing grew rapid. She bent over, lifted the hem of her skirt, and pulled out her knife, holding it aloft so that its blade flickered green in the light of the corona. Her hand trembled, as did her half-deepened voice.

— Better stay where you are, pendejos.

The silent one chortled, the ugly one in the middle whooped, and the one on the right revealed more metal and black spaces.

And then they were upon her, feeding like degenerate wolves.

{26}

FRANCISCO RAMIREZ HAD TAKEN TO WALKING THE
streets late at night, his only goal to exhaust himself and permit
the arrival of sleep. He always varied his route, and he started
that night by heading towards the ancient Spanish mission at the
southeast corner of the village. After touching its cool walls, letting the passage of time they represented put his own problems
in perspective, he headed north along the eastern edge of town,
his route skirting the plazita containing the desecrated Pozo de
Confesiones. Here he paused to give a thought to his old amigo,
the molinero Roberto Pántelas, who had recently started walking with the use of a cane. *Really*, thought Francisco, *I must call
on him tomorrow and see if there's anything he needs.*

Francisco continued in the direction of the river, a route
that took him through the ejido. He stumbled past the sleeping families of his students, who often slept outside to take
advantage of the breezes that blew over the desert in the middle of the night. Stepping around one slumbering clump, he
heard a raspy voice whispering in the relative quiet.

— Ay, Francisco, what are you doing out so late?

It was a question he had no answer for, except to say that sleep wasn't coming easily these days.

He then circled past the decimated home of the hacendero Antonio Garcia, where he paused to feel a degree of admiration. When the rest of his ilk had fled back to Europe, when even his wife had decided that she'd had enough, Antonio Garcia had refused to abandon the sorrowful majesty that is México, and for this he would always have Francisco's respect.

Upon reaching Avenida Cinco del Mayo, Francisco had a choice to make: either turn right and follow the roadway to the bridge, where he sometimes stood and watched the lights of Del Río reflecting on the waters of the river, or turn left and head back into town. He chose the latter. As he neared the town hall, the number of people living on the street increased, and Francisco had to step around lolling bodies in order to traverse the northern edge of the plaza. He walked past the lineup of gringos waiting to get access to the House of Gentlemanly Pleasures, eventually reaching the point at which Cinco de Mayo petered down to a single lane leading out to the tower. It was Francisco's plan to spit on the base of the incessantly blinking tower — this was becoming a nightly ritual — and then return to his home.

He heard a noise. It was so faint that at first he could barely distinguish it from the moans emanating from within the walls of the brothel. The only difference was that it was coming from a different direction. Francisco took a few more strides and heard it again; for a moment he wondered if the curandera might be lurking somewhere, intending to unnerve him again with her maniacal utterances. He stopped and placed a hand to his ear. This time he was sure he'd heard some sort of feral groan, and he wondered if perhaps a she-wolf had been struck by another hit-and-run driver. Francisco hurried towards the origin of the sound, and as he did the moans became louder, and more human in tonality. Upon reaching the mouth of a tiny laneway running south, he spotted a body that, judging by the marks in the dust, had been dragged into the alley and left amidst a scattering of junk.

— Dios mío, he uttered while scrambling towards the body, only to discover that it was the man-woman they called Maria del Mampo. Her face was grotesquely swollen, her right leg was bent unnaturally to one side, and her skirt was torn in a way that revealed what her assailants had done to her. Her hands, meanwhile, gripped the sides of her body, as though trying to stem a torrent of pain originating in her ribs. When she heard Francisco's approach, she turned her head in his direction, moaned again, and mouthed the words *Help me.*

Francisco ran as fast as he was able to the House of Gentlemanly Pleasures. There he rapped on the back door. When no answer came, he pounded on it, yelling *Por favor, por favor, there's an emergency!* Maria de las Montañas answered, her angelic blonde hair falling over the left side of her face.

— Francisco Ramirez! she exclaimed with a smile. — What a surprise! Really, you should be lining up with the gringos, but since it's an *emergency*, maybe I could talk to . . .

— No! he exclaimed. — Maria, please, get Madam.

— *Francisco!* She retired years ago, you know that. You sure you wouldn't prefer someone a little closer to your age . . .

— Maria, please. It's Maria del Mampo.

Maria de las Montañas blanched. — What is it?

— She's been hurt.

Maria closed the door and ran to get Madam, leaving Francisco to wait on the street, hopping from foot to foot, aware that any delay might result in loss of life. The door pushed open, and a moment later he was hustling along with Madam, Maria de las Montañas, Maria de la Noche, and a new, strong-armed Guadalajaran called Maria del Cielo. Upon seeing her downed sister, Maria de la Noche ran to the victim's side. When the rest of the gang pulled up, she looked at Madam with an expression that could only be described as accusatory. The two other Marias ran forward as well, each dropping to her knees and attempting to fan air over Maria del Mampo's battered face. Every few seconds Maria del Mampo groaned, though in all other respects she seemed barely conscious.

— Can she walk? Madam asked.

There was no response.

— I said, can she walk?

— We don't think so, Maria de la Noche said stiffly.

— Well then, carry her.

— Sí, said Francisco, stepping forward. — Somebody help me . . .

With that, Francisco and Maria del Cielo lifted the battered victim and guided her back to the brothel, her feet raising wisps of dust.

— Put her in room number seven, commanded Madam. — It's the biggest.

As these instructions were carried out, all the other Marias came rushing, many of them quitting in the middle of agreed-upon acts. Predictably, this angered their clients, who started hollering for either a refund or a different Maria. Madam ignored them and ordered whichever girls were working to continue doing so. She then ordered Maria de la Noche to get the injured Maria something strong to drink, and she sent Maria de las Rosas outside to petition the waiting gringos, offering a free interlude to any hombre able to produce a valid medical licence. In this way, a bespectacled doctor from Brownsville was hustled into room number seven to attend to poor Maria del Mampo. Those Marias between clients, meanwhile, huddled around the entrance to the room, sniffling and remembering times when they didn't feel so hated.

As for Francisco Ramirez, the moment came when he realized that there was nothing more he could do to help, and that his presence in the brothel only threatened to get in the way. Without saying goodbye, he slipped out the same door by which he had entered and began walking back towards the plaza. He had taken only a few steps when he heard his name being yelled behind him. It was Maria de las Montañas, leaning out the door of the house.

— Francisco, she called again. — Come here.

Francisco obeyed, thinking that they must need his assistance in some way that hadn't occurred to him. When he reached the door, Maria reached out a thin hand and took him by the wrist, guiding him down the main hallway of the brothel towards a door bearing the number nine. She closed it behind them, the clamour of the hallway immediately diminishing.

Francisco looked around the little room. There was a small bed, a wicker chair, and, against one wall, a bureau holding a small basin filled with water. A kerosene lamp was burning on the bureau, the wick turned down so far that the room was all but cast into darkness. Maria de las Montañas remedied this by stepping towards the lamp and turning the small brass knob extending from its side. The room bloomed with light, allowing Francisco to see the room's other distinguishing feature: the walls were painted a scarlet red.

Suddenly it occurred to Francisco why Maria might have led him there. — Ay, Maria, he stammered. — I . . .

Maria, who seemed not to be listening, gathered thick tresses of blonde hair in her little hands and then shook them, her hair tumbling over her shoulders. She was wearing a skirt and a simple cloth blouse tied at the front by a thin pink ribbon. Looking into Francisco's eyes — eyes that had lost the ability to either blink or look away — she pulled on the end of the ribbon, and the blouse tumbled to the floor around her feet.

— Francisco, she said — Madam has asked me to give you a little reward for helping out this evening. These days, not too many young men are willing to stick their necks out for the town's fallen women.

— Ay, Maria, he stammered. — I am afraid I am still . . .

— Sí, sí, you're still in love with Violeta Cruz, everyone knows this. But first let me ask you something.

She took a step towards him, stopping close enough that he could detect the lovely rosewater perfume she put behind her ears, on her wrists, and in the dimpled recesses that exist where the back meets the swell of the buttocks. She looked up into his eyes, craning her neck to do so.

— When you win back the affection of Violeta Cruz, and she accepts you into both her heart and her hammock, wouldn't you like to know how to please her with something other than your chiselled good looks?

Maria was standing sufficiently close that the tips of her breasts touched the material of Francisco's shirt, creating an effect similar to the one achieved by placing a match to a mound of dried leaves.

— Well? she purred. — Francisco?

She then rose to the tips of her toes and kissed him with a passion that, feigned or not, caused Francisco Ramirez to ponder the existence of God, his alter ego the Devil, and the possibility that both could, at least on a physical level, successfully coexist.

— Sí, he answered when their lips finally parted. — I think you might be right.

{TRES}

{27}

AFTER ANOTHER SUMPTUOUS MEAL, VIOLETA CRUZ
and John Romulus Brinkley retired to one of the mansion's
other bedchambers, this one located at the far end of the long
dark wood hallway that served as the central passage of the
mansion's second storey. This time, their congress occurred
directly across from a painting by Saturnino Herrán, in
which the artist had faithfully captured both the nobility, and
the vulnerability, of a pre-Columbian Native.

Through her tour of the good doctor's art collection,
Violeta was learning that there were different experiences to
be had with the physical expression of love. With Brinkley,
there was an almost a regal sense of protection; in his arms
she felt sheltered, coddled, pampered even, and definitely
impermeable to all the indignities thought up by the world at
large. As well, she felt a calm that she had never before known
in her life on the other side of the border, and she was finding
that this feeling had an almost narcotic effect on her — the
more she learned of its taste and texture, the more she wanted

it. (Whereas with Francisco — ay, Dios mío, the effect that muchacho had had upon her. Huddled in their desert lee, his thick arms around her, she often found that lurid images formed in her mind — of unbroken horses, of dragons loosed upon a town, of lightning scampering along a desert floor in sheets of buzzing, intense electric blue. And even though these images presaged a loss of control that frightened her, it was nevertheless true that, when in one of the doctor's art-festooned bedrooms, she occasionally wished she was with Francisco, struggling to survive the bubbling cauldron into which he had pitched her.)

Violeta dined with the doctor the next week as well, their post-meal conjugation occurring in his other other bedroom. This room sported a mural painted by José Orozco, whose stylized depiction of strong, virile Mexicanos made her think, yet again, of Francisco, so much so that, at the moment when the doctor blurted *Te amo, Violeta, te amo!* she was a long way away, thinking of things that made her feel two-faced and shameful. That night, immediately after the doctor's culmination, Violeta crawled out of bed and found one of the mansion's many spotless washrooms. There she cleaned herself with a potion she'd acquired during a midnight trip to the house of the curandera, who'd given her a prophylactic wash composed of herbs, sotol pith, and a mild emetic found in the pineal glands of the desert sidewinder. She'd then returned to bed, feeling guilty about the way she could not give herself fully to one man only.

Violeta returned the following Saturday evening for yet another staff appreciation dinner, her ambivalence thankfully lessened by a week spent in Corazón de la Fuente, which seemed to grow more chaotic with each passing day — one of the Marias had even been attacked, all manner of sordid actions committed against her body. That week's coupling took place in yet another room, this one graced by a mural by David Alfaro Siqueiros; it was a rendering of México's revolutionary leaders, and quite frankly it made Violeta nervous. This was more than made up for the following week, when they made amor just inches from a night table supporting a tiny line drawing of an oleander. When Violeta inquired as to its authorship, the doctor smiled and told her that it was by an up-and-coming female artist who, it was rumoured, had a moustache, a single eyebrow, a twisted spinal column, and a romantic involvement with the great Diego Rivera.

— I love it, she told him.

— It now belongs to you.

The following Saturday, however, her doctor was not himself; when he met her at the door, he merely backed away, saying *Ah, Violeta, you are a sight for sore eyes.* He barely ate his dinner, and throughout he complained that he was at war with forces determined to put a cap on both individual initiative and the march of science. When Violeta asked what he meant, he clammed up and seemed to fume. She resolved this by giving him a rudimentary massage and pouring him flutes of champagne.

— Violeta, he said after barely touching his dessert. — I have one more room to show you.

He led her upstairs, and they reached a short passageway that bisected the second floor of the house. At the end of this passageway was a door. The doctor opened it, revealing a winding staircase. Violeta began to climb it, emerging in a room that the doctor referred to as the belvedere. The chamber was hexagonal, with large windows interspersed with wall space. She walked along the windows. Through them she could see the distant lights of Del Rio, moonlight gleaming off the Río Grande, and, from a window facing south, the smouldering street fires of her own little village. Occasionally the distant landscape flared green.

— No, he said. — You're missing it. My pride and joy . . .

The doctor pointed to a small painting of a bull's head.

— It's by Pablo Picasso, he said.

— Who?

— Picasso. Soon he'll be the most famous artist in all the world.

— It's beautiful, Violeta said, though in truth she found the painting disturbing. From whatever angle she chose to regard it, the bull still stared her straight in the eye, as though benefiting from some demonic ability.

There was, of course, a bed in the middle of the room, directly beneath a pane of glass that looked upon the stars. According to the doctor, this most special of rooms had hosted governors, titans of industry, and famous authors. She blushed, and kissed him as he fumbled with her petticoat. They lay together, slowly proceeding to the point at which two become one, a conjoining that was accompanied this night by a strange metallic taste in her mouth — it washed over her lips and tongue as surely as the rush of a stream.

They lay admiring the heavens, Violeta feeling as though the night sky was a gift she'd been given. Around midnight she rose and dressed, a cue that the doctor should alert the chauffeur. Instead he lay looking at her, his petulance having clearly returned.

— Violeta, he said to her. — Can't you stay just this one time?

— My mother would kill me.

— I will give you caviar and eggs for breakfast. We can swim in my private pool. I can shower you with riches. I can give you anything you want.

— Ay no, amor. I can't.

— It's just that . . . it's just that I have to go out of town for a while. A professional obligation, Violeta. The thought of being separated from you kills me. It absolutely slays me. Don't you see? I need to have you here with me now. I need to have you here right this *instant.*

The desperation in Brinkley's voice further melted her heart, and made her feel certain that his love was something she would enjoy forever.

— You don't have to worry, she said. — I'll be here when you get back.

— But Violeta . . .

They embraced inside the front door of Brinkley's mansion. Fortunately, it was late, and Brinkley's servants were, in almost all cases, in their quarters. They parted, the doctor holding her shoulders in his small hands while his eyes roved over her features, as if trying to commit every detail of her face to memory.

A few days later, Violeta awoke in her room in Corazón de la Fuente. While normally this would have filled her with an aching, low-level regret — all the noise, all the filth in the streets, "Will the Circle Be Unbroken" broadcasting from the rain-barrel spigot — she was imbued with an odd elation. It was as though there were some gaseous elixir in the air, leaving her giddy and carefree. As she went about her day, she caught herself smiling at the sight of children, or at the way the sun filtered through the branches of trees, throwing spiderweb shadows upon the earth. Other times she smiled at nothing at all. Around midday she decided to visit the store of Fajardo Jimenez: the latest news was that he'd acquired a freezer, and that the miracle of ice cream had finally come to the little village of Corazón de la Fuente.

She left her home, humming as she walked through the crowded, filthy streets, the calls of *Mamacita!* and *Ay, qué bella!* failing to deflate her blissful mood. The store bell chimed when she walked in.

— Violeta Cruz! Fajardo said by way of a greeting. — So lovely to see you. Usually it's your mother who does the shopping.

— And it's going to stay that way. But a little bird told me that . . .

She didn't have to finish her statement. Fajardo was already beaming, his teeth gleaming through the hair matting his face.

— So you wish to try some ice cream? I have vanilla and chocolate. Tell me which you'd prefer, Señorita Cruz. Or should I call you Miss Rose Dawn, high priestess of the Secret Order of the Maya?

Violeta giggled. — Pues . . . can I have a little of each?

— How can I say no to a priestess?

Fajardo walked over to his freezer, extracted two tubs,

and spooned a portion of each in a small glass dish. He then handed it to her along with a long, slender spoon that, like every other metal object in Corazón, was broadcasting the signal of her beloved's radio station. Violeta accepted the dish and spooned a tiny bit of the vanilla into her mouth.

— Dios mío! she exclaimed. — I have never, ever tasted anything as delicious!

— Now try the chocolate.

— Mmmm. It's impossible to say which is better!

— In that case, enjoy them both.

Violeta took another spoonful, and then another, and another, finding that the surface of her tongue had actually come alive, had turned into a ravenous, pleasure-demanding infant who could only be satisfied by yet another mouthful. As Fajardo looked on, she ate away, humming all the while, her vocal cords drowning out the music coming from her spoon.

Suddenly she stopped and peered at Fajardo. — Honestly, she said. — This is the most delicious thing I have ever tasted. But do you know what would really go with it? You know what would make it taste even better?

— What's that, Violeta?

She paused, as if to confirm her suspicions with her taste buds. She then smiled and said: — You wouldn't . . . I mean . . . you wouldn't happen to have a pickle to go with this, would you?

When the inevitable, and not entirely subtle, physical changes began to occur in Violeta's body, her mother noticed.

— Violeta, Malfil exclaimed one afternoon. — Am I just crazy or is your hair getting even thicker?

— Mami, you know this happens every year around this time. It has something to do with the barometer.

— Well, if the barometer keeps changing, pretty soon there won't be a brush in all of Coahuila that will tame it.

A few days after that, Violeta walked into the main room of the house wearing only a camisole. Malfil looked up, and her face tightened with confusion.

— Violeta, she said. — Is it my imagination, or are your senos getting bigger?

Violeta glanced at her bosom and smiled. For once, she was pleased to possess these fleshy encumbrances, items that had always done nothing more than turn the boys of the town into salivating hogs. But now, thanks to the curandera's useless prophylactic rinse, she would soon need her swollen breasts to feed the life growing inside her.

— It's my time of the moon, Mami. This always happens.

— Maybe you had better cut down on the tortillas just to make sure.

And then, one morning just past dawn, Violeta awoke with the absolute certainty that she was about to be ill. She leapt from her hammock, raced through the room where her mother slept, and made it to the expanse of desert backing her house. The sound of her retching soon awoke the dogs in the Callejón of the Sleeping Curs, who all lifted their snouts skyward and started crooning. This in turn roused Malfil. She emerged from the rear of the house to find her daughter on her hands and knees, the first rays of the morning sun turning her back orange.

— Mija! she exclaimed. — What did you . . .

Her voice trailed off. Seconds ticked by. All those little clues had suddenly added up to something that was not in any way little. — Oh, Violeta, she muttered in a voice turned brittle with exhaustion.

Violeta stood, indecorously wiped her mouth, and prepared for the row that was about to come. Instead, Malfil's eyes filled with tears. She turned and walked slowly back into the house. Violeta followed, saying *Mami, I'm sorry, I'm sorry.* Malfil seemed not to hear. She crawled into the hammock in the main room, her back to her daughter. There she lay, weeping. When Violeta went to touch her shoulder, she batted it away. It was, Violeta thought, the cruellest thing that Malfil could have done, and recognizing this inspired tears that were nearly as plentiful as her mother's.

{28}

IN THE MAYOR'S DREAM HE WAS RUNNING FASTER than was possible for a human, over plains stretching to the point of disappearance, his breath inexhaustible and his muscles impervious to pain, unbothered by heat or sand or infirmity — it was as though he were soaring, his perfect feet touching down in only the most cursory of ways. He ran for kilometres and kilometres, never tiring, never caring, his body made newly whole, outrunning buzzards and roadrunners and the rays of the sun and, most of all, the responsibility that now pursued him like a posse of lawmen.

Miguel Orozco awoke with a start and sat straight up in his little adobe room just down from the plaza. He was perspiring, and he could still feel the remnants of his dream course darkly through his blood. After catching his breath, he rose from his hammock and walked out to the little mesquite-stick porch that extended from the rear of his casa. There he kept a large tin bucket filled with river water. He bent over and dumped a ladleful of water over his head, his black hair drying quickly in the sun creeping through the slats of the ramada.

He dressed in the same garb he'd worn to Laura's funeral a week ago: gabardine trousers, a white cotton shirt that looked perpetually bleached, a donkey jacket, and a homburg. He then drank charred coffee and ate a leftover tamale filled with calf's brains and green pepper. When he had finished, he checked himself in the mirror and limped down his street towards Avenida Cinco de Mayo. As he walked, his neighbours all noticed his garb, rightly concluding that the mayor was about to conduct important business, quite likely on the gringo side of the border.

When he reached the avenida, Miguel Orozco turned right and limped towards the bridge, where the Mexican border guard, upon hearing an explanation of the mayor's mission, let him pass without the usual fiduciary demands. Miguel thanked the man and walked across the wood-slat bridge. In the middle he paused and looked east, closing his eyes against the heating orange glow of the sun. He let the soft, aloe-scented air drift gently against his face. How wonderful, he thought, it would be if the whole world existed *between* countries, in places unmolested by the governments formed by people.

He sighed, continued walking, and greeted the toll keeper on the other side of the bridge, who wore a customs uniform, an identification badge, and an air of proprietorship. After enacting the obligatory negotiations, Miguel paid him one dollar and entered los Estados Unidos. A small lane connected to the paved road that ran into Del Rio. The mayor stuck out his thumb and was picked up within minutes by a

Mexican-American driving a truck filled with undocumented yard workers. Miguel nodded his thanks and crouched in the back with the workers and several dozen flats of marigolds. By the time he was let out in front of the Roswell Hotel, his knees were stained orange, and he briefly considered returning to Corazón to change. Instead he again thanked the driver and went inside the building that housed Radio XER and Dr. Brinkley's medical practice.

The reception desk was manned by an attractive young woman with thick eyelashes.

— I very much would like to speak with Dr. Brinkley, Miguel said.

She blinked. — And you are?

— Señor Miguel Orozco. I am the mayor of Corazón de la Fuente.

— Señor Orozco! I'm so sorry . . . I didn't recognize you! Please, please, sign in and I'll give you an identification card and you can go straight up to the fifth floor.

A minute later the mayor entered the first elevator he had ever been in. Around his neck was a visitor's badge on which the receptionist had misspelled his first name. The doors closed and his heart began to pound, for the elevator was coffin-shaped and the air inside it clammy. As he rose towards the top of the building, he was nervous that something would happen so that the doors of the elevator would not open. *The lengths*, he thought, *that gringos will go, just to avoid a few stairs.*

Miguel stepped into another reception area, this one staffed by another attractive woman who, the mayor thought, could have been the sister of the receptionist on the first floor.

— Buenos días, she said.

— Good morning.

—I'm told you would like to see Dr. Brinkley.

— Sí, that is correct.

She smiled. — Well, I know the doctor will be more than glad to make time for the mayor of Corazón de la Fuente. How are things across the river?

— They are no so good, he said. — That is why I am here.

— Well, I'm sorry to hear that. Such a pretty little town. Dr. Brinkley is always telling us what a marvellous little gem it is.

As she spoke she flipped through the pages of a large leather appointment book. She stopped and looked up at him.

— Tell you what, I could slot you in for, mmm, one-thirty on Friday. Would that work for you?

— I can no seeing him now?

— I'm afraid not, Señor Orozco. As you can imagine, Dr. Brinkley is a very, very busy man.

The mayor paused, as if to mentally sift through his own schedule. This, of course, was for show; he had owned an appointment book about three years earlier and had used it only to remind himself of Christmas and the celebrations surrounding the Independencia, both of which he would have remembered anyway. He'd ended up giving it to a local orphan, who put the book to good use as a kindergarten scribbler. He eventually nodded, tipped his homburg, and found the stairs.

That Friday, he again dressed in his funeral suit and crossed into los Estados. This time he had no luck thumbing a ride; with a start, he remembered it was the national holiday known as el Día de la Raza, on which Mexicanos either celebrated the arrival of Christopher Columbus or, depending on their point of view, lamented it. In either case it meant the same thing: every Mexicano in the whole of the north was at home, preparing for a day of parades, piñata bashing, and binge eating. Meanwhile, car after car piloted by gringos passed by. The mayor began walking in the direction of town, his bad foot already aching. By the time he reached the Roswell Hotel, he was tired, thirsty, and forty-five minutes late.

He stepped into the first-floor reception area.

— Señor Orozco! called the receptionist. — We were beginning to wonder what had happened to you . . .

— I had . . . mmm . . . I had car troubles.

— Well, that's too bad. I'm afraid Dr. Brinkley assumed you weren't coming, and after waiting for many minutes he decided to attend to his next piece of business.

The mayor's mind clouded with self-accusations, the majority of which involved his stupid, stupid decision to be born Mexicano. The receptionist, meanwhile, wrote down the date of another appointment on a slip of paper and passed it to him with a grin that bordered on the patronizing. He walked to the border in a sulk and trudged, exhausted, to the town hall, where he hid his face behind a newspaper for several hours, refusing to speak even to the old woman who brought his mid-afternoon sweet roll.

One week later, to avoid the fiasco of his previous trip to Del Rio, he left early. Naturally, a truck filled with itinerant garbage pickers stopped to pick him up even before he had a chance to stick his thumb in the air. As a result, he arrived at the Roswell Hotel before the sun had completed its transition from a blazing orange ball to a solid white-light sphere. He entered the hotel with the cleaning staff and waited for a full hour, only to be informed that Dr. Brinkley had been called away to perform an emergency procedure on the governor of Mississippi, who was suffering from an inflammation of the excretory tract. They rescheduled, yet again. The mayor left, his skin purple with anger.

When he returned five days later, this time punctually, the receptionist again apologized for Brinkley's absence, explaining that he was in his native state, scouting locations for a new clinic.

— Señor Orozco, she said. — I tried to contact you but you didn't leave your telephone number. Really, I'm so dreadfully, dreadfully sorry, but I'm sure that if we reschedule your appointment, Dr. Brinkley will do everything in his power to make himself available. Although it had better be soon: the doctor will be taking an extended leave in the near future. Expanding his base of operations, I'm happy to say.

The mayor stood there, speechless and reddening, his fingertips twitching at his sides. He was about to say something when, surprising even himself, he turned without responding. As he dragged his bad foot towards the door, he felt as if the eyes of the world were upon him, their collective judgement an arrow.

Late that afternoon he sought out Father Alvarez, the cantina owner, and the hacendero and asked them to come with him to his office. Though it was an unprecedented request, they each nodded grimly, and did not ask why the mayor wanted to see them. Under shimmering greenish skies, Miguel unlocked the chain that now maintained the security of city hall. They marched wordlessly up to the mayor's office. Miguel took his chair while the other three stood. Outside, the sun shone brilliantly over the vagrants, whores, thieves, beggars, and malcontents crowded into the plaza.

The mayor let a few seconds tick by, during which he looked from amigo to amigo.

— Brinkley won't see me.

The others did not look surprised.

— I think he knows what's going on in our town, and is embarrassed. If you ask me, I think he's packed up and buggered off already. I could be wrong, but I think he's washed his hands of us.

There was a long, freighted pause.

— Compadres, said the cantina owner, — you know what we are? We're a town of mujeres. First we got fucked by Porfirio Díaz, then we got fucked by the revolution, and now we're getting fucked by that pendejo Brinkley. Listen to me, primos. We're becoming a town of weak, whimpering, womanly cowards.

No one said a word, and in that extended moment of quiet there was sad agreement.

— So, Father Alvarez said with a deep, shuddering breath, — what do we do?

— I'll tell you one thing, said the hacendero. — I won't put up with it this time.

— No, said the cantina owner. — Me neither.

Again there was a long, drifting silence, during which the men mulled over their own, individual reasons for hating John Brinkley and the rancour he had brought to their once quiet pueblo.

Just a week and a half earlier, as he crept over to Margarita's side of the bed, the cantina owner had been visited with renewed visions of that leering captain. Suddenly nauseated, he'd retreated from his wife's surrender, complaining of fatigue, his face burning with frustration, his will molested. Since then he'd been forced to conclude that the benefits of the Compound Operation were temporary, if not out-and-out illusory.

The hacendero's stallion, meanwhile, had recently started raking his ears against the earth, causing them to bleed and attract bugs. In response, the hacendero was now ridding his house of all metals, his last meal eaten with a spoon he'd carved, rather roughly, from a huizache branch. As for the father, his mood was only further darkened by the Pentecostal nonsense beaming out of Brinkley's tower — on the way over he had passed a house topped by a metal weathervane from which he could clearly hear an evangelist ranting about the Four Horsemen of the Apocalypse.

— I have an idea, the hacendero finally said.

— What is it? grumbled the father.

— I know how we're going to get that hijo de puta.

The men listened as the hacendero solemnly voiced his idea. It was a simple proposition, savage and brutish and alive with finality. It was the resort of desperate men, and he used few words to describe it. When he was finished, his friends looked downwards, as though afraid to see the reaction of the others. They all knew that, under normal circumstances, they would have done nothing other than play with the idea, enjoying the temptation it represented, revelling in the lushness of its timbre. Yet the mayor and the father and the cantina owner kept their eyes fixed on the knotted, splintering floor-boards, their heads filled with the echoes of past humiliations. Outside, voices rose from the crowded, filthy plaza — some sort of violent commotion was occurring outside, of a sort so common now that it didn't even occur to them to go to the window and look.

The mayor opened the bottom drawer of his desk and pulled out the bottle of tequila he had bought to replace his recently looted mescal. In the drawer he kept a single shot glass; he put this on his desktop next to an empty coffee cup. The cantina owner spotted a pair of water glasses on the mayor's filing cabinet, and he put them on the desk as well. Miguel Orozco poured four tequilas; he kept one and handed out the other three.

The men lifted their tequilas and downed them in a sin-gle, warming toss, their toast having to do with the rescue of their town, their old lives, and their sense of themselves. Then they solemnly walked down the chipped hallway stair-case. Once on the street they turned left, in that way avoiding the dirt-faced throngs living in the plaza. At the next street they turned south and entered the store operated by Fajardo Jimenez, who was known to keep certain contraband items in his cellar, items that included explosives, hallucinatory roots, various models of handguns, and playing cards featuring photographs of naked Chiapan women.

Fajardo, upon seeing them, smiled through the fur cover-ing his otherwise handsome features.

— Hola, said the hacendero. — Qué onda?

— No mucho, said Fajardo. — I heard it was thinking of raining.

— I heard that too. It's been a while.

Fajardo looked at the men. — So. Are you looking for something?

— Sí, the hacendero said.

— Well, don't keep me in suspense.

— Do you remember last spring, when I had to clear some stumps from that land out behind my paddock?

— I do.

— Well, I have some more to get rid of.

— So you need some dynamite. Why didn't you just say so, hombre? How many stumps do you need to clear?

The hacendero paused, thinking. He looked to the others, who shrugged their shoulders in a way that was barely perceptible. Finally he turned to the store owner and answered.

— Pues . . . hundreds and hundreds?

— Hundreds and hundreds! You must have enough stumps to fill a . . .

Fajardo stopped, an understanding slowly dawning across his shaggy features. A series of brazen robberies at his store, coupled with the death of Laura Velasquez, had turned him against Brinkley's tower as well. He lowered his voice and leaned towards the men, his eyes shifting in either direction.

— I hear you, hombres. I'll have to order some more from my cousin across the border. But if you can wait a week or two, I can promise you this: I'll sell you enough dynamite to clear every paddock in México.

{29}

FEELING THAT SHE NEEDED SOME QUIET TIME TO think, Madam made the unprecedented decision to close her House of Gentlemanly Pleasures for a single night, spawning a riot that, after raging for about fifteen minutes, extinguished itself in the general clamour of the plaza. Throughout the uproar, she gazed at Brinkley's tower through the window of her bedroom, cursing herself. For the first time since its arrival, she was beginning to feel she might have been wrong to support it so unconditionally. She put her face in her hands and fought a wave of self-pity. Her choices were obvious. She could denounce the tower, refuse to service Brinkley's patients, and gradually win back the town's approval. Or she could do what people inevitably do when angry, bitter, and under extreme stress: surrender all reason to the dictates of instinct. The deciding factor was her long-held vow to watch over her Marias, to care for her Marias, and to make sure nobody had the effrontery to touch a hair on their beautiful heads ever again.

She stayed awake for hours, finally resorting to an opiate draught she'd been given by an Oriental client. Her dreams were cascades, and she came awake feeling ragged. After several cups of black coffee, she dressed in her riding suit and retrieved the pearl-handled revolver she kept in a locked box beneath her bed. She placed this in the folds of her petticoat and summoned Maria del Alma and Maria de la Mañana. They came immediately, looking pink-faced and anxious.

— We are going on a little trip today. We are going to sort out this business with the town. Now go pack a lunch. Tacos al pastor. And frijoles. Filling food. Do it now. We have a long day ahead of us.

As they packed the lunch, Madam asked two other Marias to hitch her buggy to the pair of mules kept in a small corral beside the House of Gentlemanly Pleasures. By ten o'clock in the morning, Madam and the two Marias were heading along the same highway that Francisco Ramirez had taken during his quest to find the brother of Violeta Cruz. They rode without incident under a thin, bleached sky. Around midmorning, they turned south off the road leading to Piedras Negras and headed into the badlands. It was around this time that Maria del Alma, a petite girl with hair the colour of straw, asked: — Where are we going, Madam?

Madam thought for a moment, debating how much she wanted to say. After a minute or two of tense silence, she figured that she might as well admit to the more digestible parts of her plan.

— I know an hombre. He used to be a client of mine, before I had the house. He's Mexican.

— Really? said both Marias.

— Sí. It was just after the revolution ended, and the country was awash with stolen money.

— Who is he? asked Maria de la Mañana.

— I'll explain. Do you remember when Pancho Villa got mad at the gringos and attacked that town over the border in New México?

The two Marias looked at each other.

— No, of course not. You were both little and still living down south, and for that you should be grateful. The long and the short of it is that Villa invaded New México and torched a town and killed a bunch of people. The gringos got furious. To get Villa, they sent thousands of soldiers into Chihuahua and Sonora and Coahuila. It was called la Expedición Punitiva, and of course it didn't work, but that's not the point. Around this time, the gringos set up camps to train hired guns to protect whatever interests they still had in México. They trained them to watch over American haciendas, to defend American businesses, and to guard American factories. They taught them to fight and use weapons, and they taught them well. When the revolutionary governments went ahead and seized control of American haciendas, businesses, and factories *anyway*, these men collected their paycheques by riding around and harming anyone they thought might be sympathetic to Villa or Zapata. When the revolution ended, the gringos cut them loose. They were called White Shirts.

— Did they really wear white shirts? asked Maria de la Mañana.

— Sí.

— Why?

— So people could tell them apart from the Gold Shirts and the Red Shirts.

— I don't understand, said Maria del Alma.

— Most people didn't. It was a time that forbade understanding. Plus, after a time their shirts got dirty and they covered them with bandoliers, so nobody could tell them apart anyway.

Madam stopped talking, as she preferred that her Marias not know the whole story: that these white-shirt-wearing paramilitaries naturally turned to the pastimes that men with their talents always resort to when released from their formal obligations — namely hijacking, racketeering, extortion, terrorism, and other acts of reckless psychopathy.

— And this hombre, said Maria del Alma. — He was a White Shirt?

— Sí.

— And you are going to hire him to protect us?

The madam let a few seconds pass.

— His name is Ramón. I do not know his last name. I hope I can still find him.

They again rode in silence. The rolling red turf of the badlands converted into a desert thick with cholla and sand the colour of rice. After a time they stopped and ate tortillas and then continued into windless heat and pockets of strange, deathly silences. A buzzard lazily tracked them. Eventually Madam turned off onto a small dirt track that wound up over a ridge and descended into a gully studded with barrel cacti and stones. Far off, next to a stream so withered by the sun it was barely a trickle, was an old settler's cabin. They could see a brazier smoking next to it and goats tethered to thick wooden pegs. There was a smell of dirt and old clothes and toasted corn. Upon seeing this squalor, the Marias were reminded of home, and couldn't help but feel saddened.

Madam halted the mules.

— Wait here, she said.

She climbed down from the buggy and walked along a dusty path towards the door of the cottage. Beneath her feet were scorpions and vole tracks and the cloven impressions made by goats. She rapped on the door. She waited. She rapped again.

The heavy door creaked open and Madam came face to face with the man she remembered. He was still tall and leanly muscled, with a moon-shaped scar below his right eye. His movements, she noted, still had a frightening coiled quality, as though at any second they might be unleashed fully. The only difference was that there seemed to be less of him. He was wearing an eye patch, he had lost all but a few oily strands of hair, and his right arm was missing below the elbow.

— Ramón, she said.

— Who the hell is Ramón? was his response.

— You are, cabrón. Or at least that's the name you used to use.

He leaned a little closer, as if to inspect Madam's face. Suddenly he grinned, revealing a mouth filled with metal and damp rot and teeth turned orange.

— Ahhh . . . I remember you now. You're that puta from Corazón.

Madam shuddered, commanded herself to breathe, and answered: — I am.

— How did you find me?

— You once told me where you lived.

He chuckled and stepped outside. He put his lone hand on the small of his back and stretched, exposing his unshaven face to the sun. He then spat onto the soil.

— Why're you here?

Madam stalled. She seriously wondered whether Ramón was up to the job, and was on the verge of saying *Nothing, my mistake* and taking her Marias home. But then she pictured Maria del Mampo, lying in her bed, covered from head to toe with indigo swellings.

— I have a problem, she said.

— We all do.

— The town's turned against me. Over some business you don't need to know about. Mostly they're making my life as uncomfortable as possible. Throwing rocks through windows and setting fires and scaring my girls. Plus one of them was attacked.

— I know the feeling. Us White Shirts weren't too popular once the gringos up and left.

— You still have your boys?

Ramón's face widened into an evil, leering grin. — You're asking me to protect your whorehouse? If that's the case, then sí, I could round up a few. At least the ones who aren't dead or in jail. But you know, señora, protection comes at a price.

— I know that. Money is not a problem.

He cackled and slapped his hand against his side.

— Well then, looks like you got yourself a deal.

❖ ❖ ❖

Madam Félix and her two Marias returned without incident to Corazón de la Fuente. Shortly after entering the town, they spotted Roberto Pántelas, the grieving molinero, who was now walking with canes in both hands and taking only the most faltering of steps. Seeing this, they turned away, there being a limit to how much sadness the human spirit can process.

As they unhitched the buggy, the other Marias heard them and came running. When Madam told them that the town would soon learn to treat them with the respect that each and every one of them deserved, they all clapped and jumped up and down like children.

Two days later, Ramón rode into Corazón de la Fuente, his left hand holding the reins of his horse, the remains of his right arm flapping against his side like a spasmodic wing. Behind him rode seven men on five horses, each looking as soiled and life-worn as his commander. To announce their presence they rode slowly through town, laughing and firing pistols and attempting to spy on señoritas through shuttered windows and calling the men on the street hijos de putas. After two or three circles, Ramón pulled his horse to a stop in the middle of the plaza and dismounted. By this point, most of the drifters and vendors who now made permanent use of the square had scattered. Those who hadn't took refuge behind benches or hid beneath faded ponchos.

But there was one homeless drunkard, sitting with his back against a wall on the east side of the square, who pointed at the desperados and said something in an unintelligible growl. This caught Ramón's attention, and the sound of his boot steps could be heard across the plaza. He reached the man, who was unshaven and half-toothless and wearing stained clothing. Ramón kicked the soles of the man's boots, causing him to jump a little.

— You say something, borracho?

The man coughed and focused his gaze upwards. — Ized . . . hoon the helleroo?

Ramón's face screwed into a grin. — I still didn't get that.

This time the drunkard took his time, and all of his energy, to form his words. — I said, who in the hell're you?

Ramón pulled a rifle out of the tether strung across his shoulders. He grinned again, and swung the stock at the lower half of the man's face. There was an eruption of red. The sky instantly seemed to darken and the winds seemed to swirl and the whole of the town was forced to listen to the drunken man's gurgling wails.

Ramón, satisfied that he had the attention of the town, walked back towards the middle of the plaza and loudly announced: — ANY A YOU COCKSUCKERS TRY ANYTHING WITH THE WHORES, YOU'LL HAVE ME AND MY BOYS TO DEAL WITH. AND THE NEXT TIME, WE AIN'T GONNA BE IN SUCH GOOD MOODS.

When they'd all finished chuckling, Ramón and his wild bunch walked to the House of Gentlemanly Pleasures. There they were offered baths, fine liquor, cigars, and a free session with a Maria of their choice. All of it was paid for by Madam Félix, who, gazing out over the plaza, felt a gratitude of which she was not at all proud.

{30}

THE SOUND OF VIOLETA CRUZ LOSING THE CONTENTS
of her stomach drifted onto the street fronting the house
she shared with her grievously disappointed mother. There
it was heard by Ramón and his White Shirts, who were out
conducting their first patrol of the day. They stopped and
listened, Ramón trying to decide whether this insipid racket
represented an insult to either the madam or her Marias.
Not being able to imagine a way in which it was, he spurred
the sides of his horse and reluctantly moved on. The others
followed.

Ramón and his thugs had been there about a week, and
their method of surveillance had evolved into a routine. Every
three hours or so they emerged on horseback from the corral
that backed the House of Gentlemanly Pleasures and slowly
loped along Avenida Cinco de Mayo, their horses treading
upon anyone who didn't have the sense to get out of the way.
After a slow, menacing turn around the circumference of the
plaza, they continued clopping along Cinco de Mayo. When

they reached its end, they cast admiring glances towards the hacienda belonging to a Spanish hacendero named Antonio Garcia, many of them making a mental note to ransack what was left of the place the next time they had a full afternoon to themselves. They then turned south and passed through the quaint plazita that was home to something called the Pozo de Confesiones, where an elderly man sat parked in a home-made wicker wheelchair, shakily drooling and staring at the ground; the other townsfolk referred to him as the molin-ero, and made a habit of leaving parcels of food and drinking water on his spindly, quivering lap.

The horsemen clopped along Avenida Hidalgo, casting threatening glances at anyone who looked as though he might be planning something. Upon re-entering the plaza central, they languorously patrolled its perimeter a second time, bull-whips looped at their sides, their holsters containing pistols the size of rolling pins. They exited via the south end, a route that took them by the cantina belonging to a moustachioed hombre named Carlos Hernandez. Here they dismounted, went inside, and ordered rounds of tequila, mescal, cervezas, and an odoriferous pulque that was routinely left too long in the sun. When they eventually stumbled to their feet, they made no attempt to recompense the cantina owner. In the minds of Ramón and his White Shirts, it was the price the town had to pay for the restoration of law and order.

The horsemen then rode towards the far corner of the pueblo, near where an old crone referred to as the curandera was rumoured to live. They had all taken note of her filthy, teetering shack, for they all knew that she would be the per-son who would treat the infections, sores, and inflammations they would inevitably contract in the brothel. The White Shirts then returned to the House of Gentlemanly Pleasures, where they watered their horses and smoked and talked of the old days. Those who had developed manly urges headed inside, where they demanded release from a Maria of choice. Thus sated, they napped until their next patrol.

With such rigorous policing, the town soon fell into a tense, sorrowful gloom, not unlike the one that had manifested itself during the years of the revolution. Graffiti denouncing Dr. Brinkley appeared on walls and fence lines, and many of the townsfolk got into the habit of tossing putrid food at the base of the tower, such that the site soon began to resemble a large open-air compost heap. Upon passing in the street, long-time residents were sure to greet each other with only the most reserved tilt of their cowboy hats, afraid that anything more might somehow offend the White Shirts.

The attacks on Madam and her Marias ceased. There were no more slurs, dismissive gestures, or unkind words. If one of the Marias felt like taking a walk, she could do so alone, at any hour of the day or night, confident that any and all townsfolk would now cross the street to avoid her. Madam, meanwhile, resumed her long-standing practice of strolling the plaza, puffing contentedly on a Honduran cigarillo, the sun falling warm across her shoulders. To be truthful, she felt bad that her fellow townsfolk, upon seeing her, now ducked inside their homes, not trusting themselves to feign the cordiality insisted on by Ramón. It was a reluctance, she hoped, that would dwindle once the ragged old mercenary left her employ. Given the way things were going, that would undoubtedly be soon.

So complete was the compliance offered by the citizens of Corazón de la Fuente that Ramón and his men soon grew bored. To counteract the monotony, they spent more time drinking at the cantina, playing endless rounds of cards, and having their way with Madam's youthful, bronze-skinned employees. These pursuits sated Ramon and his pistoleros for a short while only; they had a yearning for action that had been growing, like a malignancy, since the death of their sworn enemy, Pancho Villa.

One afternoon, Ramón and two of his White Shirts were lazing on one of the plaza's wrought-iron benches, passing a bottle of tequila requisitioned from the cantina. Shortly after they'd tossed away the emptied bottle, one of the town's chicas, a relatively plain girl of no more than thirteen years of age, hurried by them, a filled laundry basket in her arms. The inevitable whistles and catcalls followed: it was the way in which the material of her skirt defined the outline of her nascent hips.

— Ay, qué bella, said one of the men. — I tell you, Ramón, there ought to be a law.

— Ay sí, there ought to be.

There was a moment of silence, during which one of them belched.

— You know, Ramón added, — that's the problem with this shitty little town: there are no laws. And no police, unless of course you count that gimpy little worm they call mayor.

— You're right, said the others.

— In fact, said Ramón, who was now getting excited,

— that's what we should do. We should give these people some goddamn rules to follow.

And so Ramón invented a code of conduct for the people of Corazón de la Fuente to disobey. Ironically, many of these bore a moralistic hue, which is always the case when laws are created by the despicable. Women who wore blouses that were at all clinging or low-cut were stopped, punitively fondled, and told to go home and change into something more befitting a good Catholic woman. If the White Shirts heard rumours of a man with a mistress — a description that applied to the majority of hombres in Corazón de la Fuente — they promptly went to the man's door, shot off the lock, dragged him out onto the street, and forced him to apologize so loudly that his frightened voice ricocheted off the town's pink and blue adobe walls.

One afternoon while sitting around a table in the cantina, Ramón's men discussed the problem of crowding in the streets. After an hour of drunkenly tabled ideas, they came up with a system of controlling pedestrian traffic that involved crosswalks, one-way streets, and a ban on unnecessary sprinting. These rules were posted for half a day. Anyone caught violating one of them was forced to imitate a chicken in the very same bandstand where the Reyes brothers had once performed chokeholds and half-nelsons. There was no shortage of offenders — Ramón's rules were so complicated and nonsensical that Ramón himself barely understood them. This, of course, was deliberate. Ramón and his men now spent entire afternoons in the plaza, firing pistols at the feet of violators who performed their punishment with insufficient zest.

Deemed a hazard, open fires were prohibited, even though the ejido dwellers and the homeless people camping in the plazas depended on them for their evening meals. Singing, energetic dancing, and public displays of drunkenness were likewise banned; the latter particularly stuck in the craw of Corazón's citizenry, given how Ramón's men reeked, at all hours of the night and day, of liquor. Marihuana was likewise illegalized, despite the fact that it grew abundantly along the banks of the Río Grande — it was Ramón's stated belief that its effects made people lazy and that anyone caught smoking even the smallest amount deserved to circle the town while tied, stomach down, to the back of a burro. Naturally, Ramón and his White Shirts smoked all of the confiscated marihuana themselves, becoming so forgetful that they often punished the same individual two or three times for the same infraction.

One afternoon, a group of Ramón's men were sitting in the plaza bandstand, passing a bottle of tequila requisitioned from the cantina. Soon they were all howling drunk. Pistols were discharged, and the air filled with the scent of gunpowder. Two of them — both had low simian brows and an odour reminiscent of hog slop — decided to visit the store operated by Fajardo Jimenez. There they picked out packs of American cigarettes, bottles of warm pop, bags of processed tortillas, avocados, ammunition, limes, bunches of coriander, and the long strips of marinated beef neck used for fajitas. The drunker of the White Shirts stumbled and knocked over a pyramid of frijole cans. The display came down in staccato thuds, each can making a small splintered divot in the lacquered floorboards.

When the White Shirt who had knocked over the cans did nothing to right the display — he even laughed, a wad of sputum gurgling in the back of his throat — Fajardo Jimenez, unable to contain himself any longer, spoke.

— Excuse me.

The men turned, eyes narrowed.

— You forgot to pay.

The White Shirts were sure they'd misheard, so remote was the possibility that this carnivalesque store owner was actually asking for compensation.

Fajardo leaned on the counter, revealing hands that looked like bear paws. — Por favor, he said. — I'm sure you just forgot.

The White Shirts regarded each other with a look tinged with adolescent joy, and then they laughed like hyenas. The smaller of the two took out the pistol he carried at his waist, pointed it drunkenly, and shot Fajardo in the fleshy part of the upper thigh. Fajardo fell to the floor, moaning. The White Shirt, meanwhile, didn't think to hurry; he levelled his pistol and was about to finish the job when the other White Shirt put a hand on the man's worn, grease-stained sleeve.

— Not so fast, primo. This hombre is clearly an insurrectionist. It's our duty to make an example of him.

— Sí, sí. A Villa supporter through and through.

They discussed possible courses of justice, not caring that a bleeding man was writhing on the floor next to them. After a minute or two, they came to the earnest decision that shooting him was too quick, lynching was a waste of good rope, and tarring and feathering would necessitate too much work. Instead they concluded that the solution lay in the rope one of them had in his saddlebag. As the shorter White Shirt sat on Fajardo's heaving chest, the taller tied an end around the store owner's feet. After admiring each other's handiwork, they dragged Fajardo out of the store, the back of his head bumping on the steps leading to the dusty calle. There they secured the other end of the rope to the saddle of a horse.

As they began to drag Fajardo through the streets of the village, the other White Shirts heard the Zacatecan's screams. They all came out and, relieved that something was finally happening in this dreary little two-bit town, mounted their horses and began firing their pistols in the air while fiend-ishly whooping and screaming old war slogans at the tops of their lungs. Even though this produced an extreme amount of noise, a peculiar form of silence also descended upon the town, a silence that existed beneath the White Shirts' sadistic revelry not unlike the underlay of a carpet. It was a silence made from impotence and fear, from noses pressed against windowpanes, from the riddance of a town's collective soul. It was the sound, they all realized, of history doing the only thing it knows how to do.

As the bandoleros charged through town, slowly killing one of Corazón de la Fuente's favourite citizens, those liv-ing in the streets and laneways kept their heads down, seeing nothing. Those lucky enough to reside in houses went back to their griddles and hammocks. The screams and whoops kept on. They echoed off the church, the hall, the cantina. Grown men cried, forcing their women to hold them, for the action in the street was inspiring blood-soaked flashbacks of the revolution. Consoling the men also helped the town's women ease their own suffering, for they all remembered the days before the tower, when everyone had been as gaunt as beggars, and Fajardo Jimenez had been known for pointing at perfectly good produce and saying *Ay, señora, some of those peppers are too blemished to sell. It'd help me out if you could take a couple off my hands . . .*

For this reason it was mostly the town's children who witnessed the store owner's demise — children who broke free from their mothers and, attracted by the noise, pressed their awed, wide-eyed faces against windowpanes, only to discover that, for the innocent, horror can be a difficult thing to look away from.

{31}

IN THE DAYS FOLLOWING THE SUMMARY EXECUTION
of Fajardo Jimenez, the town's gloom worsened, becoming
an icy, deadened calm. The sounds of living that had previously emanated from the ejido and the plaza after nightfall
turned to a sombre, almost sepulchral, quiet. The homeless
living on the streets of Corazón de la Fuente, too exhausted
and poor to travel, sought refuge in the town's nooks and
crannies, such that it was no longer possible to traverse an
alley or peer down a dead-end lane without encountering
a penurious family from the south, attempting to cook tortillas over low white embers. Long-time residents of Corazón
rarely left their casas, emerging only to forage for food, wash
their clothes in steaming outdoor tubs, or attend to their
jobs as day labourers over the border in Del Rio. Mothers,
who as teenagers of the revolution had taken sanctuary in
the gulches and gullies surrounding Corazón, escorted their
daughters to their old hiding places, often breaking into tears
along the way.

Shortly afterwards, Corazón de la Fuente was visited with another debasement, this one in the form of a harelipped gringo businessmen who, one wretched morning, crossed over the bridge between nations. Accompanying him were an old donkey and a cart so teetering with firearms that pistols and handguns kept falling into the street and accidentally discharging, in one case wounding a woman hanging laundry to dry. While in peaceful times the gun peddler would have been told he was unwelcome and forcefully removed from the village, on this day he was surrounded by mercenaries and homeowners alike. They stood side by side around his cart, looking at Colts and derringers and even a few requisitioned Lugers, ignoring the fact that they would likely be using the weapons on each other. Included amongst that day's customers was the cantina owner; as he looked into the man's arctic-grey eyes, he suffered the chilling, and most likely accurate, sensation that this hombre represented the heart and the soul of all wars everywhere. Beset with this impression, he yearned to take the sidearm he'd just selected and dispatch the salesman to whatever death pit he'd crawled from in the first place. Instead he counted off a roll of pesos and grumbled his thanks.

Time lurched. It seemed as though the whole town was in mourning. Women who had lost husbands during the revolution once again donned the black dresses of grieving widows. At midday, those obliged to walk through the streets of the town reported the eerie feeling that unseen eyes were watching them, peering diabolically from cracks and fissures in the adobe. At night the village somehow seemed darker, the blackness of the skies overwhelming the frog-green corona produced by the tower's colossal signal. Everything became dulled, as if coated in a depressive moss. The town's blue and pink adobe walls seemed muted in hue, and vultures could be seen circling languorously overhead, as though awaiting a bonanza. Rumours arose that translucent presences had been spotted rising from the graves of the municipal cemetery, an apparent attempt to flee to other eternal resting places; even the spirits of the dead, it seemed, could not bear to watch the ruination of Corazón de la Fuente.

On one such day, the sky was overcast with rainclouds that would no doubt hover, produce not a single drop of moisture, and then dissipate into finely spun wisps. Ramón and a few of his thugs, insane with boredom, entered the town's only saloon. Without so much as a nod towards the proprietor, they sat around one of the bigger tables and pounded their fists. The cantina owner brought them a round of cervezas. They drank these within minutes and again thumped the butts of their hands against the table. The cantina owner gritted his teeth and brought another round. The White Shirts consumed these as well, and then started barking for tequila, or mescal, or whisky — anything that offered a little kick. Suffering particularly acute visions of the night when the Villista captain had put a gun to his head and set his bar on fire, Carlos swept up every remaining bottle from behind the bar and impudently carried them over. He roughly dropped them to the table's knotty surface and said *Knock yourselves out, primos*. The cantina owner then went back to his seat in front of the cracked mirror, where he watched and seethed and nervously wound the tips of his gargantuan moustache, all the while thinking *Not again, you cabrones, you pendejos, you hijos de putas. Not again.*

The White Shirts drank until the only ones not lolling in their seats were a pair of scoundrels who had lost consciousness and were sleeping with the sides of their faces in pools of condensation. The floor was graced by puddles of partly digested stew, the pissoir tacked to the wall ran with a foul, bubbly release, and the air inside the cantina was acrid with expelled, mescal-soaked breath. It was at this point that Carlos Hernandez emerged from behind his bar, walked up to the White Shirts, and pounded the tabletop so hard that a pair of bottles fell to the floor and broke with a crash.

— That's it. You've drunk me dry. No more. I'm finished. The cantina's closed forever. I have *had* it.

Ramón, one of the few men in the cantina sober enough to understand the impudence of the cantina owner's statement, took out his pistol and shot into the ceiling and the floor. He was about to shoot the cantina owner when Carlos, eyes blazing, hands shaking with adrenalin, produced his newly purchased Smith & Wesson. He then joined in Ramón's shooting, whooping like a desperado, firing so wantonly at the walls and floors and ceiling that by the time he was finished his cantina was little more than a splintered accumulation of sawdust, spilled liquid, and smoke. The cantina owner stood panting in the middle of the ruin. Plaster dust adhered to the perspiration coating his skin, causing him to look like a wide-eyed ghost.

— That was the most fun I've had in years, he said as he reloaded his pistol. — Now get out, you filthy, grunting pigs. Your smell is making me ill.

Rightly concluding that the cantina owner had lost his senses, those White Shirts still graced with consciousness rose wobbling to their feet. They then backed out with their hands held skyward, even the most insensate among them noticing that the cantina owner was grinning like a rested house cat.

Now that this sort of insolence existed in Corazón, Ramón and his White Shirts reduced the number of their patrols. Instead they spent their time brooding in their encampment behind Madam's bordello, feeling resentful that they were forced to serve in a town with neither a cantina nor a place to buy even the most basic of supplies. The Marias began giving Ramón's men the most hostile of looks every time they went inside the house to demand a quick pleasuring; they had begun to feel that dealing with the White Shirts was more onerous than dealing with the town's resentfulness. Thus came the day in which Madam, regretting the frenzy she'd let loose upon the town, called Ramón into her office. A pile of gringo dollars, held together with elastic bands, rested on her desktop.

— Enough, she told him. — You've done enough. Here's your last pay, along with a healthy bonus.

Ramón walked up, took the money, and rapidly counted it, looking neither pleased nor disappointed. He then looked at her and winked.

— I got a better idea, he said. — How's about we leave when *we* think the job is done.

He left her office and exited the brothel. — Cabrones! he barked. — Full company, report. Now.

The men all groaned, rose from their bedrolls, tied on their holsters, attached spurs to their boots, and wrapped themselves in the bandoliers worn by soldiers, bandits, and revolutionaries alike. They all mounted horses that, like their owners, had grown lethargic and grumpy with age. The animals expressed their displeasure by whinnying and attempting to bite their riders on the calf. In return they were spurred and smacked hard on the flank and whipped on the rump and in this way were reminded who was boss. Someone opened the gate, and Ramón's White Shirts clopped onto Avenida Cinco de Mayo.

As the White Shirts lazily rode towards the centre of town, the gringos lining up for the House of Gentlemanly Pleasures all sensed trouble and scattered. As always, Ramón and his men rode slowly around the plaza, one of them exhaling deeply and grumbling *Ay, qué feo es éste pueblito*. Mostly, however, they were quiet. The sun felt hot on their necks and coat sleeves. The sky was a bleached, cloudless blue. Above them an eagle floated lazily, hunting for mice. There were nine men slowly riding that day, and in their heads ran nine different thoughts — money, food, the past, the future, women they had known, sons and daughters who had gone off to live in los Estados, how nice it would be to leave Corazón, how nice it would be to have a cool bath, how a cerveza might go down well about now. They all grew hot and restless. Two of them even fell into that place halfway between sleep and wakefulness, where the muscles lose their tension and thoughts turn illogical. The only sound was the gentle, rhythmic clop of hooves on packed road dust . . . that is, until gunshot ricocheted through the plaza, and the head of one of the company members, an older hombre named Pedro, erupted in a funnel of pink.

They heard a second report, and then a White Shirt named Alfredo was holding his upper arm and yelling *I've been hit, I've been hit* and the company charged towards the shelter offered by a laneway, where they all drew their pistols and fired madly in the direction from which the bullets had come. This lasted for minutes and minutes. When they finally stopped shooting, the town smelled of gunpowder and the air was clogged with risen dust and the only sound was the groaning of a few innocent transients who had been shot while attempting to flee for safety. The White Shirts all listened for movement; upon hearing nothing they charged back to the corral. There they regrouped. Alfredo, who had suffered a flesh wound only, had his bullet dug out with the heated blade of a camping knife, his only anesthesia a wad of denim clamped between his teeth. When the ordeal was over, he muttered *Gracias, amigos,* slumped to the earth, and succumbed to the fever that would kill him a few days later.

To the backdrop of the downed man's delirious groaning, Ramón paced back and forth, his half-arm flopping. His eyes blazed scarlet, a consequence of rage and of having spent the entire afternoon smoking pipefuls of confiscated marihuana. That afternoon played out with nauseating familiarity for those who remembered the revolution. The remaining White Shirts, invigorated by their own interpretation of justice and morality, went from door to door searching for sympathizers. At each house they bullied and interrogated and frightened and spat accusations and struck hombres in the solar plexus with the butts of their rifles and conducted full-body searches on any woman not hiding in the desert.

Dusk came that night with flies and the rotting of flesh. Ramón and his desperados retired to their encampment. This time, Madam was waiting for them outside her place of business, her expression one of abject disgust.

— Ramón! she spat.

The surviving White Shirts stopped.

— I've asked you to leave already and this time I mean it! All of you. Pack your things and get out of my sight.

Ramón dismounted. He approached and slowly circled her, his shuffling steps raising dust. From the back of the house, the assembled Marias could hear the spurs on his boots clink. He finally stopped, regarded Madam, and spat onto the ground.

— You ain't getting this, he said. — There's an insurrectionary presence out there. Probably some old Villistas who heard we're still in business. Come to town to make themselves known — just the sorta thing those damn communists would do.

— I don't care. You work for me. Or you did. I've paid you enough. I paid you enough a long time ago. Now leave.

This time, to further communicate her request, Madam unclasped the handbag she was carrying. She reached inside, extracted the small pearl-handled revolver that she used in moments of emergency, and trained it between Ramón's beady reddened eyes.

— Whatta you gonna do? he challenged. — Shoot us all?

— That would not be possible, said Madam. — But I know you'd be a dead man.

— I would? Well, lemme remind you of something. Anything happens to me and a hell's gonna rain down on your sluts the likes of which they ain't never seen.

He then nodded at one of his goons, who was upon Madam in a second. A shot whistled through the air, and then two more of Ramón's men beset Madam, who screamed and yelled and attempted to kick her assailants in the shins. In response, the biggest of the thugs slapped her hard across the face, a stinging, welt-inspiring attack that converted her screams to soprano whimpers. She was then dragged through the back door of the House of Gentlemanly Pleasures, where the goons stopped at a closet filled with brooms, cleaning fluids, and the sadomasochistic toys used by Maria de la Noche. *Please*, Madam begged, her words falling on ears deafened by years of gunplay. They opened the door, shoved her inside, and turned the key protruding from the lock. The Marias could hear her pleading and pounding against the door, a sound that converted them into a group of cowering schoolgirls.

Ramón walked past them, pleased with the way in which his lackeys had defused the situation. He turned to the Marias.

— Now, all you whores. Get outside and stay there. It ain't safe for us to camp out there in full view. From now on, we live in here and you do all a your fucking outside, you understand? It's the war all over again, ladies. You should feel lucky we're here to protect you against them godless commies.

With that, the Marias were given a few minutes to collect their things and head to the White Shirts' filthy encampment. That night, word spread on both sides of the river that the famed Marias, owing to some skirmish in Corazón, were now plying their trade from pup tents smelling of sweat, old socks, and seminal emissions. It was news that spurred all but the most faithful of their customers to decamp for bordellos in Sabinas or Piedras Negras.

Ramón and his men spent the early part of the next day indoors, drinking fine amber cognac that, once upon a time, Madam had served to the hacendero Antonio Garcia. As the morning wore on they grew indignant, their instinct for self-preservation overwhelmed by boredom and alcohol-fuelled bravado. Ramón's men soon started insisting that they rush out and start firing, overwhelming their foes with a combination of surprise and ruthlessness. Ramón thought about this and agreed, his one condition being that they wait until nightfall, when the cover of darkness would also be theirs.

Time slowed. Trigger fingers grew itchy and muscles twitched. By half past two Ramon and his wild dogs could stand it no longer. They ran whooping into the street, forgetting that nightfall and the element of surprise were to have been the cornerstones of their strategy. Firing at everything that moved, they made their way to the central plaza, where shots rained upon them from a rooftop at the southeast corner of the square.

— Take cover! Ramón yelled, and the paramilitaries ducked behind the bandstand. There they dug in.

The ensuing gun battle proceeded languorously, with long periods of inactivity interrupted by brief, intense moments of bloodletting. Every hour or so, one of the sides would attempt to change positions, resulting in mad scrambling and a consequent loss of life. In time Ramón determined that their enemies wore hats, black shirts, bandanas over the lower half of their faces, and — a sure sign they were communists — the huaraches commonly worn by peasants. This enraged him even further, such that he stopped fighting on behalf of principles, or ideals, or even the desire to acquire material goods.

Oh no. When Ramon next ordered his men to charge out from behind the bandstand, guns blazing at everything that moved, he was enraged by the same bitter reciprocity that fuels all war: you have done that awful thing to me, and I have done that awful thing to you, and both of us have done awful things to each other, and so on, and so on, and so on, and so on . . .

Meanwhile, inside his tiny house, a heartbroken molinero named Roberto Pántelas listened to the battle wax and wane outside his window. He was confused, for the revolution had ended long ago, though you would never have known it, not with all the infernal racket outside (*Can't they let an old man expire in peace?*). If there was one thing the molinero had learned in his long, long life it was that men will always find something to fight about, the rationale not mattering nearly so much as the fighting itself. This was just one of the reasons he so preferred women, and with this sweet yet sorrowful thought running through his head, he took a laboured breath and lay back, and he placed a hand over the pain emanating from the centre of his chest and he thought *Ay, viejo, you've had a good run, even if you never had a wife or children, life hasn't treated you so badly, you always had something about you that attracted the fairer sex like flies to spilled honey, you shouldn't ever forget that.* And as he lay looking at the dim wooden rafters above, he thought of some of the women he had known throughout his long, long life. He thought of women with hair as light as marigold petals and he thought of women with hair as dark as Coahuilan evenings. He thought of women with a scent so sweet you'd swear they were made from honey and he thought of women with a scent so musky it made your mind race with wickedness. He thought of women who liked to laugh and others who behaved as solemnly as widows, and *Ay, ay, viejo, remember that time in Saltillo, when a rubia invited you to bed only to be discovered by her best friend, who then asked, using the formal* usted *no less, if you minded very much if she joined in? Sí, molinero, those were the days, and don't forget that woman in Monterrey who asked for rope and lanolin and then used them both with the cleverness of a professor.*

Of course, those times had meant nothing in comparison to the episodes of real love, for he had been in love so many times, and so many times he had been *this* close to the altar when, as little as a week before (or, on one shrill and awful occasion, the very day of), someone else had come along, someone a little more charming, a little more beautiful, just a little bit younger. And how could he make them understand that he really did love them all, each and every one of them, be they young or old, pretty or plain, rich or poor, lusty or otherwise? It didn't matter — if anything, it was their differences that he celebrated, the variation to be found in the world of mujeres (whereas with hombres, *ay*, so alike, so lacking in nuance, so simplistic in their desires, for which reason he always thought that if he had been born a woman he would have become a lesbian, so that he could still make love to other women even if it did mean burning in hell). In fact, by the age of twelve, when he first discovered the pleasures of the flesh in a brothel in Villa Acuña, he'd known what his grand passion in life would be, knew the manner in which his existence would have purpose. Few men could say that, and if he had some regrets, it is also true that all men have regrets, for what is a life without regrets and mistakes and tumbles taken in the road? And it was not as though he hadn't been able to settle down and love a single woman, even though for most of his life he had thought it beyond his capabilities. On the contrary, his life had been a funny thing, for in the last year he had met a woman who replaced all women in the depths of his old and irregularly beating heart, a woman who made him forget that other women existed, a woman whom he'd wanted to marry and who, despite his advanced years, was more than happy with their plans to have as many children as they could manage (*and you could have managed plenty, couldn't you have, you old rooster, you old rascal, you feverish old billy goat*). So how could she have gone before him? How was it that God — who couldn't possibly be upset by his years of giving pleasure to others, who couldn't possibly begrudge the way He had made the molinero — could have taken away the grandest love he had ever known?

To show his displeasure, the molinero committed his first and final act of Catholic betrayal. He closed his eyes and did not think of the countless miracles that God provides, from sunsets to flowers to animals, from days spent resting to the taste of a well-made flauta to the dense, spongy feel of a young woman's tetas, from the wonder of light over the desert to the dusty pine taste of tequila to the shock that is thunder to the mystical sound of wind blowing over sand. Instead he just let himself go, he just let himself drift away, and as he did, it was with the spiriting thought that he would soon be joining his amor, his mujer, his Laurita.

He then took his final breath, his soul becoming air, his blood the moisture of clouds, his thoughts the presence felt in the shadow of ancient places.

{32}

THE FOLLOWING DAY, RAMÓN DISPATCHED A RIDER
into the surrounding countryside. A few days later, the rider
returned with a half-dozen more fighters sympathetic to their
old cause, all of whom yearned for the excitement of days gone
by. They were offered lodgings in the House of Gentlemanly
Pleasures, the new recruits laying out their bedrolls in small
rooms with dark red walls and ceilings. They unpacked
changes of clothing and found a place to spit their chewing
tobacco. Cigarillos were lit and guano-encrusted boots placed
on fine furniture. Soon Madam's previously well-kept brothel
was littered with old saddle blankets, half-empty bottles,
and underpants. Having lost its scent of rosewater and fine
tobacco, the house now smelled like the whiff one gets upon
passing the partially opened door of a public latrine.

For a few days Ramón's army ruled the town, the enemy
now outmanned, outgunned, and not daring to engage the
opposite side. This hesitant peace lasted until the Villistas
sent away a rider of their own, who promptly returned with

his own posse of gunslingers sympathetic to *their* old cause. For those townsfolk who dared leave their houses, it was common to glance up and notice men in dark bandanas and bandoliers taking cover behind chimneystacks. Now that the two armies were on even terms, the fighting continued with a renewed vigour, one side firing up into the sky, the other firing down into the streets. The plazas and avenidas of Corazón de la Fuente refilled with gunfire, shouted orders, and the groaned misgivings of men who not only lay dying but had chosen that moment to understand the ways in which they'd squandered their time on earth. The people of Corazón de la Fuente, meanwhile, responded in a manner that had become second nature during the throes of the revolution. They gave a depressed communal sigh, formed groups of volunteers, and, to avoid an outbreak of cholera, dutifully cleared the streets of bodies whenever there was a lull in the fighting.

One night, as the street cleaners performed their grisly duties, Francisco Ramirez climbed out his bedroom window. He stood for a moment, peering in either direction, and then headed towards the molinero's tiny house. It had been days since anyone had seen Roberto Pántelas, and with Laura Velasquez gone there was nobody who routinely visited the old man. Francisco was concerned.

He moved along the rear walls of houses, conscious that, despite the apparent calm, he was nevertheless putting himself at risk. Still, it was after midnight, and there was a good chance that any White Shirts or socialists who happened to be out would be drunk; Francisco was confident that he would detect them before they detected him. Sticking to shadows wherever possible, he darted across the plaza and reached the Pozo de Confesiones. He knocked quietly on the molinero's door, looking quickly in every direction to ensure he'd not been heard.

When there was no answer, he tapped again, this time daring to softly call out the molinero's name. There was still no answer, so he moved to the window of the one-room house and gazed in. He could see the old man on his bed, hands clasped over his chest, a look of frozen contemplation on his face. Francisco smelled the faint odour of decaying flesh seeping through the pores of the adobe walls, and he noticed that the molinero barely made any impression on the mattress beneath him. Francisco rapped daringly on the window, despite knowing full well that a combination of heartache and cancer had swept the courtly old man to heaven.

My old amigo, he thought. *I should have come earlier.*

Francisco's eyes dampened. He moved along the façades of the houses, finding a tiny alley leading to the rear of the homes. As in most dwellings in Corazón, the molinero's kitchen extended from the back of the house, protected only by a wooden awning. Francisco tried opening the back door, only to find that it too was locked. With a single kick, the door splintered and flew open, smashing against the wall on which it hung. Again Francisco froze, alert to possible reprisals. He heard the far-off call of a coydog and the faint signal of Brinkley's damnable station and a rustling of desert breezes, and that was all.

He entered, the stench forming a vinegary liquid on his tongue. There were flies buzzing in the heated air and a half-consumed cup of coffee on the molinero's table. Francisco crossed the floor and went to his old friend, his fear of death and all its cold incarnations overshadowed by the love he felt for the molinero.

— Señor Pántelas, he murmured as he kissed the old man's cold forehead. — I'm here. Don't worry, I'm here now. You're no longer alone. I should have come earlier but I didn't, and for this I am sorry.

He gently covered his old amigo with a blanket, straightened his hair, and made sure his hands were in a comfortable position. Then, as a final tribute to the molinero, he tried to summon the heartache he would feel were it his own father before him — he hoped that this feeling might ease the old man's passage to the next world and make him feel as though his time spent in the world of mortals had not been without purpose or meaning. Francisco felt an ache in his chest and throat. He thought of non-existence, and the way it always loomed on the horizon, sullying the experience of living; better to be a dog, or a toad, and have no consciousness of your own mortality. When a tear finally loosened and dribbled down his pink, burning cheek, he swiped at it bitterly.

— Señor Roberto Pántelas, he said in a voice weakened by sadness. — It has been a pleasure to know you. No matter how long I live, I will never forget you. Tomorrow I will tell Father Alvarez that you have gone to heaven, and we will somehow find a way to bury you in the middle of the war that has broken out in your beloved Corazón de la Fuente. So do not have fear. I promise that your final passage will be graceful, and that you will rest in eternal peace, and that your legacy here in Corazón will be one of kindness, and obedience, and faith.

His throat began to close against the smell, making it difficult to speak. He thought of all the little talks he'd had with the molinero over the years, and the way that he had come away from each one feeling as though life's little challenges were just jokes, played upon us by someone or something with a magisterial sense of humour. He also remembered the day that he and the old man became friends: Francisco had been a little kid, attracted by the sound of grinding corn, and he'd impishly asked the old man if he could help. *Cómo no*, the molinero had answered. *I'd be glad for the company, hand me that bucket of corn, my goodness you're strong, how old did you say you were? What? Just seven? My goodness you're going to grow into an hombre and a half, verdad?*

Francisco shuddered, for it seemed like that was just yesterday; the frenzied way in which time passed was as bitter a reality as mortality itself. A darkness invaded his heart. Gazing down at his old friend, Francisco Ramirez understood that there were times when goodness, while a necessity for gaining access to heaven, was also a hindrance in the world foisted upon men and women. With this realization came a further understanding — what the curandera had meant when she'd pointed a warty, crooked finger in his direction and said *You're the one.*

He took a deep, shuddering breath and spoke with a stronger voice.

— I will make one other promise to you, my old friend.

He took another breath, this one designed to fight off a mild dizziness.

— Before the week is out, I am going to get the goddamned cabrón who did this to you.

{33}

VIOLETA CRUZ SWUNG SLOWLY IN HER MOTHER'S hammock, savouring the love that every woman feels for her unborn child. She could feel it raging within her, churning in her stomach, simmering in her veins, replacing the marrow of her bones with a burning, mucilaginous lava. It pulsed in every part of her, in the arches of her feet and in the whites of her eyes and in the tender channel existing behind her slender kneecaps. It was a feeling so profound it almost hurt, albeit in places where discomfort feels lovely. Her maternal instincts thus awoken, they now possessed her, and she could not help but think to the time when she'd be raising her child — boy, girl, she didn't care — on the beneficent side of the river.

She couldn't wait to tell her bespectacled lover. He'd informed her on many occasions how much he liked children, and how much he wanted to have an entire houseful. He'd also confessed that this had been the main source of friction in his pitiable marriage — his wife's inability to give *him*, a four-time recipient of the Compound Operation, a baby. Violeta smiled and felt awed. He did not have to worry any longer. She would do this for him. She would grant him this gift, this miracle, this unabated joy.

Surely he'd be back by now.

Violeta rose and poked her head out her bedroom door. She looked from side to side, and wrinkled her nose at the smell left behind by the homeless who were using the back lane as a lavatory.

—Mami, she called

She listened, and heard nothing.

—*Mami?* she called again, her voice louder this time and filled with the wonder of possibility. Again she heard nothing. Her feet danced against the floor. She ducked back inside her room and dressed to please her doctor: long skirt, snug white blouse, a necklace. She brushed her long hair till it gleamed and she pinched the sides of her face with thumb and forefinger, even though pregnancy had left her with a continual flush. She rubbed a paste of crushed sand berries over her lips, leaving them the colour of a sunrise. She did so in a hurry, for she did not know when her mother would return.

Violeta took a single step into the dusty street. Though it was early in the day and the streets gravely quiet, she understood what fate would befall her should she run into an errant mercenary. More of a concern was her mother; she could well imagine how Malfil would react were she to catch her daughter trying to visit the man who had not only deflowered her, but created new life within her. For both reasons, simply waltzing across the bridge separating the two countries was out of the question.

Instead Violeta crept along the rear of the block, past ramadas and chicken coops and torn outdoor hammocks. She emerged in the Callejón of Resting Curs, which at that time of the day was thankfully still. She tiptoed around mangy, flea-bitten dogs, some as tiny as hamsters and some as large as the deer that roamed the plains of Coahuila, careful not to tread on any tails or accidentally kick a sensitive milk-filled teat. Poking her head into Avenida Cinco de Mayo, she hustled to the far side of the street and flattened herself against an adobe wall, her white cotton blouse picking up smears of light blue. After a brief rest, she moved along the laneway in which she was hiding, carefully climbed a wooden fence, traversed a stretch of brambly desert, and arrived at the southern bank of the Río Grande.

She paused, caught her breath, and slipped into the murky, slowly drifting water. The far bank was only a few hundred metres away, a distance she covered by aping the movements of deer who sometimes plunged into the river on afternoons when the heat grew oppressive. She entered the land called el Norte spewing grey water. Breathlessly she crawled onto the bank and lay in full sun, letting her clothes and hair dry enough that they were no longer dripping water. With her clothes still slightly damp, she climbed the bank and found her way to the road leading into Del Rio. It was there she discovered that a beautiful young Mexicana dressed in moist clothing had no trouble catching a ride with one of the Hispanic gardeners who plied that stretch of tarmac in old, coughing pickup trucks.

She was let off in front of the Roswell Hotel. After cross-ing herself, she lamented the way her wet hair had soaked through the back of her white cotton blouse — she felt like a walking cliché, a slur come alive. No matter; she didn't have time for such trivialities. As soon as she reached her doctor and told him of her condition, and of the conflict that had broken out in Corazón, he would usher her to his palace and she would start her life as the spouse of a respected American doctor. She straightened, took a deep breath, and walked through the reception area, drawing glances from those who were surprised to see Rose Dawn at such an odd hour. At the elevators she pressed the button for the fifth floor. As she rode upward she was visited by visions of her future, a future that included a riverside mansion and a brood of beautiful children. She closed her eyes and felt faint; it was too much for a young Mexicana to imagine, let alone experience. The doors opened. She walked quickly, so excited she had to struggle not to break into a run. She reached the outer room of Brinkley's office, where she was greeted by the doctor's secretary, a fair-haired woman named Sheila.

— Rose! she said. — How *are* you? I hear that things are difficult across the river.

— I am good, good. The doctor . . . is he in?

A puzzled expression came to Sheila's face.

— Haven't you heard?

— Haven't I heard . . . what?

— I can't believe no one's told you yet!

— Sheila, Violeta said, with a note of impatience. — Where is Dr. Brinkley?

— Why . . . he's *left*, Rose. He's setting up another clinic, this one in a small village back home in North Carolina. He says he's going to build a recreation centre for underprivileged children. He says it's his way of helping the place he came from. Mrs. Brinkley is there with him as well. He told me he wouldn't be back for six to eight months. From now on, his centre of operations will probably be there. Isn't it wonderful, the way he likes to help people?

Violeta's world tilted and turned wavy, and the first thing she felt was a strop-honed anger with herself, just for thinking that wonderful things could happen to a simple muchacha from a poor brothel town on the border. Her child would be fatherless now, a squalling little cabrón, Violeta its shamed and stupid mother. She felt tears fighting to escape whatever place produces them.

— Sí, she said, her face draining of colour and warmth. — It is.

She turned and walked out of the room. As she rode the elevator to the first floor, her feelings of self-contempt were replaced by a sudden realization. *Of course*, she thought. *How could I have been so stupid?* Often she had noted the way that Sheila looked at the doctor: admiringly, desirously, her eyelids batting the unconscious rhythm of one whose heart has been warmed. This confirmed it — Sheila was in love. Using the intuition granted by God to all women, Sheila had figured out that Violeta had graced the doctor's art-festooned bedchambers. Brinkley had not left. He wouldn't have done that. It was all a ruse, a swindle, a dissemination spawned by jealousy. In Violeta's turbulent mind, the fact that Sheila had uttered this fabrication with such a cheerful smile only added credence to her theory.

Well, thought Violeta. *We'll just see.*

With a palpitating heart, Violeta ran out onto the street

and found Del Rio's lone taxi driver, a pot-bellied gringo named Johnson who made a living mostly by taking old ladies on shopping expeditions. He was leaning against the hood of his Ford, drinking a cup of coffee.

— Hello, she said.

— Can I help you, missy?

— I am wishing to visit the house of Dr. Brinkley.

— It's quite a way.

— Jess, it is.

Johnson thought it over. — It'd cost put-near ten dollars.

— Ten dollars is fine.

Two minutes later Violeta was in the musty back seat of the car, gazing fearfully out the window as they left the town limits. As Johnson drove, she recalled the first time she had visited the doctor's mansion, and the feeling of airy limitless-ness that had possessed her. They passed all the landmarks that Violeta, over the past month and a half, had grown to take for granted: the furrowed grape fields, the old wooden livestock barns, the wavering pasture land, the cypress trees touching over the roadway, the algae coated swamp. This time she took note of each and every one.

Finally Johnson pulled up in front of the mansion. Violeta looked out, and felt a sickness invade every nook and recess of her being.

— Wait here, she said as she stepped out of the car and gazed up at the darkened house. Noticing that the tall wrought-iron gates were ajar, she walked up the path leading to the front doors of the mansion. She knocked, and knocked again. She then peered through a window into the gloom. All of the fur-niture was covered with sheets, and where oil canvases had once hung were now large rectangles of bleached wall space. She moved around the house and gazed miserably into the dining room where the doctor had first entertained her with champagne, fine food, and tales of his boyhood. The dining room table was covered as well, and it looked as though some-one had yanked the immense crystal chandelier from the ceiling, scattering bits of plaster and dried paint.

Violeta heard footsteps. She turned and saw two men, both dressed in dark suits and wearing sunglasses, come around the corner of the house. As soon as they saw Violeta they paused, only to then quicken their pace. They stopped when they reached her, looking breathless. One was carrying a clipboard and a pen.

— Good day, said the one who had been writing.

— Good day, Violeta answered.

— Tell me, would you know the owner of this house? asked the other.

Violeta hesitated. — I do.

— So you know Dr. Brinkley?

— I just stated that I did.

— Do you know where he happens to be?

Violeta shook her head, and for the next few minutes the two parties eyed each other, as though unsure of what to do next. Finally, the first dark-suited man cleared his throat and said: — Ma'am, I'm going to have to ask if you have any identification.

Violeta's heartache was immediately supplanted by panic. Though she did not know who these men were, or why they were lurking around the darkened house, she did know one thing. At no point had Brinkley ever arranged a work visa for her, or so much as mentioned the necessity of one, and it occurred to her that this may have been imprudent of him.

— Jess, she said. — I do. It is in the car. I will retrieve it.

She turned, commanding herself to walk as calmly as possible. Upon reaching the taxi, she looked back and saw that the two men were now peering at the upstairs windows, as though trying to glimpse a phantom.

— We will go, Violeta said.

— Who're them fellers? asked Johnson.

— I said *go*, Violeta barked, in a way that reminded her of her mother.

Johnson turned and saw the torment in Violeta's eyes. After studying her for a moment — her skin had reddened and her lips had started trembling — he turned back to face the dashboard and put the car in gear.

As they pulled away from Brinkley's mansion, Violeta forced herself to enter a cold, distant, emotionless place so that she wouldn't embarrass herself by dissolving into hysterics. Twenty minutes later, Johnson stopped at the bridge separating the two towns.

— We are no there yet, Violeta protested.

— You kiddin' me? With all the trouble y'all are having over there? I wouldn't cross that bridge if my life depended on it. Uh-uh, señorita. End of the line.

She paid the driver with dollars still damp from her swim in the river. She then tipped both guards, though not without telling them what she thought of their low, extorting ways, and how they would not be able to do this in a civilized world, and how one day God would cast a judgement upon them. Upon reaching Mexican soil, she began to run. She ran past starving campesinos and short, squat-shouldered Indians and sleeping, knife-hiding villains. She ran past vagos and borrachos and patrolling White Shirts, who grunted *Mamacita!* as she hurried by. She ran past Chiclets vendors and grubby-faced children and sellers of Indian corn-husk dolls. She ran past the town hall and she ran past the spireless church and she ran through the dark, dark shadow cast by the tower. She ran past the house of Francisco Ramirez and felt worse, knowing that, had men in black suits come looking for *him*, he'd have stayed and taken his medicine rather than abandon her. She then burst into her house and ran to her room, wailing.

She cried and she cried, her tears falling through the mesh of her hammock and pooling so prodigiously on the floor beneath her that, after a while, they began to drip through the floorboards, surprising the voles scurrying over the contents of their earth-walled root cellar. This went on for either minutes or hours, Violeta wasn't sure; she knew only that the point came when her eyes dried and she felt overwhelmed by thirst. Still she didn't get up. The door to her home opened and closed, and hearing this, she wished herself dead.

When Malfil entered her room, Violeta was staring into nothingness. She couldn't even roll over to avoid the brunt of her mother's fury.

— Violeta! her mother began, her voice as coiled as always. — What in the name of Jesús is going on?

That is when mother, employing both logic and instinct, came to understand what had happened to her daughter. Malfil's expression softened, and as it did she looked almost pretty. Her shoulders dropped and her eyes turned moist. She left the room and returned, carrying one of the chairs from the main room. She placed it next to her only daughter. A moment later, Violeta felt her mother's long, lye-scented fingers running through her hair.

— Your doctor, said Malfil. — He's gone, verdad?

Violeta's voice, when it finally came, was a gurgle. — Go ahead and say it, mami. Tell me I've been a fool and a tramp.

— Maybe tomorrow.

— You know you want to.

— What I want doesn't matter, mija. Not at this moment.

There was the longest of silences, during which Violeta started to blubber anew.

— Mami, she sputtered. — I feel so ashamed.

— I know.

— I feel so *stupid*.

Malfil took one of Violeta's hands and squeezed it. — Men do that to us, amor. They can't help it. It's like blaming a dog for scratching at fleas.

Violeta snuffled. Time elapsed. Outside, life carried on, unconcerned by the tribulations of people.

— What am I going to *do*? Violeta finally asked.

— Today, you do nothing. Tomorrow, we'll figure this out.

Violeta gulped air and sat up, strands of hair sticking to the tears on her face. Malfil raised herself up beside her. Violeta then did something that, just one day ago, she would have thought impossible. She rested her head on her mother's shoulder, an action that transported her to her days as a young child, the family not yet destroyed by revolution, Malfil relieving the hurt caused by a broken toy.

— Everything, Malfil assured her, — will look better in the morning.

A few seconds passed.

— And if it doesn't, we'll just wait for the morning after that.

{34}

FRANCISCO RAMIREZ RAISED HIS BEDROOM WIN-
dow, paused to see whether the attendant creak had woken
his brothers, and climbed into the laneway backing his casa.
He stood for a moment, peering in either direction, listening
for the sound of gunshots. After a minute he concluded there
was nothing out there beyond a slight breeze and insects and
the raspy panting of dogs.

He moved along the rear walls of houses, conscious that,
despite the apparent calm, he was nevertheless putting himself
at risk. Sticking to the shadows, he traversed north, towards
Avenida Cinco de Mayo. After a few minutes of dodging from
alcove to alcove, his shirt lit green with each darting movement, he snuck past the radio tower and followed the avenida
until it dwindled into a rutted lane. As he walked, he was careful not to turn an ankle or trip over debris. After a few hundred
metres, the path curved towards a dusty, rock-strewn incline.

Carefully, Francisco climbed the hill. As he approached
the hovel marking the summit, he saw small bats, attracted by

the presence of rotting fruit, hanging upside down from the roof's crooked overhang. He reached the cabin and knocked forcefully. From inside he heard rustling, followed by footsteps. The door opened slightly and the curandera peered out. In her mouth were three peggy, pale orange teeth. Her skin had so many wrinkles it looked like the surface of an apple left too long in the sun. She scrutinized Francisco with the eye that still worked.

— Francisco Ramirez, she croaked, opening the door wider.

— Sí.

— So. You have come.

Francisco looked at pale earth and felt a discomfort that surprised him. Unable to locate words, he let the old woman continue.

— Another man has put a little cabrón in the belly of your one true love.

— Sí, he said.

— And this same man has, in his own indirect fashion, helped kill Laura Velasquez, Fajardo Jimenez, and your dear old friend Roberto Pántelas. It's no wonder you hate him.

The curandera produced a sly, wrinkled grin that illuminated the craggy nuances of her face, in the same way that a light shone into a well will reveal the lichen proliferating at its bottom.

— Come in, joven. It's good to have a visitor. Now that the revolution has returned to Corazón and the streets are running again with blood, old Azula has been getting restless. To tell you the truth, I want to get rid of Brinkley's tower as much as you do. There is something of the devil about it.

Francisco walked into the gloomy, odoriferous cottage, his nose filling with the stench of bile and simmering frogs and floor beams turning to a flaky rot. The room was lit with candles, and everything flickered orange. He squinted to see. There were newspapers spread all over the floor, and beneath them, a scurry of mice and vermin, which gave the impression that the papers were moving of their own accord. Along the far wall was a soot-blackened fireplace in which a few logs were smouldering, filling the house with a smoky mesquite scent. In the fire itself, suspended by a charred black chain, was an old cast-iron pot. Inside the pot, a noxious bromide bubbled and seethed and, every few seconds, popped, filling the cabin with a stench that reminded Francisco of horse urine. He looked around. The roughly hewn table in the middle of the room was piled with food-crusted dishes and, upon these dishes, the hurrying presence of cucarachas. In the corner, next to a broom rack, was a ratty caged owl that, if Francisco wasn't mistaken, was missing its beak.

— Have a seat, said the curandera.

Francisco looked around. There were no chairs in the room, and the table was so alive with insects and the remains of past meals he was hesitant to approach it.

— Ay, said Azula. — Give me a second.

Mumbling to herself, she began clearing the table of dirty dishes, a task involving three trips to the open-air kitchen that projected from the rear of the house. She then took a broom and swept the table surface in such a way that many of the roaches jetted into the fire, where they hissed and flamed green and released a smell not dissimilar to burnt corn.

— Now sit. I've assembled everything.

The curandera laughed to herself as she shuffled towards the fireplace. One by one she began pulling down a selection of the glass jars from the soot-covered mantel. *Esto*, she kept mumbling, *y esto . . . y esto.* By the time she was finished, Francisco found himself sitting before a row of medicinal flasks, each containing a mysterious powder. He turned to ask Azula what she was planning, only to see that the whiskered old woman had trundled off again towards the kitchen. She returned carrying a large wooden bowl, which she plunked down beside Francisco. For a moment she rested, her gnarled, filthy hands resting upon the jutting protuberances that were her hipbones.

— Bueno, she said.

Again Francisco cast his eyes over the accumulation of powders. Oddly, he felt a sudden nervousness, and he had to fight the temptation to say *I don't know if I can go through with this.* He overcame this weakening of his resolve by imagining Brinkley kissing Violeta's tender lips. Immediately his nervousness was replaced by cold fury.

The curandera took a seat across from him. He noticed that the old witch's face bore a streak of charcoal that started at the corner of her mouth and travelled directly north, to the bottom of a watery, reddened eye.

She grabbed the first jar and, with a sudden jerk that revealed her strength, twisted off the lid. She dumped a little of its contents into the wooden bowl.

— What is it? asked Francisco.

— Pulverized bat wings. An old bruja staple.

Francisco nodded, and watched as the curandera opened another jar. This time, when she sifted out a pinch of granular white powder, she explained without prompting. — Dried armadillo sperm. Explosive as hell, and it burns at the temperature of a blast furnace.

She reached for a smaller bottle, this one filled with a thick liquid. She poured no more than a few drops into the mixture.

— Cactus resin, she announced with a satisfied grin. — I harvest it myself.

She proceeded to a medium-sized jar filled with a furry substance. She tipped some in, informing Francisco that many had tried to make incendiary powder without the wiry hair that rings a burro's muzzle, only to see their efforts amount to nothing. She then added mashed jumil bugs, dehydrated vole snouts, and the salivary glands of a Hercules beetle, which were an indigo blue and no bigger than flakes of dandruff.

Azula looked at the contents of the bowl and said: — Now we just need the secret ingredient.

— Which is?

— If I told you, joven, it wouldn't be a secret.

The curandera rose and again disappeared into the diabolical mystery that was her kitchen. From where he sat, Francisco could look out and see stars and the green-lit night sky and the sawtooth outline of the distant sierras. After a moment or two Azula reappeared, dragging a large jute sack behind her. Francisco jumped out of his seat and helped the old woman haul the bag into the room.

— Gracias, she said. — Azula isn't as young as she used to be.

— What's in the bag?

— Like I said, the secret ingredient. Fertilizer. The hairy Zacatecan keeps some on hand for me. Or at least he did, the poor bastard.

The curandera nodded with satisfaction, reached into the depths of her peasant skirt, and pulled out a blade. She slashed it across the corner of the sack, creating a generous aperture. Francisco helped her lift the bag so that it was immediately above the mixing bowl.

— Now, the old woman croaked. — Pour until I say stop.

Francisco tipped his end and watched the bowl fill with the greenish granular substance. Then they put down the sack and admired their handiwork: the mixture now looked like something one might use to bake a mint-flavoured cake. Both Francisco and the curandera were breathing hard.

— Now *that*, said Azula, — is incendiary powder! Trust me, this will give your Dr. Brinkley something to think about.

Francisco watched as the curandera gingerly stirred the mixture with a long-handled wooden spoon. As she worked, Azula sang in her native Kickapoo, the melody sorrowful and haunting. Her arms were thin and bony, most notably in places where you'd expect a muscle to flex with the effort. Finally the old witch put down the spoon and grinned, revealing her trio of peggy, yellowing teeth. The fertilizer was now roiling slightly, and emitting a scent that reminded Francisco of toothpaste.

Again the curandera trundled off, this time returning with a measuring cup. She dipped it into the powder, which began to spume over the edge and drip onto the ragged wooden floor. Francisco followed her out the rear of the cabin, into a stretch of desert bramble covered in rocks and huizache and the remains of small animals torn apart by she-wolves. He let the door slam behind him. This disturbed the bats hanging inverted from the roofline, all of which came alive and fluttered into the night, their movements accompanied by mouse-like squeaks.

The curandera stopped beside a huge boulder that was oddly pyramidal in shape. She motioned towards it.

— Old Azula has hated this thing for years.

She sprinkled the frothing potion around the base of the rock. Just then the clouds shifted, and the silver of the moon mixed with the light green corona rippling through the sky, coating the desert with a sea-green illumination.

— You see? she said, looking up. — Mother Nature wants to lend us a hand. Now we can see what the hell we are doing.

The old witch backed up, Francisco following, until both were standing about twenty metres from the boulder.

— Can you believe I have lived here for seven decades and never done anything about that rock? Now. You have to put your hands together, close your eyes, and touch your fingers to your forehead. Like this. In this way the forces of clarity are summoned.

The curandera put her hands together as if in prayer and lowered her eczema-coated forehead to her fingertips. Francisco did the same.

— Now, she said. — The hard part. I need you to fill your heart with dark thoughts and hostility. Do you understand? I need you to summon all the hate you have ever felt, even for those you love. This will not be easy, as you are embarrassed by these emotions, and have been told your entire life that these emotions are bad, despite being ones to which we all must lay claim sooner or later. Listen to me: you must let your heart run with bile and enmity and the darkest of sentiments.

Otherwise, the next step won't work. As I say, this won't be easy, but you must try.

Francisco thought of the molinero, lying withered and dead in his straw-mattressed bed. He was tempted to say *Ay no, señora. It won't be hard at all.*

— Repeat after me, said Azula. — O Mother Earth, giver of all things magisterial.

— O Mother Earth, giver of all things magisterial.

— Forger of rivers and oceans and seas.

— Forger of rivers and oceans and seas.

— Creator of mountains and valleys and plains.

— Creator of mountains and valleys and plains.

— We beseech you to lend us your powers.

— We beseech you to lend us your powers.

— So that we may combat a presence that has darkened our lives.

— So that we may combat a presence that has darkened our lives.

Both looked up. Francisco watched as Azula stared at the boulder, which was still lit silvery green even though the clouds had passed back across the moon. A full minute passed, during which the curandera didn't blink, flinch, or draw an apparent breath. Francisco, unnerved, finally spoke up.

— Curandera?

Azula kept staring forward. — Sí?

— What do we do now?

She reached into the folds of her skirt, this time extracting a tiny pistol with a bleached wood handle. In a single clean motion, she levelled the gun, aimed, and fired at the powder surrounding the immense rock.

There was a muffled explosion — it sounded more like rushing air than an actual burst — followed by a fountain of sand, root, and pebble. Simultaneously, the boulder that had for so long annoyed the curandera turned from stone to levitating dust. Francisco watched, eyes wide, as this residue floated to the height of a barrel cactus and then leisurely settled back down to earth, forming a slightly mounded accumulation that shimmered under the mysteriously coloured sky.

— Ha! Azula exclaimed. — It works! What did I tell you, joven?

She looked up at Francisco and chuckled.

— So, she said after a few moments. — Now comes the fun part, sí?

{35}

EACH DAY ARRIVED WITH THE CROWING OF ROOST-
ers, the whirring of insects, the chatter of awakening birds,
and a scarlet banner stretched across the horizon. As the
sun rose, the cool of the night burned off like butter in a pan
and turned to a thin, dry heat. For the first hour or two, the
people of Corazón de la Fuente hurried through the streets
and avenidas, anxious to perform any chores requiring them
to leave their homes. Around ten o'clock, both the Villistas
and Ramón's paramilitaries began to awaken as well; all over
town you could hear them coughing and groaning. Any citizens still on the street took this as a cue to return to their
homes and batten their doors with improvisations of mesquite planks and nails.

By eleven o'clock, gunshots began to echo off the adobe
building fronts. As time passed, these interchanges would
escalate into bloody running pistol battles. The citizenry
took to their root cellars just as they had done during the
revolution, surviving off potatoes and pickled cactus. The

fighting — long interludes of silence interrupted by brief, vicious episodes — continued all day and then worsened at nightfall, when the rage of the combatants was sharpened by the swallowing of mescal and psychotropic roots. Finally, around midnight, when the violence had settled, those men unlucky enough to be on cadaver duty would load a donkey cart with that day's bodies, douse them with lime, and then dump them into a large grave that had been created in a field beyond Brinkley's despised tower.

Indigent families, who had been leaving Corazón de la Fuente in a trickle, now began to flee in earnest, their pitiful belongings lashed to the backs of Sicilian burros, their way lit by moonlight and prayers for the future. Madam's few remaining clients finally said goodbye to their beloved Marias, explaining that fear for their personal safety had forced them to make a choice they didn't want to make. For the first time since Brinkley had started broadcasting, there was no lineup of customers at the House of Gentlemanly Pleasures, all eager to test the success of the Compound Operation. This was appropriate, given that the brothel was now occupied by only the most unsavoury of specimens: Ramón and his men had begun to suffer from exhaustion, poor nutrition, and, in some cases, delirium tremens. News of their condition spread, not only through Coahuila, but also to Nuevo León, Chihuahua, Durango, and Zacatecas. Each day, new blood arrived in the guise of former White Shirts, paramilitaries, fascists, Porfirists, and even the odd American freedom fighter, all pleased to resurrect an older, psychopathic way of life.

The enemy — Ramón heard they were captained by an old radical named Patricio Jigán — had set up on the east side, near the town's smaller plaza, outside the one-room dwelling where the molinero had once lived. Of course, news of Jigán's campaign had spread as well, and his beleaguered forces were bolstered daily by old Villistas, socialists, communists, Gold Shirts, Zapatistas, Trotskyites, anarchists, and even a few good old-fashioned train robbers, who had pilfered and looted so exuberantly during the revolution that they had once shut down passenger rail in all of México. They too had an atavistic longing for those times.

With so many gunmen in town, the running gun battles ended. The truth was that all of the fighters, be they left or right, pro-revolution or anti-revolution, White Shirt or Gold Shirt, looked pretty much the same — same huge moustache, same bandolier marking an X across the centre of the chest, same filthy embroidered sombrero, same disturbed glint in the eye. After a while, both sides came to the sobering realization that the majority of deaths on the battlefield — a.k.a. the streets and plazas of Corazón de la Fuente — were being caused by friendly fire. To remedy this, they established battle lines, just as the Allies and the Germans were said to have done in France. The Villistas piled their sandbags along the eastern edge of the central plaza, while the White Shirts piled their sandbags along the western edge. Every day at noon, three p.m., and dusk, they'd show up to shout insults at one another and fire at anyone foolish enough to lift his head above the line of sandbags. Many died with their hands cupped around their mouths, the words *Your madre takes it in the culo* left to fade with the sound of gunshots in the thin, hot air.

Aerated by pistol rounds, the trees surrounding the plaza bled sap and slowly dropped what little foliage had grown back since the end of the revolution. The building façades sprouted new bullet holes — the Villistas in particular liked to take potshots at the church, as this inflamed the enemy and tended to make them do things that were strategically unwise. Faced with the food shortages that always accompany times of war, the townsfolk began killing off pigs and chickens and even the odd nag, such that the animal population of Corazón de la Fuente soon expired. Without the sounds made by penned livestock, the village became something unreal, something no longer meant to sustain life. The plazas, streets, avenidas, and back alleys cleared entirely, save for dented cookware and filthy old clothing left behind by those in a hurry to leave. Even the Callejón of Narcoleptic Bitches emptied, the dogs of Corazón all heading to the desert, where they either perished or began producing broods of mangy, distempered coypups.

Throughout all of this, Madam remained locked in the closet, her fingertips bloodied from scratching at the door, her voice hoarse from screaming for release, her clothes pathetically soiled by her own waste, her body kept alive by whatever food and water Ramón's men deemed fit to occasionally throw in to her. Worse was the knowledge that she could have killed Ramón — there was a second, just before his goons jumped her, when she had a clear shot at his grimy forehead, and only the slightest pull on her trigger finger would have dispatched him to hell. And yet she'd hesitated. She was not a killer. She had let Ramon's thug bat her arm down so that the floorboards took the bullet instead of that festering White Shirt. This hurt most of all. Having given up hope, she now lay in a curled ball and awaited the arrival of her own protracted demise.

And then, as if by miracle, the door of the closet was thrown open wide. The light assaulted her eyes, and she pushed herself, whimpering, to the back of the fetid space. She could hear the sound of boot steps retreating along the floorboards, along with a ragged voice yelling *You got thirty seconds to get that whore outta the closet. She's starting to stink up the place.* And then two Marias were there, Maria del Alma and Maria de las Rosas, saying *Madam, please, hurry.* She nodded and said nothing and tried to stand and couldn't. Each Maria took an arm, and with their help she rose to her feet, Madam so foggy-headed she was conscious only of the wooden floor moving beneath her toes. This turned to dusty, pale earth, a change coincident with the sensation of the low orange sun warming her back. Madam let herself be dragged to the first of the pup tents erected by Ramón's men. There, two more Marias washed her with dampened cloths and dressed her in a clean, if unglamorous, smock. They gave her small bites of tortilla and spoonfuls of a tepid meatless broth. A cooling towel was placed upon her forehead.

Madam Félix fell into a deep, tormented sleep. When she finally awoke, she did something she should have done long, long ago. She wept. She wept for the hacendero, and she wept for the loss of her house, and she wept because she was barren and a long time ago a husband she could no longer picture had thrown her, wailing, into the street because she couldn't give him a child. Mostly, she wept because that bastard Ramón wasn't lying dead in the broiling sun, his features ornamented with a bloody third eye, smack dab in the middle of his forehead. At first her sobs were quiet, almost reverential, though when they began to build in intensity she did not attempt to muffle them in any way. Her cries drifted through the canvas of the tent and filled the yard and unnerved the Marias, who felt powerless in the face of such sorrow. This went on and on, the madam ridding herself of a poison that had infected her system for years.

It was pitch-black when she finally stopped. She felt around, her left hand coming upon the cool, glassy surface of an unlit kerosene lamp. After a little more fumbling she found a box of matches and lit the lamp, the inside of the tent erupting in a nectarine glow. She lowered the flame to a cool, soothing blue. Though she was dressed in someone else's nightdress — she recognized it as belonging to Maria de los Sueños — her own clothes lay cleaned and folded beside her. She stood and dressed, which was difficult, given the low ceiling of the tent. Before pushing open the flaps and stepping into the arid night air, she took a few breaths to collect herself. In a moment she felt imbued with a new resolve.

The Marias were all sleeping, worn out by a day of servicing the needs of Ramón and his cutthroats. Some were in their pup tents, and others were sleeping around the twinkling embers of the fire. The first one she came to was Maria del Alma. Madam kneeled and brushed the hair off the girl's slender forehead. Again, she had to fight against a flaring of tears. She could remember, as though it had happened yesterday, the day Maria del Alma first knocked at the door of Madam's house: sixteen years old, thin as a sapling, as pretty as a dove, her family so poor that she and her siblings had grown up taking turns wearing each other's clothes.

Madam smiled ruefully as she stroked Maria's forehead. *I broke my promise to you*, she thought. *I can no longer protect you,*

I can no longer feed your family. But this will not last, I promise you this, mi niña, mi linda, mi preciosa Maria.

Gently she shook the girl's shoulders. Maria came awake silently and looked up at Madam. There was, as always, trust in her expression.

— Qué pasa? she whispered.

— Shhh, mija. Don't say a thing. We are going. Collect your things. We are leaving Corazón.

Maria blinked, her eyes still bearing a glimmer of innocence. As Maria silently collected her things, Madam went around to all of her Marias, including Maria del Mampo, who was now well enough to travel, albeit marred by scars and disfigurements that would prevent her from ever working as a Maria again. Before waking each of her young wards, Madam silently recalled how she had met each girl, and she forced herself to remember as many pleasant moments as possible involving her and their lives in the House of Gentlemanly Pleasures. This helped, for it made her feel as though her life in Corazón hadn't been wasted. *Shhh, mija*, she whispered each time, *we are leaving this place*, and each time the Maria would nod and begin gathering her belongings (the lone exception, of course, being Maria de la Noche, who grinned and saucily whispered *A todo madre, Madam. It's about time*).

They all worked quietly, in absolute silence. Then, like the proverbial wind, they slipped away without saying good-bye to anyone in the town that had forsaken them, not even the hacendero, though Madam did stop her train of Marias in front of his battered mansion. There she forced herself to remember how safe she had felt whenever he was in her bed, scenting her pillows with brandy and tobacco. She indulged herself this way for only a minute, her Marias understanding why they had stopped behind the ramshackle old hacienda, and why Madam's lips were trembling.

Following instinct and the light of the corona, Madam's caravan of Marias walked east along the riverbank, where they could stop and drink whenever they felt tired. After a while the landscape was lit a natural silver and not the green of high-powered radio frequencies. This pleased them and made them feel as though their new lives had begun.

They existed like nomads, camping under the stars and dining on nopal blackened over fires. They ate soup brewed from jumil bugs and smoked cigarettes rolled from wild punche. These hardships didn't bother them, as they were all savouring a freedom that had nothing to do with male clients and a reignited revolution. They travelled for three days, in no hurry. They admired the skies and drank milk from hacked-apart cacti. At night they huddled for warmth and said prayers in Latin. For the first time in ages, they had time to think about God, the purpose of life, and the meaning of eternity. In this way their journey felt like a gift. Some even acted upon affections that had existed for years, their first Sapphic fumblings occurring under a wash of starlight.

They finally stopped at a stretch of uninhabited desert that was strategically located across the border from Laredo, Texas. There was nothing but chaparral and prickly pear and a sympathetic view of the river, and, in the other direction, a distant sierra. They bathed in cool waters, built a fire, and erected the tents they'd wisely commandeered from Ramón. This, they all realized, was the new way in which decisions would be made: wordlessly, organically, without the issuance of commands. By nine o'clock the next morning, coffee was bubbling, by ten o'clock their stomachs were filled with grid-dle cakes, and by eleven o'clock an ad hoc sign had been fash-ioned. It read, appropriately enough, *The House of Gentlemanly Pleasures II*. By noon Madam's new, makeshift brothel had its first customer, an itinerant seller of encyclopedias who often ducked into México for just such a purpose, and who was giddy with delight that there was now a brothel *here*, just over the border from bustling Laredo. His choice was Maria del Sol, whose gentle, fawn-like movements made the man think of things normally not associated with bordellos, including rainbows, the taste of ripe fruit, and the laughter of children. He left vowing to return.

To mark the occasion, Madam made an announcement.

— Mijas, she said to her Marias. — This place is a good one. We will live here as a family and we will prosper for years to come, and we will all grow wrinkled and rich together. But there is one thing we will do differently here.

— Sí? echoed the Marias.

Madam fought to suppress emotion. — You have all been given the name of the daughter I always wanted but, given the caprices of God, could never have. Instead, you became my daughters. You became my family. This fact has existed for years, even if none of us chose to acknowledge it. When I was locked in that infernal closet, it occurred to me that I no longer wanted to partake in this . . . in this charade. All visitors, clients, and callers will continue to address me as Madam. You, however, will refer to me by another term.

She paused, and looked adoringly at each one of them.

— From now on, you will all call me Mother.

This made all of the Marias smile, including Maria de la Noche, whose left eye brimmed with the beginnings of a tear.

{36}

JUST AS MARIA'S TEAR OVERCAME THE RESISTANCE
of her lower eyelid, tumbling down her cheek like a child
rolling down a hill, Madam's long-time amor entered the
grand room of his hacienda, a place in which his parents had
once hosted luxurious affairs attended by aristocracy from
all over northern México. He rarely went in there and never
spent much time when he did — the ceiling bowed and the
north wall had been riddled by mortar fire, giving it a riveted,
undulating quality. Everything smelled like damp wool and
mould, and the few pieces of furniture that remained were
covered with old bedsheets. Everything else, more or less,
had been sacrificed to looters.

The hacendero found this difficult to bear. He still shuddered every time he considered that his great-grandfather's
fire irons, which had borne the Garcia crest as proudly as a
ship flies its flag, had probably been melted down to make
rifle pellets. He still felt a painful rumble in his stomach
every time he thought that the room's immense sofa, a piece

hand-created by Galician craftsmen, had no doubt been hatcheted and burned for warmth. He still felt the onset of manly tears when he imagined that his family's china, which dated back to the Inquisition, had been purloined so that rebel cooks would have something on which to slop tripe stew and refried beans.

He sat in a huge draped chair where, it was said, a visiting Galician bishop had once sipped tea and commented on matters of the Church. Across one wall was a procession of gilt-framed paintings, each one depicting a member of the hacendero's ancestry. They too had been desecrated during the revolution, no doubt by leftist thugs possessed by feelings of righteousness. There was his great-great-uncle, a magistrate who sat with the royal court in Madrid, his face slashed by the blade of a resentful communist. There was his grandmother, a woman whose ancestors, it was said, had helped plot the Crusades; in an act of political commentary her face had been smeared by rebel excrement. There was his father, a man who had the ear of Porfirio Díaz and the respect of all who knew him, a pair of glasses and horns drawn on his magisterial face. Finally there was the hacendero's wife, Doña Prudencia, the outline of an erect member drawn so that it was about to enter her slightly parted mouth.

The hacendero dropped his head and felt particularly moronic. He could still remember the day she had stood before him, looking officious in her riding boots, a long tan dress with a high lace collar, and the black kid gloves she always wore when embarking on a journey. Her steamer trunk was packed and waiting on the porch.

— You're a fool, Antonio.

Of course she was right. Every other hacienda owner in northern México had sold up and gone back to Spain, or had paid paramilitary groups for protection. He had done neither, thinking it a poor way to repay the country that had hosted him since he was a boy. The simple fact was that he loved México, and always had. He loved the sense of excitement in the air, the passion expressed so easily by its people. He loved the space, and the taste of tequila. He loved cacti and endless skies. Of course, there was one other consideration, one that he'd downplayed at the time. His heart had alighted elsewhere.

As the hacendero regarded his gallery of defaced paintings, it occurred to him that each portrait was sitting in moody judgement. For some reason he had never noticed this before. Yet it was as plain as the arrival of a new day: the slight air of condescension in their eyes, the stiffness caused by disappointment in their carriage. A barely detectable whiff of anger.

He thought *I deserve your censure. I do. I have failed the Garcia name. I have done nothing less.*

From far off he heard a flare-up of the fighting that had taken control of Corazón de la Fuente. He heard the ricochet of bullets and the hollers of downed men needing help and the mad scramble of those trying to get out of the way. It was a medley of sounds he heard two or three times per day, lasting each time for no more than a few minutes, only to be followed by a leaden silence. This time, however, he also heard a desperate equine scream.

The hacendero leapt from his chair and ran through the length of his house, and when he made it to the paddock, he knew exactly what had happened. Frightened by the fighting, Diamante had made a run at the wood-plank fence that the Reyes brothers had constructed to replace the wire enclosure. The poor horse now lay on his side, mouth frothing, eyes wide with fear, clearly in pain. His right foreleg was crooked and trembling and clearly shattered. His nose dripped a thin pink gelatin.

The hacendero kneeled and took the horse's head in his hands. For the first time in weeks, the horse didn't fight him — he merely closed his eyes and took slow, rasping breaths. The hacendero patted him gently, his fingers tracing the diamond between the animal's glorious burnt-orange eyes. He spoke gently to his horse, describing a world where there were no such things as wire fences or bad weather or pain. Diamante, he noted sadly, seemed to be listening, and so he kept talking of a different world in a different time and all of the wonderful, pleasing things that were to be found in that world.

As he comforted Diamante, the hacendero thought about his life with horses. When he considered the time he had spent in that world, he understood that the moments in which he had felt most free, and most impassioned by the act of living, had been atop a caballo. He smiled. Images of the horses he had owned, going all the way back to a pony his father had presented to him when he was a boy of just six, flashed through his mind, a galloping procession of palominos and pintos and galiceños and mustangs.

The hacendero paused for a moment and listened to the rise and fall of his horse's ribs. They made a soft, restful *shhh* that reminded him of the waves of the ocean, and he couldn't help but think of the time he had ridden Diamante all the way to Matamoros and dipped his boot in the Golfo de México. Though they'd followed the Río Grande all the way there, the hacendero had decided to follow a canyon back through the sierras. It was a glorious decision — the air was fresh and the peaks were alive with birds and for dinner they pulled fresh fish from a stream they found halfway through the range. The next day, towards the end of morning, the canyon narrowed and they came upon an encampment of mestizos. There were dozens of them, living in itinerant poverty, their day revolving around a sooty mesquite fire. The hacendero was nervous; banditry and even murder were not unheard of in the mountains of northeastern México.

A couple of older men had approached.

— Hola.

— Hola, primos.

— That's a nice horse.

— Gracias.

— Where are you going?

— To a small town near Piedras. It's called Corazón de la Fuente.

Their eyes lit up. — Where they have that radio tower?

— Sí.

The men digested this information. Both had weak, watery eyes and dirty clothing.

— You still have a ways to go. Would you like to share lunch with us?

He'd sat and accepted a metal plate towering with tortillas, beans, and armadillo meat charred over the fire and then sprinkled with lime juice and salt. They were drinking a warm homemade cerveza that tasted like sweet earth and barley. It was, he thought, the most delicious meal he'd ever eaten. When he finished, a dark-skinned woman appeared and asked if he'd like more. He thanked her, and halfway through his second serving realized that there was no reason in the world why these poor Mexicanos, assaulted by poor government and bad soil, should be so solicitous and kind to a wealthy Spaniard. And yet they were. If there was a soul of México, the hacendero thought, he had found it here, around a fire of low embers, in the company of giving strangers.

Diamante chuffed with pain.

— Caballo, he whispered. — On the morning of his death, Fajardo Jimenez gave me a cache of dynamite the size of a large stove. Today I am going to use it. It is a promise I am making to you. Perhaps it will go all wrong and I will die and I will see you soon in heaven. This could happen, and if it does, at least I will have gone down fighting.

Because of the conflict in town, the hacendero had started wearing a holster, even when sleeping in his huge, perpetually creaking bed. He withdrew his pistol and felt the wooden handle rest heavy and warm in his hand. His tears flowed with abandon, for the rules regarding manly behaviour were different when the death of a beloved animal was involved. He crossed himself and prayed, not just for his own soul and the soul of his horse but also for the soul of Madam Félix and his long-departed wife and, most of all, for this beautiful, tormented country called México. He lifted the pistol and placed it against the horse's temple. He could tell by looking into Diamante's eyes that the animal fully knew what was happening; he was facing his end with a courage that the hacendero doubted he himself could equal.

— I am sorry, said Antonio Garcia before he pulled the trigger.

He stood, walked back into his house, and buried the pistol in a hole in the earthen floor of his root cellar, never wanting to see the wretched thing again. Choking back tears, he walked through the ejido and emerged on Avenida Cinco de Mayo. He turned west, towards the village where he had lived for all but six of his years on this planet. Before reaching the plaza, where he ran the risk of catching a stray bullet, he cut around behind the town hall. He knew of a back door there that, once upon a time, had been used by cleaning staff; a few weeks earlier, a looter had broken the lock by striking it with a rock, and it had remained open ever since. He entered and walked up a cool, silent staircase, past families who were now camping in the hall itself. When he reached the mayor's office, he found Miguel Orozco standing at his window, looking sadly over the plaza. The mayor turned and looked at the hacendero.

— Antonio, he said. — What has happened?

— Tonight is the night, was the hacendero's response.

{37}

FRANCISCO RAMIREZ LAY IN BED, FULLY DRESSED
under a thin cotton blanket, until he felt certain that the rest
of his family was asleep. He stood and looked at his sleeping brothers, marvelling at the way they could be such devils
during the day and such restful little angels at night. Without
really understanding why, he kissed them both lightly on the
forehead and said, Just in case, *Take care, hermanitos.* He then
paused outside his grandmother's room, listening to the telltale snores she produced when asleep. This left him with one
last obstacle: he had to pass by his father, who slept in a hammock slung in the main room.

Francisco crept to the entrance of the room, aware of the
way in which his boots creaked against the floorboards. The
room was dark, though green light pulsed through gaps in
the front window curtain. He listened for low, regular breathing, and then tiptoed past his motionless father. Upon reaching the casa's front door, he put his hand on the latch.

— Mijo.

Francisco turned, and realized that his father had been watching him from the start.

— Are you going out? Francisco the elder asked in a low voice.

— Sí, answered the younger, who then watched as his father slowly climbed out of his hammock. He was wearing a plain white night smock, and as he walked his narrow feet barely made a sound against the knotted floor. He stopped before his son.

— Are you going to do something I don't want to know about?

— Sí, papi.

— Francisco. If, in your wisdom, you feel it is something you really must do, I will not question you.

— Gracias.

— Would it make a difference if I told you to be careful?

— Tonight, papi, careful has nothing to do with it.

— I know that, mijo.

His father turned, walked back to his hammock, and climbed in, the ceiling rafters groaning. Francisco turned and, his face burning, walked into the quiet street. As he'd done a few nights earlier, he darted from alcove to alcove, his movements timed to match the moments in between the pulsing of the corona. Halfway along Avenida Hidalgo, he thought he heard the sound of a pistol being cocked. Francisco froze and listened intently; the only thing he could hear was the dull roar produced by his ears. He continued, ducking from alley to alley, undeterred by the occasional dog bark or flutter of bat wings. Upon reaching the edge of town, he broke into a cautious run, such that by the time he reached the door of Azula's shack he was out of breath.

The door flung open.

— It's about time, said the curandera. — I thought maybe you'd lost your nerve.

Francisco shook his head.

— Good. Well, the powder is on the table. You're young. You get it.

Francisco gulped. The bomb the curandera had used to destroy the boulder had been the size of a small stack of tortillas. Tonight she'd filled an entire burlap bag with the devilish powder. Easing it onto his shoulders caused him to grunt with effort.

— Good thing you're big, said the curandera. — My recommendation is that you don't drop it. It'd be a waste of time if we blew ourselves up instead of the tower.

With such perilous cargo on his back, Francisco had to choose his steps carefully, for the path leading down the hill was scattered with rocks and brambles and tree roots. The weight of the bag pressed on his shoulders, causing a burning pain; meanwhile, the curandera hopped down the path with the litheness of a mountain goat. At the bottom of the hill, she waited.

— What's the matter, joven? Can't keep up with an old woman?

Francisco struggled. When he finally reached her, he gingerly put down the bag and said: — Por favor, I need a rest.

Azula snickered. — Heavy son of a puta, isn't it?

— Sí, said Francisco as he worked to regain his breath.

— Well, don't wait too long. You don't want someone to spot us.

At which point they heard voices. They both turned and peered through the kelpy gloom. Moving towards them was a quartet of figures. Francisco's heart raced; if they were Ramón's goons then their lives would be over. But as the figures approached, Francisco noted something familiar about the way each of them walked. One, he was sure, had the hiccupping stride of Mayor Orozco. When they got a bit closer, he realized that it *was* the mayor, and that he was accompanied by Antonio Garcia, Carlos Hernandez, and Father Alvarez (who, Francisco noted with extreme surprise, was wearing the garb of a priest). Each was carrying a large package.

The four men spotted Francisco and Azula, and stopped.

— Dios mío, hissed Alvarez. — What's in the sack, bruja?

— Her *name*, Francisco interrupted, — is Azula.

The four hombres looked at one another, rolling their eyes.

— For the love of Jesús, the hacendero exclaimed. — What's in the sack, *Azula*?

The curandera surveyed the four pairs of eyes looking at her.

— Incendiary powder, she croaked.

— And would you mind telling us, said Father Alvarez, — what incendiary powder is?

— Cómo no, the curandera gurgled. — It's a bomb, and a hell of a big one at that. With the help of this muchacho, I'm going to blow a hole in that tower the size of a truck. And understand one thing: I told each and every one of you that the tower would come to no good. But did you listen to me? Did you listen to that crazy old witch who lives on the hill? Ay no, nunca. Not one word.

The men, Francisco included, all looked to the green desert floor, each made uncomfortable by the fact that she was right. Moments passed. The hacendero walked past her, looking justifiably tense.

— Well, señora, in that case you're in good company. I suggest we keep moving.

The four men took the lead, the mayor struggling to keep up. Francisco picked up the sack and hefted it over his shoulder, his strength stimulated by the fact that they were no longer alone. With Azula beside him — she, too, was beginning to huff — he followed the men down the slight incline that led past the edge of town. There the path approached the western edge of Corazón de la Fuente. As they neared town, Francisco could hear the twanging signal of Radio XER, and he felt justified in his actions — soon it would be silenced, and the people of Corazón de la Fuente would never again have to listen to that grating, infernal song about the unbroken circle. This knowledge led to a quieting of his mind, such that he was truly walking in silence. Above, the skies shimmered with an alien, salamander green. That, too, would soon come to an end, and for this he felt noble in his actions as well.

At the point closest to the town, the troop was just one block away from the house where Malfil and Violeta Cruz were sleeping; at a certain point Francisco could even make out their flat clay-tiled rooftop. It was strange — Francisco had actually been the first to suspect that Violeta was with child. Before the rumour spread, he had sensed that Violeta was transformed into a different person, into someone who was no longer partaking of childhood. As Francisco followed along behind the hacendero, he realized that, sometime over the past few weeks, he had undergone the same metamorphosis. Even though he was intent on sabotaging the man's tower, he realized that he felt a slight, begrudging gratitude towards Brinkley for forcing this change upon him.

The group had mixed up and spread out. Francisco was now walking closest to Father Alvarez, with the hacendero and the cantina owner leading the way. The mayor had fallen behind, a victim of his damaged left foot. The curandera, meanwhile, had drifted off by herself; Francisco could hear her muttering in the green-hued darkness. Soon the path veered so close to the town that it brushed against the spot where Avenida Cinco de Mayo and Avenida Hidalgo looped into one another. Here the hacendero paused beneath a row of mesquite trees and looked for White Shirts and Villistas alike. The mayor and the curandera pulled up, the group becoming one again. One hundred metres away stood the tower. The hacendero turned.

— I think the coast is clear.

Francisco nodded, his body so flooded with adrenalin he no longer felt the weight of the bag slung over his shoulder. The group scuttled along a roadway littered with spent shells and chips of adobe and mounds of earth kicked up by wayward fire. The tower stood high above them, a megalith of bolts and dark steel girders. Soon the avenida had dwindled to yet another footpath — this one barely wide enough to allow the passage of a cart — and then the hacendero turned right and guided the others into the desert, pulling up beneath the immense steel beams that formed the lower struts of the tower base. There was garbage everywhere, left behind by those who had come looking for prosperity, only to flee at the reignition of war.

The hacendero waited as the others drew up.

— I'm going to place the dynamite, he said.

— And what about my incendiary powder? croaked the curandera.

— Por favor, said the hacendero. — Be reasonable . . .

The mayor, who had just drawn up, spoke. — We'll use both, goddamn it.

Everyone looked at Miguel, surprised by the resolve in his voice.

— It'd be a hell of a charge, said the hacendero.

— Plus, said the cantina owner, — we wouldn't be able to make a powder line that's long enough. We'd blow ourselves to bits in the process.

The curandera laughed. — No, we won't. I brought this.

She reached into the folds of her skirts and, after rooting around for a moment, pulled out her pistol and waved it in the air.

— This'll set off my powder, and I promise you when that happens, your packets of dynamite won't just sit there applauding.

The rest of the group went silent. Eventually, the cantina owner spoke.

— I thought we just wanted to disable the tower. If we use all of the explosives, the whole damn thing might come down. Do we really want this?

There was something about the ensuing silence that proved the existence of miracles and the presence of the Almighty and the watchful protection of the Virgin. Though nobody spoke, the moment being too reverential for words, they communicated nonetheless. They communicated through glances and alterations in posture and boots nervously drawing lines in the dusty earth. In so doing, they discussed the placement of the explosives and they discussed where the tower might topple and they each suggested places where they could take refuge if it should fall. They discussed all of these matters, revealing shades of personality and character that surprised the others. They reached an agreement in a few solemn moments.

— Sí, said the mayor. — We want this.

Francisco and the four older men approached the western base of the tower. They set down their respective packages side by side in the sand, directly beneath the support beams holding up the rear of the tower. This way, if the tower did fall, it would topple harmlessly into the desert. They all crossed themselves and walked towards the river, where they hid under the lip of the south bank.

After they'd settled, the hacendero turned in the direction of Father Alvarez and said: — Perhaps you would like to say a few words, Father?

After a few moments, he nodded and stood next to the bank, a fully bedecked priest illuminated by the green light in the sky.

— O Lord, he started. — We do beseech you, for we understand that our actions on this day are a violation of your teachings. Yet we still ask for your forgiveness, and your understanding that we are not blessed with your grace, your wisdom, or your eternal patience. On this evening we ask for your pardon in the full knowledge that you, and only you, can find it in your heart to give it.

He turned to the others. — I believe a moment of silence would be appropriate.

They all nodded and closed their eyes for a full minute, each alone with the burden of his or her own thoughts. Father Alvarez concluded with a solemn amen, then stepped back down below the bank.

— Thank you, Father, said the hacendero. He then turned to the curandera and asked: — Are you ready?

The old woman raised the pistol and rested her spotty, wizened arms on the bank of the river. She took aim, and they all heard the shot ricochet harmlessly off a chip of rock.

— Mierda, she croaked.

— Steady, said the cantina owner.

— Sí, echoed Father Alvarez. — Take your time.

Again the curandera sighted the mound of explosives waiting at the base of the tower. With one eye narrowed, such that it was only slightly more creased than the other, she again squeezed the trigger. This time the bullet flew over the plane of the desert, unobstructed by the tower, producing a playful whistle that slowly faded to silence. The others released their breath. The curandera closed her eyes, lowered her head, and seemed to enter a momentary trance.

— There's a reason, she mumbled. — There's a reason I can't do this.

Her face brightened with realization. — Oh, she said, — I know.

She passed the gun to Francisco and, in a voice ringing with seriousness, said: — The spirits have made their decision, joven. Now blast that tower to hell.

Francisco accepted the pistol and, with a cool breath, sighted the explosives. Though he did not consider himself a good shot, like all méxicanos he had done some shooting in his life, mostly at gophers and birds, both of which the women in the village would bake into pies. But this was entirely different. His hands were trembling, and he struggled to breathe away his nervousness. Taking aim, he found, was difficult; a bank of clouds had drifted over the tower, blocking the moonlight and obscuring his view of the explosives. He decided to wait for the skies to light up with a particularly strong flare of the corona.

— What's the problem? asked the hacendero.

— Just wait, answered Francisco, in a voice so icy it gave the others pause.

Seconds ticked by, though in the compressed world of that moment, time itself ceased to exist, transforming into something more akin to pure electrical energy. For some reason Francisco was visited with images of his young life in Corazón de la Fuente. Though some of the memories were good ones, the majority involved the revolution, and the ills it had brought to his family. He could picture the worry on his father's face the day the rebels came to town and torched the cantina. He could picture his infant brothers in their little bed, crying at the sounds of artillery. There were days in which they'd had nothing but rice and beans to eat, and he pictured those meals as well, his grandmother doing her best to dress up the food with oregano and an extra ladleful of cooking oil. As Francisco waited, he understood that this moment was not about Brinkley or what he had done to

Violeta Cruz, or even what the tower had done to Corazón de la Fuente. No, this moment was Francisco's cry in the face of México's ravaged history. This moment was Francisco's way of announcing that he would not stand for any of it, not willingly, not any longer.

As though delivered by God, the grandfather of all coronas ignited the skies, the entire Coahuilan desert a sudden pea-green moonscape. Francisco grinned and willed the tremor to leave his shooting hand. He then whispered two words so quietly they existed in his mind and his mind only.

— *Eso es,* he said, and pulled the warm metal trigger.

{38}

THE HEAVENS LIT WITH FIRE; THUNDER PUMMELLED his ears; the sky turned from a shimmering green to a dense, smoke-filled blaze. As they'd expected, the two bombs removed the anchors supporting the rear of the tower. What they had not anticipated was that the explosion would be sufficiently powerful to knock out the foundations on the other sides of the tower as well. They had also not imagined — not even in the wildest recesses of their imaginations — that the explosion would cause the tower to actually lift a few metres and then hover, like an immense dart, as though trying to decide how best to enact its apocalyptic punishment.

There was a thunderous boom, followed by a concussive wave that travelled along Avenida Cinco de Mayo, shattering windows and fragmenting adobe walls and reducing rooftops to bits of floating thatch. Dust rose from the roadway, so thick and chalky that the people rushing outside in pyjamas and night robes had to narrow their eyes and breathe through shirt fronts and bandanas. The risen dust soon mixed with all the adobe and straw in the air, forming a cloud so thick that the assembled, after a few minutes, couldn't so much as see their hands in front of their faces. People coughed and called out the names of loved ones. There was not the barest hint of a breeze; as a result, the impenetrable haze hung resolutely over the town, refusing to let its occupants gauge what had happened.

The cries of children eventually petered out. People began to return to their homes, a task accomplished by taking one treacherous step at a time through the airborne murk while simultaneously swishing their arms in front of their bodies. Others remained rooted to the spot, praying for the soul of the town known as Corazón de la Fuente.

At daylight the slightest vestige of a wind began to stir, inspiring the worst of the cloud to drift in the direction of the river, which quickly gummed up and stopped flowing. Those still out of doors were left coated in shades of blue, pink, and camel. Visibility returned, albeit slightly, so that everything appeared as though in the midst of a sandstorm. The entire populace of the town gathered on the stretch of Cinco de Mayo extending west from the plaza — this included the combatants in town, who were so amazed by the spectacle before them that they seemed to forget they were standing shoulder to shoulder with men they had been attempting to kill just hours earlier. Each and every one gazed upwards, all hatred and rivalry supplanted, if only for a time, by the impossibility reaching into the sky.

After much gasping and prayer, there was an outbreak of whispered discussion. A minority viewed the event as sheer fluke, evidence of the anarchic forces ruling such things as destiny, comeuppance, and the functioning of the universe. There were others who saw it in purely physical terms — according to these individuals, the force of incline exactly matched the force of gravity; ergo, the fate of the tower, albeit somewhat unlikely in appearance, was not in any way glorious. The majority of those bearing witness, however, were practising Catholics. For them it was nothing short of a miracle, a testament to the way in which celestial powers guided their lives. For as they all stood there gawking, not one among them could deny that the tower had landed upright in the parched desert soil, an inch or two away from where it had originally stood, remaining aloft without the benefit of guy wires or foundation or supporting beams. In this, they literally imagined the fingertips of God, coming down from the sky and guiding the tower's placement.

There was one thing, however, that everyone could agree on. Even in the slight breeze blowing over the desert that morning, the tip of John Brinkley's tower was wavering. With each rustle of air the tower's steel fuselage groaned, sounding not unlike the gringo clients who until recently had attended the House of Gentlemanly Pleasures. This inspired more gasps and sub-audible prayers — it was clear that the next time a decent storm kicked up, the tower would topple and crush anyone sufficiently stupid to have lingered in its path. That was not the issue. The issue was where, precisely, that path would lie.

A frightened calm descended over the town, a tranquility born of the knowledge that any significant noise or commotion might not only bring the tower down, but bring it down upon the heads of whoever produced that noise or commotion. People behaved as though somnolent. All movements were considered and slow, and whispering became commonplace. Steps were taken lightly, and only when necessary. The Villistas and White Shirts stopped fighting, as they realized that the initiation of any battle could be their last — guns were holstered, ammunition buried, bombs defused. Without an enemy to shoot at and atrocities to perform on the ideologically opposed, they were faced with crushing questions of self-identity, questions that drove them from the town as surely as enemy reinforcements. The paramilitaries wandered off to the rank, festering snakepits from whence they had come, and the Villistas rode back to whatever communist safe houses they had lived in prior to the fighting in Corazón.

A few days later the hacendero went to the homes of the mayor, the cantina owner, and Father Alvarez. One by one, he invited them to come to his ruined hacienda, and one by one they said *Claro* and put on their boots. They were just about to cross the plaza and continue towards the hacendero's house when Antonio stopped and turned to the closest friends he had on the planet.

— Primos, he said. — There's one other I should include.

The others then followed him to the house of Francisco Ramirez, who answered the door with a surprised expression on his face.

— Mijo, said the hacendero. — We are having a little meeting. I must insist that you join us.

Francisco Ramirez stared at them numbly. Aside from his own father, they were the four men he admired most in

Corazón de la Fuente, and to be included in their ranks was an honour he had never thought would be his. A minute later he was walking with them, causing those townsfolk who were looking out from between their shutters to understand that the social position occupied by Francisco Ramirez in Corazón de la Fuente had altered forever.

Moving slowly so that Mayor Orozco could keep up, they traversed the central plaza, trudged through the mud of the ejido, and reached the hacendero's bullet-riddled mansion. The hacendero beckoned them into his study, where a half-bottle of brandy and a carafe of water were sitting on a small table — he had donated every other stick of furniture to the people of the ejido, who would no doubt admire it for a few days and then use it as cooking fuel. The hacendero poured five glasses of brandy.

— Caballeros, he said. — I wish to make an announcement.

— Go ahead, said the others. — We are listening.

— With the revolution, the men of Corazón de la Fuente lost something that no man should have to lose. When we lit that explosion, aided by our young friend Francisco, we got it back. For your role in this, I thank you all. Salud.

The men drank.

— I have one more thing to say. Tomorrow I will board a bus that will take me to México City. Then I will take another bus to Veracruz, where I have arranged passage on a ship that will return me to the land of my birth.

His three oldest friends nodded, having expected this news years earlier, when the hacendero's wife had first fled México. Francisco, meanwhile, looked on, irked by the way in which life never failed to operate. Just as he had gained

DR. BRINKLEY'S TOWER   401

the hacendero's respect, and possibly even his friendship, the
Spaniard was saying goodbye.

The hacendero continued. — I need you to know that I do
not make this decision lightly. I have lived in this house since
the age of six. These four walls inform me who I am, and all
that I feel for this little world of ours. Please understand that
when I arrive in España, I will not be doing so as a Spaniard,
or anything resembling one. I will tell my loved ones that my
blood is now fully Mexican. I will live as a foreigner amongst
my own people, and furthermore I will be proud to do so.
Adiós, amigos. I will miss you most of all.

There came the most profound of silences, followed
by manly embraces. When the hacendero approached
Francisco, there was a moment of reluctance on the part of
the younger man.

— Antonio, Francisco said in a halting voice. — I am sorry
for killing your old nag.

The hacendero grinned.

— Mijo, he said. — She died in the pursuit of adventure.
She died in the middle of a quest. You gave her a great gift. For
this, I should thank *you*. Goodbye, my new friend, it is too bad
we couldn't have more time together.

It then grew deathly quiet, both inside and outside the
house; they all accepted this as an invitation to reflect. After a
minute or so, the cantina owner cleared his throat and spoke.

— Compadres, he said. — I have some news as well.

The next morning, Carlos Hernandez went into the desert,
to an old cholla he'd partially uprooted so as to produce a

small black cavity in the scrub. From there he fetched a lock-box containing all the money he'd made as a saloon keeper during the construction of the tower — minus, of course, the dollars he'd spent on a .44 calibre pistol and the all but useless Compound Operation. Standing above the village, he thought of his years as the town's lone saloon keeper, and was pleased to be leaving.

He and Margarita packed as lightly as possible and caught a lift on the highway running across northern Coahuila. Just before sundown they reached the site of a new brothel, one that rumour had told them was just across the river from Laredo, Texas. Already there was the most rudimentary of buildings, no doubt tacked together by workers who were eager to be paid in services rendered.

It had been a long walk from the highway, and the two felt hot and tired. Carlos knocked on the door, Margarita standing nervously behind him. After a moment it swung inward.

Madam Félix blinked, and then smirked. — Cantina owner.

— Hola, Madam.

— And his wife, of all people.

Margarita lowered her head and grinned bashfully.

— What brings you to Nuevo Laredo? asked Madam.

— You do.

— I don't think I understand.

— I am thinking that this place . . . this Nuevo Laredo, as you call it . . . could benefit from other amenities. Do you not think that the gringos would be more likely to visit if there was a drinking establishment? A place where they could have a cold cerveza and a nice hot meal? Perhaps a few beds in which to actually spend the night? Do you not think the gringos would feel more anonymous if there was an entire town here?

— You are telling me you wish to build a cantina here?

— I am.

— And you have the capital to do this?

— Sí.

— In that case, said Madam, — I grant you my best wishes. I will do everything in my power to aid you.

The cantina owner and his wife were busy that evening. They borrowed some planks, nails, and floorboards left over from the upstart brothel and tacked together a lean-to that allowed a view of the river and the sort of tanning performed beneath moonlight. The next day, Carlos would scout the nearby town of Rodriguez for men who had sturdy backs and wanted to make a little money. When he had recruited a workforce, he'd travel to Sabinas and arrange for the delivery of building supplies. Then, over the next few weeks, the frame of his new saloon would appear out of thin air, each plank and joist offering the promise of new life. Shortly after that, the fledgling town of Nuevo Laredo would attract other residents, who would appropriately start small businesses of their own.

But that was all to come. In the meantime, the cantina owner lay next to his wife and listened to the trickle of the Río Grande and the distant sound of voices and light traffic coming from Laredo. A delicious, tingly fatigue invaded their bodies — the kind of fatigue that feels well-earned, the result of a productive day. Their feet extended from the lean-to and were lit silver instead of sea green; this fact alone imbued them with gleeful optimism. From within the upstart bordello they could hear sighing and the noises made by those pressed hotly together, and these sounds inflamed the cantina owner with a desire for something other than rest.

Carlos Hernandez turned to his wife. He kissed her slowly, as though all the time in the world were in their possession.

— Margarita, he said. — I believe we will be happy here.

— Sí, Carlos. .

— And I believe we will have so many little ones that you will never know the sound of peace.

— Sí, said Margarita. — I believe that God wants this as well.

Francisco Ramirez continued to follow Brinkley's exploits in the newspapers available in the Del Río library. He was not surprised by what he discovered (or rather, he was not surprised by *most* of his discoveries). After a long and determined manhunt, it seemed that John Brinkley had been located by the gringo organization called the Internal Revenue Service — he'd been hiding in a place called the Smoky Mountains, in a shack known only to a few family members, sporting a hillbilly beard and hair bleached the white of a skunk's stripe. They arrested him for tax evasion and wasted no time putting him on trial. Brinkley's crimes, it seemed, were serious enough that the good doctor faced the possibility of spending the rest of his life in jail.

The Texas papers also detailed the concoctions upon which Brinkley had based his operation: the fictional medical degree; the pharmaceutical products made from water, sugar, and gelatin; the invented science upon which the Compound Operation was based. Even his time spent in South America had been a fiction, his Spanish learned during a lengthy boy-hood stint in Monterrey — apparently his parents, both of whom were carnival grifters, had exiled themselves to avoid some rather unsavoury criminal charges. Once that particular fact was unearthed, many of the nation's reporters smugly noted that, as was generally the case, the apple had not fallen far from the tree.

Yet the case of John Romulus Brinkley was a tricky one, one that confirmed that life's rules are unknowable, and lacking in parameters or consistency. For when the charlatan doctor's trial began, a series of national charity directors all testified in Brinkley's defence, a few of them tearfully. For years, it seemed, Brinkley's donations had comprised a significant portion of their annual budgets, and without them they weren't sure how they were going to survive.

And still John Brinkley's dislodged tower stayed upright, despite the winds that ordinarily came to Corazón in the months preceding winter. The harmattan that normally appeared each fall, originating from somewhere in the Gulf of México, was abnormally tame that year. The sirocco that ordinarily blew down from Oklahoma raged so timidly that Christmas that most didn't even register its arrival. The zephyr that usually arrived in the new year, perfuming the town with the kelpy scent of the Pacific, failed to make an appearance as well.

Yet every person living in Corazón de la Fuente knew that the tower would one day come down — it was an event that was now central to their lives, one that granted their existence both shape and a fretful texture. Soon those who stayed would be called upon to rebuild the damage caused by the tower's imminent toppling; for the majority it was a sense of duty that kept them rooted to the soil that had hosted them since their days in the cradle. It was, they all knew, the way of war, the innocent left to tidy up the aftermath of the vicious.

Violeta Cruz felt this beckoning as well. Around the time her morning sickness began to wane and her belly began to inflate, she experienced a shift in both her priorities and her understanding of what is truthful in this bedazzlement called life. Late one afternoon she dressed in a black skirt and white cotton blouse, and she knocked timidly on the door of the house belonging to her one-time novio.

Thankfully, Francisco answered.

— Hola, Francisco, she said in the cautious, lowered tone that had become second nature to those still living in Corazón de la Fuente.

— Violeta.

She bit a minute obelisk of nail that had managed to take root on the baby finger of her right hand. She tried to speak and found that she couldn't. When her words finally took root, they sounded like a plea.

— Francisco . . . I know I don't deserve to ask you this, but would you take a walk with me? Please?

The two moved silently and carefully, a bank of air between them. Instinctively they meandered along the path leading past the mission, towards the lee where they used to have their assignations. There they looked out over a plateau turning gold in the falling sun. There was the occasional call of a hawk and, in the distance, the rustle of wizened tree branches.

— Francisco . . .

She glanced at him, then returned her gaze to the desert, which was changing hue with every passing minute. Her voice was a murmur. A ball of shame formed in her throat.

— I know that you helped bomb the tower.

— How did you find out?

— I just did.

— I see.

— I also know why you did it. Or at least I . . . I know what the rumours say.

— I did it to punish the man who disgraced you.

There was a pause, during which Violeta began to sniffle. When she next spoke, it was in a voice breaking with emotion.

— I need to know that you didn't do it because you pity me. I need to know that you have never felt sorry for me, not even for a second. I will not allow this. I am a wealthy young woman, thanks to the money Brinkley paid me, and already I love my baby as deeply and as richly as any madre has ever loved a niño. I was never disgraced. I am not to be pitied. It would be unfair. Do you understand me, Francisco Ramirez? I will not allow it.

Her voice broke and trailed away. Francisco kept looking forward, understanding that this was the moment he had hoped for — the moment in which he could tell Violeta that she shouldn't have toyed with his affections, that she shouldn't have fallen into the arms of the first rich gringo to come her way, that any predicament she now found herself in was entirely of her own making. He had rehearsed these lines so many times that they popped into his head fully formed, and with a savage degree of righteousness. A few weeks earlier he might even have given them voice. But the brutality he'd witnessed during what had come to be known as the War of the Tower caused him to realize that without such things as forgiveness and understanding, life was little more than a thing made of chaos.

Instead of speaking, he placed three fingertips on Violeta's forearm. He did this so lightly that he was only sure she felt their presence when he saw the fine auburn hairs on her arm rise and tremble gently in the breeze. The couple sat this way for several minutes, their eyes following the apparitions that hover over a desert during the twilight hours. Neither initiated the kiss that ensued, their mouths seemingly drawn together by forces magnetic in nature. Their heartbeats synchronized, their body temperatures rose to precisely the same level, and they both lost the ability to gauge time and space.

And then, slowly, in the manner of those who have lost themselves in love, their corporeal selves melted away, freeing them from the self-consciousness that, at all other times, defines the act of living.

Just as it was ordained to happen, the mothers of Corazón de la Fuente awoke one morning and lit fires and made coffee and kissed their children and stepped wearily onto their stoops. There it was: a slight yet discernible moisture clinging to the air. A diminishment of the sun's normal intensity. The fractional drop in temperature that always presaged the arrival of a desert tempest. The scent of ozone, carried on the wind.

Given the gathering motion of the air, most predicted the tower would come down within six or seven hours. They all went back inside and explained to their families that they'd be taking a little trip that day. Hampers were packed, picnic baskets stocked, carts dusted off. Mules were watered and bicycle tires inflated. Soon a procession of townspeople, using any and all methods of transportation, headed to the nearby towns of Rosita and Piedras Negras. There they would wait for the fall of the tower, after which they would return home and deal with the mess. Included among those returnees would be the town's priest and the town's mayor, both of whom would guide any reconstruction required once the tower finally came down. If the tower fell to the southwest or northeast, that reconstruction would be minimal. If it fell to the east, it would be considerable. The two hombres felt prepared for either eventuality, one emboldened by a new-found decisiveness, the other invigorated by a reborn trust in God's ways.

Sometime around noon, Francisco Ramirez told his father that he had something to do. Thinking his son was going to fetch Violeta — the two families planned to travel together to Saltillo, using the tower's collapse as an excuse for a little holiday — Francisco Senior told him there was no shortage of chores to do before their departure, and that he should hurry. Francisco nodded and pledged to return soon. But instead of walking to Violeta's house, he followed the path to the house of the curandera.

She greeted him with a snort. — Well, if it isn't the mad bomber.

— Señora, he said. — I need to see you.

— Of course you do. You need to thank me because Violeta Cruz now sees you in a different light, and she likes what that light is showing her. You have come to thank me because, the night before last, she led you into the desert and made amor to you in the feverish manner of a woman who's decided who she's going to spend the rest of her life with. Isn't that right, joven?

— Azula, said Francisco. — How could you possibly know this?

— I am a witch. I have a crystal ball and magical powders and a broom that trembles with omniscience.

— Ay sí.

— I am joking. I wandered into the village and heard the talk.

Francisco didn't chuckle; instead, his eyes reddened. Seeing this, the curandera's demeanour softened.

— Mijo, said the old woman. — Life has sent much in your direction these past few months. Life can do that sometimes. It's all right. It doesn't mean you deserve it.

— No, Azula, Francisco managed. — It's not that.

He paused. He knew that giving voice to his worries would leave him feeling shaky.

— If that tower falls on the town, you and I will be responsible.

— It won't.

— But how can you be certain?

— I am a witch. I told you this already. I have a crystal ball and magical powders and a broom that trembles . . .

Still Francisco did not laugh. The curandera sobered as well.

— Do you know just how old I am, Francisco Ramirez? Do you have any idea how long I've been taking care of this town?

— I do not.

— And you never will. So trust me. This town will be fine. Now go. Marry Violeta Cruz. Be good to one another, and be good to the children you're going to have together. And especially be good to the little cabrón Brinkley put in her belly. It'll have a tough enough row to hoe without your resenting it. Oh, and by the way, I won't be here when you and Violeta get back. I've decided to move on to greener pastures.

Thinking that the curandera was finally quitting for a town that might appreciate her, Francisco nodded.

— I will, Azula Mampajo. I promise. And farewell. I will miss you.

— And I'll miss you, you lovesick dummy.

Soon after, the exodus began in earnest. By early afternoon Corazón de la Fuente was a ghost town: tumbleweeds rolled lazily over the deserted streets, shutters knocked against one another in the quickening breeze, and the only other sound was the light whistle made by air rustling over sand. By the hottest part of the day, in fact, the only person left was the curandera. She smiled. Many, many years ago, in a Kickapoo peyote ceremony, it had been foreseen that she would one day be the last being in Corazón de la Fuente, and it pleased her that this prediction had finally come true. She stepped out of her hovel and looked down at all of Corazón.

— Ay, she said out loud. — At times you've been a real horse's ass. Still, I suppose I can't complain. But I have to be honest. I've grown into a tired old woman, and this last jam you got yourself into just about did me in. It's time we ended this dance, don't you think?

She descended from her fetid little knoll, switch broom in hand. She cleaned the original Franciscan mission, the Roman arch over the Pozo de Confesiones, the floor of the bandstand, and the entranceway of the town church. Then she swept the town's two plazas — one large, one small — until they were clear of huizache needles, vole droppings, and mesquite branches. As she worked, the arthritis in her joints began to flare, a product of both her labours and the gathering storm. Upon finishing, she smiled to herself, feeling the turbulence in the air, and thought *Won't be long now.*

She went back to her property, where she burned a small pyre of witch hazel while meditating. She then packed a mochila containing a small amount of tobacco and corn, put it on her back, and stepped outside. After placing a finger in her mouth, she held the moistened digit aloft and thought *Hmmm, the winds will come from the southeast. It's about time this town got a break.* Again she smiled. When she thought of some of the things she had seen in her lifetime . . . Glorious things. Horrific things. Funny things. Puzzling things. Things that revealed the way in which true meaning existed only in the absurd.

As she had done so many times in her life, she trundled down the path leading towards town. Already the tip of the tower was beginning to jostle and pivot and heave. The curandera saw this, and felt at peace. Instead of turning towards town, she marched into the very desert where she had been born next to ululating elders and a smouldering stinkweed fire. After some consideration, she chose a nice spot directly northwest of the radio tower, one that looked sandy and clear and free from biting spiders.

She then sat cross-legged, her face lit white by sunshine, and waited for the winds to come.

{Author's Note}

In 1939 the American government passed a law making it illegal for an American-owned radio station to broadcast from Mexican soil without permission from the government of the United States. It was called, appropriately enough, the Brinkley Act.

Facing numerous indictments, criminal charges, and malpractice suits, John Romulus Brinkley declared bankruptcy in January 1941. He died penniless on May 26, 1942, having suffered three heart attacks and the loss of one leg due to poor circulation. His mansion still stands in Del Rio, Texas, though it is closed to the public. Likewise, the ruins of his broadcast facility are still to be found on the outskirts of Villa Acuña, México, though they too have fallen into disrepair.

{Acknowledgements}

This book owes its existence to my interest in Mexico, radio, and the art of the long con. It couldn't have come to fruition without the help of my agent, Jackie Kaiser; my editor, Melanie Little; and House of Anansi's Sarah MacLachlan, who decided to take a chance on it. I'd like to thank the people of Guerrero, a tiny pueblo in northern Coahuila that served as a model for Corazón de la Fuente. But mostly, I'll thank my wife, Susan Greer, who routinely has more faith in my abilities than I do.

Dr. Brinkley's Tower by Robert Hough

1. How do you think Señora Azula Mampajo, the town curandera or healer, is viewed by the citizens of Corazón de la Fuente? Do those attitudes change by the end of the story? If so, why? If not, why not?

2. How is the colour green used, with increasing intensity and pervasiveness, in *Dr. Brinkley's Tower*?

3. What is more insidious: the physical effects of the transmission of Radio XER, or the mental and spiritual?

4. Who is the most foolish or gullible character in *Dr. Brinkley's Tower*, and who is the most savvy and resourceful? Who is toughest, perhaps the most hard-hearted? Who is most tender and compassionate? Which character surprised you the most, for good or for bad?

5. Where do the satirical barbs of *Dr. Brinkley's Tower* best hit their marks? Is it with individual human pride, hubris, and folly; collective human pride, hubris, folly, and duplicity in conflict or commerce; the differences and conflicts between men and women . . . or something else entirely?

6.   Compare the business acumen and managerial styles of Dr. Brinkley and Madam Félix.

7.   Who tells the most damaging lie in *Dr. Brinkley's Tower*?

8.   Will Francisco and Violeta live happily ever after? What will strengthen their bond and what might challenge it?

9.   Does knowing that Dr. Brinkley is based on a real-life figure change your perception of him? Why or why not?

10.   Will Corazon de la Fuente rebuild, or is its future as Nuevo Laredo?